THE GATES

THE GATES

CHUCK WACHTEL

VIKING

VIKING
Published by the Penguin Group
Penguin Books USA Inc., 375 Hudson Street,
New York, New York 10014, U.S.A.
Penguin Books Ltd, 27 Wrights Lane,
London W8 5TZ, England
Penguin Books Australia Ltd, Ringwood,
Victoria, Australia
Penguin Books Canada Ltd, 10 Alcorn Avenue,
Toronto, Ontario, Canada M4V 3B2
Penguin Books (N.Z.) Ltd, 182–190 Wairau Road,
Auckland 10, New Zealand

Penguin Books Ltd, Registered Offices:
Harmondsworth, Middlesex, England

First published in 1994 by Viking Penguin,
a division of Penguin Books USA Inc.

1 3 5 7 9 10 8 6 4 2

PUBLISHER'S NOTE
This is a work of fiction. Names, characters, places,
and incidents either are the product of the author's imagination
or are used fictitiously, and any resemblance to actual persons,
living or dead, events, or locales is entirely coincidental.

Copyright acknowledgments appear on page 405.

LIBRARY OF CONGRESS CATALOGING IN PUBLICATION DATA
Wachtel, Chuck.
The gates : a novel / by Chuck Wachtel.
p. cm.
ISBN 0-670-83886-1
1. Man-woman relationships—New York (N.Y.)—Fiction. 2. Italian
Americans—New York (N.Y.)—Fiction. 3. Lower East Side—New York
(N.Y.)—Fiction. 4. Afro-Americans—New York (N.Y.)—Fiction.
5. Americans—Travel—Nicaragua—Fiction. 6. Teachers—New York
(N.Y.)—Fiction. 7. Family—New York (N.Y.)—Fiction. I. Title.
PS3573.A29G38 1994
813'.54—dc20 94-5795

Printed in the United States of America
Set in Janson
Designed by Katy Riegel

For Jocelyn Lieu

The universe, which is not merely the stars and the moon and the planets, flowers, grass and trees, but *other people*, has evolved no terms for your existence, has made no room for you, and if love will not swing wide the gates, no other power will or can.

James Baldwin

I am standing on the threshold about to enter a room. . . . I must shove against an atmosphere pressing with a force of fourteen pounds on every square inch of my body. I must make sure of landing on a plank travelling at twenty miles a second around the sun. . . . I must do this whilst hanging from a round planet head outward into space, and with a wind of aether blowing at no one knows how many miles a second through every interstice of my body. These are some of the minor difficulties. Then again it is necessary to determine in which direction the entropy of the world is increasing in order to make sure that my passage over the threshold is an entrance, not an exit. *Arthur Stanley Eddington*

Again I am struck nameless, unable to name,
. . . silent in this terrifying moment under all moonlight,
all sunlight turning in all our unfree lands.
Name them, name them all, light of our time.

Muriel Rukeyser

For their help and their support I wish to thank:

Dore Ashton, Brian Breger, Philip Herter, Hettie Jones, Beena Kamlani, Deborah Karl, Lisa Katzenstein-Gómez, Margot Livesey, Matti Megged, Michael Manley, Neil Myers, Dawn Seferian, Lisa Springer, Eileen Sutton, Robin Tewes, Paul VonDrasek, Ed Wachtel, and Ann Rizzotti-Wachtel, who dreamt this book before I wrote it.

—C.W.

Acknowledgments will be found on page 405.

PART I

THE ABIDING CITY

1

Primo Thomas, about to give his order to the counterman in D's Dairy Restaurant, is pushed a step backward by a short, wide-shouldered man who shoves himself between Primo and the counter and then sets an empty Seven-up can on its Formica top. He lays a drinking straw, still wrapped in paper, beside it.

Primo taps him on the shoulder but he doesn't turn around. Primo had not seen his face but could sense from his movement that all the man saw was the point of the wedge he was driving between Primo and the counter, and the narrow column of space he was about to occupy.

Primo taps him again, and again he doesn't respond. He's wearing a thick flannel shirt, too heavy for this hot, early-June afternoon, and knee-high galoshes, the kind with clamps that close the front.

He picks up the straw again. "I didn't even use this," he says to the counterman. "You can use it again."

The counterman hits a register key with the side of his hand. "What'll you have?" he asks Primo. He reaches into the cash drawer as it slides open, takes out a nickel and hands it to the man in the flannel shirt.

The man turns and Primo takes another step backward. "Hiya," he says to Primo. His round face seems small above his wide shoulders. Having gotten his nickel, his movements are relaxed. "Hiya," he says, as if they know each other.

The counterman waves to Primo to get his attention, then says, "You can't eat it, if I can't make it."

The man in the flannel shirt heads toward the door but is stopped as two young women enter. He taps his foot, sets his hands on his hips and looks angrily down at the floor. When they clear the doorway, he shoves himself out onto Second Avenue.

"And I can't make it if I don't know what it is." The counterman holds up his empty hands and smiles at Primo.

"Tuna, lettuce and tomato."

"I haven't seen you in quite a while."

"Two years," Primo says.

"*That* long?" He shakes his head, then holds up a slice of dark bread in one hand, an ice cream scoop of tuna salad in the other. "Whole wheat, if I remember correctly."

Primo nods, smiles.

"Where you been?" he asks.

"Out of town."

"That's a relief. I thought it was a boycott." He walks down the counter. As he walks back he splits apart a fresh head of lettuce with his hands. "What were you doing *out of town?*" he asks.

"Teaching," Primo tells him. "A small college up in Massachusetts."

"What do you teach?" He smiles down at the sandwich as he wraps it and folds a pickle into the top of the wax paper. "No, wait. Let me guess. . . ." He looks up at Primo, still smiling, and squints as if to see him more clearly, as if he were guessing his weight. Primo looks down at himself. They are both looking at the front of his sweaty, soot-gray sweatshirt. The sleeves are cut off at the shoulders and his arms, hanging at his sides, are still tingling from carrying his belongings up the five flights of stairs to his apartment.

"Astrophysics," the counterman says. "Those guys are all slobs."

Primo shakes his head.

"Let's see. . . . You don't look like you teach history. Not biology neither. I can't see you cuttin up dead frogs. . . . You're a tough one." He bends down and reaches into an icebox below the counter. Primo briefly has a clear view of the menu, written on paper plates taped to the quilted-tin wall.

He comes up with a can of Pepsi. "You still drink this?" He sets it beside the sandwich on the counter. Then he says, "I got it. The three R's. Am I right?"

"The first two," Primo says.

"Reading and writing. I knew it all along. I was just playin with you."

"You're full of shit," Primo says, smiling.

"You're right," the counterman says. "But tell me, Professor . . . If you're so smart, how come you came back to all this?" He waves him arm toward the window, toward Second Avenue.

Primo doesn't answer. He looks through the dirty glass, the top half covered with a transparent sheet of green plastic. It doesn't soften the upper half of the view like sunglass lenses, it liquefies it, as if you were looking through a loaded water pistol.

"Well?"

Primo doesn't answer. He becomes entranced with the busy street. The sunlit avenue is made up of distinct, shifting corridors: people, parked cars, moving cars, parked cars, people. He doesn't see it the same way. He's been out of town a long time and he's happy to be back.

The counterman packs the sandwich and soda in a paper bag.

Primo reaches for his wallet, lets it fall open in his hand and slips out a five. He is still smiling. "You haven't changed," he says.

"Don't have the time." He slips a folded napkin into the bag. As he does this he whistles a tune that starts off being "Take the 'A' Train" but then becomes something else. He whistles with a beautiful, steady vibrato. Then he picks up the straw left by the man in the flannel shirt. "How do you suppose he got it back into the paper wrapper?"

Primo looks at it. "He never opened it," he says.

He slides it into the bag with Primo's lunch. "In that case it's yours."

That morning, at ten a.m., the frondescent branches of the ailanthus trees along the Houston Street exit of the FDR Drive—the calm undulation of the thick compound leaves, just above the motion and exhaust fumes—were, to Primo, after a short and restless night's sleep, preceded by a day of packing the rental van, preceded by two years of living in the town of More, Massachusetts, population seven thousand, including the student body of More college, preceded by his first thirty-five years, all of them spent within New York City, the welcoming arms of friends and relatives, the little flags waved at train stations for soldiers and home-coming athletes: they were, he realized, seeing them through the windshield when he finally slowed down enough, after all this time, all this time, to focus on any single thing clearly, a vision he has had out the windows of every house—nearly every room—he has ever lived in.

Welcome: the tan-brown bricks of the housing projects that begin on Avenue D, so clear in the bright midmorning sun you can see each one. Welcome Avenue C, *Avenida Loisaida*, the increasing heat as he moved farther from the East River, welcome the tall clumps of grass that burst through the paving stones of the traffic island, welcome Avenue B, where Primo swung the van to the right.

Welcome.

Primo had to drive around the block and back the van up to the front of his apartment building because a film crew was blocking the entrance to East Third Street at Avenue B. Normally this would have annoyed him, but today he was a small-town kid arriving in Manhattan, where people don't just *live* life, they dream it on film. After he parked, he walked to the corner to see what they were shooting. Trucks and vans lined the sidewalks on both sides, feeding out wires and cable. Mylar mirrors magnified the sunlight, directing it into the open doorway of the building on the corner. A camera had been set up on top of one of the vans. Nothing else was actually happening. Neighbors, many of them familiar to Primo, and the film crew, were just standing around. He asked a few people but no one seemed to know what they were filming. Sitting on a beach chair was an old man he always greeted when they passed each other but never, in the ten years Primo had lived on the block, spoke with. Primo asked him what they were filming.

"The girls are over there," he said, pointing to a long camper bus parked across the street.

"What girls?" Primo asked him.

"The girls in the movie. I saw em when they first got here."

"You know the name of the movie?"

"My granddaughter's better-looking than the both of em put together." He looked back at Primo. "No one knows what the movie is. All they're sayin is that it's for TV."

Primo walked back up the street and began unloading the van.

Among his belongings was a squash racket he bought when he first arrived at More College. His friend Manny, who'd first told him about the job, insisted he get one. This was part of it: his new life would mean a slower pace, cleaner air, getting into shape. But Primo had barely used it, and felt less likely to do so here, in New York. It also was the best thing at hand to prop open the heavy outer door of his building. The handle slowly thickened beneath the head and formed a tight, secure wedge in the space between the bottom of the door and the dirty, scuff-worn tile floor.

The woman who had sublet, a friend of Mariah, his ex-wife, had cleaned and dusted before she left, and left a note with her new number in California along with the money for her last month's phone and Con Ed bills. Primo had left nearly all his furniture—he wasn't sure if he would stay at More or not—and taken only the things he'd need for his daily life: books, clothes, stereo, TV, etc. The windows were clean, the bed was neatly made and his four chairs were set evenly spaced around the table. The sparse order was monklike and pleasing. He had lived in this apartment for ten years, most of them with Mariah. The disorder he and his belongings would bring to this arrangement would be a clean, new disorder—not the familiar dust and clutter he left behind two years ago—and it would be all his.

On one of his trips down to the van he stopped to watch the mailman fill the boxes. Last week he'd put a mail-forwarding card in the post office at More and was hoping something would be here already.

Mrs. Karbash, on her way out for a walk with Lady, her Chihuahua, also stopped to wait for her mail. Mariah used to say that Lady reminded her of Granny on *The Beverly Hillbillies.* Mrs. Karbash smiled at Primo as if he'd never gone away. He smiled back. Lady stretched the leash so she could sniff the squash racket, a new and unfamiliar object in her small world.

The mailman handed Mrs. Karbash a postcard with a picture of a motel on it, and something official in a brown, windowed envelope. As she was leaving, another familiar tenant, a man about Primo's age, carrying his young son on his shoulders, passed her on his way into the building and stopped to wait for his mail.

"What do you think?" the man said to his son.

The child laid both his hands across the top of his father's head and smiled. He had been an infant when Primo moved out. Now he was old enough to sit atop someone's shoulders, and to be talked to.

"I agree," the father said. "They're gonna shoot a movie on *our* block and not tell us what it is. . . . no *way* we're goin to see it."

Primo laughed. The child watched him.

"They're not tellin nobody," the mailman said.

"All I could find out was that it's for TV," Primo said.

"Then *we're* not watchin that night," the neighbor said, looking up at his son. Then he said, to Primo, "You been away?"

"Two years."

Just then the mailman said, "Ssssshit!" He'd been trying to shove a rolled-up magazine into one of the mailboxes and had scraped his knuckles on the edge.

"You got a lot of new neighbors while you were away," the mailman said. "People with credit cards, charge accounts . . . They get mail order catalogs, lots of junk mail, magazines . . ." He brought his hand to his mouth, sucked the back of his forefinger. The child watched this with a focused interest. "They get all kinds a shit." He then closed and locked the boxes.

Primo decided to take a walk to the corner and see what the film crew was up to before he finished unloading the van. The crowd of onlookers had grown. Not only were the mirrors aiming light toward the doorway, there were now tall spotlights as well. Everyone's attention was focused on the area bathed in light. In the century or so this building has stood here, its entryway, and the small patch of concrete leading to it, had never been seen in such intense and brilliant light. The bricks, pavement and metal were no longer the structural components of a familiar bit of architecture, they were the parts of a scene's composition, a scene that will occur within this molecule of a neighborhood that, for a moment, has stopped being theirs. Primo squeezed into the crowd to watch.

A man kneeling on top of one of the vans spoke into a walkie-talkie, then waved his arm in a forward motion. Two young women, followed by two young men, suddenly emerged from the building. They looked almost like neighborhood teenagers. None of them spoke. They walked as though they were headed somewhere important. After walking a few steps beyond the field of light, they stopped and relaxed. They held their bodies like anybody, on any kind of job, taking a break, and seemed unaware of the people watching them. Primo recognized one of the men—he had seen him in a designer jeans commercial—doing just what he was doing here: walking. Only in the commercial it was in slow motion.

A woman approached them and, for a moment, they all huddled together. She then spoke into a walkie-talkie and they walked back into the building.

Later, while Primo was unloading the van, the old man he had talked to earlier walked slowly by with his folding chair.

As Primo stepped past him, with a carton of books on his shoulder, the man said, "They shot that scene four times. They got here before sunrise and that's *all* they did."

Primo stopped, smiled and faced him, wobbling a bit from the weight of his load.

"Each take it got worse. They shoulda asked me, *I'd* tell em. They got it best the first time."

"Did you find out what it's called?"

"They wouldn't say, but I'll tell you this. . . . They call it *Gone With the Wind*, it still ain't winning no Oscars. Hear what I'm saying?"

Primo laughed.

He looked at the carton on Primo's shoulders. "That looks pretty heavy."

"It is," Primo said.

After Primo brought up the last load, he pulled the squash racket out from under the door and let it swing closed. He was starving and tired. His plan was to drop the van off at the rental agency, get a take-out sandwich at D's and eat it in the park. He leaned against the van for a moment, twirling the racket in his hands. He couldn't decide what to do with it. At the moment, it didn't seem worth a trip up five flights of stairs and he wasn't going to carry it around with him. Besides, he'll probably never use it. It belongs to the life he just left, not the one he returned to. He laid it on top of one of the garbage cans lined up in front of his building. Then he got into the van, rolled down the window and started it up. He knew it would be gone before he rounded the corner.

Primo was born in Harlem on the thirty-first of December, 1950, to Dr. Samuel Thomas—a black physician who was the son of schoolteachers who migrated to New York from North Carolina during the Depression—and Giovanna Leo, daughter of Neapolitan immigrants who arrived here after the First World War. His mother, certain he would be a boy, gave him his first name before he was born. She said he could be called nothing else. She said the name was a blessing. Primo because he was their first—as it turned out, their only—child, and Primo because his actual due date was the first day of the year. The fact that he pushed himself into life a day early didn't change the propitiousness of the name, since *prima*, in Italian, can also mean before. To his mother's way of thinking, the more appropriate a name, the luckier the name is. His father used to say that luck had to do with timing, and that it's much luckier to be born at the beginning of something, rather than at the end of something else.

When Primo was a young child, his parents moved to South Queens where, with the help of a GI Bill mortgage, they could afford a home large enough to house both the family and Dr. Thomas's practice. Their block, 135th Street, was also the service road of the Van Wyck Expressway. Their house was perched on the brink of a canyon. Brick-and-concrete steps, the nightmares of mailmen, descended from the front doors of the houses on his block and cut through sharply down-sloping front lawns that were barely held in place by retaining walls, crabgrass and the roots of ailanthus trees. In South Queens, the Van Wyck Expressway serves as the eastern boundary of Richmond Hill, solidly white, working and lower-middle class, where the only black people you saw worked there, were bused in for school, were passing through or lived, as did Primo's family, along one of the frontiers. Across the river of traffic lay Jamaica, predominantly black and poorer, and the source of most of the patients Primo would find sitting in his father's waiting room when he'd pass through it, on his way deeper into the house, weekdays after school.

When Primo, as a child and later, as a teenager, looked out his bedroom window, across the small, flat backyard and across the unending forest of two-story housetops, he felt he was looking inland.

In the last few years before he left, Primo's life became more and more contained within himself, and had less to do with where he was. He hadn't expected to miss New York. He wasn't even sure he'd return.

Familiar things: traffic lights, mailboxes, the same stretches of pavement, parked cars, storefronts, things that for a decade had become, increasingly, his, simply because each day he walked past them, were becoming less and less *there.* As they lost their presence, they bored him, they made him angry. They had somehow begun to reassert their definitions as uncharged objects, without meaning beyond their specific function. They could have been anywhere. *He* could have been anywhere. They were no longer his.

This process began two years before he left, when Mariah accepted a teaching job at a college in Southern California. She had become increasingly successful as a poet. Her poems were appearing in magazines, a small volume had been published and, the year before she left, she had won a state arts grant. They'd lived together since their sophomore year at City College, and had been married since the year they graduated. Although they did not acknowledge it at the time, they both knew her leaving would be a coincidental manifestation of the process of separating that had begun years before. Mariah was always a bit ahead of Primo when it came to acceptance. In a poem she sent to him her second year away she wrote:

If you look closely
at the first cleft
in a tree trunk you
will see it begins
long before
the branches
separate.

At the beginning of his first summer living alone, he went to the festival of Saint Anthony in Little Italy. He was with friends, people he was teaching with at a community college in Manhattan, all of them white. They were drinking beer and eating *zeppole.* Primo had won a green stuffed turtle by throwing three darts into a target shaped like a red apple.

They came upon a small crowd gathered around a long wooden table that had posters of Sophia Loren hanging along the front. A middle-aged couple and their teenage daughter were sitting behind it. They were handing people copies of a petition on clipboards, and the people were laughing and signing them. At that time Sophia Loren was serving a thirty-day sentence in an Italian prison for tax evasion. One of Primo's friends read the petition aloud. *Nice people don't go to jail. Sophia Loren is a nice person. So* please *pardon her and let her out.*

They all laughed. The teenager behind the counter said to the crowd, "Other people don't pay their taxes, but they're discriminating against her because she's a big star."

Primo and his friends all signed the petition. The man behind the table gave a speech. He asked the crowd if they noticed how much rain had fallen in the last week.

No one could remember.

"Much more than it ever does in June. And you know why? Mother Nature is crying for Sophia."

Again everyone laughed.

Suddenly Primo noticed that the teenage girl behind the table was staring at him. Her look was serious, vaguely angry. Then he noticed her parents were also staring. The look on their faces was direct and undisguised: hatred. He felt as if everyone else, the whole street, the whole afternoon, went into slow motion. He was the only one to keep moving at the same speed.

No one else noticed. They continued laughing and talking among themselves.

Primo walked closer to the table, stood right before them and smiled. Then he said, "When my mother made *moolinyam*, she'd never use too much cheese. She used to say real Italians know that God made eggplant so you could taste it, not disguise the flavor."

The woman began to smile, then stopped.

Primo asked her how she got the orange-colored stains off *her* Tupperware. "My mother gave up trying," he said. He looked back at the father, who was furious but silent. He gave him a big smile.

Then he leaned toward the daughter. "My mother also used to say that the dark, shiny skin of an eggplant was beautiful. It was a mystery to her how anyone could make a bad word out of something so beautiful. She liked to kiss my arms when she said it. Your mother ever kiss *your* arms?" He looked at her. Then at her mother and father. "Not all mothers are the same," he said. "Who can figure . . . ?"

He then handed her the turtle, turned on his heels and walked off.

That night one of the friends he was with called him. "What happened?" she asked. "One minute, we were all just standing there, next minute you were gone."

He tried to explain it to her. She didn't understand.

"Look," he said. "Someone throws a rock at you, you know you should duck. Someone calls you a name, they're telling you where they're at. But this kind of shit . . . Who can laugh. Who *can't* laugh. This kind of shit's worse than evil."

Over the next two years the friends he and Mariah had known since college moved away, or moved deeper into their own lives. Although he and Mariah visited occasionally, and communicated, they grew increasingly separate. The deep sense of alliance they had shared for years had dissipated. It felt as if Mariah, in leaving, had walked into a forest he vaguely comprehended as *everyone else*. And she intended to stay there. They filed for a divorce. They got one.

During the first decade Primo had lived in the neighborhood, the same pair of work shoes—ankle-high, shiny brown leather, wide toe with a single thick seam across the top—had been on display in a shoe store on Avenue A. They were formal work shoes. Depression work shoes. The kind you can shine. They must have been regularly dusted, even polished. Ten years and no one had bought them. Primo had the sense they'd been there a long time before he got there as well. He'd walk past the window at least once a week. He never paid them much attention, but he liked them being there. They reminded him of the shoes worn by the men who used to sit in his father's waiting room. They were serious shoes, meant to come in direct contact with the surface of the planet. They belonged to a time before heavy, more permanent objects gave way to lighter, temporary ones.

He was walking past one afternoon and saw that the window was soaped over. He rushed up to it, pushed his face against the glass and tried to look in. He couldn't see much, but he could see enough. The entire place was being renovated, the shoes were no longer there. That was all he could see until he took a step back. Then he saw the reflection of his own angry face.

He stopped in the liquor store on his way home.

That night—Primo was beginning his second bottle of wine—his friend Manny called from Massachusetts and told him about the job at More College.

"I know you don't want to leave New York," he said, "but let me tell you about it anyway."

"Guess what," Primo said. "Sophia Loren's outta the slammer."

"What?"

"Free as a bird. They gave her her walking papers."

"You drunk?"

"I'm celebrating."

"I'm usually the one who's drunk. This is a change. What are you celebrating?"

"Sophia's freedom."

"Wasn't that two years ago?"

"Yeah. But it wasn't a moment too soon. Life in the cooler was hell on her. Know why?"

"I can't imagine. What the hell are you up to?"

"Know why? They made her wear work shoes."

"There's a job here, Primo. Listen. That's why I'm calling. To tell you about it."

"I'll take it."

"You'll take it? Primo, I hope you're serious."

"I'm serious. I'll take it. But it was awful. She looked like Li'l fuckin Abner."

"Who? Sophia Loren? That was two years ago."

"And not a moment too soon."

Today Primo feels there is no place else, for him, to be. He's happy to be back.

He's walking east down St. Mark's Place toward the park. The early-summer crowd is mixed, young, pretty. It's not yet humid, not yet hot. In his sweatshirt and jeans it feels as if it is no temperature at all.

At First Avenue the crosswalk is blocked by a Con Ed van and an open manhole cover encircled by yellow rubber cones. As the stream of pedestrian traffic slows and curves around, Primo finds himself walking directly behind a young woman wearing a long many-wrapped necklace made of spent .22 caliber cartridges strung together. The crowd slows even more and he finds himself pressed close enough to her to see the small impressions left in the rim of each shell by the firing pin of the gun that fired them.

None of the workers are aboveground and as he passes the open manhole he hears a woman's voice singing Marvin Gaye's "If This World Were Mine" in a sweet voice measured to a steady, breathy tempo by the exertion of whatever work she is doing. He's beginning to feel *back*, to pick up the sense of being here he left behind two years ago.

The block between First Avenue and Tompkins Square has a gently civilian quietness. It feels like the main street of a small town on a weekday afternoon. There is little movement in the storefronts, the upper branches of the young sycamores stir slightly, three people are walking dogs.

As he nears the corner a teenage girl on a bike swerves toward the curb beside Primo. He's walking at a place where no car is parked and she comes within a few feet of him. "Sens, speed, hash," she says. Like one word, "*Sens-speed-hash.*" Primo offers no response and she gracefully arcs away from him, shoots between a parked car and another waiting at the light and swings onto Avenue A. He knows no policeman could ever catch her. He'd have to see her first, and there are very few things less visible than a dark teenage girl riding a bicycle on Avenue A.

Primo sits on one of the benches that face the outdoor band shell across an open space filled with the oldest, widest elm trees in downtown Manhattan. The center of the park and his favorite spot for alfresco lunch on warm afternoons. He watches four men trying to drag a doorless refrigerator up the short flight of steps into the band shell. Its platform is already covered with cardboard, blankets, clothing, sleeping bags.

There's a young man, barely more than a teenager, asleep at the far end of the next bench. He's lying on his side, his knees up, his head against the hard slats of the bench seat. He appears to be hugging something. Primo notices his dark swollen belly, pushing out between the flaps of a green flak jacket.

A woman on Rollerblades, wearing a Walkman, shoots out of the path Primo had just walked on, does a 180-degree turn, then glides past the benches skating backward. The refrigerator is now back on the ground and one of the men is sitting inside it, rocking back and forth, groaning and moving his arms like he's pulling oars against a strong current.

Primo sits cross-legged and leans his weight into the bench. The sky is a clear, rich blue between the upper branches of the trees. He's been in motion, nonstop, for two days, and his muscles have just begun to relax and loosen. Before unpacking he'll take a long nap.

The man on the next bench mumbles in his sleep and turns onto his back. His jacket falls open and Primo can now see what the man is hugging: a squash racket. *His* squash racket. He holds it with the handle at his waist and the flat, wide head, like the head of another, smaller being, pressed against his chest and neck.

Primo moves to the bench the man is sleeping on and sits beside him. He wraps up the uneaten half of his sandwich and sets it between the man's feet.

Primo then leans his head against the back of the bench and closes his eyes. Before he falls asleep he makes a loud kissing noise. He feels like he has just thrown a rope across the wide canyon of the last two years, lassoed a stump on the other side and, with the epic strength of Pecos Bill, pulled the facing cliffs together.

At the moment the two sides joined, they kissed like lips.

Smack.

2

Primo hears the phone ringing as he climbs the last flight of stairs. He unlocks the door, rushes inside, shoves a kitchen chair aside as he crosses the room and grabs the receiver. "Hello?" He hears the click of the caller hanging up. He's sure that the span of silence after the last ring had not yet reached the point where the next ring should start. The person calling must have been ringing a long time.

He sets the phone back into the receiver and falls onto the bed. In the park he quickly fell into a deep sleep. After an hour or so the afternoon sun found a space through the treetops. Before waking, he could see it through his eyelids. It was like looking at a light bulb through a glass of red wine. He never fully awoke during the walk home. At first, he didn't even notice that the film crew had left. The police barricades were piled on top of each other on the corner but otherwise the block had the same look and feel it always had in late afternoon. Then he saw the trailer with the dressing rooms, as long as the rear portion of a semi, the only thing they hadn't taken. Coming upon it half awake, without all the equipment and people, made watching them film that scene, just hours ago, seem like a dream he had while asleep on the park bench. And the trailer was now simply a mobile home, covered in white aluminum siding, parked on a side street in downtown Manhattan, with no apparent reason for being there. A large and quiet fish very much out of water.

The small burst of energy that asserted itself when he heard the phone is passing. He has not looked up at this uneven square of plaster ceiling in two years. The edges of its surface soften as he falls back toward sleep. He'll finish the nap that got interrupted when the afternoon sun woke him.

The phone rings again.

"Hello?"

"I thought I heard someone pick it up," a woman's voice says. "But my arm was already in motion. By the time my brain got the message, the phone was hung up. Hiya Primo."

"Who is this?" The voice is familiar, but he has no idea whose it is.

"What were you doing before, sitting there watching it ring?"

"I just walked in. *Who* is this?"

"Who the hell you think it is?"

"I don't know. But now *my* arm's in motion, and it's getting ready to hang up this phone."

She laughs. "Men's arms are always in motion." He then hears a child in the background. "Hold on a second," the woman's voice says.

He hears the two-part clunk of the receiver being set down. He hears a scraping sound: a chair being moved. He hears her speak to the child. "Felicia, wait. . . . Wait till after supper."

Pamela. Now he knows who it is.

"Look at the time," he hears her say to her daughter. "If you start painting now, you'll only have to stop and clean up in ten minutes."

Pamela. He hasn't spoken to her in years. Not since Mariah left. In all the years he's known her they've never spoken over the phone. She's a poet, and has always been more Mariah's friend than his. Felicia was maybe three years old the last time he saw her. That was just before Pamela left her husband and got an apartment up in Westchester, near the college she taught in.

When she picks up the phone he asks her how she knew he was back. "In fact, how'd you know I was away?"

"How many people do we know in common?"

"This call would cost you a lot less if you answered questions better."

"I can afford it. And of all the people we know in common, how many knew you were out of town teaching literacy to the children that couldn't get into Harvard?"

"I haven't heard from Mariah in a while. Not even a poem. She sends me all the poems she writes about me."

"I like the one where she compares you to a dolphin. You like that one?"

"Pamela, I'm happy to talk to you. And I'm also tired. Is there a specific reason you called?"

"I'm inviting you to dinner. A welcome-back dinner." He hears Felicia's voice in the background. Then Pamela's voice, at a distance from the phone, telling her she'll be right there. "A let's-see-who-changed-the-most dinner, a beginning-of-the-second-half-of-your-life dinner." Again, he hears her voice aimed away from the phone. "I'm coming," she says to Felicia. "I gotta go. When you get hungry, call. Hear me?"

Between the time he hangs up the phone and the time he finally falls back to sleep, he receives three more phone calls.

Manny calls from More. He asks how the trip was. He tells Primo that there already exists a memorial on the shelf above the coffee maker in the English Department office: the Harlem Globetrotters mug Primo used. "It will remain there, never again to be drunk from, but to contain the wooden stirrers and, more important, the memory of the two years Primo Thomas graced this institution with his presence."

His Aunt Olivia calls. She is his father's sister, and the only living relative Primo has any contact with.

Primo's father died when he was sixteen. Two years later, when Primo began college, he moved out on his own. Soon after he married Mariah, his mother sold the house in Queens and moved back to Harlem, where she lived with Olivia, who had never married and remained, on her own, in the large apartment that she and Primo's father had lived in since they were children. Like her father and mother, Primo's grandparents, she was a teacher. She's now retired and has lived alone since Primo's mother passed away seven years ago. He always visits her during the Christmas holidays, and once or twice during the rest of the year.

Primo's mother had been forbidden by her family to marry his father, and was rejected by them completely after she went ahead and did so. Primo met her parents, the Leos, only once, when his mother brought him to Mass at Our Lady of Lourdes Church, in Harlem. He called it Lady of *Lords*, until his mother taught him to say it the way Italians do: *Lurr-de*, she had told him, *Nostra Signora di Lurr-de.* She'd had a dream, she told Primo. She was a child again and she was kneeling at the altar waiting to receive her first Communion. In the dream Primo knelt beside her. That was when she knew she had to bring him. He was seven at the time. "We are all children to God," she told him. "To Him, we never stop being children."

She never told him if she had known her parents would also be there. She did not act surprised when she saw them, but he felt her whole body stiffen. She greeted them as if she barely knew them, not touching other than to lean toward her mother and quickly kiss her on the cheek. The whole time, she held Primo close beside her with her arm around his shoulder. Then she presented him to these strange old people. "This is your grandmother," she said. To them as well as to Primo. "This is your grandfather."

Afterward, they all walked down the wide center aisle and, after genuflecting, slid into pews on opposite sides of the church.

Primo watched the old man during Mass. His hard, wrinkled skin added to the severity of his expression. What Primo remembers most from that morning thirty years ago is the fact that his face never changed, not when he first looked at Primo, and not later, when Primo watched him, across the width of the church, kneel, genuflect, make the sign of the cross, speak the prayers. It was as though he lived his life deep inside his dark, wrinkled, worn-out face. The man Primo was watching was not his grandfather, he was someone who had once been his mother's father. When his mother was his age, she lived in the same home as the man who lived inside that face.

Olivia had called to find out how he was and also to invite him up to dinner.

"Been back one day and already I got two dinner invitations."

"If she's young and good-looking you have my permission to see her first. But then you better be heading uptown."

"I'm not heading anywhere for a while. I feel like I'm the engine on a train whose caboose is still in Massachusetts."

"When all your cars pull into the station, you come up and see me."

"It's a date."

"Who else you having dinner with?"

"I didn't say I was having dinner, I said I was asked."

"Who asked you?"

"A friend of Mariah's. You don't know her."

"Oh no. Don't tell me it's the one with the three rings in her nose."

"Aunt Olivia, you really don't know her."

"You're the only who can address me as *aunt.* I'm Olivia or Ms. Thomas to the rest of the planet. A sweet designation, aunt, but only when uttered in proper Black English vocalism: *Ahnt.* Listen: My *ant* came to the picnic. What's the first thing that comes to your mind?"

"What I was saying, dear Aunt Olivia, is that you don't know this woman."

"You're just like your father. You never say anything about anything. When you *do* open your mouth, it's like you're giving away something valuable."

"What do you want to know?"

"That you're happy, Primo. That my nephew is happy."

"I'm happy."

"You're happy. . . . You're flying an airship. That's what you're doing."

"I'm what?"

"That's what your father used to say. When he was young."

"Why?"

"Because people used to use that word. *Airship.*"

"No. Why'd he *say* it?"

"Because he was older than me, and because he was a boy. He could come and go as he pleased. Church and school was all I ever left the house for. He'd come home looking all excited and preoccupied, like he'd been around the world and back, and I'd ask him what he was doing and he'd always have the same wiseass answer. *Flying an airship.*"

"I *am* fine. I'm just sleepy."

"You're flying an airship."

The third call is for the woman who sublet while Primo was away. It's from a guy named Dennis who sounds angry and incredulous, hearing a man's voice answer the phone.

Primo tells him she went back to California.

The guy won't believe it. "But she didn't say nothing."

"That's the way it is," Primo tells him, before he hangs up.

"That's the way *what* is?" the guy asks him.

"One minute everything's righteous, next minute they fly off in an airship."

3

Primo unpacks a Boston Celtics photo calendar from the top of a carton of books and tacks it to the kitchen wall. It had spent the first half of the year in his office two hundred miles to the north and would delineate the remaining six months on a kitchen wall in downtown Manhattan. The photographer for June is artier than the ones chosen for the previous months, who preferred midair collisions and shattering backboards. Three pairs of dark legs, high-top sneakers at their bottoms, ascend toward heaven. Behind them, a vague wall of audience, the faces barely discernible in bright, damp air.

He changes the channel on the portable TV. It has been on all morning. As he unpacked, he watched the news, *Transformer* cartoons and a talk show. He now decides on a bilingual, Spanish/English program on public TV. A family are sitting around their kitchen table, having a conversation about the things in the room. They are unusually polite. They always address the person they are speaking to and constantly refer to everyday objects by name.

"Pablo, could you please pass me a spoon?"

"*Anita, ¿prefieres una cuchara o una cucharita?*"

"I'd like a teaspoon please. Thank you, Pablo."

"*Mamá, ¿prepariste arroz con frijoles hoy?*"

"Of course, Anita. I know it's your favorite."

As Primo unpacks and carries stacks of books and clothes into the bedroom he repeats aloud the phrases from the program. *Pablo, ¿te gustan las nuevas sillas? Yes, Papi. They are very comfortable. Y Pablo, ¿puedes ser un pendejo en dos idiomas? Yes, Papi, I can be an asshole in two languages. Es muy fácil . . .*

By early afternoon he has unpacked nearly all the boxes and stacked them in the hall. The only one remaining is the Del Monte canned peaches carton the TV is sitting on. All the other cartons were from the supermarket in More, but this one he had brought with him two years ago. It sat in the back of his closet the whole time, holding the things he never used: a health food cookbook and a blue wool sweater with a reindeer on the front his Aunt Olivia had given him as a going-away present, a deck of cards and the squash racket. Now it's filled with books and papers from his office at More, things he won't need until next month, when he starts teaching again. He decides to leave it packed. It will make good temporary furniture.

He sits on the couch and watches the TV. A series of aerial shots of beautiful rocky islands surrounded by glass-blue sea, interspersed with drawings of the Trojan horse, Poseidon with his trident, Socrates, men wielding spears, bunches of grapes, chariots. An educational program on Greece. Then two children, one Greek, one American, are walking toward the ruins of the Acropolis. The Greek child tells the American child that the Parthenon was here long before we were—cut to the city below, streets swelling with automobile traffic, then to a jet, crossing a blue sky—and will be here long after we're gone. Both children feign a serious and awed expression. There is a shot of a drawing of what the Parthenon must have looked like in ancient times, a shot of the current city below, then the children again, standing in front of the ruins.

Suddenly Primo is crying. His mouth is open. His mouth is open and he's crying aloud.

What is this shit? He stands, walks to the TV, back to the couch. *Before we got here . . . long after we're gone.*

He knows what it is. *The oddest fucking thought. Out of nowhere. His father is no longer on the same planet the Acropolis is on.* But he's known *that* for twenty years. *Shit!*

He hates the sound of his own crying.

He walks into the kitchen and drags a chair back into the living room. He stands in front of the TV and lifts it over his head.

How do you like the new motherfucking chairs, Pablo? Shit, Pablo. How about I break this new motherfucker over your head?

He sets the chair back down. His mouth is open, but he is quiet now. He walks around the room, then stops, stands beside the chair. He sits on it. *Shit, Pablo. What's wrong with you?* He starts laughing. *You live on TV. Don't you know this shit's fake?*

It's insincere, Pablo. . . . It's counterfeit, it's fallacious. He's laughing and shaking his head. *What's wrong with you, man?*

He turns the chair so he faces the TV. He leans forward, his elbows on his knees and his palms cupping his chin, and talks to the children on the screen. *He was here sixty years.* They're now walking inside the ruins of the Parthenon. *Sixty years.* There is no roof. They look up at the sky. *How long* that *fucking thing been here? Maybe five thousand years? How many?*

Don't answer me. It don't matter. However long it's been here it couldn't've become longer ago *in his short lifetime. Know what I'm saying? I'm saying years can't measure shit been around that long. Human years can't. Dog years can't either. Even elephant years can't and those motherfuckers are like a thousand days long. . . .*

The children are now in a classroom standing beside a big globe. *Now listen to me children: Time is big! That fucking thing was as old as it is now when he was born. When you and I were born, too. It might have been a little younger when my great-great grandpa was born on a plantation and it might be a bit older when Captain Kirk gets his ass born two hundred years from now. . . .* He stands, walks up to the screen. *But us? The way time sees it, all of* us *are in the same photograph. If we could've known each other, even a minute, we're playing in the same ball game.*

I can't see why this should be of the slightest interest to either of you. He turns off the TV and goes back to the couch.

What the hell is going on? He died twenty years ago.

He leans back. It must be all the traveling. He must still be tired.

What is going on? First, the phone kept ringing while he was trying to fall asleep. Then later, in the middle of the night, he awoke for no reason at all. But he was tired so he just lay there, listening to the street sounds, and waited for morning. After two years of emptier nights the sounds were welcome: the voices, spinning tires, the sirens, each delimited their own presence within the collective, energetic whir, the enormous dome of outside world.

He's unwinding. *Shit.* That's what it is. In over thirty-six years, he's learned a few things about himself. One of them is that during periods like the last two and a half days, his life becomes pure motion, and what he's doing becomes *all* he's doing. The shit that could be on his mind drifts upward and stays up there until he finally stands still. Then it drops back on top of him like a ton of bricks. Until he rights himself he staggers a bit from the shock. Unwinding. A couple of days and he'll find his stride.

He decides to get dressed and go outdoors. Get some fresh air. Maybe lunch, maybe a movie. He flattens the empty cardboard boxes, stacks them and ties them into a bundle with cord. Then carries them down and leans them against the garbage cans out front. The next neighbors who move somewhere else can use them. Maybe Anita and Pablo will move out on their own. It's time they entered the real world, where you don't address people by their names each time you say something to them.

They're good boxes. Pablo, Anita, they're yours. *Mi caja es tu caja.* If you don't use them someone else will. We recycle things in this neighborhood. Squash rackets. Drinking straws. Shit can stay around a thousand years that way.

4

The film crew trailer is still there. It's the only thing in his line of sight that could alter a first visual impression identical to the photograph he develops from memory of the block five years ago, ten years ago. There have been a lot of changes. They began before he left and continued while he was away. But so much stays the same, and that's what he's looking for now.

In early spring, when he decided to leave More and return to New York, Manny, disappointed, responded with a string of platitudes. They were sitting in a bar called Big Tad's, the only place with live music in town, when he told him.

"Don't look back. You can't go home again. What do you want to do, cross the same fucking river *twice?*"

"Save it for your students."

"What's back there for you?"

"What's here?"

"Me. And the wise sayings I use as essay topics."

"I'll miss you, too."

"*We have no abiding cities here . . .*"

"That's a new one. Where's it from?"

"Old Testament, I think. Van Gogh liked to say it."

"Your students understand it?

"Not at first. They thought it was just bullshit until I told them David Letterman said it. That brought them around. Do you know what it means?"

"I never watch David Letterman."

"If you think you live somewhere, you don't live anywhere. There's no *where* about it. Life is *in* you, or it's in people, friends, *not* places. So stay."

As he walks past the van it annoys him. Aluminum siding belongs in Queens, where he grew up, or on the outsides of the small houses and trailers clustered on the edges of towns like More. Not in downtown Manhattan. To look beyond it at the dark brick and fire escaped walls is to frame the exterior surfaces of suburban, rural and inner-city lower-income life in the same field of vision. And that's not the film they were making.

The same white siding began to appear on the houses in the neighborhood he grew up in, in the early sixties, when the wood and shingles of the turn-of-the-century row houses began to molt from age and rot. He remembers getting off the bus, after school, walking down the street and enjoying the brightness of the first few houses that had it. From fifty yards off, to a child, the layered plank design was indistinguishable from newly painted wood. The clean, light surfaces, among the dingy, sooty walls, gave him pleasure. He liked to look at them. Now, after two years at More, it's impossible for him to see it without an entourage of attendant images: weeds, cinder blocks, old tires, a barking dog, a shopping cart chained to a sagging hurricane fence . . . The presence of the newer, even-edged, smoother surfaces cannot hold back a larger deterioration.

He walks across the street and is pleased to discover that the other side of the trailer, the side uninterrupted by doors or windows, had been graffiti'ed during the night. It says *Dr. Light 'n' Lisita* inside a big red heart. Instead of Cupid's arrow, it's pierced through with a blue dagger. Red and blue blood drips from the two wounds it makes. Nearer the front, riding a lightning bolt, are the letters *BB*.

If they leave this trailer here a few days longer it will look like a permanent part of the neighborhood. The *abiding* neighborhood. They might not even be able to find it.

He heads uptown on Avenue A and sees Gladys García, a young woman who lives in the corner building with her mother and grandmother. She was three when he and Mariah moved in. Now she is walking toward him, half a block away, pushing a baby carriage. On warm days she'd sit in front of the building with her mother and grandmother and their dog, an old cocker spaniel, and sometimes they'd bring out their small portable TV and run an extension cord through the open window. Their presence gentled and made comfortable the outdoor space on the entire block. Primo and Mariah always greeted them when they walked past and sometimes Mariah would sit with them and chat.

Gladys is wearing a black sleeveless T-shirt with something written in silver glitter script across the front. As they near each other Primo wonders if she'll recognize him. She was fifteen at the most when he left, still a child, and now she's a mother. Her waist and hips are still wide from her pregnancy. On the front of her T-shirt it says *Atlantic City.* He smiles at her when he's sure she's close enough to see him. He can't tell if she's noticed. The carriage has a gauze curtain but he can see the child. It is very small. Sleeping. Underneath the glittery lettering on her shirt, in faded, flatter colors, are the symbols of a heart, a club, a spade and a diamond.

He sees her notice him looking at the baby, but he's still not sure she recognizes him. He looks straight at her.

"Yo," she says.

"Gladys," Primo says. "Hi."

She smiles, slows down, but doesn't stop. Then she says, "How's Mariah?"

"She's fine."

"Do me a favor," she says. She turns her head as they pass each other. The high, off-white side panel of her matronly brassiere hugs the U shape of exposed skin in the open side of her T-shirt.

"Sure," Primo says. He stops, to slow the growth of distance between them.

"Tell her my mother's dog died."

"I'll tell her," he says.

She leans over the handle of the carriage and says something to her baby.

"I'll tell her," he says again.

FOURTH OF JULY

5

As a child, Primo understood there to be a kind of beauty, a thing he desired in other people and that drew him to them, in their ability to inhabit the things they said. People could send out words in contained, isolated bubbles, like in comic books, or in streams of sounds wet with pleasure, or curiosity, or desire, or anger, that seemed to issue not only from their mouths but from their whole bodies, and that could fill the space between them and Primo, and change it to a pleasing substance.

There were, in his earliest years, few people consistently around him, and most of them were adults. Of them all, his father had the deepest, most substantial connection to the things he said and did. Primo would wait at the edge of his father's clenched silence for the words he'd speak. His anger had great power. And also had the most beauty. Primo wanted to draw out that power and gather it in. It had in it something he wanted. It seemed so unlike his own withdrawn, tentative inclusion in the life around him.

As he got older, spoke more and was spoken to more, he began to distinguish two kinds of people. Those who said things simply because they wanted to, and those who spoke because silence, often the silence he learned to consciously invoke, was unbearable to them. Their voices added no charge to the air, and when he looked for meaning in the words themselves, he found none. *What grade are you in, young man? I have a daughter your age. You want to be a doctor like your father?* Then he, on his own, would have to give definition to everything in the room—the lamp *he* saw, the table *he* saw. The fools standing in front of him, bending in his direction, were not even there. He'd become bored, lonely, angry. The light would feel thinner and drier. Time stopped passing. He'd have no way to occupy the moment and no way to end it.

It is in these last things that this has realized itself into memory. A lamp, a table, light filling a room. The refusal of time to pass.

Primo is standing in front of the train station in Ayrwood, New York, facing the road that winds uphill toward the heart of town. Pamela said she'd be waiting for his train but she's late. It's a clear, bright, hot evening. A profusion of thick treetops are crammed into the squares and rectangles that fill the spaces between the houses and small buildings on the rising hillside. He's never been in this town. Its name, as it appears on the signs on the station platform, is Ayrwood-on-Hudson.

In the fifteen minutes or so he's been waiting, the cars that had been idling by the station exit or parked in the small lot have gone. He was the only rider not traveling the familiar, well-worn path of the evening commute, the last leg of which, for them, is the short drive up that hill.

He begins to pace. The gravel in the parking lot is made of the same round ballast stones that support the train tracks. They press into the bottoms of his sneakers. He is the only thing moving.

He walks to the edge of the station building so he can see, across the tracks and just beyond the southbound platform, the Hudson River. The sun has come to a standstill, hours above the river and the opposite shore. The flat red path it sends toward him lies still across the heaving blue-green surface. If he were standing alongside the next station, at the next suburban town, the same path of sunlight would find him. In fact, if a million people stood in line along the eastern bank of this river they would each see it, an aisle of red light that stretches from the New Jersey shore all the way to their feet. And they'd each see it as their own. His restlessness is tightening into anger. "Shit," he says aloud.

He hears the quiet crunch of tires, slowly approaching from behind. "Shit," he says again, then turns.

Pamela has stopped her car ten feet behind him. She is leaning her head out the driver's window, squinting and smiling into the sunlight.

"Well what do you know. . . ." she shouts as he walks toward the car. "Another dark man has found his way out to the suburbs. It's nice, seeing another one of us, in this gentle village." She leans across the seat and opens his door. "Get in, pilgrim."

Primo hasn't seen her in over four years.

"Sorry I'm late," she says.

She appears the same. Her hair is in the same loose, irregular braids that curve upward and then fall over both sides of her head. Yet the first sensation he has in seeing her is that she has changed. Perhaps her cheeks are a little fuller, her eyes set more deeply, older. Maybe that's what it is, maybe not.

"I had to pick up some things last minute." She points to a plastic shopping bag in the back seat. At a glance Primo can see that it contains onions, a bottle of grape juice, a six-pack of beer. "The line at the supermarket was endless."

The road winds upward, away from the river, and opens up into the town's main road. They pass a drugstore with buntings slung across the top of the window and, from the wall above, strings of red, white and blue pennants that reach to a lamppost out front.

Pamela uses it to illustrate what she's saying. "That's why I took so long at the market. Tomorrow being the Fourth, the whole town's stocking up on hot dogs." She turns to Primo and smiles. "Twenty-four hours from now, a cloud of meat molecules and charcoal smoke will darken the sky."

"Very poetic," Primo says.

"And very true," Pamela says. "This holiday gets more serious every year."

Primo speaks aloud the names of the businesses they pass. "DiPalma Meat Market, Kay's Dry Cleaning, Sid's Video, Lieu's Bicycle Shop . . ."

Pamela smiles, then says, "Nice town. We got one of everything you're supposed to have."

The only relationship they've ever had was in their separate relationships to Mariah. Husband and wife's friend. It's not the absence of these roles that feels funny to Primo, it's that without Mariah they have no past. They are familiar, casual, driving toward a dinner table through this gentle small town, and they don't really know each other from Adam.

"I brought wine," Primo says. This follows nothing they've said but fits the next space in the rhythm of conversation. He holds up the bag he'd carried with him from the city. In it there is also a gift for Felicia, a Slinky he bought in a store on First Avenue.

"Good," she says. "We'll drink it."

They pull into the driveway of an old, white Victorian house. The paint on its front porch has worn and peeled, and the patches of wood it exposes are gray and dry.

"The house is now three apartments," Pamela says. "We send the rent to Florida." She drives around the back and parks in front of another, smaller porch. Chained to its banister are a ten-speed bicycle and another, much smaller, with training wheels.

He watches her as she shifts into neutral, pulls on the emergency brake.

She notices. She smiles at him.

"So how you doing," Primo says—he extends his hand and they shake—"after all these years?"

The back door swings open and Felicia comes out onto the porch. She sets her hands on her hips, taps one foot, and smiles a parental I've-been-waiting-a-long-time smile. Primo smiles back as he walks toward the porch.

She says to him, "You're gonna tell me you haven't seen me since I was real little, right?"

"I had that in mind, but I think I'll skip it."

"There's no point, is there? I wouldn't remember anyway."

"You're absolutely right."

"Grape juice?" she asks her mother. And then answers for herself by lifting the bottle out of the bag Pamela had set on the kitchen table.

They sit at the round dinner table in the kitchen. The windows over the sink and drainboard and the back door are wide open. A welcoming in of what is outside that rarely happens in Manhattan. The sound of someone sawing wood and the news from the small speaker of a portable radio float in from a nearby backyard. There's a crock of chili set on a bamboo trivet in the center of the table. A bowl of salad and another of rice.

Primo tells Pamela and Felicia that they shot a film on his block last month.

"Were you in it?" Felicia asks. Beside her plate is a jelly glass with a Smurf on it. It has about one sip of grape juice remaining at the bottom. On the other side of her plate is the Slinky Primo gave her.

"In it? No. I watched them though."

"Not even a walk-on?"

"I'm a teacher, not an actor."

She frowns slightly.

"You going to finish your salad?" Pamela asks her.

She picks up a spinach leaf, rolls it into a wide cigar shape, takes a bite of it, then pushes the rest of it into her mouth.

"Thank you," Pamela says.

"What was the name of it?" Felicia asks, chewing. "The movie, I mean."

"I don't know. All they were saying is that it's for TV."

"You watched them filming and you weren't curious?" She then looks at her mother. "What's wrong with him?"

Primo tells her that all he knows for certain is that he's seen one of the actors, a guy about sixteen, in a designer jeans commercial.

Felicia asks which commercial.

Primo looks at Pamela for help. She reasks her daughter's question. "Which?"

"I don't know *which*. . . . There's just these guys, in jeans and

T-shirts, walking in a line through a cloud of steam. They got these looks on their faces like they're going to kick somebody's ass."

Felicia smiles. "That's the one," she says. She looks at her mother, then back at Primo. "Okay," she says. "The first one's got an eagle on his T-shirt and a blond crew cut."

Primo laughs. Her careful watching, her memory are amazing.

"The second one's got the cut-off sleeves, real dark skin, V-cut neck and uses too much hair relaxer."

"He the one carrying the football?"

"Uh-uh, that one's like fifth or sixth. Anyway, he don't matter. Now the third . . ." She smiles at Pamela again. "The third. He's got on a white T-shirt, no sleeves at all, high-top fade."

"That's him," Primo says. He feels like he blindly dropped his finger onto a page of an open phone book and it landed on the name of someone everybody else already knows.

"He's her favorite," Pamela says. "He's also in a Michael Jackson video."

"Two." Felicia shows him two fingers.

Primo is laughing.

"*Two* Michael Jackson videos. I'm glad to see he finally got himself a serious dramatic role."

Everyone is laughing.

"Did they at least tell you when they were going to show it?" she asks.

"No. But if I learn anything I'll call you."

More often than not, for Primo, tense, curious, ordinary moments like this one can, on their own, expand outward, away from him, and away from everybody else he's in them with. Then the time just passes, or rather, is simply endured, until he finds himself in the next moment, with whoever he is in it with and whatever new things are happening within it. It feels like something had funneled their wandering, uncentered communication to this single, shared reference point. A single star in the immeasurable constellation of strangers whose faces we have casually seen on screens, pages, even in person.

Primo helps himself to more chili. Felicia slides her glass forward and he refills it with grape juice. She starts laughing again. Primo starts laughing again.

For each thousand short, solo, barely rememberable voyages through time, which is emptier than space, you land on an inhabited planet. One such as this: the simple yet unlikely possibility that three people—adults or children, strangers or family—would actually find themselves talking about the *same* thing. And know it's the same thing. That's what life is always like at the movies.

The setting sun has fit its entire self behind the bulk of the house opposite the kitchen window. It generates a steamy red fire from the shingles on its sloping roof.

"Everybody's got the right to enjoy a summer evening," Primo says. "An ordinary, yet special pleasure in these odd times."

"Amen," Pamela says.

Felicia looks at them both. Raises the side of her lip in curiosity. "*Amen?*" she says.

After dinner they watch a film on the VCR. Primo and Pamela are sitting on the living room couch. Felicia lies on the floor between them and the TV.

The movie begins in a small town in the years just after the Second World War. It's shot in a bluish black and white that has the visual feel of old photographs. The main character is out of work. A guy he knew from high school has become manager of the local bank while he was off fighting the war. He asks him for a job. The guy asks if he has a suit. He doesn't but he'll buy one, two if need be. But the guy isn't encouraging. He tells him he doesn't think he'd fit in with the bank's image. The main character tells the young bank manager that he was a jerk in high school and he's a jerk now. Then his girlfriend decides to accept the marriage proposal of another man. So the main character, along with his dog, leaves town in search of a job and a new life. As they drive, he talks to the dog. He complains that if the dog is going to fart, it should open a window first.

They haven't driven far when they come upon a crowd gathered at a spot where the road crosses a river. He pulls over to see what's going on. A car has driven off the small bridge and is slowly sinking in the river. He can see that there are people trapped inside. He dives in and helps two children out the open rear window of the car. Then he brings them to two men, one black, one white, standing knee deep in the water at the shore, both of them wearing overalls and work shirts and worn, soft-rimmed fedoras. Then someone on the overpass above shouts, "She's still *in* there. She can't get out!" He swims back and slides his body through the car's rear window. There are vague, frantic movements inside the car, which is sinking faster now. The rear end is now all that remains above the surface. Just before it is swallowed by the water, a woman escapes and then, startled and gasping, swims toward the two men at the shore. The entire car, with him inside it, has slid underneath the water. Everyone's eyes are riveted to the roiled, foaming surface where the car had just been. Then the water begins to grow calm again. His dog, sitting at the edge of the road above, begins to bark.

"Why are we watching this?" Primo asks Pamela.

Felicia rolls onto her stomach and faces Primo. Then says, "Because it's the first movie in the world with a dog that farts."

"So *that's* why," Primo says.

"I like this director," Pamela says.

"He's a great director," Felicia says.

As they speak, the screen becomes dark. Bright colors appear and form into tornado shapes that swirl across a field of night-dark blue.

"The light looks like a Slinky," Felicia says. Then she says, "Wow, now it's a color movie."

"It is," Pamela agrees. "Now it's in color."

Felicia slides nearer to Primo and her mother and sits with her back against the couch.

The main character is now standing in a bright, empty room with black and white floor tiles. He is looking at his own fingers, confused. He smiles briefly. He frowns. The camera pulls back and we see him from behind, naked.

"Wow," Felicia says.

"Wow," Pamela says.

"Why are we watching this?" Primo asks again.

Pamela's engrossed in the movie and doesn't answer.

The main character's aunt, who died years before, has shown up and given him a pair of pants and a shirt. She tells him he's dead. He gets upset, he won't accept it. She tells him to face it. "You kicked the bucket. You bought the farm."

Felicia turns to Pamela. "Mama," she says, "he's dead?"

Pamela reaches down and runs her fingers over her daughter's hair. "He is, honey."

"It's okay," she asks, "that he's dead?"

"It is, honey. In the film it is." Then she says to Primo, "There's two reasons I like this director. He makes goofy, unusual movies that actually mean something, and even though he doesn't make movies *about* black folks, he knows we're in the world."

"That's a pretty hard thing *not* to know."

"Not when it comes to the movies. In most films about white folks, a sister or brother shows up along with their reason for being there. They're cops . . . you're on a bus or a subway . . . you're in a bad neighborhood, a jazz club, a prison . . . And if it's a birthday party or a wedding reception, you got to have one or two black couples on the dance floor. And maybe a chic, stylish Asian lady to establish the scene."

"Wow," Felicia says. "Do you believe this school?"

In the movie the main character is being led around some kind of heavenly school by a beautiful young woman. Children are sitting at computer terminals, singing, playing musical instruments. The beautiful young woman opens the door to a room that is actually a jungle. Inside, a teacher, wearing a pith helmet, is teaching children the names of tropical birds.

"I'd go to that school," Felicia says. "I'd go to that school in a minute."

"It's simple," Pamela says. "A small thing, but it makes a big difference . . ."

On the screen, the man and woman are now lying beside each other on the bank of a gentle dreamy river.

"It's like when you're there, you're just *there.* It don't really matter . . . Or *not* there, even. What matters is that you don't feel measured in, like a part of some recipe."

"Two cups of dark folks," Primo says, then smiles.

"A simple thing, but a big one. When the world feels *that* real, people just *being* there, it's easy to let go, and just stroll into the make-believe world of the film. Even when all the falling in love and car chasing and mystery solving goes on among the white folks. You know the rest of us are nearby. At least on the same planet."

"Or the same heaven," Primo adds, nodding toward the screen.

The young man and the beautiful young woman have fallen in love and are about to get married. A choir of children is singing and their voices sound not only like children's voices but like bells and horns as well.

Felicia, without turning from the screen says, "My school sucks."

"Where'd you learn that?" Pamela asks.

"Everybody says it."

"Not everybody *I* know. Don't go telling your teacher that."

Felicia turns to face her mother and Primo. "I could tell her that if I wanted. Mama, she's cool. It's the *school* that sucks."

During the heavenly wedding, the beautiful young woman becomes invisible, just for a second, then returns to view. It turns out this means she is about to be born. She will enter life on earth and he will lose her.

Pamela walks into the kitchen. She comes back in with two cold beers.

From this moment on, the three of them remain absorbed in the movie. There is a small, strange man in heaven, a head angel, some kind of boss. He tells the young man that if their love began in heaven they will meet again, during some future life, and they will love each other forever. It could be a thousand years from now, but it's slated to happen. He says, be patient, but the young man can't wait that long. He wants to be reborn now. The small man finally relents but adds that if he doesn't find her in thirty years of life, it will be too late. "Will she be born a woman?" the young man asks. "She will," the small man says. "Then make me a man."

Their paths intersect several times while living their very different lives. But each time, they do not meet. And each time, Felicia shakes her head in disappointment. The day of his thirtieth birthday arrives, and Felicia climbs up on the couch. Pamela lifts her arm and

Felicia fits herself into the space next to her and beneath it. The two lovers, who haven't even met in this life, are in danger of losing an eternity of love.

They walk along the same street. They stand beside each other at a stoplight.

"Are you blind?" Felicia says to the young woman. She buries her head in her mother's shoulder. "I can't stand it," she says.

He walks ahead of her, maybe a block or so, and then stops.

"Look," Pamela says.

Felicia turns to the screen.

The man turns and walks back in her direction. They stop and face each other. They don't speak with words, they speak in thoughts.

There are tears in Pamela's eyes.

"All *right*," Felicia says.

"Whew," Primo says. He extends his palm to Felicia and she slaps it.

"I knew they were gonna find each other," she says.

"You weren't sure a moment ago," Pamela says.

"Whew," Primo says. He takes a sip of beer.

While the credits are running, Felicia snuggles up to Pamela.

"In a minute you're going to start getting ready for bed," Pamela tells her.

"Not yet, Mama."

"You sit with us a few more minutes. Then, young lady, you'll get that little behind into bed."

They all sit there, the three of them on the couch, as the tape rolls beyond the credits into bright electronic snow. Then Pamela gets up, turns off the VCR and rewinds the tape. She leaves the TV on with the sound turned off.

"Let's get ready," she says to Felicia, who remains motionless on the couch, pouting and smiling at the same time. "Come on," Pamela says. She extends a hand to Felicia. "You can come out and say good night to Primo after you get ready."

While they're inside, Primo watches the news without sound.

Over the talking head of the announcer are the words *CRACK BUST*. Then footage of police, some in uniform, some not, gathered on the stoop of a row house. Although it is July, the house has a Christmas wreath hung in its picture window. One of the plain-clothesmen is holding a shotgun. A cordon of orange ribbon holds back a small crowd of onlookers. Next, the words *Dow Jones* appear over the announcer's head. The words are set one above the other, with the letters in *Jones* crammed together so the two words form a perfect square. Then a commercial and, after that, footage of a short man, most likely Latin-American, talking to reporters and men in gray uniforms. The man looks back and forth between the camera and the woman sitting beside him, who appears to be translating the questions he is asked. The camera cuts to a view of a rail bridge spanning a river, then a close-up so that the bridge, now in the background, is blurry but a green sign that says *Río Grande* is clear. In the next scene men, in the same gray uniforms, lower body bags, on stretchers, from the open door of a freight car. In the final scene a single uniformed man is inside the freight car, pointing out for the camera a canteen, a half-dozen empty food cans, a small hole gouged through the wooden floor.

They're running footage of a Yankee game when Felicia walks back into the room, wearing a T-shirt that comes down to her knees with a blue dinosaur on the front, and sits beside Primo on the couch. She hands him two photographs. Pamela has also come in and stands behind the couch, looking over Primo's shoulder at the photographs.

One of them is just of Felicia, wearing shiny gray pants and sweat-shirt. She is also wearing a silver-gray disk that appears like an oval halo behind her head. Beside her is the bottom half of an adult wearing jeans.

"She's going to be an actress," Pamela says.

Primo asks if she was playing an angel, like the angel children in the movie.

Felicia points to the other photo, as if it holds the answer. In this one she is holding hands with a little boy who is wearing the same outfit with one difference: instead of the halo, there are some kind of spikes rising from the back of his collar to a height just above his head.

Felicia looks at him. Pamela leans over them, her hands on Primo's shoulder.

"*Well?*" Felicia says.

Primo looks up at Pamela, then at Felicia.

"I was a spoon," Felicia says.

Pamela leans around, looks right at Primo. "Maybe his eyesight isn't so good," she says. "Or maybe he just ain't too smart."

Felicia puts her face right up to Primo's. He opens his eyes, wide as he can, and stares back.

"I think he's just dumb, Mama." She kisses him on the cheek.

"I think you're right, honey," Pamela says.

While Pamela puts Felicia to bed, Primo opens the wine he'd brought with him. When Pamela walks in, she flips off the TV and sits next to him on the couch.

"So tell me," she says. She lifts her wineglass and clinks it against his. "Whose mother's dog died?"

"I see you've been talking to Mariah."

"You called her to tell her somebody's mother's dog died?"

"It was Gladys's mother's dog. Gladys asked me to tell her."

"That explains it."

With Felicia gone to bed, and with the TV turned off, the room is shrinking down to the couch they're sitting on and the light spilling over it.

"That's what I like about you two," Pamela says. "You still talk."

"How is she?" Primo asks.

"She asks about you, too. I envy that. You two have the best divorce." She takes a sip from her glass, washes it around her mouth like a wine taster and swallows. "Good," she says. "It feels warm after the cold beer." Then she says, "Mariah's fine."

"Ever hear from Randall?" Primo asks.

"You kidding? He couldn't give a shit if I live or breathe. Then again, it's mutual. Even *more* mutual on my side."

"Mariah and I don't really talk much," Primo says. "We keep each other informed of where we'll be and when. She sends me poems sometimes. It's a habit."

Pamela leans toward Primo, about to say something. Then shakes her head, and waves it off with her arm.

"What?" Primo asks.

"Nothing. Go on with what you were saying."

"I just said what I'm saying. You didn't."

"Just Randall. That's all. I just mention his name out loud—let it get outside of me—and the shit *inside* starts to rise." She waves her arm again. "I open that door, you're on the receiving end of a yearlong blues . . ." She spreads her arms apart, palms facing, as if measuring.

"When we met—must've been twelve years ago—you were with that other guy . . . an actor or something. What was his name?"

"Ronald. Yeah, he was an actor all right." She starts laughing. "If his life depended on it, he couldn't even play a fork. Not if he had to read lines. You know he first asked Mariah out?"

"No." Primo smiles, turns his head. "She never told me."

"You two being newlyweds, she just spun him around and aimed him at me. He didn't stay around too long, though. I was just Saturdays and Sundays. . . . He was bouncing two other beds on weeknights."

Primo can respond to either the anger that tightens her forehead or the humor mixed in with it that lightens her eyes. The balance of the two communicates to him not only the two separate things she feels, but that she is older, that they are both older.

"Felicia is beautiful," is what Primo says.

"For her, I'm more than grateful. I'm working hard on forgetting anything else having to do with her father."

Primo pours himself some wine, then holds the mouth of the bottle over Pamela's glass. She nods, smiles, and he pours her some too.

"I think Mariah sends me poems when there's stuff in them she can't tell me directly," Primo says.

"She does. But can't you see? Even *that's* good." She looks down into her wineglass. "Even that's good."

Primo doesn't answer. The room fills with the sound of a passing car. Its sound pushes ahead of itself, then builds to a loud *whoosh* just before it breaks past the house.

"Besides, if she never wrote another poem about you, you'd be pissed off. I'd like to send some of mine to Randall. I'd fry his ass with them. But he doesn't deserve even that, knowing I'd give him a thought."

Primo raises his glass. "Here's to not giving *any*-one a single thought."

"Not a single, *in*-consequential, no-account, don't-mean-shit-to-a-tree, shrimpy, micro-fucking-scopic, whisper of a thought." She nods to add emphasis and drains her glass.

"Not even a thought one *tenth* that size," Primo adds, and drinks.

"However," Pamela says, "the thoughts start getting *that* small, we're getting down to a size Randall can understand."

"*Up* . . ." Primo says. "Be careful. You just gave him a thought."

"I did, didn't I. This *not-thinking* shit is a lot harder than it looks."

"This not-thinking shit's complex," Primo says. He pours them both some wine.

"The idea's to stay in the here and now."

"We can chant," Primo says. He leans his face close to Pamela and smiles. "Know a good mantra?"

"Wake my daughter, you're out of here."

"You know anything else, anything quieter, could keep our minds from wandering out of this room?"

Pamela lightly pushes her forehead against Primo's. "I think this conversation's coming in for a landing."

Blood is rising in his face. They have crossed a border and have begun touching, like islands, under the surface. He presses her cheek with his palm.

She pulls his head beside hers. Inside Primo a clenched hand is opening.

Pamela kisses his temple, his cheek, his neck. Then she says, "But you'll have to leave before Felicia wakes up."

———

Primo is resting his head on Pamela's soft, bare stomach, and trying to read the titles on the books that line one entire wall of her bedroom. The upper half of the wall is in shadow, the lower half is softly lit by the light that escapes beneath the shade of the bedside lamp. When she inhales, her skin presses upward against his cheek and ear. She moves her fingers slowly through his hair.

"Gwendolyn Brooks, Roget's Thesaurus, The Norton Anthology of something . . ."

"You weren't interested in my library a half hour ago."

"I didn't know you *had* a library a half hour ago."

Perhaps their occasional, barely memorable, brief lookings at each other, small curious exchanges, had, over the years, added up to some kind of unspoken familiarity: their sex was easy and fluent.

"Maybe we knew each other in a past life," Pamela says.

"Yeah, in prehistoric times. I used to come over to your cave to watch TV."

"No. I think we were birds. Living somewhere nice and tropical. One afternoon after lunch—I had just enjoyed a tasty dragonfly—you landed on my branch. You gave me one of them bird looks. You know . . . wide-eyed, no blinking. You don't remember?"

"Can't say I do." He's lying with his left arm under the small of her back. With the fingers of his right hand he lightly rubs the skin on the inside of her thigh, slowly back and forth, between the soft, damp, sticky skin and the smooth, drier skin lower down.

"Then you start fanning your tail feathers and puffing your neck in and out. You were so good at it I thought I was hearing a rumba. Next thing I know, I feel these wings wrapped around me."

"What happened next?"

"What do you think happened next? We shook the branch till half the leaves fell off it. Then you flew off to I don't know where. Now here we are, fifty lifetimes later, and you're doing an inventory of my library."

"Sounds a little like the movie we just saw."

"Only better."

Primo combs her pubic hair upward with his fingers. With each upward stroke it stretches a little higher.

"What are you doing?" Pamela asks. She begins to move her fingers through his hair the same way.

"Styling your hair. I'm going to keep teasing it till I block out the entire view."

"What?" She laughs. His head bounces on her stomach.

"I'm obstructing the view, building a little privacy fence. I'm about to erase a whole shelf of books."

"You *must* know that you're crazy."

He stops combing upward and begins to shape the hairs in the cup of the palm of his hand. Then he says, "I'm finished."

"Oh yeah? How does it look?"

"I wish you could see it."

"So do I."

"It's like sitting behind Jimi Hendrix at the movies."

She is laughing so hard now that Primo can no longer keep his head on her stomach.

"Come up here," she says. "Forget about hairstyling. I want you to show me again how a spoon and a fork can fit together."

Primo rises and lies beside her again. He rubs his hand, upward, along her leg, and as he does so, she lifts it at the knee. He reaches under her thigh and lifts her leg higher and she tilts herself toward him and he presses into her from the side. He reaches over her and continues combing her pubic hair. She moves his fingers slightly downward, to her clitoris.

"You know a lot about silverware," she says.

"That's why they call me Primo."

"What does *that* mean?"

"Not a thing," he says.

"Uhhmmm," she says. "I didn't think so."

Primo is looking under the bed for his watch. Pamela is in the kitchen making coffee.

By one of the legs is a clump of dust shaped like a sea lion with its head and neck raised. Beside it is a walnut shell. The rest of the dark square of floor is smooth and bare.

Pamela walks back into the bedroom. "Primo," she whispers.

He is kneeling on the floor. He turns and looks up when he hears her. She has a mug of coffee in one hand and his watch in the other. He starts to speak and she raises her finger to her lips. Outside it is still dark.

"I found it on the couch," she says softly. "Between the cushions." She hands him the coffee. "We'd best hurry." She holds up his watch by the band and turns its face toward her. "The train leaves in, like, fourteen minutes."

They are both quiet on the way to the station. They had slept less than an hour. It feels as if days have gone by in the ten hours since they drove this route in the opposite direction. There isn't a soul on the streets and all the houses are dark. It's cool and their breath fogs the windshield.

Primo is holding his coffee mug in both hands between his knees. He has sipped it down to half full. He notices, on the outer surface of the ashtray, a diagram of the shifting pattern of the four-speed transmission. They had come together easily and quickly. There had been no series of playful, tender contacts. He doesn't know what to do now, afterward, in their last few moments together.

"So," Pamela says. "You think Gladys's mother got herself a new dog?"

"Don't know," Primo says. "But if you like, I'll look into it."

"Do that." The road begins to wind downward; they are now passing along the main street. The night-lights in the storefronts project dim rectangles onto the sidewalks. "What was that dog's name, anyway?"

"Queenie."

"Nice name."

"Sometimes Gladys's grandmother would call it Reinita. It liked me when it was a puppy. When it got older it got real fat and started to growl at me. It always loved Mariah, though."

Pamela smiles, sets her hand on Primo's knee. "Sorry about making you leave so early," she says.

"No problem." They are on the last, level stretch of road before the station parking lot.

"Felicia's just beginning to accept that Randall's gone. How *far* away that really means. And he don't help any. He hasn't called her since New Year's. And I don't know how long before that. Both times he told her he'd call again real soon."

She parks the car in the empty lot. The station house is dark and empty, but there are lights on over the platforms.

"It's okay," Primo says. "Really." He sets the coffee mug on the dashboard. His arms and legs are tingling, like his blood is slightly carbonated. "It was a great dinner. A great night, start to finish."

Pamela leans over and kisses him. Then she pulls her head back, smiles and kisses him again. "I'm glad I got to know why they call you Primo. Now get your ass onto that platform. You miss this train, you got two hours till the next one."

Primo gets out and stands still a second before closing the door. He presses his feet into the gravel, feels the pebbles press back. He walks around to Pamela's side of the car. He motions his head toward the passenger's seat and says, "Just a second ago I was sitting right there. . . . Now I'm standing here."

She is leaning out of the window. She looks up at him curiously. He bends toward her and they kiss again. He tries, self-consciously, to bring an effort to it that implies he is urgently present. He is. And that she can rely on him to not just leave without acknowledging that something meaningful has happened.

He then takes a step back and is surprised to find her looking at him angrily. He hears the train, at a distance, approaching.

"What?" he says.

"Don't be an asshole."

"What?" He turns, briefly, and sees the train's single headlight, about a quarter mile from the station. He knows *what.*

Her look softens, but not all the way to a smile.

"See you," he says. He just stands there.

"You're a good egg, Primo," Pamela says. She then points toward the train.

Its headlight has grown larger. He's beginning to feel the tunnel of sound it pushes ahead of itself.

"You best hurry," Pamela says.

6

Primo, jolted from a thick sleep, opens his eyes. His cheek is pressed against the smooth, cool back of the train seat. He faces the window.

Although he doesn't yet remember how he got there, he's neither surprised nor curious. He doesn't move. He doesn't disturb the thick air of his own sleep.

His body is curled into the palm of the seat, one leg on the seat opposite, the other crossing it, with both hands folded on top of a newspaper that sits on his lap. He hears his father's footsteps, even-paced and deliberate, crossing the wood floor of the wide living room, approaching his bedroom. . . .

The train lurches into movement, then, quickly, comes to a halt. As he wakes he sees, through the window, between the backs of two brick buildings, an enormous yellow shirt hanging upside down on a clothesline, its arms nearly touching the ground. It was dark when he boarded the train. He had raced across the overpass to the southbound track and, on a bench at the bottom of the stairs, found a *New York Times*, folded neatly, as if it hadn't yet been read. He saw, across the tracks, the headlights of Pamela's car as she pulled backward out of the lot, turned, and began the uphill drive back through the town. Then the roar and vibration of the incoming train. As it came to a stop, it widened the frenzied cluster of moths surrounding the yellow platform light over his head.

Primo lifts his arm, looks down at his watch. They must be somewhere in the Bronx: he boarded the train only half an hour ago. The sun has half risen in that time and it lights up the fabric of the yellow shirt like stained glass. He is now fully awake. It's becoming Saturday morning. It occurs to him that the skin of the *New York Times*, folded on his lap, is less conductive of the cold, conditioned air, than the leatherette upholstery against his cheek.

Primo looks down at the front page of the paper and is reminded that today is the Fourth of July. He wonders who had left it there, for him to find, so neatly folded on the bench. Perhaps it was someone who'd planned to take the same train but suddenly remembered, just moments before Primo got there, a flame still burning under a coffeepot, a wallet left on a dresser, an unlocked front door. Or maybe it was someone who, like Primo, just looked down, read the front page and was reminded that today was the Fourth and in that moment decided to stay in the suburbs rather than endure the noise and violence and crowds that overrun Manhattan on this holiday.

Primo's earliest memories of sleeping and waking are memories of his father. Primo often heard him rise in the middle of the night. He'd then hear a lamp in the living room click on, sending a thin sheet of light under his bedroom door. Sometimes his father would switch on the TV with the volume turned down to a soft hum. Sometimes he'd read the library books or medical journals that were always stacked on the end table beside the couch. Primo imagined that most often he'd just sit there, as Primo, in bed, would just lie there, also unable to sleep. Sometimes his mother would call him. He might then walk across the floor in the direction of the bedroom, or he'd call back to her, in a sharp, hushed, breathy voice that would shape the words into small beads of sound Primo could hear but not understand.

It was also his father who'd wake him. *Rise and shine.* He'd press his shoulder with a heavy hand, shake him awake. *What are you, a prince? Get your ass out of bed.* This *is what life is.* Waking up. *We* all *have to do it.*

Not wanting the train to move, wanting to keep his eyes on the radiant yellow shirt until they closed again, he is thinking that his father had spent his whole life fighting the desire to go back to sleep.

By the time Primo began school, the sound of his father's approaching footsteps was enough to cause a wave of sensation to enter his body and lift him from sleep.

The train staggers into forward motion, then settles into a slow, heavy glide of about five miles per hour. Primo takes his foot off the opposite seat and sits up. The movement causes a breath of Pamela's smell to waft upward from his open shirt collar. A voice comes over the P.A. system and apologizes for the delay. Signal problems.

He pulls open the top of his shirt with his finger. He wants to liberate whatever remains of Pamela's smell on his chest and stomach.

In the course of a lifetime, half a lifetime, a person must experience ten thousand occasions of brief, casual, unspoken and barely, if at all, remembered longing. Moments that happen in situations in which nothing, beyond a quick wave of desire, could occur. This thought spreads itself across Primo's mind as he watches the slow, arcing rise and fall of the wires slung between telephone poles, and the sluggish procession of the brick backs of buildings and the alleys and thick-weeded lots between them. How often does someone send out a tiny signal of curiosity and desire—in an office, a bus, a restaurant, a hospital, a police station, at a funeral—usually a single fiber in the spun thread of a larger and more abstract communication: *What time is it? . . . Did you know the deceased? . . . Hot, isn't it?* Often it's transmitted solely with the eye. And how often, although of this one can't be certain, is a similar message transmitted back?

Usually, you never see the person again, or if you do, it's under different terms. You never expect to. The odds are worse than a sucker's bet that your life would ever afford you the opportunity to realize and follow up on the impulse.

Perhaps something deep inside your mind sees the future and knows which encounter—the one in a thousand—has a reunion in store. And maybe it keeps those memories in the *Active* file. Something inside him was ready and waiting and familiar. Not from knowing Pamela—he never really did—but from a small, quick, long-ago self-acknowledgment of wanting her.

Or does each one of these encounters, simply because it happened, form its own little convolution, like a groove etched in a record? Then long after they are out of reach of memory, the unconscious mind can play them back as often as it likes. That would mean that he—and every other asshole on the planet—walks around nurturing ten thousand unconsummated relationships. Add to that all the other kinds of encounters, remembered and not, people now dead, from kindergarten, on the opposite subway platform, in dreams even . . . *Shit.* He's an island with a population larger than Manhattan. . . . Too much to think of.

His mother once took him to the Barnum and Bailey Circus at Madison Square Garden and it made him restless and angry. He couldn't watch what was going on in one ring without trying to watch what was going on in the other two. He couldn't watch one, and he couldn't watch all three. . . . He falls back to sleep.

In a dream he is dark and shaped like a worm or a finger. Something no nearer to the shape of a man. He is thin, shadowy, nothing like the dense matter of flesh. He moves around in the core of something hard and vaguely mineral, and the space he occupies is barely larger than himself. He doesn't feel imprisoned, it's just where he is. He isn't happy or unhappy. He picks up sensations, like electrical charges, from the hard inner walls that contain him. The one he is feeling now makes him calm. He has no idea what the structure he is inside of would look like from the outside. He might not even recognize it if he could see it. That's okay, he thinks to himself.

While he was asleep another passenger boarded the train: a middle-aged man, who sits at the opposite end of the car, leaning back into his seat, reading a hardcover book with a bright, red jacket. From where he's sitting, Primo can't read the title but sees something that looks like a dragon, and beside it, a hand holding an Uzi. The man slips his shoes off and sets his stocking feet lightly on top of them.

A wave of fear suddenly passes through Primo. He realizes that this man must have checked him out, somehow, before making himself so comfortable, in a train car carrying just him and a sleeping black man. Perhaps he just watched from his seat farther down the car. Perhaps he walked nearer, watched Primo sleeping, maybe assumed the *New York Times* on his lap gave this stranger enough in common with the world he himself was familiar with for him to feel safe enough to relax. Primo wonders if it's this man's fear he feels, or his own.

They are now crossing the Harlem River between the Bronx and northern Manhattan. Primo imagines the man is a commuter—that's also why he seems so comfortable—has been for thirty years and knows each inch of this trip like he knows the rooms of his own house. He probably lives in a small, quiet town like the one Pamela lives in, though on a more affluent street, with larger homes and larger spaces between them, and every day makes the trip between this gentle village and an office, somewhere within the hard towering geometry of midtown or Wall Street. Perhaps, this morning, there is something at the office he must look into before the long holiday weekend.

He's fifty-five, perhaps sixty. The time of life Primo's father was in when he last knew him. His gray hair is thick and cut in a youngish manner that sweeps both ways across his forehead. Even in this relaxed position, his bearing is authoritative but friendly, as if he spent his childhood and youth consciously trying to present the appearance of someone who has won at many things and with little effort, and this has long since become his natural, permanent demeanor. His bearing more than compensates for the elderly, feminine impression made by his reading glasses, riding low on his nose. He could be a corporate lawyer, a banker, a judge. He could even be a senator.

The train stops at 125th Street. No one gets on or off. Primo was born just west of here, on the other side of the park. His Aunt Olivia lives in the same building, in the apartment she and his father had once lived in, and that his mother shared with her during her last years.

For the moment the train pauses in the station, Primo can see, out the window, the upper floors of the old, abandoned *National Geographic* building that rises from Park Avenue below.

"Food for thought," he says to himself. He looks into the tangled darkness behind its gaping windows and says, "A sinful shame. A sinful shame *and* food for thought."

He remembers sitting at the dinner table between his mother and father. He was five years old. His aunt and grandparents were there. They were talking about this same building. It had been vacant since some indefinite time before Primo's childhood. His aunt, who passed it each morning on her way to the subway that took her into the Bronx, to the school she taught at, said, "A shame, a sinful shame. A building that beautiful and *nobody* living in it." Then his father said, "That building provides us with food for thought. It used to have in it a magazine that filled its pages with pictures of black and brown people, but then left the neighborhood the minute those same people moved in too close. . . ." Primo was too young to have any idea what he was talking about. He never got past the words *food for thought.* He couldn't equate them with the baked potato on his plate. "*Food . . . ?*" he said. His mother first began to laugh. Then everyone else at the table. In the years that followed, his mother would call potatoes *food for thought.*

Later, at dinners with his mother and aunt in that same apartment, he was told the rest of what his father was talking about. In those years, after his mother had moved in with Olivia, they tried to introduce Primo to the man he might comprehend his father to be had he lived into Primo's adult life. They did so in fragments related to special occasions: holidays, outings, snowstorms . . . Primo didn't feel curious. He'd listen, but barely respond. Yet somewhere, inside, he was assembling the pieces into a never completed portrait; the parts held themselves in place by a kind of gravity, and he'd keep rearranging them in attempts to explain the gravity's source. As a young child, he felt magnetized to his father's presence. When he'd leave a room, Primo felt the tug. Twenty years ago, when he died, the force lost its center but didn't seem to decrease. Even so, during the years that followed, the first years on his own, when he met and then married Mariah and began inhabiting his own adult life, it came to seem, more and more, that his father's absence didn't begin for Primo at sixteen, when he died, but sometime long before. If he looked straight at the thought of his father, at the *thought*, it would seem he had never been there at all.

His mother had told Primo it was the Army that had done it, made him so angry. He was easier to be with, calmer, happier, before that. It was the war.

Olivia said he was angry long before that. "Let's face it," she said. "The war black Americans fought had nothing to do with Rita Hayworth, or Gene Kelly tap-dancing on the deck of a ship. And there's no excuse for what they did to him, a doctor. But he was angry ever since I was old enough to know what a brother was. The war just gave it a shape and a reason for being." His father had rarely spoken of his Army experience and it was this, too, that went into the portrait he gathered from these dinners with his mother and aunt.

In 1941, the year Samuel Thomas first tried to enlist, the medical journals were filled with recruitment ads—*Doctors: Uncle Sam Needs Your Special Skills*—and articles about how small towns had to ration the few physicians not serving in the armed forces. He was told that, at thirty-three, he was too old. He informed the recruitment office that the Army was accepting enlistees up to the age of thirty-six and, in cases of individuals with especially needed, noncombat skills, much older. He was told they were not, at that time, accepting new medical personnel. This made no sense. He then wrote to the Department of the Army and received a brief letter informing him that the matter did not fall within their jurisdiction, but within that of the Medical Officers' Recruiting Board. He wrote to them directly. They told him that their plan, at the time, was to recruit primarily from medical and dental schools. Only after that would they recruit from the private sector.

That year, Olivia showed Samuel an article in the *Daily Worker* about a Harlem surgeon, a Dr. Charles Filer, who'd been trying to enlist for the last year, who'd even had military experience in Spain, but had been refused at every turn. Samuel wrote letters to both him and the reporter who wrote the article. Soon after, the three met in the East Twelfth Street office of the *Daily Worker*. They became friends and, working together, discovered that only three, out of two hundred, Harlem doctors had been called to active duty.

After Samuel died, Primo's mother gave him copies of the articles, signed with the names of all three men, that had been published that autumn in the *Daily Worker*. They also published a copy of a telegram they'd sent to Major General James Caree Magee, Surgeon General of the U.S. Army. *Who is keeping immobilized the skill of patriotic Negroes who are anxious and willing to contribute toward keeping our soldiers in fighting condition?* Primo, as a teenager, was unable to hear his father's voice in the odd, formal language. The pieces of newsprint had dried and yellowed, but his mother had placed them in clear plastic envelopes, each page separately, so they could be read without being damaged. She also gave him, in the same plastic envelopes, his father's diplomas from high school, college and the Howard University School of Medicine.

Within a month both doctors received draft notices. The reporter, Adam Sidney, did as well. Charles Filer and Samuel Thomas were called as ordinary draftees, not as physicians, and both served as corpsmen. Filer was sent to North Africa and Primo's father to Italy and, later, the invasion of southern France. After the war Filer moved to Detroit. The two men communicated less and less over the years, but his wife would send an annual Christmas card. Beginning in 1960, her name appeared alone on the cards, which continued to arrive. Primo was given those more recently, after his mother died, along with the letters she had received from his father while he was overseas. Most of them were short, about the food, weather, living conditions. He'd thank her for a book or some cookies she'd sent. In one of them, however, one of the few that were longer, he wrote: *My punishment, for having my name on those articles, is to sterilize and field-dress wounds, inject men with morphine, transport their living or dead bodies to aid stations, where their wounds are re-dressed by other doctors, or where my task is to quickly withdraw blood from the newly dead to transfuse into those still living. They could have punished me in other ways. But they wanted me to hear something loud and clear: in or out of the army, I'm an enlisted man. Maybe, at first they thought, "We could just shoot him down like a dog on the street. That way he wouldn't even have to leave Harlem." But then they must have thought about it some more. And they decided to do it this way.*

His mother had kept all their letters in a shoe box, dated and ordered so that the letters she sent were interspersed with the letters he sent in response. This letter was written just after he had received from her a letter in which she included the notice published in the *Daily Worker* that announced the death of Adam Sidney, who had fallen in heavy ground fighting that week in the Solomon Islands.

"He knew he was special," Olivia later told him. "*Everybody* thinks they know more about life than anybody else. And they're right because it's *their* life. The truth is, Samuel Thomas knew even more than that. He did, even as a child. But he had to live a life measured to the size of people who lacked the capacity to understand this. Add to that his lack of humility . . . But why should he *be* humble? The man was brilliant. Being a doctor wasn't even half of what he could be . . ."

At thirty-six, there is little room in the fabric of Primo's life for the presence of a father twenty years gone. Yet, just in the last month or so, as if returning to New York were returning not just to a place but to a time, something has jogged loose and risen upward, like something remembered from a dream long after you dreamt it. If presence is something measurable, then his father's, at this point in his life, is quantified by zero. Unless someone else brings him up, he doesn't give him a thought. He thinks of his mother much more and knows her memory with dimension and clarity. Her absence with pain. Yet, at times, especially in these last weeks, the surprising thought occurs to him that it's his father's voice he talks to, and that talks back to him, when he talks to himself.

The train has again come to a halt. They are now inside the Park Avenue tunnel, less than a mile from Grand Central. The windows reflect the inside of the car. Primo waves his hand at his own reflection and that of the empty seat on the opposite side of the aisle. The evenly spaced bulbs on the tunnel's inside walls diffuse their light into the Plexiglas, and spread into columns inside the images. They're like the faint bars of color and light behind the action on the screen of a TV.

When the train eases back into movement, the man farther down the car puts his shoes back on, slips his book into his briefcase and sits up straight. They're nearly there.

As the train slows, the man stands and walks to the closed doors at the middle of the car. The platform is brightly lit and filled with people waiting for the train to pull in. Families with children carrying picnic baskets, thermoses, baseball bats, shoulder bags. Primo walks over and stands beside him. The crowd is energized and anxious. Wherever this train will go on its next run, there will be open space for picnics and baseball.

The train stops again, just before moving the last few yards to the end of the platform. Primo and the man stand facing the crowd. Just outside their door are a young couple with a tiny newborn child in a large, old-fashioned baby carriage with lace hanging from its canopy, and another, older child, a little girl, squirming in her father's arms. One of his top front teeth is missing, and there are wide spaces between the others. He's wearing a red baseball cap backward. Primo notices a Band-Aid on the inside of the little girl's bare forearm. She must have recently had a blood test. The train is a half hour late and the father stares angrily at the man and Primo as if they had something to do with it.

"I bet it's going to be hot," the man says. He'd put on his sports jacket when he first stood up, and now he slips it off again, shifting his briefcase from one hand to the other, and drapes it over his arm. He then laughs quietly and turns to Primo. "Looks like we're the only ones not having a picnic."

"Guess so," Primo says.

The man just outside the door sets his daughter down on the platform. He places his hands on her shoulders. He has not taken his eyes off Primo and this man standing beside him.

"They've got the right idea," the man says. "Maybe *we're* going in the wrong direction. Maybe we should stay on board."

The train starts to move again.

At first Primo is silent. Then he says, "That's food for thought."

"What?" the man says, preoccupied but still smiling.

"Food for thought."

"Could be," he says. The train inches about five feet. The doors slide open. "At last," he says, shaking his head, exhaling breath.

Primo follows him along the path his fast walk clears through the crowd. When they pass out of the gate and into the concourse the man quickens his pace and the distance between them increases. The bright, dense shafts of light that fall through the terminal's upper windows form square chambers of brightness and shadow on the marble floor. This man, his briefcase in one hand, his sports jacket slung over his shoulder, breaks, smoothly, into and out of each one, as if he were projected onto a screen like film, alternately shot in color and black and white.

7

Primo and Manny are sitting on the concrete bank of the East River, eating sandwiches from D's, drinking Heineken from cans, waiting for the sun to finish setting and the Macy's fireworks display to begin. It's seven-thirty. Manny insisted they get there two hours early. "The crowd gets so thick," he said, "by the time it starts you can't get any nearer than First Avenue. That's no better than watching on TV." Manny's portable radio/cassette player is squeezed on the ground between them, playing a Tracy Chapman tape. Later he'll tune it to the channel that plays the music choreographed to the fireworks. "You got to have the whole effect," he told Primo last week when he called from More to tell him he was coming in. "If I'm driving all the way to New York, I'm getting the *whole* effect."

There's a row of long barges, packed with fireworks, spaced evenly along the river from Twenty-third Street to Fifty-ninth. The surface is bustling with tugboats and fireboats, moving north and south, or crossing and recrossing between the barges. They keep the water too busy to hold a recognizable reflection of the industrial buildings on the Queens waterfront across the river.

A strip of people already lines the river's edge, and families with folding chairs and blankets are quickly filling in the fifty-foot aisle of pavement that runs between the river and the FDR Drive. At the edge of the drive vendors are selling hot dogs, beer, T-shirts, plastic tubes shaped like wands and halos that glow in the dark, and small American flags.

A teenage couple is sitting beside them. The girl is wearing five or six of the glow-in-the-dark halos around her neck. Her boyfriend is sitting cross-legged and she sits sideways across his lap. They share a quart of Ballantine ale, laugh, speak softly into each other's ears and kiss. Sometimes, when she moves, the bottoms of her sneakers press against Primo's leg.

Manny has been filling Primo in on life in More since he left. "I saw that motorcycle guy, you remember, the one that offered you his girlfriend. He was in Big Tad's again. Don't think he remembered me."

"Was she with him?"

"The girlfriend? Nope. He was flying solo."

"Maybe she got smart," Primo says.

"Maybe she found a guy who could walk upright."

The guy they're referring to sat next to Primo one night last year at the bar in Tad's. Manny was with Jill, his girlfriend at the time, and Primo was with a woman named Helen, who worked as secretary to the dean. They'd gone out together a few times during his first year at More.

The guy was oddly fascinated with Primo and kept trying to start a conversation. Manny had thought the guy was weird and kind of funny. Primo later told him he thought the guy wanted to kill him. That was why he was nice to him. Primo was probably the first black person he'd seen in Tad's that wasn't playing an instrument. On top of that he was with a white woman. The guy couldn't just ignore Primo. He wasn't built that way. So he sat down and started talking.

First he introduced himself, extending his hand, and asked Primo his name. Then he asked if he'd ever heard of Primo Carnera.

"Was he a wrestler or something?" Primo asked him.

"Yeah," the guy said.

At this point Manny leaned over Helen, who sat between them, and briefly entered the conversation. "Wasn't he in that movie *Mighty Joe Young*?"

"That was him," the guy said.

"He flexed his arm and broke these steel bands around his biceps," Manny said, smiling, making a muscle. "Then he had a tug-of-war with a giant ape."

"Who won?" Primo asked.

"The ape," the guy said, and smiled. He reached over Primo and shook Manny's hand. "That's the only other Primo I ever heard of."

"His last name's Thomas," Manny told him. "You might want to ask him about the English muffins."

After saying this Manny returned to his conversation with Jill and Helen.

The guy asked Primo if he wanted to play pool with him and Primo declined. He then introduced his girlfriend Deedee, who was sitting beside him, to Primo, and Primo introduced Helen. Then the guy bought a round of drinks for everybody. Time passed. Somebody played Prince's "Little Red Corvette" on the jukebox and the guy was quiet for a while, tapping his foot to the music. Then he asked Primo if he wanted to dance with Deedee and Primo said no. He thanked them both for the offer but Deedee, who never really entered the conversation, didn't know what he was thanking her for. The guy then became embarrassed and hurt and angry. Primo bought them both drinks. Then, luckily, the jukebox was turned off and the live music started.

Manny lights a cigarette and drops the smoking match into the top of an empty Heineken can. Then he says, "Doesn't sound to me like his girlfriend, what was her name, Ginger . . . ?"

"Deedee."

"Deedee. Doesn't sound to me like an evening with her could compare to the hot date you had last night."

The young woman next to Primo stands up, stretches and asks her boyfriend, in Spanish, if he would like something to eat. He shakes his head. Then she squeezes into the thickening crowd and walks toward the vendors at the edge of the drive.

"I hope you at least practiced safe sex," Manny says.

Primo still doesn't follow up and talk about Pamela, so Manny changes the subject. "I was thinking of setting a scene from my novel here. At the fireworks display. What do you think?"

"Good idea," Primo says. "How's the work going?"

"Without you around to distract me I'm getting a lot done."

For the past five years, Manny has been working on a novel about a conceptual artist who is one of the wealthiest men in the world and who, at the same time, is a committed anarchist. His works of conceptual art, which he calls *interventions*, are happenings meant to disrupt and destroy the class system.

"Henry O's latest opus is a masterpiece. Listen to this. He starts an endowment that provides, for each cashier in each Woolworth's in the entire country, a raise in salary so that they are now earning two hundred and fifty thou a year. . . . What do you think of that?"

"Sounds like he's getting a lot subtler," Primo says. "But what I think of it depends on what happens."

Henry O's last intervention was to buy mansions in Beverly Hills, Greenwich, Connecticut, and Beacon Hill, and give them, anonymously, through invented inheritance schemes, to three homeless families he found living in Grand Central Station.

"I'll tell you what happens," Manny says. "Woolworth's cashiers begin entering society in a big way. They get season box seats at the ballpark, they eat in the right restaurants, they get invited to parties with the fat cats, their names start showing up in society columns. Real estate agents in exclusive neighborhoods are climbing all over them, American Express invites them to become members. But the big scene happens at a cocktail party in the home of a famous plastic surgeon. You'll love it. A corporate lawyer and a bank V.P. corner this Woolworth's cashier on the balcony and try to strike up a conversation with her." He takes out a pocket notebook. "Can I read some to you?" he asks, and then, without waiting for an answer, proceeds. He uses a different voice for each character.

"*What's your workday like?* the bank V.P. asks her.

"*I take the subway, pick up a coffee and cinnamon doughnut on the corner, then I ring up stuff until lunch. . . . Is that the kind of thing you want to know?*

"*Fascinating*, the V.P. says.

"*Wow*, the lawyer says.

"*Sounds awfully demanding*, the V.P. then says.

"*It's pretty easy. . . . Boring, though . . .*

"*Easy!* the lawyer says. *How could it be . . . having to remember all those prices?*

"*No*, she says. *They stamp the prices right on these little tags—*

"*But*, the V.P. interrupts her, *they forget to sometimes, don't they? I often see things on the shelf with no prices on them.*

"And now the lawyer interrupts *him*. He can't help himself. He pushes the V.P. aside to make sure he has center stage when he makes his point. *But tell me.* He's smiling now, already nodding in anticipated agreement. *How often do they get those darn prices wrong?*"

Primo laughs. "It's funny," he says.

"I hope it's not too funny?" Manny asks.

"Just right," Primo says. He then feels a tap on his shoulder. The young woman has returned. She is holding a half-eaten hot dog and needs Primo to move so she can squeeze in beside him.

Manny goes on reading. "The bank V.P. tells the cashier he's thinking of encouraging his son to start training in the operation of cash registers. *What are your thoughts on this?*"

Primo has lost his focus. In such a crowded, public moment it's hard to concentrate on any single thing for long. His attention is drawn to the young woman who is now sitting on the pavement next to him, leaning against her boyfriend with her arm around his shoulder. She's telling him that her father, whom she lives with, doesn't want her going near her mother. But she sneaks over to see her, when he's at work.

"*Carajo* . . ." the boyfriend whispers, and she laughs.

Yesterday her father found out. Her mother had stupidly told a mutual friend.

She is shaking her head. "Do you believe it? She *would* tell that chump Willy, right?"

"*Carajo*," the boyfriend says again. She buries her head in his neck.

". . . *since the MBA's already under his belt*," Manny, as one of his characters, is saying, "*he might take some time for cashier training before he enters the job market. I hear it's faster now, with the new zebra-stripe things and price scanners coming in. But that could mean more prejob training? Well, you'd be the expert on that. How long you think it might take . . . ?*"

Primo is staring straight into the water and Manny is still unaware that he's barely listening.

"So he comes home, right?" the young woman says. "*Y lo me dijo*, why you *go* by her? So I tell him, she ain't *your* mother. I tell him, listen, slick, she's *my* mother . . ."

At this point Primo turns toward her. He wants to see her expression, saying this.

"Are you listening?" Manny says.

Primo turns back, faces him. "Kind of."

"Well, what do you *kind of* think?"

"It's great, man. It's funny. Problem is, it's better than the rest of it."

"I was thinking that too. I think maybe I'll have to revise the earlier stuff . . . you know, make it as good?"

"Sounds right," Primo says.

The crowd has been steadily gathering and now extends out into the drive. Police barricades are set up to allow one lane of traffic, each way, to squeeze through.

It has grown darker. A slight coolness lifts off the water. Manny turns off the cassette tape and turns on the radio. A news announcer is describing an incident that occurred yesterday in Texas. Eighteen men died in a locked boxcar while trying to sneak across the border at El Paso in order to get to jobs in Dallas. The train had been delayed several times and held at sidings under the hot sun. There was a single survivor.

"Do you believe this?" Manny says.

Primo is hearing the words he didn't last night, sitting on Pamela's couch after the movie, watching the rhythmic flow of images play on the screen with the sound turned off. He also remembers reading the headline on the front page of the paper he found on the platform this morning, at the beginning of this overlong day, before the sun, now setting, had begun to rise. *One Man Survives Boxcar Ordeal.* His sleepy mind was too crowded to read further, or associate the words with the images he'd seen on the TV.

Mr. Rodríguez told officials that he survived the 120-degree heat by breathing through a hole he and the others punched through the floor with a spike.

Since last night, his knowledge of this event, this terrible thing, far away and apart from his life, has been assembling itself, piece by piece. "So much happens," Primo says.

"Do you believe this?" Manny says again. He shakes his head, lights a cigarette. "A fucking nightmare . . ."

"I saw it on the news last night. And in the paper this morning."

Manny looks at him. Then says, "So when are you going to tell me about this woman you spent the night with?"

"She's a friend of Mariah's. I hardly knew her before last night."

"Have any plans of *knowing* her again?"

"Don't really know."

"You think she wants to?"

"Don't know."

"You sure got a lot to say about it."

"Sorry," Primo says. "I'm just not sure *what* to say about it."

A bottle rocket, set off somewhere behind them, whizzes over their heads, falls through its arc about halfway across the river and drops into the water.

"Wow," the girl beside Primo says. "Wow," she says again, and taps Primo on the arm. "What do you think would happen if it landed on one of those barges out there?"

"I don't know," Primo tells her.

"You think it would start off the whole big fireworks?"

"I don't think so."

"*Oh*," she says, disappointed. "I wish it would. I'm tired of waiting."

"Me too," Manny says.

Another bottle rocket squeezes into the air above them. It rises higher than the first, leaving a faint, thin trail like a thread following a needle, then falls into the gathering darkness above the river. Primo turns, as if to see the person who launched it. The thick crowd now extends across the drive, up the side streets and beyond the range of sight. "You're right about the crowd," he says to Manny. "This year it may go even farther west than First Avenue. It may go clear across the island."

"Don't change the subject," Manny says. "We were talking about your rendezvous last night."

"Manny, you're a pain in the ass. I really don't know what there *is* to say about it. I'm sorry," he says again.

"Don't apologize," Manny says. "Maybe it's *my* fault. Maybe it's my approach. Not direct enough." He smiles, then says, "Did you slam the ham? How many times? Did she hum softly afterward? Light a cigarette? Is it love?"

Primo smiles, shakes his head. "There really *isn't* much to say about it. That's what was so unusual, so pleasing. It felt good. It was easy. She's lovely. We enjoyed ourselves."

"Your powers of description amaze me," Manny says. He takes a pen out of his shirt pocket and turns to a blank page in his notebook. "May I write this down?"

Just then the first volley of rockets explodes into three enormous green-and-red carnations. No one had seen them lift themselves from the barges or soar upward. The flash is followed by a collective, humming *OOOOOOHHHHH*, the sound of a million people seized with awe at the exact same moment, a sound that owns the whole world for the half second before the thunderous report, and the whomp of an airless wind you could actually feel.

STANDARD TIME

8

Primo is sitting at a window table in La Tasita, a small Dominican restaurant on Rivington Street, just two blocks from *Solidaridad Humana.* He began the ritual of morning coffee here, before class, in July, when the summer semester began. This is his first Monday morning since the clocks have been reset to Standard Time. The rising sun has been pushed an hour ahead of the clocks; the shaft of light that falls through the windows is denser, brighter, but covers six inches less of the tabletop than it did the last time he sat here passing these same minutes before his first class. All last week, the light had extended just beyond the stack of exercises, torn from his students' workbooks, and the white coffee mug in front of him. Now, the bright gold stars in the Formica tabletop that surround and appear between these familiar objects are shadowed in dim, interior room-light. He slides himself and his whole operation nearer to the window. It's nine-thirty.

His first class, from ten-thirty to twelve-thirty, is Level One English. For most of the students, this is their first encounter, aside from immigration officials, advertisements, street signs, radio and television, with the English language. For some of them, it's their first class after completing a two-semester course of basic literacy skills in Spanish. Most of his reading for this class consists of simple question-and-answer dialogues. *Where are you going, Paul? I am going to the store.* They are less than a month into the fall semester and the students are still borrowing the verb forms from the questions. *Who owns this book, Mary? I owns this book.*

Outside, a young man walks by, closely along the window, sliding his shadow across the window tables, and then stops at the public phone that stands at the edge of the glass where the next storefront begins. He has long sideburns and a stiff, thin ponytail. Primo watches him lean into the nichelike enclosure and set a take-out coffee cup, his keys, a pack of Marlboros, a stack of change and some folded-up sheets of paper on the little counter beneath the phone. He constructs this small environment carefully.

Do you have any children, Jane? I have a children. Her name is Magda.

When the guy at the phone leans his head forward to see the numbered buttons he presses, his tight ponytail rises like a pump handle. Before bringing the receiver to his face, he rubs the earpiece and mouthpiece against the sleeve of his denim jacket. Soon after he begins talking, he takes a pen from his jacket pocket and begins writing things down.

In class, they will first go over the exercises Primo is now reading, then they will talk. They'll discuss everything—weather, headlines, family, the countries they come from, the subways, their electric bills, music, boyfriends, drugs, air pollution, astrological signs, Wall Street—anything that will enable them to use their small vocabularies and enlarge them, which amounts to anything they haven't discussed before in English. The subject is a language, the only one he speaks fluently, his country's container of everything.

Students who have been educated before coming here usually advance more quickly. They make comparisons and learn from them. They want to know how you can read a question aloud if it doesn't *begin* with a question mark. Some of the students who have just completed the basic literacy skills in Spanish can have difficulty holding a pen. In this way, Level One is mixed. For all of them, adults learning both a new language and the strange and complex culture that speaks it, the work is hard. As hard as medical school, as hard as astronaut training, as hard as raising children, as hard as constantly threading needles, as hard as walking long distances carrying heavy weight.

Level One meets four days a week. As does Level Two, afternoons from three-thirty to five-thirty. Level Three meets three nights a week, from six to eight-thirty.

He has just read the same questions, the same answers, often written with the same mistakes, nineteen times. He has with him the *Daily News*, the *Post*, and the *New York Times*. He will read some of the headlines aloud and discuss them after they have gone over the exercises. It is important to select them carefully. What seem the simplest phrases in journalese shorthand can be very confusing. In Level One you can waste valuable classroom time untangling phrases like *Cabby Slain*, or *Prez Nixes Aid Package*. The morning after Darryl Strawberry hit two home runs, the headline read, *It's The Kid!* Partway into the journey toward the meaning of the phrase, Jacinta, a woman in his summer Level One class, decided it meant that someone important had a baby. Most of the class came to understand its meaning, but Jacinta preferred her own. "*Bebes son noticias. Béisbol es béisbol, nada mas.*"

Primo pays his check, pulls on his sweater and walks out front. The clear October morning has warmed in the last half hour. He takes his sweater off again and hangs it over his arm. The guy on the phone, who is still talking, still writing things down, sees this and understands it to be an unspoken message: he presses the receiver between his cheek and shoulder and snakes himself out of one side of his jacket. As he is doing this he frowns into the phone, and says loudly, "It's the best I can do." He then moves the phone to the opposite side and strips down to his white T-shirt. He has a tattoo of a hawk or an eagle on his forearm, and at least a half-dozen rubber bands around his wrist. "Yeah, I got Sony," he says into the phone, "and yeah, I got Toshiba, but for four hundred I got shit. The fucking *speakers* cost more than that . . ."

There were no usable headlines in today's papers, and last week they discussed the World Series, the change of seasons and resetting the clocks. So today, as they often do in Level One, they will find the source of their discussion in the mural, painted by a student several years back, that runs the entire width of the classroom, from the top edge of the blackboard to the ceiling.

On its left side, a dense crowd of men and women are leaning into their journey across the wall. One of them is carrying a Spanish/English dictionary. In the center of the mural is an eagle, its wings painted in stars and stripes, and the letters *ABC* across its broad chest. To its right is a skyline of New York City, above which a small flying saucer hovers in a light blue sky. Mixed into the rich assemblage are the gears of industry, a range of mountains on a distant horizon, flags of several of the Americas, and across the foreground at the center, half within, half outside of the composition, is a long cornucopia, spilling out an endless fortune in gold coins.

Primo often finds students staring at the mural and can even know, by the tilt and direction of their eyes, which of its images they are focused on. It's nearly impossible not to stare at it, or into it. The hand that painted it articulates each separate image with demanding immediacy. When your eyes are on it, it *is* the world outside the classroom, as irresistible as a large picture window or a movie screen. If your attention is not focused, it inevitably becomes the territory into which your mind will wander.

Those people in the painting, where are they all going? Home. To work. To take their driver's test. To Colorado. To a birthday party. Nowhere, they are not real. To my house. To your *house? Yeah, too many people come to my house. . . .*

As the discussions find their collective motion, they rise into invisible structures that fill the classroom. The students begin to speak to each other as much as to him. Primo enters to ask and answer questions, to correct things, to steer them back to English and to add his own two cents when the subject engages him.

How come there's an flying thing? A *flying thing. A what? El platillo volador. Teacher, that is a UFO? Yes. ¿Cómo? Un OVNI. ¿OVNI? Objeto Volador No Identificado. I saw once an OVNI, Unidentified Flying Object, in my country. You were dreaming? She was in movie theater. ¡Claro que sí! Theater? El cine. ¿Una telenovela? No. You know, Steven Spielberg.* E.T.? *Yes! He made this picture? I don't think so. I like* The

Godfather. *I like* Passionaria. *Steven Spielberg? No, there would be children. I think it is very much like him. I think so. Magda. I do not think it is like him. Magda? ¿Sí? Steven Spielberg hizo la pintura. English, please. . . . He made it? You mean* painted *it.* When *he is here? Sometime when he made that.* Painted *that. ¿Cuándo? But there are no children. . . .*

9

Solidaridad Humana is a five-minute walk from Primo's apartment. He often spends the time between classes at home. Today, when he walks in after morning class, Mrs. Karbash is standing in the entryway with Lady, watching the mailman slip the letters into the boxes.

He pauses to wait with them and Lady jumps up on her hind legs, sets her forepaws against Primo's knee and wags her tail. After Primo bends down and scratches her head, she walks over to the mailman and sniffs his foot.

He taps each envelope on the edge of the door to the open boxes as he searches for the name. Whenever he can't find one, Mrs. Karbash helps him. His Walkman earphones, hanging loosely around the collar of his shirt, emit a soft, thin, indiscernible music.

"How come you like my shoes so much?" the mailman says to Lady. He lifts his toe and pushes her away.

Mrs. Karbash pulls her back with the leash.

"She smells my shoes every day, like she never met me before."

"Lady's a good girl," Mrs. Karbash says.

Primo notices a white postcard go into his box.

"I walk the same filthy streets every day but to her it's like . . ." He looks down at Lady, smiles, shakes his head. "It's like Old Spice or somethin . . ."

"Isn't she a good girl?" Mrs. Karbash asks.

"You're Thomas, right?" he asks Primo, then hands him a manila envelope. It's from Mariah. It feels like it has a slim paperback book inside. He spoke to Pamela on the phone last week and she told him Mariah had a new collection of poems coming out.

"Is there a . . ." The mailman pauses, looking down at an airmail envelope. "Ma-gin-niss?" he asks.

"I don't know," Primo says.

"MacGuiness?" Mrs. Karbash asks.

"Yeah," he says, then turns, briefly, to her.

"Three F," she says.

He then hands Primo a letter-sized envelope. This one from Manny.

"Isn't she a good girl?" Mrs. Karbash says again. Lady wags her tail and stretches the leash toward the mailman.

Manny'd crossed out the More College return address and written in his own.

"I just thought of somethin," the mailman says. "I carry *your* mail in these." He turns around, holding an envelope in his hand. "But for Lady, the mail's on the bottom of my feet."

"Do you hear that, girl? You get mail too," Mrs. Karbash says to Lady. Then she looks at Primo and purses her lips. "What's he talking about?"

"I walk all around the neighborhood, right?" the mailman tells her. "Then I come here and maybe she can smell if there's like half a Big Mac lyin in the gutter on the corner, or if a new dachshund just moved in on Avenue B."

"It's like she reads her mail by sniffing," Primo says.

"She's a good girl," Mrs. Karbash says.

"She gets the *news* from my *shoes*," the mailman says.

Before he lifts and closes the door to the boxes, he pulls the postcard out of Primo's box and hands it to him. It has a yellow mail-forwarding sticker with his address on it. It's a reminder from the dentist he went to in More. Six months have passed since his last cleaning and exam.

"So what do *you* think?" the mailman asks Primo. "Is Lady a good dog or not? I'm dyin to hear your opinion."

"The best," Primo says.

"She really *is,*" Mrs. Karbash says.
"The best," the mailman says.

The title of Mariah's new book is *All She Wrote.* No letter accompanies it. She inscribed on the title page, *I trust you'll remember the occasion of the first poem. I'm lucky you were there. Love, Mariah.*

He left the book on the table, checked his answering machine for messages, dropped the postcard into the garbage can in the kitchen, made himself a sandwich and carried it back to the living room.

HOW MY BOYFRIEND AND I GOT FIRED FROM OUR JOB IN THE BOOKSTORE

The boss thought that we
were talking about him, when actually
we were discussing the execution,
by hanging, of thirty-eight Sioux
warriors, in 1862, for taking
part in the Minnesota Uprisings.
Our boss said, Who? I said,
Not who, I said, What. *What?*
he then said, and I said, The largest
single execution in the history
of the United States. He was now
taking it personally. I said, There's
no mystery. I lifted my empty
hands, None none none what-so-
ever, and again he said, What?
and I said, Mystery, and he
said, That's it, You two are
fired, and I said, That's
not it, *that's* all. *He then*
said, All? That's right, I said,
All, *as in, That's all,*
folks, or, more to the point,
That's all she wrote.

More than fifteen years ago, when Primo and Mariah were living together but not yet married, they worked for a time in a bookstore on the Upper West Side. Both of them were paying their tuition for graduate school by teaching remedial writing, part-time, for the college's new open-enrollment plan. But the rent also had to be paid. Another graduate student, Nazz Jacobs, who was their age and already a parent, had been putting in as many hours as he could in the bookstore. Primo asked if he'd let him know the next time they had an opening, and he did. "Only don't tell the manager you know me," he said. "He won't hire friends. He's got this thing about it. He thinks all they do is talk and conspire to steal books."

A month after Primo was hired they had another opening. Mariah applied and got the job. Right from the start the manager was suspicious that their relationship was more intimate than the ordinary relationships between co-workers. Primo knew his suspicion was intensified by the fact that they were the only two black employees.

One day, while shelving books, Mariah began leafing though an oversized book titled *History of the North American Indians.* She came across the fact that Abraham Lincoln had, in 1862, ordered the mass execution of thirty-eight Sioux. She walked over to the aisle Primo was working in and showed him the picture of the block-long structure of the gallows.

"This the same Abe Lincoln wrote the Emancipation Proclamation and the Gettysburg Address?"

"Same guy," Mariah said.

"You sure? I read about another Primo Thomas once. This one burned down twenty-one orphanages somewhere in Louisiana."

"I heard of him too. I also heard about a Primo Thomas who'd always start talking to his girlfriend just when she sat down at the typewriter. Sometimes he'd even interrupt her just cause he was horny. You heard of that one?"

"Can't say I have."

"And I've never heard of another Abe Lincoln."

"Kind of reminds me of what they say about Babe Ruth."

"And what's that?"

"He not only had the record for home runs. He had the most strikeouts, too."

"Interesting," Mariah said. "But we're talking about a mass execution. I don't think there's an actual correspondence here . . ."

At this point they realized that the manager was standing beside them. In Primo's memory, the conversation that followed was longer, and louder, than the version in Mariah's poem. But it is an accurate distillation.

Losing a job meant little to them. Nothing could stop their lives, or their relationship, from enlarging. And besides, there were plenty of minimum-wage jobs around. The world was changing, for the better, and they were changing with it. Maybe even abetting the transition.

Mariah had read in a psychology class that the first act of a family was the coming together of two future mates. The final act was its dissolution. Primo remembers a poem she wrote at that time: *Last year's nests / empty in the branches of trees / are still important. / Especially because you can't / live in them.* If that was true, then for them a new family was at hand. And it was easy. You *made* a family, you didn't just find yourself within one. And you made it by wanting it. You just had to want it. As easy as taking baths together, eating Hamburger Helper, as easy as the pleasure they found in each other's bodies.

Everything was changing. The whole world. An apartment with dyed sheets for curtains, two old chairs, a radio, a mattress and a cable-spool table was at the very least a household: it was anything you wanted it to be.

He closes the book. He doesn't know what he'll find in the rest of the poems, or what they might make him feel. After lunch he has two more classes to teach. During the workday it's best to anticipate complicated feelings, and to head them off at the pass.

He opens Manny's letter.

Dear Primo,

The 2 following lists are (A) the words and phrases my (your ex-) students most often spell correctly and (B) the words and phrases they most often misspell.

A: Aerobics, *Days of Our Lives*, Golden Retriever (though often as 1 word), BMW (it *is* 1 word), video, alterations, I'm tired, She's tired, He's tired, Racket (as in tennis), Love (as in tennis), Frisbee, Lotto, NutraSweet, Checkbook, Plane Fare, Virus, Cost Effective.

B: Hemisphere, Wyoming, Nelson Mandela, Cellophane, Chile (sometimes as Chilly, more often as Chili), Catherine Hepburn, Sandinista, Detroit, Handkerchief, Ambiguity, Senator, Egypt, Guerrilla, Brooklyn.

I have compiled and sent the above to you as a reminder of the life you have left behind, to express my ever-growing weariness, and as preface to the following:

I have just learned of, and already signed us both up for, a delegation of teachers that will visit Nicaragua this January. We'll travel around the country with members of their teachers' union, learn how they do it, see the sights, get the runs, soak in the sun, and learn about what they call The New Education. It's cheap and all you have to do is bring your own toilet paper and anti-malarial pills. Included with this special offer is a 1-piece set of 2nd-hand luggage: the self-same duffel bag you borrowed, and haven't yet returned, when you moved back to New York last June.

I'm talking the adventure of a lifetime.

You must come!

Listen to this (I know you can't actually *listen*—you're reading—it's a figure of speech): "The New Education is a dimension of the process of liberation of the great popular majorities from the material and ideological conditions in which they are reproduced as exploited and oppressed classes."

Wow, huh?

Now this brings me back to the students referred to in lists A and B. Do we want our system—The Old Education—to reproduce them? Or do we want to learn how to free them from their bonds, enlarge their minuscule horizons, enable them to freely choose their futures, and get them out of our faces. We must learn what this New Education is all about!

Whaddya say?
Manny

10

Between the moment, at three p.m., when Primo's alarm goes off, and the moment, a few seconds later, when he actually wakes up, he awakens twice in his dream. In the first moments of his third waking, he is surprised, and then relieved, to see the familiar walls and ceiling of his room.

The first time, he awoke in an enormous dormitory, a sea of beds wider than his range of vision, and in them other people, none of them people he knew, were sleeping. Out of nowhere, children appeared and began playing around his bed. They held hands and danced. They urged him to get up and join them but he didn't want to. They had on their faces the same mock-angry look people use to urge reluctant dancers out onto the floor. He shook his head. It was then he realized he was dreaming and closed his eyes so he could fall more deeply back to sleep and wake again, but this time not be in this dream. The second time, he awoke in the same room. The other sleepers were still there but the children were gone: it was as if, between wakings, real time had passed. Now there was an aluminum ladder set up beside his bed. A woman was standing on its top step, hanging strips of colored crepe paper from the ceiling. They were for some kind of celebration but he didn't know what it was.

The fact that this woman was there, and that she could have been there the whole time he was sleeping, caused him to feel an unbearable sadness, then, suddenly, an angry desire for privacy. He didn't want anyone else to be awake in this room.

A moment after opening his eyes for real, he loses memory of these two false awakenings. His first conscious thoughts are images from a dream he'd had earlier, just before the dreams of waking up: driving in an open convertible with Mariah. They passed trees and telephone poles and, occasionally, houses. Each of the houses had people standing in front of it, adults and children, and more people looking out the windows. He and Mariah were heading somewhere and they were late. Every time they made a turn or rose to the top of a hill, they expected to see it. They were certain they hadn't passed it, and equally certain they should have been there already.

Primo sits on his desk, facing his Level Two class, listening as they read the short autobiographical sketches that were their weekend writing assignments. They most often write about the countries they left, their families, and the lives they have begun to live since arriving in the United States. First they read them aloud, then Primo asks the other students if they understand. After that, if they thought anything had been written incorrectly. The discussions that arise are rarely about language. Most often, they are about the countries written about: comparisons and disagreements about weather, crops, foods, where things are, when things happened.

The pearls from Cuba are inferior.

Puebla has three hundred and sixty-five churches and in the world that *is the greatest amount in one place.*

The subways in Mexico City are clean and quiet but not so much as Luisa says.

Carmen, who had been in his Level One class in the summer, reads: *My country is really Manhattan because all of my family is now here. We are very very happy. My home is beautiful. My husband is Victor. My mother is Luz. My son is Ronald. I am Carmen.* She then passes around the Polaroids she took over the weekend of the family carving a pumpkin into a jack-o'-lantern. The photographs record each step: Her husband cutting the top off as her son holds the thick stem while her mother, sitting beside them at the table, looks on. Carmen scooping out the seeds and pulp. Her husband cutting out a triangular eye. Her son holding his head beside the big carved pumpkin, mimicking a wide, toothy grin. The finished pumpkin with a lit candle inside. There are three people in each picture. Either Carmen or her husband took them.

"I saw three of the *Halloween* movies in Panamá," a student named Luis says, after looking at the photographs. Luis, in his mid-forties, is a draftsman, but is working as a messenger until his English improves. "It's nothing like your pictures, Carmen." He laughs.

"I saw a *Halloween* movie too," another student, Regalo, says. "That knife your husband has might be the same one in the movie."

Everyone laughs at this.

"You saw only the first one. With the knife. I saw two of them. The one with the dolls . . . that's the best."

"There's a new one this year," Primo says. "It's the third or fourth." Then he says, "And after the fourth . . . ?"

"Five."

"That's the number. What's the adjective?"

"*¿Número ordinal?*" Luis asks.

"Correct."

"Fifth?"

"Very good."

"Sixth, seventh, eighth, ninth, tenth . . ."

"Luis," Regalo says. "They will never make *that* many."

"I would never see one anyway," Carmen says.

A student named Rubén reads: *My country is Colombia. Colombia is very nice. It is very beautiful and has many intelligent women. Colombia has many beaches, volcanoes and rivers. It produces good coffee, gold and big emeralds. People dance merengue, cumbia and American. I love my country!*

A discussion arises about the merengue that evolves into a discussion about which dances Rubén meant by *American.*

As the students are talking, a wave of soft, vague light, of sleepy distraction, passes over Primo. When it recedes it leaves the image of him and Mariah riding in a car. He is in the car with her, driving, and he is out of it as well, seeing them both, as if through the lens of a camera. He sees her arm, folded over the door top, smooth and beautiful, extending out of the short sleeve of her T-shirt.

Pastora asks if she can read what she wrote.

Primo tells her she can, then takes a sip from the take-out coffee cup set beside him on his desk.

Santo Domingo has beaches, mountains, fruits, many volcanoes.

He's suddenly angry at Mariah. There is a wall around the past, around their past, and when you're just looking back on it a wide, open gate appears. But if he turned and took a single step toward it, the gate would slam shut.

Has beautiful gold and silver, poor people, pineapple. Has tomatoes, potatoes, cauliflower, garlic, carrots, mushrooms, lettuce, onions and tropical fruits.

"Where do they have carrots?" Carmen, who is also from the Dominican Republic, asks.

"There are carrots."

"*¿Zanahorias?*"

"What?" Primo asks.

"Carrots. I never saw carrots in Santo Domingo. Have you?" she asks Primo.

"I've never been there."

"We had carrots."

"*Sí, en lata, sí.*"

"We had them fresh."

"In the market?"

"In the garden we had them."

"In your dream you had them."

He and Mariah have been apart for years now. She'll write poems about them, sometimes she'll call him for no reason. He doesn't call her. Only when there is some purpose for the call. Even a stupid one. *Gladys's mother's dog died.* When they were together, they both knew how to live just in the present. To *make* the present. Now he can't do it as well. He's forgetting how. It still seems easy for her.

"I know about English," Primo says, "not about carrots."

"You should go there," Carmen says. "So you can find out."

"He should go there for carrots?" Luis asks.

"He should go there because it's so beautiful."

"He then should go to Mexico City."

"I might be going to Nicaragua," Primo says. "Anyone been to Nicaragua?"

"Guatemala. *That* is beautiful."

"*Sí, y pobre.* He should go to Atlantic City."

"Héctor is from Honduras," Carmen says. "It's close to Nicaragua, like New Jersey."

Héctor sits in the back seat of the front row, nearest the door. His written English is progressing, but he is reluctant to speak aloud.

Primo asks him if he has ever been to Nicaragua. He answers no.

Primo then asks him if he knows anything about Nicaragua, since the two countries are neighbors. He wants to know something. It will help him decide, make it real, set this one thing, a place, in his near future.

Carmen raises her hand. "Luz is my neighbor on Bergen Street. But I did not know you use that word about countries."

"Like New York and New Jersey," Luis says.

"I can't believe she doesn't know that," Pastora says.

"Nicaragua is a bad place," Héctor says. "Why would you go there? It's not happy."

"I'd go with other teachers from the United States to meet teachers there."

"Are we neighbors with them?" Carmen asks.

"Brooklyn and Manhattan are neighbors," Rubén says. "Am I right?"

"Exactly," Primo says. "Do you understand that, Carmen?"

"Thank you."

"Why isn't it happy?" Primo asks Héctor.

"They are poor. They have war. They never fixed things after the . . ." He pauses. "*Terremoto* . . ."

"Earthquake," Luis says.

"Wasn't that ten years ago?" Primo asks.

"That was more. Fifteen years maybe. Since then it has never been happy."

"Don't go there, teacher," Carmen says.

"I might learn to be a better teacher."

"You're already a better teacher," Pastora says.

"Visit your neighbors. It's better," Carmen says. "Come to Brooklyn." She starts laughing.

"Take the F train," Luz says.

"I tell you this," Carmen says. "You come to Brooklyn and that's where you find carrots."

11

Primo is sitting at one of the front-row desks, waiting out the time between his Level Two and Level Three classes, staring into the mural. When lit only by the electric lights, the large figures in the foreground appear thicker, more dimensional. The light raises the rigid grain of the brushstrokes and bounces back from the wide, smooth patches of shoulders and faces and hats. In this light the images lose their stories. And if you don't concentrate hard enough, or if you concentrate too hard, the masses of color will break away from each other.

If you stare at the flying saucer long enough it begins to vibrate. Then you can move it between the tops of the buildings.

He has been feeling that something is about to happen. Not in the next instant, but within the range of future he comprehends as soon. This feeling launches another that sails like a radio wave through the last five months since he came back to New York, bounces off a wall of time, sails back over the string of days, homing on the future, and as it passes overhead it drops a single word from the sky: *same.* His life has been uneventful. His life has been a hand slipping into a new glove that is the same size and shape as its previous one.

The sky of the mural is a softer, more daylightish blue in the electric light. The real sky, outside, is a black mirror pushed right up against the windowpanes. Last week at this time, during the moments before Level Three, it was still dusk.

He knows that once he has this sensation of impending change, he has already, somewhere inside, begun to make it happen. It's like setting the clocks back. What really happens is that the surface of the planet stays still for an hour, while the inner globe, pulling at the roots of everything, continues its rotation through the next thirty degrees. Over time, the outside catches up with the inside, the separation corrects itself and the planet resumes spinning, like a top, through its unified days. It's like Mariah's poem about the branches of a tree beginning their separation before the tree even knows about it. Something is stirring. He'll know where he's going by the time he gets there.

12

Primo is packing the folders and green-covered workbooks into his briefcase as the last of his Level Three students file out of the room and into the hall.

On the outside of the front door of the classroom is a poster of Elvis Presley, on the back door a poster of Beethoven. Primo associates their faces, in smoky black and white, with the moments just before class and just after, as now, when the doors are opened inward and he can see them. As students walk past them on their way out of class, the language of their ongoing conversation usually changes from English to Spanish, like a melody dropped by a piano and picked up by a saxophone.

He notices that Carolina Benavidez has remained in her seat in the back of the first row. She isn't writing or reading or occupied with anything but he can't sense if she is waiting for his attention. She sat in the same seat during the summer when she was in his Level Two class.

She isn't looking at him, nor does he feel from her a sense of waiting, of expecting, but her remaining is the beginning of some kind of communication. In a moment they will be the only people in the room.

She rarely speaks in class and had refused to write the short autobiographies the other students in Level Two were writing. She said she would not write about herself until her English grew stronger. Instead she wrote about things from the news: a fire in the Bronx, a visit by Lady Diana, new changes in rent control laws. She also researched odd, useful bits of information, which she recorded in short clear paragraphs that she read to the other students: days when alternate-side-of-the-street parking rules were suspended, the number of votes needed for a bill to pass through Congress, the different rates offered by long-distance phone service companies, what number to call when you smelled gas in your hallway. She wrote a one-page paper on preventative medicine, another on how stuffed animals were made.

She would not write about the crops and weather and food in her country, or how many brothers and sisters she has. "That is like saying I have two arms and two legs, I sit down when I am tired, I cannot fly. I will write about myself when my English can tell you more than my laundry can, or the things I throw in my garbage."

It wasn't the fact of her distance that kept Primo from trying to further engage her in class discussions, but the power with which she maintained it.

He hears the voices and footsteps of the other students echoing off the painted concrete walls of the stairwells. Carolina is watching him. He snaps closed the top of his briefcase and looks back at her.

From her seat she says, "Are you going to Managua?"

He hadn't spoken of Nicaragua in this class, only earlier, in Level Two.

"I've been thinking about it."

"Carmen told me you are going."

"She told me to go to Brooklyn instead."

"*Are* you going?" After she says this she gets up and walks toward the front of the room.

Primo sets his briefcase on the floor and sits on the edge of the desk.

"Why would you go there?" she asks him.

"To meet their teachers, and learn how they work. I'd be traveling with other teachers from the United States."

She doesn't respond to this, and she doesn't seem uncomfortable about the silence.

"Why are you asking?"

"My father and my sisters live there, in Managua."

"You're from there?"

"No. We're from El Salvador. A city called Aguilares. When we left there, I came to Miami, then to here. They went to Managua."

Her skin is smooth and taut; she is on guard but calm, as if she is used to being alert, even when relaxed, as if the two conditions depend on each other. She waits for him to speak and only speaks when he cannot. She is perhaps thirty.

"I bet you miss them." He smiles. He has no choice but to be teacherly and superficial. Her eyes are also, oddly, calm. Calmer than he feels his are.

"If you go there, would you bring something to them for me?"

This is not what he expected her to ask. But he doesn't know what he expected her to ask.

"You don't have to," she says, ready to close down the discussion.

"No. I'd be happy to. As long as it's smaller than a piano."

She laughs.

This is what he wanted. That the moment evolve from an exchange of words toward a conversation.

"It's a lot smaller," she says. "A small box." She describes the approximate length and width of a shoe box with her hands. "Would this be all right?"

"No problem."

"Thank you," she says.

"But this depends on if I go."

"If you go . . . thank you."

"If I go . . . you're welcome."

They leave together and Primo walks her to the subway station on Delancey Street. On the way she tells him that the mail to Nicaragua is unreliable. Many of the things she has sent never got there. Everything that has arrived appears to have been opened and closed again. As she speaks she addresses him as *teacher*. This is something most of the students do. He tells her to call him Primo.

They stop at the subway entrance. "Good night," Primo says.

"You're not taking the subway?"

"No, I walk. I just live on Third Street."

"You walked here but you're not taking the subway?" She is surprised. She smiles. Then she says, "Thank you."

"It isn't far."

She buttons her denim jacket. There are small patches with the emblems of sports cars sewn at odd, playful angles on the front.

She notices Primo looking at them and says, "This is something I can't understand. This jacket cost much more money if it doesn't have these . . ." She touches the small colorful patches with her index finger, and laughs. She isn't asking a question, she is making this small mystery the point.

An ambulance, siren blaring, hovers for a second behind a half-ton truck waiting for the light on Allen Street. The driver slowly pushes his truck into the crosstown traffic, the ambulance swings around and shoots past them heading west.

"Good night," Primo says again.

She extends her hand and they shake.

She then looks down at the front of her jacket. "I've never even seen most of these cars."

"I don't think I have either."

"I knew right away it wasn't the cars," she says. "It's to make people look like they have fun." She smiles, then says, "And the one for people who don't have fun is much more expensive. For the same price they sell them with motorcycles or the names of radio stations. The colors were brighter on those. That's why I got this one."

"I think it looks beautiful on you," Primo says.

"It does not," she says. "It's . . . *no-place* clothing."

"No place?"

"If you wore this in my country people would think you were trying to look like you were from the United States. If you wear it here, it tells people you're from somewhere else."

"And where's that?" Primo laughs.

"A big foreign *no-place* where people can't afford the ones without the patches."

"Your English has gotten very strong," Primo says. He knows he is smiling stupidly.

She laughs, reaches for his hand and shakes it. "Thank you," she says. "You are a good teacher."

On the way home Primo notices that the window of the storefront that had originally housed the shoe store has been soaped over again. Before he left for More it had opened as a small art gallery. The night of their first opening, the crowd spilled out onto the street, holding wine in plastic glasses. After that, the place always seemed empty. Primo stopped in one day to see a show that had caught his attention from the street. A woman sitting behind a desk smiled at him when he walked in without losing a beat in the conversation she was having over the phone.

The walls were covered with windshields. They were from different makes of car, but all of them, set in old, thick chrome, some with vent windows, seemed to date back to the fifties and sixties. They were cracked and shattered as if they'd been removed from cars that had been in accidents. Some of them were streaked with dried blood and hair. Some had cigarette butts, ground glass and bits of cloth glued to their inside surfaces. One of them had a rear-view mirror with a pair of white baby shoes hanging from it.

The one that had caught his attention from outside had a web of cracks that reached like routes on a map from a hole, about the width of a forehead, on the driver's side. The zigzagging cracks caught every color of light in the room. Standing right in front of it, he could see that the hole was made by some kind of tool, some object harder than flesh. It annoyed him that anyone would go to so much trouble to create an object that was meant to appear real and to cause the person looking at it, him in that moment, to feel something—horror? fear? sympathy?—and to have done it so badly. With so little regard or connection to actual experience, either that of the invented person whose head was supposed to have crashed through the windshield, or that of the real person looking at it.

The presewn patches on Carolina's *no-place* jacket are much more pleasurable to look at. Immeasurably more beautiful.

In June, when he came back from More, the gallery was gone and a restaurant had replaced it. The new owners had completely redone the place. Exposed the original brick walls, hung lamps with straw bonnets for shades, put in a small mahogany bar. The space appeared to have always been a restaurant. Now it's closed again, dark behind the thick curtain of dry soap, where it's in the process of becoming something else.

He thinks that going to Nicaragua would be a good idea. There are no classes in January and he's made no plans. It would be nice to be somewhere warm. His last two winters in Massachusetts were serious, long winters. Might be nice to be somewhere warm, even if it's a *not-happy, bad* place as Héctor said. He tries to remember the word he had used . . . *terremoto?*

Another reason for going is that he now has a mission. He's a courier. He will bear a parcel from the mysterious, lovely, *no-place*-jacketed Carolina. He remembers a line Mariah used to quote from a poem by Pablo Neruda. He called Central America *America's slim waist.* He likes that. Beautiful. Sexy. He will give the ex–shoe store–gallery–restaurant and ex-whatever a chance to change once again and surprise him when he returns. While it undergoes its metamorphosis, like a moth in its cocoon, he will travel from the huge, noisy, cold shoulder of this hemisphere to its warm, slim waist.

NEW YEAR'S EVE

13

Primo is standing in front of the TV in his Aunt Olivia's apartment. She'd kissed him hello at the door, then rushed back through the dining room and deeper into the apartment. There is a black-and-white movie in the VCR on hold. "Happy birthday," she shouts from the kitchen. "And Happy New Year." A riderless horse, frozen in midgallop, flickers on the screen. "Sit, relax. I'll be in in a minute."

"What are you watching?" he asks, partially turning his head, aiming his voice in her direction.

"Cowboys and Indians. The usual revisionist junk."

"How come you're watching it?"

"I'm not. I just keep it on hold."

"You're watching it on hold?"

"I'm making turkey," she says. "Salad, greens and sweet potatoes, just the way my sweet nephew likes them, cut small before they get baked. A meal that's the first part of your birthday present."

She walks into the living room, holding a cooking fork in one hand and the remote control for the VCR in the other. She's wearing an apron with two turtles embroidered on the front. The TV screen stops flickering, the horse tries to complete its stride, but Olivia presses the hold button and stops it again. She then walks back into the kitchen.

"Bout a half hour ago, I stopped it to answer the phone. When I came back into the room I saw the horse, held like this on the screen, and it looked just like one of those cave paintings."

Primo sits on the couch and watches. The saddled horse is shot on an upward angle. There's nothing else in the scene but flickering desert sky. It would be a pale, empty blue were it filmed in color.

"I've been watching it like this since. This one image is better than the whole movie."

The living room walls are covered with photographs, posters, plates, oil paintings—some real, some prints—framed letters and memorabilia. Since his last visit she has framed the letter that arrived with some magazine subscription sweepstakes. It's as formal-looking as a diploma. *OLIVIA THOMAS HAS ALREADY WON A BRAND-NEW JAGUAR*, it says in bold, Gothic letters. One entire wall is devoted to photographs of the various sixth-grade and junior high school graduating classes she taught over the years.

Above the mantel is a dense constellation of family pictures. At the center, his grandfather, as a young man, stands behind a chair in which his wife sits. Their act of posing is an act of refusal to relinquish a single aspect of the meaning of their lives to the viewer. Two serious, devoted teachers, two colored Americans of the Early Twentieth Century, staring into a camera and dictating how you will see them long into the future. He, in a dark high-collared suit and vest, one hand firmly on the back of his wife's chair, the other on his hip; she, hatless, in round, wire-frame glasses, in hard, white Victorian waist and bosom, her hands, one atop the other, holding a small book on her lap. Seventy-five years after this lens had gathered them into it, they're still in control: still wholly *what* they are in every visible and deliberate aspect of their lives. People who each time they set a book down on a table knew, consciously within the act, that *that* was what a table, *their* table, was for. They were young children in a world where most of the adults had been born slaves, a world without electricity, cars and airplanes. They were young children under a sky that was empty of electromagnetic waves. They had seen Booker T. Washington speak from the back of a train car in Charlotte. They had seen four Clydesdale horses, harnessed by ropes to a system of pulleys, hoist a grand piano up to the third-floor windows of the Oak Park Inn in Asheville because the composer Bela Bartok was coming to stay there. They had known an ex-slave who, as a child, was waved to by the elderly Thomas Jefferson, being driven past in a carriage. They had no secrets, not from themselves or any human, black or white, and this was what empowered them. They had the imagination of their times and the literal seriousness required for the absolute invention of their entire lives. They would be nothing but what they knew themselves to be, and would not turn sideways to streamline their passage through the abrasive atmosphere of a world that had not welcomed them.

In the first ring of photographs surrounding this one, like the planets nearest the sun, is one of his father and Olivia as children. They are sitting on the wooden steps that lead up to the front porch of their house. Olivia has a cat curled in her lap. Primo remembers his grandmother talking about the cat that his father and Olivia had brought home one day as a kitten, and that had lived with them until it died eighteen years later, after they'd moved here, to Harlem. The children had named it Winter because it was as white as snow. But his grandmother wouldn't allow it. She modified the name to Windy. *It was a very nice name*, she had told Primo, pointing at it in the photograph, *but then, what could we have called it in the summer?*

There are more photos of his father and Olivia when they were children, his father in uniform, his father and mother together, with him as an infant, as a child, as a teenager, a picture of him and Mariah the day they were married: Mariah wearing a *Black Power* T-shirt as a wedding dress, both of them with wide Afros and him with long sideburns as well. It was the photograph his mother had brought with her when she moved in with Olivia. He remembers the antique gilt frame. It had in it a vague and clouded photograph of *her* mother and aunts, taken somewhere in Italy, near the end of the last century. Soon after Primo got married she removed the old picture and replaced it with this one of him and Mariah.

"I think we can give the horse a rest during dinner," Primo tells Olivia, when she walks back into the living room, remote control in hand.

"See you, Trigger." She aims the remote at the screen and hits the stop button and the image of the horse is replaced by broadcast TV. James Stewart is doing the Charleston with Donna Reed as the floor they are dancing on, without their knowing it, begins to slide out from under them, like the leaf of Olivia's dining table when there were more people to sit around it, and continues to do so until one of James Stewart's feet can no longer find anything beneath it and he falls slowly and clumsily backward, comically swinging his arms in an attempt to impel his weight forward, and finally falls into the swimming pool below.

"*It's a Wonderful Life*," Primo says.

"No it ain't." Olivia hits the power button this time and the screen darkens. "Help me set the table."

Sitting, eating, facing each other, these are the first moments in which Olivia has been still long enough for Primo to look at her. He has seen her only once since he came back to New York and that was last summer. He noticed how much she had aged then, and he notices, now, that she has aged since.

He doesn't see her often enough to not notice the changes time brings to her appearance. Her eyes, between her bright, ironic smile, and her short, white-gray hair, seem tireder, more deeply set in their sockets, and the skin on her cheeks and throat has become looser, softer, less able to protect the inside from the outside. When you see someone occasionally, someone you've known for a lifetime, you collect into a sudden, sweeping movement each minute of progress in the clock's hands that has occurred in the unmarked hours since you last observed them.

As if she knew this thoughts, Olivia says, "I'm seventy-four, you know. I guess you *do* know. . . . You sent me a card." She points her fork at his plate. "That's all you're eating?"

Primo takes another slice of turkey and a spoonful of greens. "Happy?"

"You know something, wiseass. . . . Today, you are half my age. Until this moment you have always been less than half my age, and from now on you will always be more than half my age."

Primo just looks at her and smiles. Even though he has no idea what she's talking about, he senses this is something she had planned to say to him today and knows she will explain further without his asking her to. "The gravy's delicious," he says.

"Today, having reached thirty-seven, you have arrived at the age I was at when you were born."

"Is that true?"

"Congratulations."

"You've now achieved some knowledge of life, as I knew it back then, when *your* life consisted of eating, sleeping and dirtying diapers." She smiles at this, then scoops up a spoonful of sweet potatoes and plops them on his plate. "You've come a long way. Which means you must be pretty smart."

"About *half* as smart as you?"

"Not even close. The acquisition of smarts accelerates. Kind of like the speed of falling objects. At seventy-four, I'm at least five times smarter than you are."

For a moment she seems to be looking at something, but not something Primo can see. She's looking backward, to find a path she has wandered from. "Thirty-seven," she then says.

"And getting smarter." Primo smiles, sets down his fork.

"My being the age I am means your mother would also be seventy-four, and your father, my God, your father would be closing in on eighty . . ." She falls quiet again. She looks down at her plate.

Primo stands. He then picks up the gravy pitcher, walks around to her side of the table and sets it beside her plate.

"Shit," she says. She looks up at him, squinting tensely, with a slight smile at the same time. "How tall are you?"

She stands up and sets the flat of her hand on top of his head, slides it off, holds it in the air above her own and looks up at it. "Shit," she says again, and then walks into the living room.

Primo remains standing beside her chair.

In a moment she walks in and sits down again. The sounds of

piano music, "Kadota's Blues" played by Oscar Peterson, follow her back into the room.

She picks up her knife and fork. "You sure you're not getting taller?" she says.

"What was the movie about?" Primo asks. "The one with the horse."

"First, the cattle guys were beating up the sheep guys. Then they both got together and beat up the Indians."

"Sounds interesting."

"A movie about friendship, according to the box at the video store," Olivia says. "But that other movie, the one that was on the TV, it's ten times worse. I always hated that damn movie."

"*It's a Wonderful Life?*"

"That's the one. This time of year every channel plays it at least twice a day. I think it's supposed to keep us happy and stupid. They have it playing on so many TVs at the same time you don't even have to watch it yourself. It's like getting lung cancer because the people around you smoke."

"It's just a dumb movie," Primo says.

"It's a piece of shit."

"I like the part where the little girl talks into the ear the little boy can't hear out of," Primo says. "Remember? She tells him she loves him and someday they'll be married."

"If you meant that, you're an idiot," Olivia says. "If you didn't, you're a cynic."

"It's just a dumb movie. A fantasy."

"Remember when the angel . . . what was his name?"

"Clarence?"

"Yeah, Clarence. Remember when Clarence shows Jimmy Stewart what the town would be like if he'd never lived?"

"Pottersville or something . . ."

"That's where the movie stops being a fantasy. Because that's what our lives are really like. That is, unless you're rich enough to never have to touch your feet to the ground. . . . But the truest part, the heart of the movie, is the life the main character lives, briefly, as someone who doesn't exist."

"But *we* know he exists."

"But nobody else does and that's the point. What really happens is that, just for a minute, he becomes black."

"Have you seen this movie lately?"

"He and Clarence get thrown out of a bar because they're strangers. They get beat up by the otherwise friendly cop because they're strangers. That remind you of anything?"

Primo nods, then starts to answer, but Olivia cuts him off.

"Except people look at this movie like they're looking at wallpaper, and see only the dumb fantasy you were talking about. And whoever's in charge of sending it across the airways knows that."

"So, when I've spent twice as much time on this planet as I have already—bearing in mind the smarts-acceleration factor—will I then be as smart as you?"

"It's highly unlikely."

"But I might get a little smarter."

"You'll have to get a lot smarter. Things are getting very weird out there. I just read in the *Post* about this town, somewhere out in Texas I think, where all the streets are named after golf players. Can you imagine such a thing? Things are getting *extremely* weird out there, and I won't always be here to explain it all to you."

"Let's get down to business," Olivia says. She holds out her glass for Primo to pour more wine into. "What's new in that sordid and complicated series of events you refer to as your love life?"

"Nothing much."

"That's disappointing. You know this is my favorite part of these occasional visits."

Primo looks at his plate and smiles.

"You telling me you got nothing to say? What about what's-her-name, up in the suburbs? The one with the little girl?"

"Pamela."

"Herself."

"I see her occasionally. We speak on the phone sometimes."

"How often is *occasionally?*"

"Once, maybe twice a month."

"That's exciting. . . . An opera. But it can't be all. Since you've been on your own, quantity has been your usual method. As opposed to quality. What else's happening?"

"There's this woman in one of my classes. We've gone out a few times. That's about it."

"One of your students? In all my years as a teacher I never did such a thing."

"You never taught anybody over thirteen."

"Even if that weren't the case, I'd never compromise the teacher-student relationship. What's her name?"

"Carolina."

"You tell her your family's from *North* Carolina?"

"Hadn't thought of it. Maybe because she pronounces it Caro-*leena.*"

"A rose by any other pronunciation . . ."

"I did tell her how many of us are teachers."

"Now *that* should win her heart. If it doesn't bore her to death first. Have you at least told her your old man was a doctor? At least give her the mistaken impression there's some money in the family."

"Haven't told her that yet either."

"Tell her you got this aunt who's an ex-astronaut. You can tell her all about the time I hit a tennis ball off the moon. Better yet, invite her to dinner. I'll tell her myself."

"Did you say there was more to my birthday present?"

"Did I say we were finished on this subject?" She smiles at Primo.

"Unfortunately not."

"I just don't want you to become one of these *afraid-of-commitment* guys they write magazine articles about. You know, a million women, Nautilus machines, malt liquor, drawers full of blue condoms that match the bed sheets. Besides, don't you want to be a father? I want to be a great-aunt. Great-aunt Olivia . . ."

"Olivia, I've been married. I know what I'd be missing if I missed it. I don't think of myself as boyfriend material, and I don't think of myself as *single.*"

"This is getting interesting," Olivia says.

"You know what it's like?" Primo says. "It's like men's shoes."

"Hum." Olivia nods her head.

"I'm serious."

"I know you are. As am I. Please go on."

"According to American shoes—what you see in the store windows—there's three, maybe four kinds of men. That's it. Any store you want, any selection: cheap, expensive, different colors, what have you, the range is still extraordinarily limited."

"What does this mean, dear nephew? More to the point, why the hell should I care?"

"I'm saying that there are only three or four kinds of relationships, just like the shoes. And I don't feel suited to the styles offered. That simple. I'm not a playboy, I'm not a husband, and I don't feel single. *Single's* the weirdest concept. It's like being some kind of victim."

"I agree with that last thing. I'm not sure about the rest." She slides her chair back and looks under the table. "Does all this have anything to do with why you're wearing sneakers in December?"

"Someone as smart as you has to understand what I'm saying."

"I do. I also know you. I think you'd be happiest living in a unit of people larger than yourself. And being a parent, too. You'd be good at that and you'd like it. I could give a shit less what you call it."

Primo reaches across the table, picks up Olivia's plate and sets it on top of his own.

"Your mother was my best friend," she says. She points at him with her fork before she hands it to him. "You *know* that. Even if she hadn't married your father, and even if I wasn't your aunt, that would be the case. And she passed you on to me. So don't get the impression I accepted delivery just because you're cute. It was for her. If you think about it, that gives me twice as much right to tell you how to live your life."

Primo brings the dishes and silverware into the kitchen.

"Just stack them for now," Olivia shouts to him. She gets up and walks in behind him. "After dessert you can have the pleasure of washing them." She turns on the flame beneath the coffeepot, and then points to a shot glass crammed with toothpicks on the highest shelf above the sink. "Could you hand me that?"

Primo lifts it off the shelf, holds it for her as she pulls out a toothpick and slips it into her mouth.

"You want one?" she asks.

"You look like a tough guy," Primo says.

"Thanks," she says. She takes the toothpick out of her mouth, then slides it back in. "Actually, I prefer to see it as a little tusk."

"Did you know that all year at dinners and birthdays your mother would listen for the mention of clothes sizes just so she'd know to get things that fit right for Christmas." They're back at the dining room table, waiting for the coffee to perc. "Sometimes she'd be sneaky and bring it up. She'd say, *Olivia, have you been losing weight?* when she knew I'd been gaining. She was always on the job.

"She wanted a family so bad she practically did it on her own. No matter how hard it was at the time—and let me tell you, it got hard—she could find a way of remembering things so it all seemed worth it. That woman *loved* to remember. *Olivia, remember your fiftieth birthday party? Your brother didn't say a word all night. Then he stands up and starts doing the twist. I couldn't believe my eyes! Remember when we all went to Bear Mountain and Primo put a piece of potato salad on his hook and caught that fish?*"

"I remember that trip," Primo says. "I remember. She cooked that bass and everybody ate some."

"And I remember when we were on the way there, the part your mother didn't seem to remember. We were waiting at a light just before the George Washington Bridge, all of us packed into your grandfather's old Ford, when a police car pulls up next to us. You and your grandma were in the front seat. Your grandfather kept you busy explaining how the streetlight worked. The police just stared into the car, at your mother, in the middle of the back seat, between me and your father. They didn't look at anyone else, only her.

Through *their* eyes, a white woman traveling in a car filled with black folks looked like a hostage. They just stared at her like she should signal for help. Blink her eyelids or something. But she just stared back at them, smiling, being just what she was, what she wanted to be: a woman sitting in a car with her family, driving to the country on a Sunday afternoon.

"As hard as your mother's life was, I never knew her to not be equal to it."

"Years later, when your mother was living with me, she had this dream about your father. I believe she had it more than once, though she was never sure.

"In the dream your father was coming home from the Army. He was arriving by train at Grand Central Station. I'm there, your grandparents are there, even you're there. But even weirder than your ahead-of-schedule appearance is that *her* parents are there too. Even her parents . . . And everyone's waiting.

"A train pulls in and the doors open. Your father, in uniform, is the only passenger to get off. He walks right up to your mother and asks her how she is. *I'm fine*, she tells him. *And you*, she says, *how are you?* He doesn't answer. He just takes off his wristwatch. You know, the one with the gold band that you have now? And he wants to give it to her. *I don't need this*, she told him. *You know I have a watch*.

"And that's the whole dream. I asked her if she thought it meant that wherever he was, it was somewhere outside of time, and he didn't need a watch. *That's probably what most people would think*, she said. *But it was the word he meant, not the thing. He wanted me to know he was watching. He was watching over me.*

"She told me about it at breakfast the morning after she dreamt it. She told me she'd dreamt it before. Later that day she said she wasn't sure anymore. Maybe she had only dreamt that she dreamt it before. So I told her, you have that dream again, you tell me about it. Since I'm not the one doing the dreaming, *I'll* keep score."

Olivia gets up and walks into the kitchen. Primo can hear the sounds she makes moving things in the kitchen. A heavy plate being set on the tabletop, then slid across it, a metal utensil set onto it with a clunk.

Olivia flips off the dining room light, begins singing "Happy Birthday" and walks slowly into the room with the coffeepot in one hand and a chocolate cake, big enough for ten people, the top crammed with glowing candles, balanced on the other. After she finishes singing and Primo blows out the candles, she says, "Leave me one piece and bring the rest home."

She leaves the room again, briefly, and this time flips the light back on when she returns. She's carrying a wrapped gift the size of a large, square hatbox, which she sets in front of Primo before she walks out a third time. The wrapping is covered with pictures of different-sized turtles, in three images, printed alternately, in horizontal lines across the paper: a turtle sunning itself on a rock, a turtle swimming under blue water amid the stems of water lilies, and two turtles on shore, facing each other, touching noses. When Olivia returns, she sets a cup and saucer in front of Primo, another in front of herself, and sits down. "Open it," she says.

Inside, Primo finds a pair of blue bikini bathing trunks, his father's stethoscope, a T-shirt across the front of which are the words *¡No joda mas!*, a roll of toilet paper, a bottle of Chloroquin antimalarial pills, a one-liter bottle of mineral water and a small photograph of Olivia, snipped from a strip of four taken in a booth. In it, she's wearing plastic Groucho Marx glasses with nose and mustache. She'd managed to get it into a typewriter and write across the top, *Happy Birthday*, and across the bottom, *Happy New Year*.

"That means stop fucking around," she says, pointing to the T-shirt.

"I know what it means," Primo says.

"I knew you did, but I enjoyed saying it aloud."

"Thank you," Primo says, looking at his gifts.

"You take one of those pills each day," she says. "And you start five days before you leave."

"Thank you."

"As you probably know, you won't find toilet paper down there. And from what I hear, if you drink the water anywhere outside Managua, that roll won't last you half an hour."

She extends her wineglass to Primo. "As your mother would say, dear nephew, *Salut*."

"Remember, if the ground starts shaking, get out of reach of anything that can fall on you. If you're inside, stand in a doorway, right inside the frame, preferably one without a door in it."

"What are you talking about?" Primo asks.

"I remember that terrible earthquake they had. Must have been fifteen years ago. And that bastard kept all the foreign aid we sent them. Never fixed a thing."

"Somoza. That was his name."

"I remember. Every time I'm in an Indian restaurant I remember—you know how I love Indian food. . . . I order *samosas* and I think, how could the name of anything that tastes so good sound so much like the name of that rat bastard."

"*El terremoto de mil novecientos setenta y dos*," Primo says. "My student Héctor told me about it."

"So many people died, so many lost their homes. . . . You just keep that wise ass of yours out of trouble." She refills Primo's coffee cup. "You know you're not going to be sitting on some Greyhound with a bathroom and air-conditioning, pointing out the volcanoes and the churches and the birds with the long tails."

"I don't know much of what we'll be doing. We land in Managua. We're going to stay there for a while. I know we're going north. To see the coffee collectives and cultural centers. They teach the farm workers at the places where they live and work. They got these teachers, Popular Teachers they call them, or *brigadistas alfabéticas*. They say they carry the schools on their backs."

"I bet *you're* a popular teacher." She smiles. "I bet that what's-her-name, Carolina, would say that."

"The way your mind works is a mystery to me."

"No mystery, I just have more cars on my train of thought."

"It's the switch tracks that confuse me."

"Someday, dear nephew, you will understand. I think we hadn't quite finished our earlier discussion. I have the feeling there's something more you wanted to say on the subject of that young woman."

"Do you know that in Salvadoran dialect the verb *pisar*, which means to step on, or tread, even like stomping grapes, can also mean having sex."

"That's delightful. Very appropriate. I think *your* train has permanently derailed, but I'll grant you this: you've revived my interest in the conversation."

"I'm telling you this because it has to do with a joke she told me."

"Go on. But if I don't find it funny, you'll bring her to dinner so she can tell me herself."

"These two campesinos are visiting the city for the first time and they wander into a building with an elevator. The doors slide open and they walk in. They're just standing there, not saying anything. They don't know it's an elevator. They just think it's a little room. So the elevator operator says, *¿A cuál piso?* Which, as you know, means What floor? but in dialect can mean, *Which one do I screw?*"

"You better get that girl up here."

"At least wait for the punch line."

"Proceed."

Primo stands up, looks to his left at an invisible man, steps into the spot he'd looked into, then looks to his right at the spot he'd just left. "So they're looking at one another," he says.

"I'm to assume it's a male elevator operator?"

"Yeah. And he's getting impatient, so he asks them again. "*¿A cuál piso?*"

"I'm on tenterhooks."

Primo, still standing, crosses his arms and points his fingers in opposite directions. "At the same time, they each point to the other and say, *Él* . . ."

"You got her number on you? I'll call her now. Or her last name . . . Give me her last name and I'll call information."

"You got it, didn't you?"

"If you have to ask, you know you're in trouble."

"Maybe it's better in Spanish."

"While you're down there I want you being careful what passes out of that wiseass mouth of yours—Spanish or English. It's a different ball game. Your friend Manny too. His mouth's even bigger than yours." She picks up the photograph of herself in the Groucho Marx glasses. "This one came out the worst. I ruined the other three in the typewriter." She looks down at her image, shakes her head. "You know, you tell a joke even worse than your father. Not that he told many. But when he did, *whew* . . . He could take the best material and turn the audience into stone." She holds up the photo and points to it. "Now *this* is funny." She drops it onto the tablecloth and leans toward Primo. "Oh, and one other thing. You see any of those rat-bastard *contras*, you walk the other way."

"So, you going to a New Year's Eve party tonight?"

"Not sure. I thought I might stay here with you."

"You kidding? And what do we do, watch *It's a Wonderful Life?* Toast the turtles at midnight? Uh-uh . . . Me and Martha and some other likely suspects are going dancing. I'd invite you along but young folks such as yourself couldn't handle the heat. Not after Martha and me get started. They'll pass an Olivia Thomas law before this year's over . . . *Stand* back . . ."

"I haven't seen the turtles."

"I moved the tank to the kitchen. They like the light better. They like to watch me cook. . . . You know they're fourteen now and they still haven't laid any eggs?"

"I assume you told them about the birds and the bees, and the reptiles?"

"I once put on a Jimmy Rushing tape, threw a couple of fresh oysters into the tank and left them alone for the day. Nothing. I don't know. Jimmy Rushing always did it for me."

"Have you tried Marvin Gaye? They're too young for Jimmy Rushing. Say, 'Sexual Healing'?"

"The problem with Pat and Mike is, they're afraid to make an investment in the future."

Primo stands, gathers their cups and saucers and dessert plates and walks toward the kitchen.

"Like my nephew," Olivia says as he walks past her. "Like everybody else these days. Everybody's afraid of the future."

When Primo walks out he tells her the turtles look fine. They were both chomping on leftover salad.

"They always enjoyed your mother's salad dressing."

"Me too."

"When she first moved in here she kept asking me why I didn't have a pet. I told her, as an adult I prefer the company of featherless bipeds. But she kept asking. *How about a dog?* she'd say. *How about a parakeet? A kitten? Goldfish? A hamster?* And I'd say no. Before I noticed she'd left a conspicuous hole in the area of amphibians and reptiles, she brought Pat and Mike home."

"I always thought you liked having them."

"I inherited them. Like I inherited you."

"Where you going dancing tonight?"

"Someplace you can't come to. A club in midtown where they don't mind old folks throwing caution to the wind. And you. What are you doing?"

"Manny's in town. He invited me to the party he's going to. I'll probably go there."

"Bringing one of your lady friends? Or are you looking to enlarge the harem?"

Primo is sitting on the living room couch, listening to his own heart with the stethoscope. It has a thickly soft, two-beat thud, like the sound of a heavy door being repeatedly opened and shut.

From behind him Olivia, using the remote control, turns on the TV and VCR, recovers the image of the horse, sets it back half a stride and freezes it again, flickering on the screen. She leaves the room, returns a moment later with two shopping bags. In one she has packed the leftover cake, in its box. In the other are his birthday presents.

She sets the bags in front of the couch and sits.

"This morning, while cooking, I remembered the summer your father and I found the cat."

"The one in the picture?"

"Her exactly. Windy, nee Winter."

"Wait a minute." Primo leans toward her. "This happens in summer, right? You sure you should be talking about it in winter?"

Olivia laughs. "Your father and I called that cat Winter anyway. When none of the adults were around, that is. It didn't mind one bit.

"Anyway, I was five or six, so anybody born that day—if they managed to come through the years—would be collecting social security. I was lying in the grass in front of the house. Every year in the first part of the summer, this mockingbird used to sit on top of the pine tree beside the house and go through its entire repertoire. I counted six different songs. I remember—I've so rarely heard one since."

The horse on the screen comes alive, along with a dense syllable of orchestral music, before Olivia freezes it again.

"Your father, as usual, was off somewhere. Today I would call what I was *bored*, but then it was something else. I wasn't asleep and I wasn't awake. I could smell the grass and the soil, and the sky was showing movies on my closed eyelids. What I remembered this morning was something I had felt *that* morning. I became worried that if I really fell asleep, the rest of the way asleep, nothing would be the same when I woke up. I had this feeling that things were always about to change, become something else, that they *wanted* to, but something held them in place. And that was me.

"But I did fall asleep. A minute, an hour, I didn't know how long. And when I woke up I couldn't understand why the grass was still the grass. It could've become a lake, or a blackboard, or cloth, or concrete, or just plain dirt. What is it makes things stay the same, or seem to? Some law of nature, or what?

"But the mockingbird was still up there, doing its greatest hits, and when I looked down, there were my knees, as skinny as they were before I fell asleep. So I decided to believe nothing had changed." She's quiet for a moment. Then says, "That cat. Did you know she lived for eighteen years?"

She presses the play button, restarts the action on the screen, rewinds it to the place it had been and freezes it again. "Maybe because it's New Years's, or your birthday, but this morning I started thinking about it again. And after all these years I realized that that day, while I slept, everything *did* change. It was the moment it all got away from me." She aims the remote at the TV. "If I only had one of these back then." She starts and stops the action again. "I don't know why I told you all that. I don't even know what it means."

"I don't know either. But I'm glad you did."

She points to the stethoscope, still around his neck. "You plan to wear that on the subway?"

He takes it off, hands it to her, and she places it in one of the bags. She then sets them just inside the front door, returns to the couch, and sits down again.

"You ever have a feeling like that," she asks him, "like you've experienced a moment when things changed? I mean really changed."

"For me, things don't change suddenly. They just sort of grow out of other things. You were asking about my love life before . . ."

"Yes, and learned little that was of interest."

"My life with Mariah grew out of my life at home. My life since grew out of my life with Mariah."

"That wasn't what I was asking, or *why* I asked. But since we're in the neighborhood, I will add that I'm looking forward to the *next* thing your life will grow into. Whatever that is."

"Why *were* you asking?"

"Just doing a comparison test. You and your father. I never knew two people more alike. If I can understand you, maybe I can understand him."

"How are we alike?"

"Answer my question directly and I'll tell you."

"Okay, I truly can't remember a moment such as the one you described."

"That's what I thought you'd say. I think your father would've said the same thing. Add to that the fact that neither of you could tell a joke if your life depended on it, and that's two things you have in common.

"Now answer this. What if you were alone in the middle of the night and something really scary or weird happened? Like the bedposts start singing a lullaby, or your shoes suddenly grow wings and start flying around the room."

"I probably couldn't see them in the dark."

"If something that scary happened, what would you do? Would you call anybody?"

"I don't know."

"You're not answering my question."

"I don't know how to. I can't even figure out what you're talking about."

"I bet you wouldn't. I bet you'd just lie there in the dark, so scared you'd wet the bed. But you wouldn't pick up that phone."

"If you know the answers to your questions, why are you asking them?"

"That's what your father would've done. Just lie there, not call out to a soul. Your father, the doctor who spent so much of his time healing people, answering emergency calls in the middle of the night . . ."

"This is getting weird. I prefer it when you ask personal questions about my love life."

"That's three things you'd have in common. I needn't mention the fourth—wiseass-itis."

"Look. The horse is running again. Looks like there's a lasso about to fall over its head."

"It's a sheepman, but don't worry. There's a cattleman coming behind that's going to lasso him before he gets the horse."

"I can rest easier."

"Listen. I'm going to tell you something that son of a bitch, your father, once told me. He said, *I don't believe we can really heal our neighbor's pain.* I think he meant it. Even though he spent his career trying to do just that. What I finally realized was that what he was saying had nothing to do with his patients, or neighbors. He was only talking about himself. He was trying to explain something he thought I'd been wanting to know. He didn't believe that in another human being, one could find relief from pain.

"No one in their right mind should believe such a terrifying thought. And worse, I think he somehow got the message across to you. He believed he controlled the world around him. It could never change without his knowing it. This world, *his* world, reported to *him*. . . . You believe it too, and I'm not even sure you know that.

"I watched the two of you grow up and I have some sense of this. You're both like trees in the park. To the casual observer, you'd look straight from root to branch, both of you kind of handsome, both of you looking enough like the rest of us. But *I* see all the twists and bumps. You look closely at a tree, you see how the shape is a history of each place a shaft of light stayed near long enough for it to lean itself into it. He got pretty crooked, your father. You're on the way yourself. . . ."

Primo looks down into the open shopping bag at the stethoscope. The chrome tubing and the thick disk his father called *the diaphragm* shine as if they were brand new, even after all these years.

"I'm going on too much. I didn't even know I had this much of it on my mind. My train of thought's hauling some weird freight, but it's real, it's mine, it's our family's. . . .

"Lately, it seems to me that this is becoming a trend. More and more people seem like they're walking around completely cut off from other people. What a dreadful way to live. There's a lot I don't know, but I'm certain there was a time when we all believed we could share pain. Heal it? I don't know. But *share* it.

"And what I've been thinking is that your father and you might be prototypes, the advance guard. I saw it in him and you first. It's not even believing this that hurts me, it's the two of you acting like it's nothing out of the ordinary. Like being alone *is* the ordinary state of things. That's what controlling things really is, it's making them ordinary, so you can live with them. That was your father's big mistake."

Primo puts his hand on her shoulder. He is moved by what she is saying, and he can't hear more, now.

"You got his good looks," Olivia tells him, "*and* his good spirit, you got your own stuff and at least half your life ahead of you. I don't want you getting any more bent and gnarly than you already are."

Olivia leans back on the couch, and presses the play button.

"I want you to see the rest of this before you go," she says, "but

I know it would take too long." She then presses the fast-forward button, and narrates the silent, sped-up story.

"That's the brother of the sheepman the cattleman had lassoed earlier. Now he's shooting from the saddle. That's the cattleman who had lassoed his brother falling dead off his horse. Now *that's* the sheriff outdrawing the sheepman's brother. And that's the sheepman's brother lying dead in front of the saloon. And finally, that's the sheepman who started all the trouble in the first place, finally acknowledging that enough blood has been spilled. It's time to negotiate with the cattlemen. On the Great American Plains there is room enough for all the white men. Why couldn't they have learned this the easy way? The end."

"I hope you have a happy New Year," Primo says to Olivia. He is standing in the hall, just outside the door.

"You too." Olivia, facing him, presses her arms against the inside of the doorframe. "Remember," she says, "if you're indoors and the ground starts shaking, *this* is where you stand."

"It'll probably take me the whole year to figure out all the things you said a minute ago."

"Don't make a big project out of it. I was just spouting off."

"Thanks for dinner, and all the gifts."

"You get any other presents?"

"Not yet. Manny said he has one he can't wait to give me. But you never know with him. When Mariah and I got married he hung a math book by a string from our fire escape."

"A what?"

"A math book. Trigonometry. He said Marcel Duchamp once did this for two friends as a wedding gift. He's not the type to give silverware."

"He's not the type to *use* silverware." Olivia steps toward Primo, stretches onto her toes and kisses him on the cheek. She then settles back on her soles, looks down into the shopping bags he is carrying, one in each hand. "Got everything?"

"I think so. Thus far, the first day of my thirty-eighth year has been great."

"Glad to have been of service."

Primo turns and begins walking toward the stairwell.

"There's one question," Olivia says to him, "I've never gotten a satisfactory answer from you on. One of these years you'll have to tell me. Wouldn't you have preferred to be born on the first day of the new year rather than on the last day of the old one?"

"It's the same to me."

"That's bullshit."

"A day's just a day." He turns into the stairway and begins the descent toward the street.

"You're so full of shit it's coming out of your ears," Olivia shouts after him.

"Happy New Year," he shouts up the stairs.

PART II

COUSIN

14

Primo imagines that the strong, hot, corporeal wind that breaks against his back is really a river of praying hands, wedged apart by his torso and forced to briefly encompass his body in their prayer before reuniting in front of him, sweeping across the trafficless stretch of tarmac roadway that serves the single terminal of the Augusto Sandino Airport, across a wide, vein-cracked field of concrete that ends at a weary hurricane fence, to the road just beyond it, sparsely, irregularly lined with palm trees that mark the end of his line of sight. The road, when he and the nine other North Americans he traveled here with first stepped out of doors, was empty, but now two half-ton trucks, their open backs crammed with standing passengers, are passing each other from opposite directions. He knows that later, when he recalls the moment, he will remember the wind, oddly humid and dry at the same time, but forget the hands. They squeezed out the door of the little theater he carries around inside memory, where he constantly plays reruns of every dream he has ever had. He is tense, tired, spacey, wide awake. He forgets apparitions as soon as the moments they occur in join the conga line of the larger experience they're a part of. He expects to. But now, while the moment is still whole and its own, Primo imagines this wind is carrying the first scent, the first broken-free molecules of himself, a stranger, out to those people riding in the trucks, and to the immense city still beyond his field of vision.

It took them over two hours to cross the short but endless distance between the arrivals entrance of the terminal to the sunlit sidewalk, where they are now waiting for the bus that will take them into Managua. For Primo, it had been the longest portion of the journey that started this morning, before dawn, when the first of the two passenger jets that brought him here lifted itself off a runway at Kennedy Airport. The waiting on lines, the gathering together after each procedure, waiting again, became the dream of approaching a shore that refused to grow nearer.

After they got their passports stamped they found themselves just inside the larger concourse of the enormous building. The only other North Americans who'd arrived on their plane—two members of a network news crew, carrying aluminum film-equipment luggage, and a nun, returning from Minnesota, where she'd spent the holidays, to her work in a community center in Managua—had quickly passed into the proximate steps of the process, nearer the exit, on the other side of which was Nicaragua.

The delegation members who could read Spanish were translating the signs and instruction posters that lined the walls and glass partitions for those who could not. There were also posters welcoming people to *La República de Nicaragua*, another that read, *VIVA el 19 de JULIO*, and public health notices for SIDA.

Primo was looking at everything with a hunger for what it could tell him, for where it could bring him: the overhead beams of the large, Spartan, anywhere-in-the-world airport structure, the worn, square-tiled floors. Most of the people there were not returning or departing. They walked, stood, gathered together, carried things—absorbed and incurious—their stances and motions designed by the various carriages of their functions, and the environment and grain of an ordinary day.

He had expected the men and women in uniforms, the sidearms and AK47s. He had also expected the heat, the broken wall fans, the alien appearance of the awkward group of strangers he was a member of. These things belonged to the past moments in which he first envisioned them, images in photographs he took in his imagination. He searched the wide room for what he now wanted: the glimpses of clear sky through the windows, the smooth-worn, unattended soccer ball resting against the wheel of an unused hand truck, the elderly couple with dark, worn faces, wearing straw hats with chin strings, both carrying red-and-blue overnight bags with the *Pizza Hut* logo printed on their sides.

He spotted a bathroom, pulled a T-shirt from his bag and headed for it. It was eighteen degrees Fahrenheit when he left his apartment this morning, it was over ninety when they arrived. The sweater and heavy shirt he wore were already soaked through with sweat. The first thing in the room to catch his attention was a shiny, coin-sized seal affixed to the side of the broken and empty paper towel dispenser. *Made in Kendallville, Indiana.* The fact of it being there, of his having to stand beside it, infuriated him. He'd been restless, impatient, hot, but his sudden anger, the extent of it, took him by surprise. He wanted to rip it out of the wall. He threw water on his face and chest, dried himself with the shirt he'd taken off. He wanted to rip it out but didn't. He felt the rage squeeze into his arms and legs. "Fuck you," he said, aloud, to the towel dispenser. "Fuck *you.*"

"Sorry." It was Manny's voice.

Primo looked in the mirror and saw him standing right behind him. He hadn't seen him come in.

Manny smiled, curiously, and turned his head. "You want privacy?"

"Do you believe this?" He pointed to the towel dispenser.

"It's broken. Is that hard to believe?"

"No, that it's *here.* . . . Read where the fucking thing came from."

"Indiana."

"Do you believe it?"

"Easily. I was made in Brooklyn—and *I'm* here. By the way, there's a new line forming. We're going to change dollars to cordobas. That's what I came in to tell you."

As they gathered at the AeroNica departures desk in the airport in Miami, the delegation's meeting place, and later, aboard the plane, everyone talked about what they knew and what they expected. Each of them had a different object in their vision. Primo had none he was aware of. He rarely believed anything the news at home said about Nicaragua. He knew they wanted him to fear the place for the same kinds of reasons McDonald's wanted him to think a cheeseburger would make him happy. Even so, something beneath the meaning, something in how they intoned the strings of words, had crept into his preconceptions: life lived here was inconceivably different from the life he lived at home. And what he'd felt with such suddenness, the moment he stepped off the plane, was that this difference, whatever it was, held something he has always wanted.

He wasn't getting here fast enough. He needed to feel he wasn't in some distant but still-attached piece of the place he'd just left. He needed to feel much farther away than that. And needed to feel it in a hurry.

He slipped in line behind Manny, who handed him a form.

"I can't believe you found that towel gadget so odd," he said.

"It wasn't the first thing I'd expected to see. That's all."

"I've always admired your sharp and curious eye, but Primo, this is not a big fact. A fart is not an atom bomb. . . . By the way, *fecha* is date, right?" He fanned himself with the form he was holding, then he pointed to it. "And this, what do you call a form?"

"*Una tarjeta.*"

"*Gracias.* Right on *tarjeta.* Like to make sure my interpreter knows his stuff." He walked behind Primo, pressed the paper against his back and began filling it out. "Everything," he said. "Every-fucking-man-made-thing has to end up someplace, doesn't it? What's weirder than that towel gadget being here is *our* being here. Am I right?"

Primo noticed the first member of their delegation on line step up to a teller's window. He watched her slide money under a plate of glass. He saw the tips of fingers slide two stacks of bills, both more than an inch thick, back out to her.

"Here," Manny said. He walked around Primo again, offered his back as a writing surface. "The weirdest thing was running into Maryellen. Do you believe it?"

Maryellen is the twin sister of a woman Manny had gone out with over ten years ago in New York. He knew she existed—she lived in Little Rock, where the sisters grew up—but had never met her. He had no idea she would be in the delegation and this morning, when he first saw her at the airport in Miami, he called her by her sister's name, Lisa. She smiled, then told him who she was. This happens to them both, she told him. All the time. That's life for identical twins. But the idea that she and someone who'd known her sister would find themselves on the same delegation, that, she said, was a new one. It was nearly all Manny spoke of on the flight down.

"Do you believe this?" He leaned his head back, talked out of the side of his mouth. "I've never seen this woman before this morning, never touched her, have said little more than hello, how are you, my name is Manny. But at the same time, having known her sister—in the biblical sense, that is—I can claim to know exactly what she looks like with no clothes on."

"I can't fill this out if you don't hold still," Primo said. "If you think about it, you can't actually claim that last statement. You went out with her sister a long time ago, right? What you maybe *can* claim to know is what this woman looked like ten years ago without clothes on."

"That's right."

"Hold still."

"It's like seeing a star that's ten light-years away and realizing that what you're seeing is what it looked like ten years ago."

"Or maybe the opposite?"

"Or maybe both," Manny says. "Whatever it is, it's very exciting. Fucking eerie, though."

Sixty dollars translated into 250,000 cordobas. No one seemed to know what to do with the thick stacks of money they had been handed.

A man who introduced himself as Alejandro, a representative of the ASTC, the Sandinista Association of Cultural Workers, had guided them through each procedure, asked them afterward to wait, disappeared for a time, reappeared again and led them to the next step. After they had all finished at the tellers' windows, he told them he was not surprised at their response to the exchange rate.

"The inflation has been out of control here," he told them. "The war, the embargo, counterfeiting . . . Many problems. If you look at the twenty-thousand- and fifty-thousand-cordoba bills, you will see just how much inflation we have experienced." He then asked them again if they would be patient and wait there until he returned.

Before he walked off, Maryellen complimented him on his English.

"Amazing," said the man standing in front of him, one of three members that teach in the same university in California. He held a fifty-thousand-cordoba bill up to the light, as if to look through it.

Twenty-cordoba bills had been restamped to 20,000, fifties to 50,000.

"What are the dates?" Manny asked.

"This one's 1985," a woman, also from California, said.

"That's a thousand percent inflation in three years," Manny said. "It's like . . . It's like a loaf of bread that cost one dollar three years ago now costs ten dollars. Is that possible?"

"It could be. But do things all go up at the same rate?"

"My God . . . prices must change every week."

"More than that. Every *day*."

Primo had drifted out of the conversation. He shoved a wad of bills into his wallet; the rest he slipped into his passport and zippered it into the pocket on the outside of his canvas bag. He was angry they had to wait again.

He walked over to the old soccer ball, scooped it up, spun it on his finger—it turned out to be flat, and only wobbled through two or three rotations—and then set it back exactly where it was, against the wheel of the hand truck.

When he got back to the line Manny asked him what he thought of Maryellen's pantsuit. "Do you believe that? Lisa wore black jeans, the tightest black T-shirts you ever saw and nothing but high-top sneakers. Could twins grow so far apart? She's standing here in the middle of Central America, wearing . . ." He pointed at her and laughed quietly. "Wearing *that.* Something the wife of a golf pro would wear to a barbecue celebrating their tenth wedding anniversary. If I look at just her, wow, if I squint"—he holds his curved hand up to his eye—"you know, kind of adjust the focus to obscure the background, I can see her pulling the saran wrap off the macaroni salad. And there's little Biff, sitting on her mother-in-law's lap. And her husband, flipping the steaks. And you know what he's wearing? An apron that says, *I Think I'll Keep Her.*"

"I like macaroni salad," Primo said.

"You're an asshole."

Just then Alejandro emerged from the door of an office across the wide, busy room, and walked toward them. "Shit," Primo said. "I hope we're getting out of here."

"Your problem is, you don't have a writer's imagination. If you did, you'd appreciate a larger portion of the great stuff I tell you. You'd know that any time spent between things, especially in new and exciting situations, is not time to simply be endured. It's not *waiting.*"

Primo picked up his bag and slung it over his shoulder. "What is it, then?"

"It's observing. It's gathering . . ."

"If you will observe," Primo said, pointing over Manny's head at the other members of their delegation, who were crossing the space beyond the tellers' windows toward the exit at the far end of the concourse, "you will see that our compañeros have gone off and gathered someplace else."

As they wait for the bus a crowd of children gathers around them. At first, they assemble a short distance away, shyly facing the adults, who wave, smile, say hello. They gradually move closer. They do not engage in conversation, nor do their faces express a desire to.

A boy, perhaps six years old, walks up to Primo. He just looks up at him for a moment, then begins gesturing with a small green plastic object Primo thinks he wants to show him. He kneels and takes it from his hand. It's a bubble wand, the kind you dip into a bottle of bubbles and blow through. Primo hands it back. The boy then points it toward the Bic pen in Primo's shirt pocket. Primo looks down at it, pulls it out of his pocket and shows it to him.

"*¿Es ésta que tú quieres?*" Primo asks him. He wonders, briefly, how this child sees him, the only black person in this group of strangers.

The boy reaches for the pen.

All at once, the children start to back off. Primo sees a woman approaching from the terminal exit. She wades into the crowd and shoos the children away. The boy takes the pen before he runs off.

Primo stands, facing her. She looks back at him angrily, then at the others.

"While you are here," she tells them, "many children will ask you for things. You must not give them anything. You can help us this way. We will not allow them to become beggars."

Her careful English has barely a trace of an accent. She is wearing jeans, tennis shoes and a blue T-shirt with faded gray lettering across the front. Primo can make out, across its bottom, the word *College*. She tells them she represents ANDEN, the teachers' union, that she, herself, is also a teacher, and that she will be traveling with them during their visit. She speaks about their accommodations and tells them that later she will answer any questions they have.

Primo senses she has said these exact words to newly arrived visitors before. She's at work. She holds a string of words up to them like a caption. When she's sure that everyone has understood them, she sets it aside and replaces it with another. It reminds Primo of the way his grandfather held the neck of a milk bottle, or a steering wheel, or the stem of a pencil: more firmly, and with more governance, than he actually needed to. Her deliberate, solid identity with her role poses a deep contrast to the smiling, anxious, travel-spacey group facing her.

As she is speaking, a small bus pulls up. She asks if everyone has all their luggage, and then introduces Horacio, the driver, who climbs out of the bus and stands beside her. Only then does she introduce herself, Angelita López, and smile. Now, when she looks at them, her eyes seem to find and respond to individual faces.

Manny, now standing beside Primo, raises a hand and asks about their itinerary. She again tells them she will answer specific questions later, at the Hotelito. She welcomes them all to Nicaragua.

Manny leans toward Primo's ear and says, "Wow, huh?"

Angelita is speaking to Horacio, who stands beside the bus. She absently scratches her forearm, under which she holds a manila envelope pressed against her side.

"We are sure as shit, genuinely *here*," Manny says.

Angelita faces everyone once more, briefly smiles and then walks into the terminal.

As they load themselves and their bags onto the bus, the children return. They know that these foreign adults have just been instructed not to give them anything, they just watch them, still and serious, from twenty feet away.

Some birds gather and peck the concrete in the space the delegation has just been standing in. Some of them are black with long tails, and some of them are light gray with even longer, bladelike tails.

Maryellen asks Manny if he knows what the birds are called and Manny asks Primo to ask Horacio.

"*Los negros son zánates. Y los otros,*"—he opens and closes his fingers like the blades of scissors—"*son tijeretas.*"

15

Señor Benavidez, Carolina's father, sitting on the couch in the sala of the Hotelito, separates the two plastic A&P shopping bags in which Primo carried the box Carolina had sent, folds them to the size of handkerchiefs and sets them on his lap. He then instructs Marta and Julia, his daughters, not to cut the sisal cord with which their sister had wrapped and rewrapped the cardboard carton.

Marta, the oldest, laughs. She then asks Primo, in Spanish, "Did she think you would drop it from the airplane?"

"You could have dropped it from the moon," Julia says. She is very pregnant, and looks just like her father. "It still wouldn't open."

It was a twelve-quart orange juice box left over from Primo's move back to New York. When Carolina gave it back to him, packed and tied, she had already placed it in the two shopping bags. She wanted Primo to keep it with him on the plane. She didn't trust the mail, which is why she'd asked him to carry it in the first place, and she didn't want it in the hands of strangers.

Marta has the same eyes as Carolina, but they seem smaller, set deeper in her older, wider face. "*Finalmente,*" she says, having untied the last knot, and hands the cord to her father, who begins looping it around his hand.

After he was shown the room he and Manny would share with a translator named Felix, originally from Spain but who now lived in Colorado, and Ken, a young high school teacher from Illinois, he went back out to the desk, just inside the open front door, to call Carolina's family.

The woman sitting behind the front desk, actually a small white table, placed the phone so that the dial faced Primo, and continued sorting a stack of papers that looked like bills or receipts and slipping them into different manila folders. Three times he dialed the number Carolina had given him and each time got only a staticky silence. He asked the woman what he was doing wrong, and instead of answering him, she turned the phone to face her again, and dialed the number he held in front of her. He noticed she was wearing two different earrings: a small coral stud in one ear and a larger green one, in the shape of a crescent moon, in the other. He watched her fingers rotate the dial. He was certain she dialed the same numbers he did. Even so, when she handed him the receiver, before walking into the shadowy interior of the hotel, Señor Benavidez was on the line.

At first he couldn't understand who Primo was.

"*Pero señor, su primo no vive aquí.*"

"*Mi nombre* es *Primo,*" he told him. "Primo Thomas." He hates speaking over the phone. He cannot use his face and hands to fill in the gaps in his incomplete Spanish vocabulary.

"Are you telling me you are *my* cousin *Tomás?*" Señor Benavidez asked Primo. He sounded angry. "Why would you tell me such a thing? You think I would not know his voice?"

"I am a friend of Carolina," Primo told him. He had said this first thing, but somehow it hadn't gotten across. The feeling had begun to arise in him that this place, the whole country within which this phone call was taking place, would not accept his presence in it.

He heard him speak to someone in the background.

Then he heard a woman's voice through the receiver. "*¿Profesor Thomas?*"

"*Sí.*"

"*Me llamo Marta. Yo soy la hermana de Carolina.*"

At last.

"*Bienvenido a Managua.*"

"Thank you."

The next problem was explaining to her where he was. The woman had not yet returned to the desk. He asked Marta to wait, walked across the courtyard and out into the street, but could find no street signs in any direction, no address on the open gate or the front door.

"I have no idea where it is." A *zánate* landed just outside the door and looked up at him.

"Are you near the place where the Pepsi-Cola plant used to be?" she asked him. "Or the flower market?"

He could be looking out a doorway that faces a street in Central America, he could be at home, in bed, dreaming. "I just got here," he said.

"That isn't a problem. Do you remember passing the baseball stadium on your way from the airport?"

He remembered passing through a ruined city. A crowd of restless, inseparable images, none of which he could yet detach from the others and give a name to. Not a stadium, not a flower market, hardly any of it appeared whole, or apart.

He remembered a scrawny brown cow, grazing among the brush and small trees in the rectangular foundation of a collapsed building. Rusted metal, bits of concrete and cinder block, patches of burnt, weedy turf. The space that had once contained things, but no longer does, outpopulates the occupied space. Not vacant, or silent, or *un*filled, it is violently empty space, and there is too much of it. That is his one, clear first impression of Managua. How could that help designate where he is?

The *zánate* at the doorstep suddenly flew upward and disappeared. The woman who'd dialed the phone for him walked in carrying a basket of folded linens.

She saw the look on Primo's face and stopped. She didn't even ask him what the problem was. She set down the basket and took the phone.

At first, she laughed as she spoke. Primo couldn't understand all she was saying. His eyes wandered out the door. The gray stones of the courtyard were damp, as if it had rained earlier or they had recently been washed. Three *zánates*, along with a dozen smaller, sparrowlike birds, were pecking in the sand-filled craters in the street, just outside the gate. Three small houses, made of painted cinder block and aluminum, faced the hotel from across the street. Their quiet intactness was soothing. *This is also where I am*, he thought. He was tired.

The woman placed the phone between her cheek and shoulder and looked down at her hands as she spoke. The coral stud was in her free ear. He imagined the green one pressed against the receiver. He wanted to understand and remember the directions she gave to Marta.

Contiguo a la casa matriz, Banco Popular, y junto al Parque del Carmen . . .

He now remembered passing a small bank just before arriving. It was actually a residential house, like the ones across the street, with a sign over the lintel and two armed guards on the front steps.

"*No*," the woman told Marta. "*Ocho cuadras al monte del estadio béisbol.*" She said, "*Sí.*" She listened for a moment and said, "*Sí*," again. Then, before asking Primo if he had more to tell them, she hung up the phone.

"Oh no," he said. "*Tenemos que llamarlos otra vez.*"

"*No se preocupe*," she told him. "They'll be here in ten minutes."

Marta smiles, then laughs when she opens the flaps of the cardboard Sunkist box that had entered Primo's life more than six months ago in a supermarket in Massachusetts, accompanied him to New York City, sat in a compartment above his head during the two flights that brought him here, to Managua, where it will spend the next and probably the last season of its existence, and pulls out two packages of hair rollers: small ones with clamps made of pink plastic, and larger, tubular ones made of thin wire.

The woman who'd helped Primo use the phone, along with another woman, come into the sala and sit beside Señor Benavidez on the couch. Julia shows them the rollers, which they examine and then hand back.

Marta then pulls out a tiny pair of baby shoes. The four women smile and ahhh approvingly. Señor Benavidez watches impassively, holding the bags and the wrapped cord on his lap. Marta then unfolds an infant-sized T-shirt and holds it up so everyone can see. Across the front, in bright red, it says, *I ♥ NY.* They all laugh and pass it around.

Next, two smaller plastic bags emerge. One has in it two large bottles of aspirin, lipstick, baby powder and a pacifier with Miss Piggy's face on the handle. The other has a collection of different-sized batteries. These Marta hands to her father.

There are three envelopes, one for each of them, containing photos and letters. And at the bottom, wrapped in the light-red scarf Carolina had often worn to class, is a Walkman. This Marta immediately knows is for her father. He examines it, figures out where to plug in the earphones, then wraps the wire around it and hands it back to his daughter, to repack along with the rest of their gifts.

The woman who had helped him with the phone asks if his name is really Primo. She laughs when he tells her it is. She tells him that was why Señor Benavidez didn't know who he was.

"My father has many cousins," Marta tells Primo. "And those that are still alive are all elsewhere."

Her father watches her tell this to Primo, as if he were saying it himself.

"He misses them very much," Marta says. "This always makes him sad."

Primo smiles at Señor Benavidez and he smiles back. For some reason this makes everyone laugh.

The other woman who works at the hotel rolls an old portable TV away from the wall and turns it on. She then settles back onto the couch. Some kind of news program comes on, in black and white. Everyone watches. Primo notices that this woman is wearing the green and coral earrings that are the matching halves of the pair the other woman has on. On the screen, Daniel Ortega, in uniform, is speaking to a crowd of soldiers in a place called Juigalpa. Many of them appear to be teenagers.

He has been here less than three hours, less than the span of a single afternoon. He is sitting in this quiet room, in front of a TV, with these people he's just met, in the middle of this mysterious, crumbling city, in a country at war.

Two of the teenage soldiers, both girls, are holding between them a banner that reads, *AQUÍ NO SE RINDE NADIE:* No one surrenders here.

"They're so young," Primo says, motioning toward them on the screen.

"*Son cachorros*," Marta says.

"*¿Cachorros?*" Primo asks.

"*Cachorros* are cubs," Angelita, who had walked in without his noticing and was now standing beside him, says.

Primo rises and stands beside her. "Hello," he says.

She reaches for his hand. They shake. He introduces himself.

"Cubs are soldiers who volunteer at sixteen," she says.

"They are children," Primo says.

"They are brave and committed," she says. Then she points to the box on the floor. "So you have been a . . . how do you say, in English, *cartero?*"

"Mailman."

"Mailman," she says. "*Mail*-man. See? We have just helped each other to learn."

Marta rises and joins them. She thanks Primo again. She tells him that while he is here, he must see *el lago*, and the Plaza de la Revolución, and the city of León, which is nearby, and the beach at Poneloya, her favorite.

Angelita tells her and Primo that nearly all those places are on their itinerary. She then asks Primo where the other members of his group are.

"When I walked in, just a minute ago, you appeared as if you came here alone," she tells him.

"They're waiting in their rooms."

"If you'll get them," she says, "we can get started."

The woman who had helped him on the phone tells Angelita they can meet in the *comedor*.

Primo points to her ear and tells her he likes it, that she and the other woman are wearing each other's—he does not know the word in Spanish, so he points at *his* ears.

"*Aretes,*" she says. Then she points to the other woman, who smiles. "She is Luisa, and I am Mercedes. We are cousins." Saying this causes them both to break into laughter.

Angelita looks at them all curiously.

"It seems my first name has been causing a big stir," Primo tells her.

"Ah," she says. She had wanted to understand the point more than to laugh at it.

"So you don't find my name unusual?" He has no idea why he asks her this.

"I remember having heard the name Primo before. But it was never someone from North America." She points toward the open door that leads into the dining room. Then she says, "We will meet in there."

She starts walking toward it, then stops, turns and walks back to where Primo is standing. She moves slowly, pensively, as if she were holding a full bowl of hot soup, but not exactly.

"Mailman," she says. She smiles, more in her eyes than her lips. "*Mail*-man. I know it is spelled differently. But to just hear it, is almost like the opposite of saying, *female* woman."

16

"I came here for one reason," Felix, sitting across from Primo and Manny, says. "To see Rubén Darío's clock."

"You could've saved yourself a trip," Manny says. He stretches his arm across the table, holding his digital watch in front of Felix's face. "Five forty-eight p.m., Central American Time."

They are in the *comedor*, sitting around a long table, waiting for Grace, John and Allen, the three professors from California, to return from their walk. Everyone is seated except Angelita, who is leaning against the wall at the front of the room, reading through some typewritten pages on a clipboard. When they got there, ten minutes ago, Luisa and Mercedes brought in two trays filled with opened bottles of soda, Coca and Naranja.

"But this clock," Felix says, "has two faces."

"Like our esteemed President," Manny says.

Felix leans across the table. A small gold swan, attached to a thin gold chain, swings out from the open collar of his shirt. "The top face," he says, "besides having the ordinary time stuff—you know, the minutes and the hours—has a third hand . . ."

"Our President has one of those too. It's always in our pockets. Or stroking our crotches."

". . . And this one measures the days of the week."

"And the other face?" Primo asks.

"The other one is just below . . . like this." He points to two damp rings, one just touching the edge of the other, left by soda bottles on the wooden tabletop. "The bottom one has two hands. One measures weeks of the month. But the other hand, the fifth hand—*that's* the amazing one. . . ."

Manny takes one of the Naranjas from the tray in front of them. "If those assholes are going to hold us up, they can go thirsty."

"The *fifth* hand?" Primo asks.

"The fifth hand measures the months of the year."

Manny holds his watch up again. "Watch this." He presses a tiny button and shows Felix the display: *Th. 1/14/88*. "So what's the big deal?"

"But Darío's clock was made before the turn of the century. No electronics, no computer technology."

Manny presses the button again: *7:05 E.S.T.* "I bet his clock couldn't do that. Now we know that up and down the east coast of the country whose taxpayers are buying weapons for the enemies of these good people, our hosts, millions of TVs have just tuned in to *Jeopardy*."

Primo takes a sip of Naranja, then rubs his fingertip down the cool, wet glass of the bottle, along the worn plywood tabletop and down the aluminum band that molds the edge. Each time he holds himself still, the restlessness that arose in him earlier seeps back from his limbs and collects in his torso. Each time, it takes up more space.

"But *this* clock, Manny, this clock is made of springs and gears. Not batteries and printed circuits. Can *you* imagine? Someone designing a clock on which a hand takes an entire year to make a single rotation . . ."

"Like the sun," Manny says.

"Like the sun. It's a great technological poem. The idea that someone would, and could, create such an instrument . . . That in itself excites me. A choreography of springs and gears so complex that on one face it describes the unfathomable, cosmic speed of Apollo, and in its opposite aspect, can punctuate each, single flyspeck of a minute."

"Wow," Manny says. "You really got a thing for this clock." He kicks Primo under the table.

"It's like having the simultaneous consciousness of the entire body and each of its cells at the same time."

"Wow," Manny says again. He looks at Primo, trying to pry some response from him, then at Felix. "You get pretty worked up about this." He looks at his watch again.

"You can look at a whole rainstorm on a weather map. Or you can measure each drop," Felix says.

"At the same time," Primo says.

"Exactly," Felix says. "And that is Darío's poetry. You light a single candle, you can create an entire morning."

"That's some candle," Manny says. He smiles at Primo, then says, "I've got to see this clock."

"And I think it's still running," Felix says. "I imagine if you stopped such a clock, you would stop time."

"What else are you here to see?" Manny asks him.

Grace, Allen and John walk in. When they see that they're the last ones to arrive, they apologize. Maryellen, who'd been sitting farther down the table, moves to the empty seat next to Felix, so that the three can sit together.

The setting sun, passing through the windows behind Primo, changes the rough wood grain of the tabletop into chains of thin flame, rivers, sawteeth. If time did stop, for the whole planet, it would always happen between things. It would have to. Between a last thing and a next thing. In at least one case it would have to occur in that microsecond just after a firing pin has struck a bullet, igniting the charge, yet before the slug has broken free of the casing.

Manny moves his hand across the table to the spot Primo is focused on. He points his forefinger downward. "These are the same kind of tables you find in bingo halls back home," he says.

"What?" Primo says.

"Bingo. You know. . . . *B-fifteen.*"

Maryellen, now sitting across from them, smiles curiously. A light knock on the door that opens into their conversation.

"They're like bingo tables," Manny tells her.

Angelita walks up to the front of the table, moves her head around the room, counting heads.

Manny leans over to Primo, cups his hand and whispers, "Can you *believe* it . . . ?" He moves his head slightly toward Maryellen. "She's actually wearing a brassiere and some kind of T-shirt thing under that peasant blouse."

"I think we're all here," Angelita says.

"Finally," Manny says. Then, smiling at Maryellen, says, *"G-fifty-five."*

She smiles.

Angelita introduces herself again. "Angelita López." She then asks that each person give their name and, if they wish to, where they are from.

"Theodore Gast. I teach Romance languages at a high school, in Roanoke."

"Felix Avila . . ."

"*Yeah*, Felix," Manny says.

"I teach at the University of Colorado. I'm also a translator. In particular, I'm interested in the work of Rubén Darío."

Angelita smiles. "Félix Ávila," she says, pronouncing his name in the Spanish way. "I have news that will please you. One of the places we will visit is his home, in León."

"Is that where the clock is?" Manny asks Felix.

"That's where it is."

"All *right*."

Grace, Allen and John introduce themselves by their first names.

"Hi. I'm Maryellen Hammer. I teach history at the high school and junior high school levels. I live in a small town in Arkansas. Breckenbridge. I doubt any of you have heard of it."

"You wouldn't believe what her maiden name is," Manny whispers to Primo.

On the tabletop, as if on a screen, Primo sees the broken, empty towel dispenser in the airport bathroom, then the same white sheet metal—the *same*—as on the shelves and flat surfaces in his father's examining room. He sees the pendulous sliding weight of the medical scale with the word *Detecto* etched deeply into it. He would face that weight, at eye level, each time he measured his height and weighed himself. He'd do it first thing in the morning because you were taller then. Stand on his toes, fill his pockets with pennies, drink a quart of water. It wasn't that he wanted to grow faster. It wasn't about getting bigger, it was about speeding up time. If he could see the groove his heavier body would balance the weight at, the height his head would cause the telescopic ruler to reach, he would see the future. He could see what he *will* see, when his life has brought him somewhere else. He remembers the glass jars filled with cotton swabs, tongue depressors, latex gloves. The triangular stone mallet, which looked like a little tomahawk, that his father would tap against his knee.

"Hartsfelder. No shit, scouts' fucking honor. She was smart to marry a *Hammer*. Gets to drop that clanky old name without having to change the monograms on her hankies."

Primo smiles at Manny. He has barely been listening. "Bingo," he says.

"Bingo," Manny says back.

"I'm Grace Berenson. I teach comp lit at Rensselaer. That's in upstate New York." In her late fifties, she's the oldest member of the group. She smiles at everyone after she speaks.

For some of them, this is their first introduction to each other, not just Angelita.

"Wow, another Grace," Allen from California says.

"We just need one more," Felix says, "and we'll have all three."

"Ken Steiner. High school. English. Deerfield, Illinois."

"You left out your rank and serial number," Manny tells him.

"Sarah Baxter. I live in Detroit. I'm not teaching at the moment, though I have taught in the public school system for twelve years. Recently, a lot of us got laid off. We're hoping to get back to work real soon."

"Manny Glass. I gave up an exciting career in accordion repair to teach freshman composition and basic writing skills at More College, in Massachusetts."

"Primo Thomas. I live in Manhattan, where I teach English-as-a-second-language at a publicly funded school called *Solidaridad Humana*."

Angelita introduces Mercedes and Luisa.

Primo tells Manny that they are cousins. He feels a resurgence of his anger. It has grown since it last lifted its head. He's tenser, more restless. He tries to overcome it by acting as if he weren't.

"How do you know that?" Manny asks him.

"My name keeps bringing up the subject."

Felix starts to laugh. "It's a great name to have in a Spanish-speaking country," he says. "You're related to everybody."

Maryellen smiles, then says to Manny, "Primo means cousin."

Primo realizes that to speak, to say something related to the larger, shared moment, is to ask for help. This makes him angrier.

Manny reaches across the table, and covers Maryellen's hand with his. "Tell me," he asks her, "what does Manny mean?"

Angelita quickly runs down their itinerary. Tomorrow morning they will go north, to Matagalpa, where they'll stay the next few days. They'll visit a community school there, another at a coffee cooperative farther north. They'll also visit a group called the Mothers of Heroes and Martyrs. She had hoped they could visit a school for soldiers, in a town called Juigalpa, but fighting broke out there yesterday and she's afraid it wouldn't be safe.

Primo remembers that Juigalpa was the place he'd seen earlier on the news.

"Shit," Manny says. "I'd hoped we were going to the front."

"Why?" Allen asks, turning his head to Manny.

"I came here to see everything."

"And put yourself in danger?" Maryellen asks.

"So he can tell his friends back home about it," Allen says.

Manny looks at him. So do Maryellen and Felix.

"Didn't I read something about an *asshole law* in Nicaragua," Manny says.

"A what?" Maryellen asks.

"It's where they round up all the assholes that visit from other countries, sit them in a room with college football pennants on the walls, bunk beds like summer camp, air-conditioning . . ."

"I never heard . . ." Maryellen starts, then smiles, with worried curiosity, at Manny.

"They play bingo, watch Disney reruns and eat Big Macs," he says. "Two weeks later they bring them to the airport and fly them back to wherever they came from."

With a dramatic and conscious deliberateness, Allen turns to face Angelita, who is still going on with the itinerary.

Then they'll return to Managua, where they'll visit the office of the teachers' union, the cultural workers' association, the Plaza de la Revolucíon, the Museo del Ejército, a children's hospital . . .

Primo loses track. He watches Manny stare angrily at Allen, who is writing things down in a notebook.

Angelita tells them that if they want to, they can attend the marathon poetry reading that each year is given in the town of Darío. It takes all day. Hundreds of poets, not just Nicaraguans but from all over the world, will read their work. They have also been invited to attend a rally to commemorate the 22 de Enero. An event that marks the date of an anti-Somocista demonstration at which nearly a hundred people were gunned down by the *guardia nacional.*

"Do we really have time to see all this?" Manny asks.

"As much of it as you want to," Angelita says. "We thought, since you will be here such a short time, that you would want to see as much of Nicaragua as possible."

"Would we have an opportunity to visit the office of *La Prensa?*" Allen asks.

"I suppose. If you wish to."

"What the hell you want to do that for?" Manny asks him.

"To see both sides."

"That's why we're here. All we've *been* seeing is the other side." Manny shakes his head.

Maryellen asks Angelita about food and water. What's safe to eat, what isn't.

Manny, his eyes on Allen, leans toward Primo and says, into his ear, "God, I wish they *did* have asshole laws."

Angelita tells them that tonight, if the lights stay on, there will be a baseball game.

"If the lights stay on?" Maryellen asks.

"They are frequently turned off at night. To conserve electricity.

And to prevent the *contra* from subverting the generators. That is why you were asked to bring flashlights."

She tells them the baseball stadium is eight blocks to the north. Then explains how to ask directions in Managua. "*Arriba* is east, *abajo*, west, *al lago* is north and *al monte* is south." She smiles, then says, "I will now act like your teacher. *¿Dónde está el estadio béisbol?*"

Maryellen raises her hand. "*Ocho cuadras al lago.*"

"*Bueno,*" Angelita says.

"I'm sure you have all learned of the earthquake we had in 1972. And if you haven't, you saw the condition of Managua on your ride from the airport. Because of the earthquake, and because Somoza bombed parts of Managua during the war, much of the city has been destroyed. So much so that addresses, as you know them, more often than not do not serve. For example, the hotel we are in doesn't have an address. If someone asks you where you are staying you could say *ocho cuadras al monte del estadio béisbol.* This makes it difficult to get around. So don't be afraid to ask. The people of Managua are very helpful."

Angelita, announcing that she will be right back, walks out of the room. Mercedes and Luisa begin bringing in dinner: plates of rice, beans and *crema*, a smoky cream cheese. Along with the food, they bring in a tray of beer in bottles.

Maryellen asks if the food looks okay to eat and Manny, offering to be her guinea pig, takes a single black bean off her plate and puts it in his mouth. He then grabs his throat with both hands, as if suddenly choking, closes his eyes and pretends to lose consciousness. Mercedes rushes over and asks if he is okay. He opens his eyes and smiles. She shakes her head and walks back into the kitchen.

"I think this food is okay," Manny says to Maryellen. He reaches for a beer, takes a sip, reads the name on the label. "Victoria. A little less body than Bud. Not bad, though."

Angelita walks back in and sets a portable cassette tape recorder on the table. "Today, I'm going to leave you with this," she says. "It is a recording that the *contra* broadcast over the radio from Honduras when medical *brigadistas* in the north were vaccinating children against polio. I think it will be instructive. It will show you the kinds of problems teachers here have had to deal with."

She turns on the recorder. "We can talk about the tape tomorrow morning on the bus. Now I will leave you to your dinner."

With that she leaves the room.

The sounds of a piano, flattened and narrowed by the small speakers, come from the tape recorder and grow steadily louder.

"That's Beethoven," Maryellen says.

"I thought it was 'Wooly Bully,' " Manny says. "Sam the Sham and the Pharaohs."

There is now a male voice, firm and authoritative, speaking on top of the music. He speaks in Spanish but bends each phrase into an arc the way North American newscasters used to back in the forties.

"What is he saying?" Manny asks.

Primo doesn't answer. He's trying to understand the tinny, emphatic, barely audible strings of words. He must apply the same kind of focused concentration as before, when he called Carolina's father. He has difficulty understanding Spanish over phones and radios. Often the chains of words are like passing trains filled with passengers. You watch each window for someone you can recognize. *Brazo*, arm . . . *Cuidadoso*, careful . . . *Aviso*, warning . . . *Escápanse*, run away . . . *Enfermedad*, disease . . . *Aviso* . . . *Brazo* . . . *Mentira*, lie . . . *Jeringa*, syringe . . .

"What is he saying?" Manny asks again.

"He is warning people not to allow themselves to be inoculated," Felix says.

"Why?"

"He says the serum is evil . . ."

"*Evil* . . ." Maryellen says. "A vaccination?"

"He says it will give them the disease of communism. He says it is a potion made from the urine of Castro."

"Wow," Manny says. "*This* is heavy shit."

Maryellen looks down at the table. She shakes her head.

Felix goes on. "He tells them they are lucky. That a laboratory in the United States was able to analyze the serum before too many people were injected. He says to tell this to any of their friends who don't have radios."

"Heavy shit," Manny says again.

The voice stops for a while and the music grows louder.

"It's the Piano Sonata in G Minor," Allen says. He smiles at Maryellen.

Mercedes sets a plate in front of Primo. He thanks her.

"It's like something medieval," Maryellen says.

"Just plain *e-vil*," Manny says.

Primo looks at his food. The voice has started again.

"You're not eating?" Manny asks.

Primo feels his back pressing against the outer edge of the entire moment, but can't get far enough away from the other people in it. Castro . . . *Escápanse* . . . *El diablo* . . . *Espíritu maligno* . . . *Laboratorios* . . . *Maligno* . . . *Maligno* . . .

"It's good," Manny says. "Eat up."

"Could you believe they would tell those people *not* to get vaccinated?" Maryellen says.

"And our colleague here wants to hear both sides," Manny says. He says it loudly enough to bounce off Maryellen and reach Allen.

The message has now played three times.

"They must broadcast it on a repeating loop," Felix says.

"Maybe they just recorded it that way," Allen says.

Primo wonders if he had to travel all the way down here just to remind himself that he spends too much time with white people.

"We wiped out polio thirty years ago," Maryellen says.

"We wiped out *our* polio," Manny says.

Primo stands up. *I have no cousins here.*

Manny looks up at him, but doesn't speak.

What is it? What is it? Primo asks himself what Manny doesn't.

The upper parts of the wall and ceiling are now completely shadowed. The last of the daylight has slipped through the window just behind Primo, like a tide of waist-high water, and illuminates the tabletop, the plates, bottles, forks and hands. It's darker where his head is now that he is standing, farther away, quieter.

Manny is still watching him stand there, but doesn't speak. Everyone else is concentrating on the tape or in conversation.

Primo doesn't want another thought from a single other person to press itself against him. He's full. He was full before he left New York. He's been full for years.

He walks around the table and out of the room.

He passes Carolina's sisters and father, who are still sitting on the couch watching television, as he heads through the sala on his way toward the hall, which leads to the front desk and out into the courtyard.

The sun has now fallen behind the uneven horizon of buildings. Beams of smoky, waxlike light, interspersed with columns of blue-black darkness, reach above the city and merge into a pale dome. Moment by moment—at increments timed to heartbeats—the darkness gets darker, and the dome and the bars of light reaching to it densify into a tangible, luminous mass.

Manny, now standing inside the doorway behind him, says, "What about the game? Assuming the lights stay on, everyone's going." Manny is quiet for a moment. Then he says, "Wow. Lightning bugs."

There is a scattering of fireflies over the courtyard, and the street and the near-pitch-black darkness of the park.

"I'm getting the feeling," Manny says, "you didn't travel to the same place I did."

Primo turns and looks at him. Manny steps toward him, hands him a flashlight and starts to walk back inside.

A humming sound Primo hadn't been aware he'd been hearing suddenly stops. Manny stands still just outside the door.

An explosion of silence. A sudden blooming of darkness from the earth to the sky.

"Holy shit," Manny says.

Every single light has gone out. The voices from inside all grow louder.

A faint light now appears behind the beaded curtain of one of the houses that face the courtyard. It flickers and brightens, as a wick is raised in some kind of lamp. At the edge of the park a match flares and lights the ends of two cigarettes.

"Nothing has changed," Primo says.

"The game is canceled. That's changed," Manny says.

"It's so quiet," Maryellen, now standing just inside the doorway, says.

A flashlight comes on behind Primo. Its beam reaches to just outside the gate and has in it two thin strips of darkness that are the shadows of his legs. He takes a step toward the gate and one of them bends, then flattens. He takes another. The beam is a carpet, a diving board, a runway. He follows it to its end, then heads left. When he gets to the corner he turns on his own flashlight and walks in the direction he remembers as *al lago.*

17

In an episode of *Little Rascals*, Stymie, one of the only two black Rascals, was left standing at the mouth of a dark cave holding a huge spool of cord. Spanky and Alfalfa and the rest of the Rascals had gone inside in search of treasure. One of them had tied the cord around his waist and Stymie's job was to hold the spool so it unreeled as his friends went deeper into the winding cave. When they found the treasure, they were going to follow it out. Of course, it got tangled and then broke, and on top of that, there turned out to be an ogre in there with a voracious appetite for the flesh of young children.

One of the Rascals had fallen asleep and this adventure had actually occurred in his dream. This was more than thirty years ago, and Primo has forgotten whose dream it was. But he remembers, as if he'd dreamt it himself, what he felt watching it. When the story followed the Rascals deeper into the cave, searching the mysterious darkness for treasure, *that* was who he was, he was all of them at once; when the camera was on Stymie, holding the spool, waiting, staring with anxious curiosity into the mouth of the cave, he was then Stymie. He became afraid, and angry, when he thought of himself as the one chosen to wait outside. If he was *that* one, he'd drop the spool and follow them inside. Or he'd go off somewhere else. Later for this. That's what he'd do, be gone.

He'd been carefully counting the number of blocks he'd walked on since he left the Hotelito but somewhere on the sixth or seventh he lost track.

It was on a block where he encountered three soldiers that he began to loosen his hold on the sequence. A woman and two men, all three of them sitting on the hood of an old Chevy Corvair. It had no tires or windshield and all four axles were propped on cinder blocks. In the brief moment he caught them in the beam of his flashlight, the woman was passing a half-filled bottle of Naranja to one of the men. Leaning against the fender, beside their booted feet, was a single AK47. Primo aimed his beam downward immediately. He expected them to react somehow—having intruded with his light—but they didn't.

By the middle of the next block he was laughing to himself. The string of counted blocks, which had snapped, had, in fact, been Stymie's cord. The episode had been playing itself out just under the skin of this real moment, the way a pontoon moving beside the boat it's attached to remains just under the water's surface. He hadn't realized it until the cord snapped. He suddenly gave up being the person he would find his way back to. Later for that. He's gone. However, he didn't become the guys looking for the treasure either. Instead, the whole show disappeared, cave and all.

More and more people have come out of doors. The absence of electricity makes being outside far less different from being inside. They're sitting on steps, or chairs, or the low crumbling stone walls in front of many of the houses. They barely take notice of him, beyond seeming to note that he is there, walking down their streets with his flashlight. Other than the single car that slowly followed its startlingly bright headlights down the street he's now walking on, the only light is the occasional flickering brightness from behind a window, or the tip of a lit cigarette, or something vague, milky, lavender, that now lines the inside of the starless sky. The streets are pitted and cracked and cratered, and he's the most likely candidate, a stranger, to break a leg. Thus, it seems fitting that he's carrying the only flashlight in the barrio.

In New York, in other cities he has been in, he would never trust the darkness to simply hold a continuation of what he can see.

Anything could be there. But as he walks, here, in this city he's never been in before, he feels increasingly sure of what lies beyond the limit of his sight. At least within the distance he is capable of walking tonight. There are just more of these people, these buildings, this odd, soft quietness. A few blocks back someone had a radio playing, but the only other sounds are the voices.

It's as if the people on this block and the people on the next one are somehow plugged into the same conversation even though they couldn't possibly hear each other. Everything *there*—the trees, the crumbling walls, the shadows—begins in their voices. Walking through an archipelago of other people's conversation—this, simply, is what being a stranger is.

He has never been outside the United States before. And rarely outside of his own small corner of it. He has no idea what the act of being here, in this city, in this country, is. Only, thus far, what the act of leaving his own is. That's what he's been doing all day. Leaving. Not arriving.

He lifts his flashlight and the beam finds the feet of a child, walking, and then the feet of the adult whose hand the child is holding. They both stop, turn, look briefly at Primo. A mother and daughter. In her free hand the mother holds something spherical: a ball or an orange. He smiles, though he knows they could not see him, then shines the beam back to the pavement just ahead of him. So this is what being a stranger feels like. A familiar feeling, and a new one. He doesn't mind this at all. On the streets of this dark, wrecked city, among its people, wrapped in their daily lives, there's a sense to it. Here he *is* a stranger.

18

After an hour of wandering through the dark in what feels like a large, complete, jagged circle, Primo asks for directions back to the Hotelito. He first gives an old man, then a young girl the coordinates he learned earlier. Both times he walks in accordance with what he is certain are the directions they gave him. And both times he becomes even more lost. Or just as lost.

He hears a car engine start. Its headlights suddenly light up the pavement farther down the street he is walking on. He tries to look beyond the car, in the direction the beam penetrates, to see if anything looks familiar, or there is anything that resembles the street facing the Hotelito with its small houses and the park along its side. In the dark he had seen so little of the housefronts or the trees or anything else he could possibly remember. He mostly saw the cracked and pitted pavement and that all looks the same. The headless bodies of a family of four, crossing the street at a distance, are lit from the shoulders down by the headlights before they cross the sharp edge of a shadow where the light strikes the trunk of a tree. One of them, a woman, emerges from the other side and walks toward the car. She stops and leans into the driver's window. Primo walks up to her and waits as she finishes speaking to the man sitting behind the wheel, then watches the car make a broken U-turn, and roll slowly down the street in the direction he just walked from.

He asks her if she knows how he can find the Hotelito and, as everyone else has done, she asks if he knows where it is.

She repeats the coordinates he gives her. *Contiguo al Banco Popular, junto al Parque del Carmen y ocho cuadras al monte del estadio béisbol.* Then, without saying a word, she walks inside the house they are standing in front of. A few minutes later a man in his early thirties appears just inside the doorway. He takes a last drag from a cigarette—by its glow, Primo can see he's wearing a short-sleeve orange shirt—and flicks the butt out into the street. He walks down the steps and stands in front of Primo. He repeats the coordinates Primo had given to the woman and which, apparently, she had given to him.

Then he says, in English, "Very near."

"Near? To here?"

"Very near."

Primo isn't sure he speaks more than these two words in English. "*¿Cerca de aquí?*" he asks him.

"I understand," he says to Primo.

"Then we're near where I'm going."

"Very near."

Primo still doesn't believe the guy actually understands English.

He points to Primo's flashlight and says, "Batteries?"

"Yes."

He doesn't say anything to this. Primo, assuming he's asking for some, tells him that he doesn't have any extras. Just the ones in the flashlight. Then he says, "You say we're very near. Could you tell me how to get there?"

The man begins walking down the street in the opposite direction the car had gone in. He stops, turns to face Primo. "I'll show you," he says.

Primo falls into place beside him, lighting the ground ahead of them as they walk. "Please?" the man says, and takes the flashlight from Primo's hand. He then turns it off and hands it back to him.

In less than two minutes they're standing in front of the Hotelito. Primo can't imagine how he managed to miss the street. The Hotelito is the brightest building in the area. Nearly all its windows are lit with candles and battery lanterns. From two blocks away you can see the light radiating up into the sky.

Suddenly, he doesn't want to go in. He doesn't know what to do. He bends down, picks up a small rock and throws it at the Hotelito. It makes a faint clack against the tile roof. The man looks at Primo but doesn't speak. Primo smiles at him. Then he extends his hand and introduces himself.

The man's name is Julio. Primo is glad they don't go through the cousin routine when he tells him his.

"I'm here with a delegation of teachers," Primo tells him in Spanish.

"Many delegations, mostly from your country, stay . . . at here." He finishes his answer in Spanish. "Last year they had doctors. They also had poets. I didn't know it was called the Hotelito."

"Wow," Primo says. Then he says, "You can say *wow* in Spanish, too. . . . Right?"

"I understand *wow*."

"Where did you learn your English?" Primo asks.

"An engineer was here," Julio says. Again he finishes in Spanish. "He was from Kentucky. He taught courses in engineering and metallurgy. I studied with him half a year."

"Wow."

"Wow," Julio says, then smiles at him. "You aren't going in?"

"Not yet."

"Okay," Julio says.

"Do you want to get home?"

"Not yet," Julio says. Then he says, as if answering a question Primo might ask, "That wasn't my home, where we met. My sister lives there with her husband's family. I live near *el lago.*"

"That's to the north," Primo says. "Right? I live even farther north. New York City."

"Wow," Julio says. Then begins humming the theme from "New York, New York."

Primo laughs and hums it too.

Julio points to Primo's watch. "What time?"

"Almost nine o'clock," he says. "An hour earlier than it is in New York."

Julio begins humming "New York, New York" again. Then he asks Primo if he'd like to have a drink.

"I'm buying," Primo says.

About five blocks *arriba* from the Hotelito they cross a wide, deserted avenue that might be a main street. There are fewer inhabitable buildings on it, but those that are there appear to have once been businesses. Restaurants, clothing stores, groceries. None of them look open. Neither does the restaurant Julio opens the door of. There is a small battery lantern lit on the bar. There are no bottles on the shelves behind it, and no one sitting at the five or six tables in the otherwise dark room. Julio calls out the name "Doroteo" and a short, middle-aged man enters the room through an open door at the back of the bar.

"Julio," he says. Then he walks back through the door, and reappears with a lit candle propped on a saucer. He walks past the two of them, smiling, and sets it on one of the tables.

Julio introduces him to Primo before they sit down.

While Doroteo is getting them a bottle of rum, Julio tells Primo that this had once been a Chinese restaurant. He points to the overhead light fixture, made of tin, shaped like a Chinese lantern. "There used to be a lot of them on this street."

Primo has seen the same light fixtures in Chinese restaurants in New York. The same characters—one like the letter *T* with two legs, another like a box drawn so the sides don't quite fit together with a short line through the middle—cut into their sides. They'd be described in the yellow white of electric light if the bulb inside were lit.

"There is a joke," Julio says, "that says the reason this neighborhood is called Barrio Oriente is not because it's the east side of the city, but that it is a piece of the east side of the world."

"So we're *arriba*," Primo says.

"We are if you are somewhere else."

Doroteo sets a bottle and two glasses in front of them. The rum is dark. The name on the label is *Flor de Caña.*

"*Y Coca,*" Julio says.

Doroteo reaches into a doorless refrigerator set against the wall across from the bar, then returns to their table with a bottle of warm cola, which Julio pours into both glasses along with the rum.

"*Nica libre,*" he says.

Primo drinks half the warm, sweet drink in a single gulp.

"Are you thirsty?" Julio asks him in English.

"Yes," he says. "And seriously so." He touches his glass to Julio's. "*Nica libre.*" He takes another big sip.

"*Nica libre,*" Julio says. "*Es un brindis, pero también es el nombre de la bebida.*"

"Ah, like a Cuba libre."

"Yes. But *Jefe Comandante Fidel*, he is the one with the ice."

Primo pours them both another drink. Along the shadowed walls are framed photographs of men and women. Most of them young and many in uniform. Now that he and Julio have achieved their goal, to find the Hotelito, then to find this place and to get drinks, they are both quiet. All day, each time he has slowed to a stop, Primo has felt as if he'd just woken up, and had to orient himself to the place he woke into.

Julio points to one of the pictures on the wall. He tells Primo it's Brian Wilson.

Primo isn't sure who it is. He's heard the name. "He's one of the Beach Boys?"

Julio shakes his head. He points down at his legs.

"I've heard the name," Primo says.

He seems a bit embarrassed that Primo doesn't know him. "*El se tendío en la vía del tren . . .*" He smiles slightly.

Primo thinks that now that they are seated and facing each other, it must be apparent to Julio how tightly strung and pissed off this man he has met on the street, in front of his sister's husband's family's house, is.

He gets up and walks over to the photograph. It had been cut from a newspaper. He's seen the picture before. He shines his flashlight on it. The man in the photograph is sitting in a wheelchair.

"I remember," he says. "Yes." He was living in More when he read about him. The man had tried to stop a train carrying arms that were to be sent to the *contras.* The same picture was in the *Boston Globe.* He lay across the track, and the wheels sheared off both legs at the knee.

Primo sits down again. Moving caused the rum to rise like vapor into his head. The candle's flicker, a steady, curled throb, makes time pass like music on a scratched record: it moves a small half-step into the future, then skips back and retraces itself. "When you live where I live," he says to Julio, "there's no end to the amount of shit that presents itself to you. One thing after another. No one remembers all of it."

Julio smiles at him. Then looks down into his drink.

"In the United States there's a lot more people than there are names," Primo tells him. "The other Brian Wilson I mentioned, he used to sing songs about surfboards and cars." He starts to hum "California Girls."

Julio joins him.

"Ah, you know it. Twenty years ago their songs were the sound tracks to the dreams of teenagers. Mostly white ones."

They hum together. They smile at each other. Primo pours them both another drink.

"You're a good man, Julio." He touches his glass to his. They drink. "You're hip," he adds, in English.

Julio takes a piece of folded notebook paper out of his pocket. He presses it flat on the table. He asks Primo to write his name on it.

Primo looks at the paper.

"I will show my friends at work tomorrow. And then put your address."

Primo sets his drink down on the table, looks up at the lantern over their heads, then back at Julio, then exhales. "*Lo siento,*" he says.

"For *what* are you sorry?" Julio asks him in English.

"For being an asshole, I am sorry."

Julio starts laughing. "*¿Por qué me dices esto?*"

"I've been sitting here talking to *myself.*"

"You don't think I understand you?"

"I know you do."

Julio smiles, then says, "You know who talks to themselves the most? I mean of the people who come from your country? The poets."

Primo laughs.

"I heard them read their poems in the ruins of the Grand Hotel."

"My ex-wife's a poet."

Julio looks worried he said something wrong.

"They talk to themselves real good," Primo tells him.

"A poet I heard there came from California . . ."

"My ex-wife lives in California."

"But you live in New York?" Julio looks at him, but doesn't say anything more.

"Why do you look so sad?"

"I have an ex-wife too. But she doesn't live so far away."

"We have a lot bigger country. A lot more room for ex-wives and ex-husbands to spread out in. Anyway, this poet from California . . . ?" Primo asks.

"He compared Lago Managua to a shining coin."

Primo sips, looks at him. Julio takes a sip, looks back at him, smiles.

"He is here three days," Julio says, "and he compares Lago Managua to a shining coin." He becomes shyly quiet again.

They both keep sipping. Primo can feel the rum that has risen into his head growing into something warm and solid.

"He comes here three days, then he goes back to California. I've lived by that lake more than thirty years. Never once, in all that time, has it appeared to me like a shining coin."

"I hear you," Primo says.

"It can look like a blanket when it isn't moving. Or the skin of an arm when the sun shines on it, but never a coin. Mostly it looks like water. What do you think?"

"I just got here. My ass is in limbo. I don't think anything." He taps his glass against Julio's again.

"Thank you," Julio says, for no reason Primo can think of.

"Thank *you.*" Primo takes another sip.

"You and your ex-wife live on opposite sides of the country. That is really far apart."

"You're still thinking about this?" Primo asks him. "We do. One of us in each shoulder."

"*¿En los hombros?*"

"That poet. His name was Pablo Neruda. One of my ex-wife's favorites . . ."

"I know of him."

"Didn't he call this part of the hemisphere America's slim waist?"

"*Sí. La cintura,*" Julio says.

"Then you might say I make my residence on the left shoulder. Assuming the continent hasn't turned its back to us."

Julio starts laughing. "*Los hombros . . .*" He runs his finger over the table, tracing the shape of a shoulder, a torso. "I think Canada is a shoulder," he says.

"Okay. I'm in the armpit."

"And your ex-wife . . ." Julio looks sad again.

"I think we're getting drunk," Primo says.

"No." Julio shakes his head.

"She lives in the other armpit. The one that other poet comes from."

"You think she knows him?"

"Anything's possible."

Julio lifts his eyebrows, slowly, as if they're heavy. "*Sí,*" he says.

Doroteo comes into the room. It's apparent in his walk and the look on his face that it's time for them to leave.

Julio stands, signals for Primo to do the same and takes the half-filled rum bottle off the table.

Primo asks Doroteo how much.

"*Veinti cinco.*"

Primo can't find a bill smaller than five hundred cordobas.

"*Veinti cinco* mil," Doroteo says.

"What, is he crazy?" Primo asks.

"That is, perhaps, two dollars," Julio says.

Primo hands him thirty thousand. Doroteo hands him five thousand back.

On the dark avenue, not a car, not a lit window. Julio, standing beside him with the rum bottle, is a stranger again. Primo realizes that the dining room of Doroteo's restaurant was the first place he'd been in long enough for it to become anywhere. Long enough that he stopped looking around, stopped measuring his relationship to his surroundings. Long enough so that who he was with, and what they were doing, was all that was happening. Enough so he can forecast what he would remember ten years from now, were he to look back on these moments: Doroteo shuffling across the dark room, himself sitting, leaning on one elbow, the sad mix of feeling from the warm rum, from Julio's sad curiosity, from the shadow that fell across the table, floating like cloth on water.

He feels the rum starting to lose its hold. He takes the bottle from Julio and sips it straight. It scrapes his throat on the way down, like a small, furry fist.

"Where to?" Primo asks in English, immediately realizing what a strange and incomplete phrase it is. "*¿Por dónde?*"

Julio points to a side street that opens onto the avenue directly across from them. He then starts toward it. Primo watches him cross, then enter the dark throat of the street.

He switches on his flashlight, aims the beam at the last spot he'd seen Julio, raises it until it lights up his orange shirt. Julio stops, turns, squints into the light.

In a few minutes they're standing at the edge of the park that runs alongside the Hotelito. Julio sets himself down on the root of a tree, leans his forearms on top of his knees. He repeats one of the coordinates Primo had given him earlier. "*Junto al Parque del Carmen.*"

Primo sits beside him. On one side of the street they are facing is the Hotelito, its windows dark now; on the other, the small houses he saw out the front door earlier when he was trying to give directions to Carolina's sister. It seems like days ago.

"I spent a week here today," he says to Julio.

"*¿Cómo?*"

Primo takes a sip of rum. "I left home so long ago I already forgot what life was like there."

Julio takes the bottle.

They hear a scurrying in the tree above their heads. Primo looks up. The branches are like skeletons of arms and fingers, perfectly still and pitch-black against the paler, gray-blue sky.

"*Un lagarto,*" Julio says. He sets the bottle between his knees, leans his hands against the trunk behind him. Neither of them speaks for a while.

Then Julio asks if he likes being a teacher. Primo says he does. Julio tells him he likes his job too. He works with sheet metal. "We're lucky," he says, "that we like our jobs."

They fall silent again.

Primo hears a sound that could be a car, miles from them, moving slowly through the city. A thin, purring, persistent breath. It could also be something he's hearing from the inside. Maybe the blood pushing itself through the vessels near his ears. Maybe a noise he brought with him from home. "You hear that?" he asks Julio.

"What?"

"Like a snore, somewhere in the distance."

"*¿Un ronquido?*" He smiles.

"Maybe."

"Maybe the lizard is snoring."

Primo takes the bottle. "That must be it."

He watches Julio listen for the sound and *not* hear it. It must be inside of *him*, his own noise. Or the kind of noise people never hear in the places they live. Like the ticking of a clock in the house of strangers. You hear it, they don't.

He sits up, takes a small sip, then asks Julio if he knows that the broken paper towel dispenser in the bathroom at the airport was made in Kendallville, Indiana.

"*¿Cómo?*" Julio looks at him.

Primo asks again.

"*¿Papel higiénico?*" he says, laughing. "Not in this country."

Primo keeps trying. He's drunk enough to think it's important.

Finally Julio nods. But at first, after the struggle to make him understand, Primo doesn't believe him. He thinks he's just being polite.

"No. I do know this company. You'll find their products in other places. They made the ashtrays on the walls beside the elevators in the Grand Hotel. But it now has no more floors, so it has no more elevators for it to be impolite to smoke in."

"The best thing about being human is the power of speech." Primo says. He takes a sip, then hands the bottle back to Julio. "We can use it to talk about absolutely fucking anything."

Julio lifts the bottle and examines it. About a quarter of the rum remains. "I have seen lots of their products," he says. "In that place . . . Indiana?"

Primo nods.

"In Indiana, they do good work with sheet metal." He starts laughing. Then he says, "Wow."

"Wow," Primo adds. "You know . . . ? All day the people in this city, the few of them I've met, that is, have been wondering whose cousin I am."

"I have . . ." Julio counts on his fingers. "I have eleven cousins."

"My name makes them curious."

"Ah," Julio says.

"Absolutely fucking anything," Primo decides to say again. Then he says, "I think that's the way you can tell if people feel at home, whatever that is. *At home.*"

Julio is looking straight ahead. Primo can't tell what he's thinking, but he knows Julio will patiently wait until Primo asks if he understands before he will tell him he doesn't.

"I think *at home* means that where they are is *theirs.* You hear what I'm saying?"

Julio nods.

"I mean the fucking people willing to say the most, even the shit nobody should want to hear, they're the ones that own the ground you're walking on. Or they think they do. Or they're crazy."

"I understand this."

Primo's been saying this mostly in Spanish, slipping in an English word wherever his vocabulary fails him. Nonetheless, he knows he's ranting, and is surprised at how Julio says this, implying he truly understands.

He turns to Julio, then asks, "Do you know who Lieutenant Uhura is?"

"*¿Ujura?*"

"*Sí*, Lieutenant."

"*¿Teniente U-urra?* Communications Officer, Starship Enterprise . . . ?"

"*La misma.*"

"*Claro que sí.* Who doesn't? *Qué hermosa.*"

"*Sí, muy hermosa.* You got to know her for the story I'm about to tell you to make any sense. You follow?"

"I follow."

"I'm telling you this cause you're my ace boon cousin. You still follow?"

Julio hands him the bottle.

"It's twenty years ago, I'm in the locker room after gym class and I'm getting dressed." Primo looks at Julio.

"I follow," he says.

Primo hands him back the bottle. "Right next to me is this guy Ralphie Fitzgerald. Every morning we get dressed and undressed together but we never talk. There wasn't many black folks in my high school and mostly we hung together. Also, this guy's conversation wasn't a thing I craved. . . . You hear what I'm saying?" Primo nods as he says this.

Julio purses his lips, nods back.

"He was like a champion fuckup. Delinquent too, but he *did* have style. Let me give you an example. Once, in broad daylight, the guy pissed off an el station."

"*No,*" Julio says, "La *estación.*"

"*Elevado. La vía del tren elevado.*"

"Ah, I hope to ride one someday."

"You come visit me, cousin. We'll do it all. Take the subway, too. Anyway, this guy's like crazy, you know, *loco*, hanging from the rafters, *demente* . . . Pissing into the air above a crowded street is just one of his exploits. So instead of leaving when he's dressed, he sits down on the bench and asks me if I know this girl Yvonne. She's a black girl and real pretty. I tell him sure. Then he tells me he likes her, but isn't sure what to do about it. 'You think she'd go out with me?' he asks, and I'm thinking this isn't such a weird thing to say, but there's something weird in *how* he's saying it. . . . Even so, I give him the benefit of the doubt. 'You won't know that till you ask her,' I tell him. You with me?"

Julio nods.

"We're running low," Primo says. He shakes the bottle, sloshing the inch of rum left in the bottom as he hands it to Julio. "You're a good egg and I know you're down for this, but I'll make it quick just the same.

"He tells me he finds her beautiful. 'I mean *beautiful*,' he says, moving his hands up and down along her rib cage and waist. An act that implied he had more imagination than I thought he had. Then he asks me if I think Lieutenant Uhura's beautiful too, and I tell him I do. So he tells me that every night, when he jerks off, that's who he's thinking of. You believe this? What did I tell you? The people who think the whole place is theirs are the ones who'll say anything. Am I right? But this ain't the half of it. This ain't even the reason I started this long fucking story. . . . By that point, I realize I was wrong to think he was even a little sane. He was the kind of guy who never flushed a toilet. On purpose."

Julio is laughing.

"You're a good listener, cousin."

He reaches out his hand. They shake.

"He's got more to tell me. He hadn't yet got to what he most wanted me to hear. He says he'd love to sleep with Yvonne, and he'd love to sleep with Lieutenant Uhura. He says it like he's real proud of himself. There's a million colored women he could sleep with, he tells me, but there's just one thing. 'One place I'd draw the line,' he says. 'I don't think I could ever eat them out. Not *even* Lieutenant Uhura. Every day I could screw one, but I'd have to draw the line there.' "

"Wow," Julio says.

"Do you believe that? He'd expect me to listen to this?"

"He had no right," Julio says. He shakes his head. "What did you do?"

"What could I do?"

Julio shakes his head again.

"One sick motherfucker," Primo says.

"One sick motherfucker," Julio agrees. Then he smiles a small smile. "I would think he never has any pleasure."

"I bet you're right. Last I heard he went into the Marines. If he's still among the living, I imagine he's still abusing himself every night to the tune of Lieutenant Uhura."

Julio offers Primo the last sip.

"You finish it," Primo says.

Julio just sets the bottle between his knees.

"Imagine this," Primo says. "I'm seeing Ralphie in a special episode of *Star Trek.* First you hear Kirk: *Captain's Log, Stardate: whatever . . .*

Lieutenant Uhura keeps receiving obscene interstellar calls. Even though we've jammed all communications frequencies, the caller, who identifies himself as Ralphie, keeps getting through. . . . Then comes the commercial." Primo squints through the small span of dark air between him and Julio. "You're still with me, right?"

"Yes. But for what product is the commercial?"

"That don't matter. Dog food. *Papel higiénico . . . Escúchame.* We come back to the show and first thing we see is the communicator screen, filled with Ralphie's face. *Oh Lieu-ten-ant,* he says, *I got something for you. . . .* You can only see his face, but he's kind of rocking, so you know he's stroking wood."

"He is cutting wood?"

"*¿Un leño?*"

"Ah." Julio smiles. "The log."

"Anyway, you can see what he's up to and he keeps calling the lieutenant and his face is getting redder and redder. . . . Then Kirk says, *Scotty, can the shields hold?*"

Julio is holding his hand over his eyes. He's laughing quietly.

"We should write an episode," Primo says. "You and me."

Julio takes his hands from his eyes and, still laughing, says, "I don't have to do this. It's dark!" He laughs even harder. Then he says, "*¿Qué te piensas en esto?* . . . 'The starship was like a shining coin . . .' "

"My ace boon cousin, you're a writer. You're wasting your talent in the sheet metal business."

Julio laughs until he stops. They are quiet for a while.

Then he asks Primo, "How long will you be in Nicaragua?"

"Two weeks. I don't think we can do half the shit they got planned for us. We're going to meet teachers all over the place, go to the house of Rubén Darío, Plaza de la Revolución. Tomorrow we're going to Matagalpa."

"Ah," Julio says. Then he starts singing. "*Matagalpa, Matagalpa. La perla de la septentrión* . . ."

"Wow," Primo says. "*¿La* who . . . ?"

"*La perla de la septentrión. El norte.*"

"Pearl of the north. I like it. But I thought *al lago* was north."

"That is also north."

"You guys are cool, but you got too many names for each direction. Whatever happened to *this* way and *that* way? Tell me, which way is *arriba?*"

Julio points to the east.

Not the slightest hint of the vague lightening that precedes the sunrise. They are still in the dark center of the night. Primo can't see a thing beyond Julio and the vague outlines of the nearest structures. He is nearly nowhere. An easy place to be.

He takes the bottle from Julio, holds it close to his eyes and examines the tiny amount of rum remaining. He figures if they both just wet their lips, and a bit more, there's a shareable nightcap. He takes his, then hands Julio the bottle. "*Matagalpa, Matagalpa* . . ." he sings.

"*La perla de la septentrión.*" Julio finishes the line. Then finishes the bottle.

Primo thinks that they are as happy and as sad as any two drunks, in any city, at any time in history, anywhere in the world. He decides not to say it aloud. He's been talking too much as it is. The noise he brought with him, on the inside, has picked tonight to rush the gates. "I wish you luck, Julio," he says instead. "I wish you luck for the rest of your life." He then asks him to teach him more of the song.

With each new line he can learn, they sing the whole thing several times up to that point. As they sing, he watches the portion of sky in the direction known as *arriba.* When the light returns, he will be right here.

LA SEPTENTRIÓN

19

A woman carrying a blue plastic washtub on her shoulder walks alongside the bus, stopped in the Plaza Española, just under the street-side windows. She walks back and forth, slowly, the entire length of the bus. Primo looks down and sees what she is selling: small, clear plastic bags of water, tied like balloons at the top, and green-skinned oranges. Leaning out the window, he feels the warm midmorning sun fall steadily through the cloudless sky onto his fore-arm and elbow, and the same dry/humid wind he first felt yesterday at the airport.

Allen, sitting a few rows ahead of the seat Primo shares with Manny, reaches down and exchanges a bill for an orange and a bag of water. Then he kneels on his seat, leans his torso out the window and photographs the woman from above. Manny looks at Primo. "The man suffers from acute asshole-itis," he says. Then he leans forward, to the seat in which Felix and Maryellen are sitting, and continues telling them about his novel.

"The title comes from Chekhov, who was like the coolest guy in the entire turn of the fucking century. It's called *Lying to the Holy Ghost.*" He then says, to Felix, "It sounds like your man Darío was up there too, cool-wise, I mean."

For several blocks the bus moves a few feet, stops, moves a few feet, stops again. There are bicycles, handcarts, wagons, an occasional car or truck. Mostly it's the pedestrian traffic, crowding the morning streets, that slows them down.

"So Chekhov gets invited to this fancy dinner on the anniversary of the abolition of serfdom. All the big muck-a-mucks were eating, drinking champagne and making speeches, while Chekhov's sitting there thinking about the waiters who were serving them, and the coachmen waiting outside in the cold—and we're talking Russian cold. He's thinking how these people's lives were hardly different from the lives of the serfs whose freedom they were supposedly commemorating. Needless to say, he had a shitty time. He hardly touched his food. He went home and wrote in his diary that he'd spent the evening watching his tedious hosts lie to the Holy Ghost. Cool, huh." He points toward Allen, leaning out the window again—Grace holding him by the belt—trying to photograph some graffiti on the side of what might have once been an office building but is now a single, jagged-topped wall, with shrubs and weeds growing alongside it. "I'll bet he'll make postcards out of it and sell them," he says. The bus jolts into slow forward movement, and Grace guides Allen unsteadily back onto his seat.

As they pass the broken wall, Primo can see what Allen was trying to photograph. A red and black stenciled image of Augusto Sandino, in a cowboyish hat and bandanna. Spray-painted under it are the words: *Sandino Vive en la lucha por la paz.*

About an hour after they'd finished the rum, Julio walked off, *al lago*, toward home, and Primo found his way back to their room in the Hotelito and slipped into bed. He'd slept less than two hours when a shaft of sunlight, passing through the window, forced his eyes open. Manny was sitting on his bed, already dressed, leafing through a copy of *Barricada*, the Sandinista party paper.

"I heard you stumble in," he said. "Find the corner bar, did you?"

Primo swung his legs out from under the sheet, set them on the floor, leaned his elbows on his knees and his head into his hands. Felix and Ken were asleep. He heard birds and he heard faint TV or radio voices from outside the door of their room. "What time is it?" he asked Manny.

"Time you had some aspirin and a very tall glass of water."

He took a shower, brushed his teeth and drank water in big gulps right from the tap. When he came back into their room, Ken and Felix were awake, both sitting up in their beds.

"Angelita's already in the *comedor*," Manny said. "Breakfast's in ten minutes. After that, a quick bus tour of Managua. Just to get a first glimpse at the stuff we'll see more of later."

"*The most beautiful ugly city in the world*," Felix said. "That's what the great poet Claribel Alegría calls it. She lives here, you know."

"You ready for this?" Manny asked Primo.

Primo sat on the edge of his bed and slowly slipped his pants over his legs, then lifted himself and pulled them up to his waist. "Ready?"

"For the most beautiful ugly city in the world." Manny walked over to his bed with a small bottle of aspirin. He opened the top and held it out to Primo.

With his weight settled back on the bed, Primo felt something in his back pocket. He reached in and pulled out some crumpled pieces of paper. He smoothed them, set them on his lap. One, a half-sheet piece of lined notebook paper with Julio's name and address. The other, a piece of yellow paper, the size of a page of a paperback book. A promotional flier someone handed him, in front of a new pizzeria, two nights ago in New York. He'd just taken it and shoved it into his pocket, then forgotten about it. *Alphabet City Pizza—Grand Opening. Eat-In—Take-Out—Free Delivery. Buy One Slice, Get a Medium Soft Drink Free. Good thru January 25th.*

"Too bad," Manny says. "We'll still be here when the offer expires."

Primo's head didn't ache too badly, to his surprise, but he felt thickheaded and dreamy, slightly roiled but physically inert. Like a dropped ball that had just completed the faster, smaller bounces that precede its coming to rest.

"What's that?" Ken asked.

Primo handed him the flier.

"And what's *that?*" Manny asked, pointing to the other piece of paper.

"The address of a guy I met last night."

"We're not here twenty-four hours and you already have a pen pal. Good for you. You'll get to tell him about all the things you'll see today. After the quick tour we head north. We'll be lunching in Matagalpa."

"Hey," Ken said, holding up the flier. "This looks like a pretty good deal."

"I knew I'd like this guy," Manny says.

Ken smiles at him.

"You could call them," Manny then said. "Maybe they deliver to Managua."

"*Matagalpa, Matagalpa,*" Primo sang. "*La perla de la septentrión . . .*"

"Where'd you learn that?" Felix asked.

Primo stood up. "My pen pal."

"Let us now enjoy breakfast," Manny said.

"I could enjoy a slice right now," Ken said.

"With a medium soft drink," Manny added.

"I'm starving," Primo said.

They have passed from Managua's streets onto a two-lane road just outside the city. During the course of the last hour, they drove quickly past the Plaza de la Revolución, the ruins of the Grand Hotel, used now as a theater, and the tombs of Rigoberto López—a poet who shot Tacho, Anastasio Somoza, Sr., during a ball he was attending in the city of León, and who, a moment after pulling the trigger, was himself killed by the National Guard—and Carlos Fonseca, ideological father of the revolution. They stopped only once, at the Museo de la Revolución. Out in front, two tanks were on display. One had been taken by the Sandinistas from Somoza's *guardia nacional.* The other, a much smaller one, had been a gift from Benito Mussolini to Tacho.

It was the smallest tank any of them had ever seen. "It's a sports tank," Manny said. "A two-seater. Just room enough for Tacho, the old devil, a few rounds for the cannon, a split of champagne and that lucky girl." He took a photograph of the sign, on the ground in front of it.

TANQUETA QUE REGALARA
EL DICTADOR FACISTA MUSSOLINI,
AL DICTADOR SOMOZA GARCÍA.

Angelita, standing beside her seat in the front of the bus, described each of the sights. She pointed out La Loma, the bunker of Anastasio Somoza, Jr., Tacho II, and the empty plinth that had held his statue until the Triumph, nine years ago. The statue had also been a gift from Mussolini, Angelita told them. "Except *he* didn't know this. It was an early example of what you call recycling. It had once stood in Italy and had on it, sitting on a horse, the dictator Mussolini. After he fell, Somoza had it shipped here and replaced the face with his own."

"A two-headed creature," Manny said, loud enough for everyone to hear.

Angelita smiled at this. "You might say," she added, "that on top of that empty pedestal lives the ghost of your two-headed creature."

Primo watched her as she spoke, pointing out the windows, balancing herself by leaning against the side of her seat. Her manner was more formal than that of a tour guide, or a teacher. He imagined she would rather be elsewhere.

She pointed to a vacant, rectangular expanse, larger than a square block. "There was a flower market here."

People looked at the weeds and shrubs, patches of brown, burnt turf and empty, dry patches of ground. She sat down, then, remembering something, stood up again. "We can see each of these things again at a later time. I thought you might like to get a quick introduction to Managua."

They drove through whole neighborhoods of destroyed buildings: caved-in, empty structures that have not been occupied in fifteen years, all of them possessed of a violent stillness. Not the dreamy, majestic Acropolis, or the steadily worsening, cold, oil-drum-fire, isolate, dangerous South Bronx . . . But mortar walls no longer joining other walls, mysterious apparitions of twisted, rusted metal, piles of dry brick and cinder block amid weeds and shrubs. Always weeds and shrubs and patches of burnt turf. So little remains of some buildings, some streets, you can no longer imagine their initial size and shape and purpose. . . . It's impossible to imagine how people once figured in their meaning: where they ate, worked, bathed, looked out of windows, passed through doorways, slept, amused themselves.

Now they are driving into a range of low hills. Higher ones appear in the distance up ahead. From here, through the bus's rear window and the dusty haze, all that remains visible of Managua are the few taller buildings that are still standing. It looks like a new city in the process of being built. Primo thinks that a neighborhood, or a city, when you are inside it, always radiates outward. It *starts* with you. Like outer clothing. Like a widening periphery of skin. The dark streets he walked on last night, before he met Julio, had no real substance other than the voices of the people on them. If they had stopped talking, everything would have disappeared.

Being within any arrangement of people and structures is like being in the center of a record album. Maybe that's why we thought the world was flat. Why we still do, at first thought—only after that do we remind ourselves it's round.

You can look at the Chrysler Building—from a Lower East Side rooftop, from the street right in front, on a postcard—and see women in thirties hats, high heels, stockings with seams; men in two-tone shoes and down-tilted hat brims. You see them crossing hallways and riding in elevators. You see gentle black men shining shoes. Out front are heavy, rounded cars, double-decker buses. Inside, the words on signs, the numbers on the faces of clocks are written in thin, three-dimensional, curving script. Everyone is moving to the rhythm of clear and reasonable purpose.

These are just some of the things Primo knows he has been told in the language of his city, before that language became more silent, less comprehensible, more insidious.

He wonders what it feels like to spend each day there, in that *beautiful ugly* city, now passing out of view—crossing its streets, traveling from one part of it to another, feeling its gravity, watching it spin around you.

They pass an intersection, where the road they are traveling on turns, increases its angle of ascent and is joined by another, narrower road. Inside the point of the triangle formed by the two adjoining roads, two barefoot children, a boy and a girl, one of them holding a donkey on a rope lead, stand beside a young man in uniform, a sentry, who sits on a kitchen chair holding an AK47, barrel up, between his knees. All three wave as the bus slows to navigate the turn.

Manny is still talking to Maryellen and Felix about his novel. He's been relating the more interesting and dramatic incidents, and reading them bits and pieces from his notebook.

"The absence of cars," Manny says. "All those streets we passed without a single car parked on them remind me of the chapter I was working on just before I left home. . . ." He flips through his notebook.

While he does this Maryellen takes a sip from a plastic bottle of spring water, then hands it over the seat to Primo. Most of the members of the delegation, sitting in twos, are looking out the windows, quiet.

"Here it is," Manny says. "Listen. . . . *Henry O, woken from a deep sleep by the sound of a car alarm that tore a hole in the fabric of night, thought of a new scheme: car alarms for people without cars. Just set them up in the empty space in front of your home or apartment house. Through a system of sound waves, the absence-of-car alarm can measure the exact amount of space necessary to contain a BMW, a Caddy, a Volvo or, for the more extravagant, a stretch limo. Once set up, anyone intruding on the space sets off an alarm, the kind that makes long, wavy siren noises, periodically interrupted by ten seconds of annoying up-curved whoops that sound like two traffic police officers having passionate sex with their whistles still in their mouths. Of course, for the homeless, they are portable. Anyone can now be a member of the orchestra that plays the ongoing sound track of material history: the 'Private Property Serenade,' that constant lyrical reminder that there are, and always have been, only two kinds of people. Those who protect the things they own, and those who would take them away . . .*"

Maryellen applauds.

"Wow," Felix says.

Angelita stands and faces everyone seated farther back in the bus.

"I hope you are enjoying the trip thus far. I thought I'd point out something interesting. If you look at the road we're driving on—in fact, if you look at most of the roads we've driven on—you'll see that they are paved with hexagon-shaped bricks."

Everyone looks. Manny leans over Primo to look out and down. Felix looks over Maryellen. Primo notices that Angelita herself briefly turns to look at the road through the front windshield, as if she, too, is seeing them for the first time.

"Looks a little like a parquet floor," Manny says.

"These are called *barricadas*," Angelita says.

"Like the newspaper," Manny says. He has his copy with him, folded on his lap.

"And I'll tell you why," Angelita says. "One of the businesses the Somoza family owned, and they owned the largest number of big businesses in this country, was the making of those bricks. All over the country, roads are paved with them. Ironically, during the civil war, they served as the building blocks for barricades. They protected the Sandinistas against the *guardia nacional.* They helped bring about the triumph."

"Wow," Maryellen says, shaking her head, smiling.

"They say *wow* in Spanish, too," Primo says.

"I bet they even say it in China," Manny says.

Maryellen then says, "Have you ever noticed how things come up in related groups, in categories? Like just now. The subject was driving. Cars, car alarms, roads, paving bricks . . . It could well be some kind of—I don't know—some kind of collective extrasensory perception."

"How?" Manny asks. He leans his elbows against the back of her seat.

"Well, Angelita can't have known we were talking about cars. Or anything to do with driving. Yet, just at that moment, she chose to tell us about the *barricadas.*"

"How about this: Felix and I happen to meet on a plane to Managua. This, of course, is not any kind of coincidence. But now I'll thicken the plot. Not only did we meet on a plane, listen to *this*—we're both bipeds, and both of us hate to pay our taxes."

"You're making fun of me," Maryellen says.

"I am not," Manny says.

"You have to use your imagination," she says. "Imagination is a *real* thing. How can you look at a bunch of stars, so far away, and so incomprehensible, *without* using your imagination? A bunch of anything for that matter: people, the lights of cities from up in an airplane, grass seeds scattered on a lawn . . ."

"What does this have to do with cars and driving?" Manny asks her.

"Everything. We look at these things and we imagine shapes and patterns. Hunters, scorpions, seven sisters. We look at the things we talk about, that come to mind, we also see patterns."

"Wow," Manny says. "Do you know what you're doing? You are provoking thought."

Primo looks around the bus, his eyes just over the heads of the other riders, following the shape of the rectangle of windows that encloses them all. Some are talking among themselves, some stare at the dry, yet green mountainsides, some are still craning their necks to look downward at the slow blur of the *barricadas*. Angelita, at the same time, looks back toward the faces of the riders, the tourists she is guiding. Primo watches her. She could be counting heads, she could be trying to imagine their thoughts.

He takes the paper from Manny's lap. On top of the *Internacionales* page is the headline *Wall Street Sufrió Caída Ayer.* The first sentence begins, *El Promedio Don Jones de Industriales cayó 57.20 puntas . . .* He wonders if *Don* Jones is what they call it, or if it's just a typo. *Don Jones.* Sounds like a football player. Probably a typo. At the bottom of the page is a picture of Coretta Scott King and her son, Martin Luther King III, laying a wreath on her husband's tomb. They had just driven past tombs of heroes. Here is another, in a grainy photograph on a page in front of him: a coincidence immeasurably more significant than the ones Maryellen and Manny are talking about. *Durante el homenaje nacional tributado el lunes cuando se conmemoró el 59 aniversario del nacimiento . . .* Yesterday he would have been fifty-nine. So young, Primo thinks. He thinks it each time he is reminded of King's age. And his son, younger than

Primo, laying the wreath *donde descansa su padre.* Where he rests. *Still* so young . . . There *is* no abiding city, yet you are never outside the city you abide within.

"That's something, what you're telling me," Manny says to Maryellen. "The imagination *is* real. Wow."

"Wow," she says, back. "I bet they even say it in China."

20

A dozen young children, all wearing white T-shirts and white diapers, sit along the base of a cinder-block wall eating peeled oranges. Above their heads the otherwise bare wall has on it the words *25 ANIVER—FSLN*, and two short, wide strokes of paint, one red, one black. Some of them look toward Maryellen and Allen, who are taking their picture. Some of them smile, not because they are being photographed—the oldest of them is perhaps three—but because these two adults are calling to them, smiling as they look though the lenses, making noises, waving their arms. One of the children holds a small, black, plastic doll in her hand. All the rest use both hands to hold their oranges to their mouths.

Two women are standing just outside what they imagine to be the periphery of the photographs. They are talking, also eating oranges, and watching as the children eat theirs.

On the adjoining section of wall, there is a mural on which men and women, farm workers and soldiers, stand among the leafy branches of coffee plants laden with beans. The incurving ridges of mortar between the cinder blocks hold the late-afternoon sunlight and make it appear as if the image were constructed like a puzzle, rather than painted across the single, continuous surface. As if the elbow and pink sleeve of a worker, the trigger plate and long clip of an AK47 and the open top of a bag filled with brown and yellow beans were a single, measured unit that existed before it was set into place to form its part of the whole.

Primo wonders if the people who live here, who are under this sun as it rises through morning into each day's late afternoon, if just one of them, child or adult, ever sees this, ever just stands here—as he, in this moment, does—taking this wall apart, reassembling it, taking it apart again.

A simple wooden kitchen chair has been left leaning against the cinder blocks on the bare stretch of wall to the right of the children. This small section is the third panel of a triptych, with the children in the middle and the mural at the left. This inactive panel, seen apart from the others, could be thought to exist nearly anywhere in the world at any time in the century. *¿Puedo sacarte una foto?* Primo hears someone say this, then says it to himself, in literal translation: Can I take away from you a photo?

They will take away pictures of the children, and will take away pictures of the mural, but no one is taking away pictures of this chair and this small stretch of wall. If they did, they'd come across it sometime in the next decade, maybe even the next month, and forget where it was taken. Cairo? Hong Kong? The Bronx? A composition possessed of too much indeterminate space is, at first, too quiet. Then too much weather, too much geography, too many different people, begin to appear. Most of the meaning of anything *taken away*—a child, a mural, a tank, a wall, a tree—is in the room you are in later when you look at its image. This image, *chair against wall*, would never stop developing—"This your brother's house on Long Island? Did the film developer mix somebody else's in with ours?"—and would be a different photograph each new time you saw it. The one thing it would always bring to mind is the largest aspect of our experience: It took place on this planet, in this century. Who could find themselves in something so much larger than their own life?

"I know what these little crumb-crushers are thinking," Manny tells Primo. He's half sitting on the seat of a moped, leaning against its kickstand, watching the children being photographed. "Who are these assholes with the cameras, making faces and weird noises?"

Angelita is describing the uses of the building, the only recently built structure on the entire *Unidad Producción Fonseca.* It is a day-care center, it is the school and, at night, the dormitory where extra coffee pickers and soldiers sleep during the times of year, like now, when they are needed.

"Children and mothers." Manny shakes his head, then slips off the bike seat, puts his hand on Primo's shoulder. "Mothers and now children. My fucking head is spinning." He is referring to their visit, earlier this afternoon, to the Mothers of Heroes and Martyrs.

Primo has been trying to keep his mind on what they are doing in this moment. Looking at the outside of this building. The children, the mural. The chair against the wall, which was the only thing to come close to helping him empty his mind. To untangle himself from the web formed by the strings of words he'd heard earlier, sitting in the dark, cool public hall in the town of Matagalpa, listening to these women, many of them old, older than his mother ever got to be, telling their stories. Why did he listen? Why give them so much airtime later on?

In this moment is the side of a building. A mural, a bunch of children, a chair. The chair's best. It reminds him of some Zen shit Mariah was once into. Imagine a sky with clouds in it. Then some wind. Then the clouds drifting away. The chair's even better. But it's not empty enough. Why did he listen to them? Before he met them he'd already learned what he came here to learn. That they live in a profoundly different world, and that they live *in* it differently. The end.

They had lunch in the *comedor* run by *Las Madres de Héroes y Mártires.* Rice and beans, and Coca in plastic cups. The plaster walls were covered with photographs of men and women who had fallen in battle. Some of them were older pictures, taken when they were children. Across from the *comedor*, at the opposite side of a wide street paved with *barricadas*, was a huge monument with statues of three revolutionary fighters, the face of Carlos Fonseca, who was born in Matagalpa, and the words Primo had seen yesterday in the Hotelito, held by the two *cachorros*, on the screen of the TV:

CON EL FRENTE AL FRENTE
¡AQUÍ NO SE RINDE NADIE!

After lunch they walked, mostly together, through the streets of Matagalpa to the ancient town hall where they met with a committee of a dozen of the *madres*. The walls facing each street were covered with painted letters and images, and gouged with lines and clusters of bullet holes.

Maryellen asked Primo to take a picture of her standing in front of the large propeller of a *contra* cargo plane that had recently been shot down. It was leaning against the side of a building, as if it were just dragged from the middle of the street where it was blocking traffic. Then she took pictures of Primo, Felix and Manny, standing in front of its crossing eight-foot blades.

It wasn't a tiny, rustic town, as Primo had expected, but a small city. Above the plaza where they were to meet with the *madres* stood a tall, bullet-pocked tower, all that remained of the *guardia nacional* command post. The air was drier and dustier and gathered itself into small gusts. Vague, spectral bursts of impressions broke against you like waves that receded before you fully knew they'd even reached you. War has been there, often, and is waiting somewhere nearby. Everyone seemed accustomed to its menacing purr. People did what they do everywhere at midday: pass to and from places, carry newspapers and purses, smile, or talk, or look down at the ground they walk on. Primo noticed that Angelita, wearing black jeans, was the only Nicaraguan woman on the streets wearing pants. Even young girls wore dresses and skirts.

The volume was increasing. Things were beginning to happen too fast. Primo could feel his fingers losing hold of the on/off switch of his intake valve. He had learned early in life to shop carefully with his senses. And to maintain control of the rate, so as to first comprehend how each new thing bears safe relation to everything already his.

They quietly faced each other. The *madres*, Angelita along with them, sat in a line on one side of the room, the members of the delegation on the other. As they waited, other women drifted in and joined the *madres*. It was hot outdoors but the large, dark, stone and tile room was cool. Some of the delegation had put on long-sleeve shirts.

Then one of the women began telling a story about how her son had fallen in battle. It had happened in 1979, just before the triumph. It was in the hills outside this town. He was seventeen and he was shot by the *guardia nacional.* She would stop periodically and Angelita would translate what she said. "When they found him they discovered that other guardsmen had come upon his body first and they fired hundreds of bullets into him. His name was Sergio, which was also his father's name." Another woman stood up, briefly, and said, "My name is Ilana Pérez. I lost my husband and my two sons, but I don't want to talk about that right now. I'm sorry." She sat down.

No one on either side of the room spoke. Some of the delegation members had begun to write in pads and notebooks. When it was quiet, the room seemed to get cooler and darker. Primo was growing sleepy.

A woman told them that a year ago they found the bodies of two young men who were not from around here, and because their *communism* had been cut out with a machete, no one could recognize them. Angelita then explained that the *contra* have said the disease of communism resides in the back of the head. "We had no choice but to bury them without knowing who their families were."

Another woman, older than most of the others, appeared at the open doorway. She stood there, leaning into her cane, until the woman was finished speaking. Two younger women then got up and helped her to an empty folding chair. She sat perfectly still, in a light-blue dress, then began wrapping the end of its thin, darker blue cloth belt around her index finger.

The woman who had just told of the two young strangers then got up and moved to the seat next to hers. "This one is historical," she said. "Her sufferings have made history here." She turned and faced the woman, pointed at her, then turned and faced the delegation. "It started when the *guardia nacional* were kidnapping children. They took them up in helicopters, very high, and then they dropped them in the mountains. She lost one then. His name was

Alejandro and he was eight. Later, her two older sons and her husband were kidnapped by the *contra* and taken to a hacienda"—she pointed with her finger—"four kilometers to the north . . ."

The story passed like refracted light from the silent woman, to the woman who told it, to Angelita, who, in a steady, matched rhythm, bent it into English. "They laid them on the floor and they walked over them until they broke their ribs. And they beat them and beat them. Someone who had been there and had escaped told her that their wrists and ankles began to swell and bleed where they were tied, and they began to smell very bad. The wrists and the ankles."

The woman telling the story leaned toward the woman in the blue dress, said something to her, then listened for a few minutes as the woman spoke into her ear. When she continued, she told the story as the woman told her, in first person. "They cut out their tongues and on the seventeenth day they all died. The person who had been there and escaped went to Managua. That was later. That was when he told me this. I lost a nephew, too. Last year. He was ambushed by the *contra.* He was my sister's. He would have become eighteen this week."

Without prompting, another woman began to speak. She said only this: "Mirta López, Sebastián López and my husband, who was named Efraín, and then Anastasia and then Gregorio."

No one spoke for a while. Then one of them would break the silence. Sometimes they would remain sitting, sometimes they would stand as they spoke.

Many of the delegation members had begun to weep. Angelita, translating, also wept.

Afterward, they all got up and approached one another. The members of the delegation embraced the mothers. Primo was too angry to talk to anyone. He slipped between the people who were speaking in quiet tones, weeping, embracing. He noticed Angelita watching him. He met her stare and she smiled. Why the fuck was she smiling? He scowled back at her and aimed himself toward the doorway. He was nearing the periphery of the crowd, when suddenly one of the mothers appeared in front of him. It was the one in the blue dress whose sat quietly as her story was told. The famous one.

He hadn't realized how small she was. She smiled, with her tired light brown eyes and then with her whole face. Inside him a heavy, flat rock was being crowbarred off cold earth.

"*Usted es una enseñante,*" he said awkwardly. He knew he was supposed to say such a thing, call her a teacher: like last night, in the *comedor*, when he tried, for a moment, to act like he was up for the same version of this shit as everyone else. But this was different. He surprised himself, being able to say this, somehow meaning it.

"*¿Por qué tú no escribiste nada?*" she said. Then she reached one arm over his shoulder and the other, the cane hooked over her wrist, around his back. She felt like a bird in his arms. "Everyone else did," she said. As she spoke, her gray hair pressed into his neck and against his chin. "If you don't write anything down, how will you remember?"

At first the hot, bright light was unbearable. Manny, leaning against the side of the building, was holding Maryellen, who was sobbing loudly. The other members of the delegation milled around, just outside the doors, still in a tight crowd, looking at each other or up and down the street, squinting.

For everyone else out of doors it was an ordinary afternoon in *la perla de la septentrión.* Allen walked across the street, took a photograph of the building and the delegation members standing in front, then crossed back again. He stood beside Primo, motioned his head toward Maryellen, who was still crying, and said, "That's just the effect they were going for."

Primo had no answer for him.

Felix, standing nearby, said to Allen, "What's your problem?"

"This whole show was planned. Meant to bring us to tears. To make sure we don't leave without knowing about all the suffering U.S. dollars have caused here."

"What's your problem?" Felix said again.

Primo noticed two boys pass them on the sidewalk. One of them, maybe eight, with a toy knife that had a blue handle and a yellow blade he flicked in and out like a switchblade. The other, maybe thirteen, was wearing worn, shiny, sharkskin bell-bottoms and a short-sleeve shirt with only one button buttoned, right in the middle. They walked off the brick sidewalk, into the street and back again, circling the crowd without looking at them.

By then, Manny had arrived in the argument. "Who do you work for, asshole . . . the CIA?"

Maryellen, standing beside Manny, put her hand on his shoulder.

"*Easy* . . ." Felix said.

"That kind of talk doesn't help," Grace from California said.

"Just someone with open eyes," Allen said back to Manny.

"Wide enough to see your own asshole."

Maryellen shoved Allen. Then walked back over to the wall, where she'd been standing a moment before with Manny, and just stood there, stiff and angry, her arms crossed, her eyes filling with tears.

"I *know* what I'm talking about," Allen said.

"You don't know shit," Manny said.

Grace from California looked toward Primo. "Can you make him stop?"

At that moment Allen shoved the hand with which Manny was pointing at him away from his face.

"*Aha.* Now it's *really* asshole time." Manny turned to Primo and Grace. "He wants to fight." He held out his hands, palms upward. "And where *he* comes from . . ." He turns back to Allen. "People can't even say *Fuck you.*"

Allen shoved Manny again, harder, against the chest.

Grace set her hand on his shoulder. "*Allen* . . ." He pushed it off.

"Who are you, fucking Solomon?" Manny was yelling now. "Who appointed you the judge?"

Primo noticed that three women who'd walked a wide arc around them had now stopped across the street. The two boys who'd passed by a moment before had returned and were standing next to him. "Go easy," he said to Manny.

"Who the fuck are you," Manny shouted, "Mr. Monroe fucking Doctrine? Who are you to decide what this"—he shook his outstretched arms in a gesture that meant the entire place—"means? What gives you the right? Is it because we got the Stealth bomber?

The space shuttle? *What?* The Hoover fucking Dam? What is it, asshole . . . ?"

Allen stood there, facing him. Then—this time with both hands—shoved Manny again, forcing him to take a step backward.

"That's it. Strike fucking *three!*" Manny grabbed the camera strap slung over Allen's left shoulder, pulled it off and began swinging the camera like a mace. Everyone in the close circle of people took a step outward. "You're a Frisbee, you're a fucking suntan, you're a soft drink with arms and legs, you're the *gaping*-est asshole in the whole fucking hemisphere."

Angelita then appeared on the stone step outside the lightless doorway. "Cameras are very expensive," she said. "Am I correct?"

A half hour later, as the bus left Matagalpa, Angelita, standing in the front, told them they were taking a short ride, six or seven kilometers north, to the U.P. Fonseca. This *Upay*, the *Unidad Producción Fonseca,* had been a plantation owned by the Somoza family. "Years ago children would sneak into the barns at night to steal eggs and to steal milk right from the cows. Now it is a cooperative. As we have told you, at this time the coffee is being picked. So it is at this time the *contra* have been causing trouble. They have been instructed that to make war on coffee is to make war on the people."

As she spoke, Primo watched the mountains slowly gather in this small bus with its twelve people on board. In leaving Managua and now the town of Matagalpa, he is going farther and farther from home.

". . . You will see more soldiers there than are ordinarily present. More coffee pickers, as well. Thus, you will find teachers. We are needed to be where the people are."

Les apestaban. They were reeking. *Reeking.* The word used by the woman telling the story of the husband and two sons of the famous woman, the woman Primo had held in his arms. *Las muñecas, los tobillos.* Their wrists and ankles were reeking. It happened in a hacienda in the hills just north of the town. These hills. *Cuatro kilometros al norte.* Her husband and her two sons. . . . *Y después de diez y siete días, ellos murieron.* She had wondered how, without writing down what they said, he could remember. *Shit. An exclamation. Shit with the fucking exclamation point on both sides.* What he thought of, as Angelita was speaking, and the bus climbed a bare, sandy stretch of mountainside, was their ankles and wrists. They swelled, they festered, they stank. This father and his two sons knew the smell of their own decaying flesh. *Les apestaban.* While they were still alive.

Manny and Maryellen were sitting together in the back. Felix sat alone in front of Primo, where he could have his own window.

When Angelita finished speaking, she sat in the empty seat beside him. They were quiet, at first. Angelita read through the sheets of paper in the clipboard she held on her lap. Then she stood again and, her hand on the back of the seat, spoke to everyone from the middle of the bus.

"Occasionally you will see, as we drive deeper into the mountains, the homes of campesinos. . . . There is one." She pointed to a concrete structure, the size of a one-car garage, with a metal roof. Instead of a door, half of one wall was missing. Two children stood in front. "The newer ones, such as that one, are sometimes called *miniskirt* houses. The roof is the skirt and the walls, to a point at least one meter from the ground, are made of concrete, or cinder blocks. Above that point, where the roof overhangs, they are made of wood."

Grace Berenson, sitting beside Ken in the front of the bus, asked, "Would you call them *mini-faldas*, or *falditas?*"

"No. We also use your word: *miniskirt.* They are designed so that the *contra* cannot shoot through the walls, nor set fire to the roof."

After saying this, she sat down again.

Primo leaned out the window, watched the house she described pass, watched the next one appear, after a mile or so of mostly uncultivated land, alongside the road just ahead of them.

What seemed unusual, in this landscape of tropical mountains, was the combination of pine trees, cacti and palm fronds. Forest, desert, jungle, are three *kinds* of places. It was odd to see them sharing different portions of the same view, even mixed up, growing in the same patch of ground. Like different seasons occurring simultaneously. Primo thought of his students, writing about the crops in the countries they come from. He wondered if what he now saw would seem ordinary to them, or was it just here, in the *slim waist*, that everything that grows in the entire hemisphere has been squeezed northward and southward toward the center. Like sand in an hourglass, simultaneously pulled in both directions by the mysterious appetite of a two-headed gravity. *Ah* . . . He said this in his throat. Then, *Shit*, meant to reach no farther than the chamber where his ears hear his voice from the inside.

He closed his eyes, leaned his head against the back of the seat. He felt the bus tilt upward. Horacio downshifted and the engine doubled its RPMs. As they climbed the hillside, the seat back transmitted the quiet, dense, metallic purr.

He heard Angelita's voice, and knew by its quieter tone she was speaking just to him, before he comprehended what she was saying. ". . . Had they been arguing long?" she was asking him.

He opened his eyes. "Who?" By then he'd realized she meant Manny and Allen, but he needed an additional second to focus his attention.

"A lot of people who've come here have the same argument. They mix up the meaning of what they see with the reasons for which they are seeing it."

"They watch too much television."

"You think so?" She thought about it for a second. Then she said, "That must be part of it. I think, also, there is some identification with the amount of power your country has. Feeling guilty about it, and being proud of it at the same time."

"That's a mouthful," Primo said. He smiled and shook his head slowly. "It's thus far been a very busy day . . ."

"But you understand."

"I think so."

"I knew *you* would understand."

"Why?"

"I thought this because you are the only black member of your delegation . . ."

"I have observed this too," he said. A familiar noise got prepared to make itself heard. "However, I try not to be black all the time." He smiled.

"You don't think I am being serious?"

"I think *Serious* is your middle name. I'm being serious too. Maybe I do understand some things better. I know I understand a lot of things *differently*. All I'm saying is that there's nothing more exhausting than being black *all* the time. Or anything else, I imagine."

"Why are you here?"

"To learn about your country, I guess."

"To learn what?"

"I'll tell you when I've learned it."

"People learn. And they *learn.* You know what I'm saying?"

"I'm the one who understands everything you say."

"You are still not taking me seriously."

"I am. And I'm also being silly. I'm sorry."

She looked at him. He could see she wasn't sure how to take what he had just said.

"Please go on," he said.

"Last year a woman from Boston who was with a delegation of teachers visited one of the *madres* at her home. It was a campesino home. Like one of those . . ." She pointed out the window toward a miniskirt house beside the road. "In this woman's house she saw that on a shelf above her bed she had a statue of the Virgin, photographs in frames, an old coffeepot in which there were fresh flowers—the woman from Boston told me all these things. . . . And there was one other thing she saw. There was also an empty dishwashing soap bottle. You know, the kind you squeeze and is made of plastic?"

Primo nodded. She smiled as she spoke. She enjoyed telling him this. He hoped they didn't get to where they were going too quickly, and that she would be talking, just to him, for a long time.

"This woman, the campesina, had painted it in bright colors. She liked to do this and she did it beautifully. She would paint anything, this old woman. An empty soup can, or . . ." She paused for a second, then held her hands and fingers so as to indicate a circle. "This part of a car's tire."

"A hubcap," Primo said.

"Yes." She smiled. "She could paint colors on anything. . . . The teacher from Boston told me that this plastic bottle was the most beautiful thing she had ever seen. In how this woman had painted it, she had changed it to a human form. She said that *it*, more than the story the woman had told, of the loss of her son *and* of her daughter, had taught her of this woman's sufferings."

"That is amazing," Primo said. Then he said, "I have the feeling you're one of the best teachers I will ever meet."

She seemed uncomfortable with his saying this. "At first, I was angry at this woman. I thought, she has learned what she knew before she left home. That there exist in our country such poor, simple and gentle campesinas as this woman. Then I thought, even if she has learned what she knew of already, she has gone to the very edge of what she already knew. And maybe, sometime later, after she goes back to her home, she will go beyond that edge."

"I think," Primo said, "I'm beginning to learn what *I'm* here to learn. And it's you who are teaching me."

"You flatter me and you embarrass me. I didn't think I was teaching you anything. I was just talking."

"Today I am learning from talk. I told the *madre* who embraced me that she was a teacher."

"I watched her head straight for you." She smiled. "I think she likes younger men."

Primo looked right at her. Throughout the whole conversation he hadn't done this.

Angelita then became serious. "Teach something to your two friends. The ones who were about to destroy the camera. Tell them the *madres* will tell their stories to each other whether anyone else is here or not. Then again, this is not what you call Club Med. If their stories persuade North Americans to write letters to your Congress, or your newspapers, we have a better chance of surviving. And our chances are very small. You understand that."

"I do."

"These women testify to liberate their suffering. At the same time, they are a weapon against more suffering."

"Now *you* are mixing up meaning and reasons."

"Yes," she said. "You are right. And I never watch television." She laughed.

Angelita smiled shyly at Primo. "And you understand."

He smiled back.

They fell silent for a while. They were passing a field filled with rows of tall, vinelike plants. He asked Angelita what they were.

"Coffee," she said. Then she asked, "What does that mean, what you said earlier, about being black all the time?"

"In my country, I prefer to be with people for whom what I say and what I do is who I am. . . . As opposed to the shape of my nose."

Angelita laughed. "I understand this. Are there many such people?"

"Millions. However, nearly all of them are black."

"I understand this, too."

"We must be getting near," he said.

"We're almost there. These plants are called *café uva.* On the *Upay Fonseca* they grow *café oro.* These belong to a private grower. He tries to export his coffee but is having bad luck." She laughed again. "Your embargo police have been following his little beans all the way to France."

"There'll be no café au lait from these beans," Primo said.

"You know something?" she said, closing her eyes slightly, but looking at him. "I think you are very funny."

Manny, using three oranges, has been teaching two of the older children, a boy and a girl, how to juggle. A younger boy, six or so, sits on the seat of the moped and watches them. Unable to speak Spanish, Manny uses two words to communicate with them: *sí* and *no.* Mostly, he moves their hands beneath the oranges as they try to toss and catch them. He has been teaching the girl to do two oranges in one hand.

Each time, after three or four up-and-down cycles, she begins to use her other hand. *No,* Manny says. The boy on the moped then laughs as Manny takes the oranges from her, shows her again, holding one hand behind his back, and then adds the third orange to show them all how doing two in one is the step before doing three in two. Primo is watching them from the chair, set against the blank stretch of cinder-block wall.

As the afternoon drew on, the children went off for their naps, and the students for the afternoon writing class, as they finished work, or duty, began to straggle in. The late-afternoon sky has just begun to darken over the U.P.'s central building, a long, barnlike structure with the same lasagna-curled metal roof nearly all the buildings have. Signs hung or painted right onto its wooden walls indicate an office, a clinic, a meeting room. It's where the children are now taking their naps. The descending sun, still hot, midway between zenith and western horizon, cannot reach the people beginning to gather on the plank benches set under its long, overhanging eaves.

Angelita walks up to Primo, tells him it's time, then over to the other delegation members sitting with the people in front of the main building. Primo then walks over to Manny, still engaged in his juggling lessons, and tells him recess is over. He hands the oranges, one each, to the children, and joins Primo, following the last of the students into the cool building.

The delegation members stand in the back of the room until Angelita invites them to sit among the twenty or so students. About half are coffee pickers and older children, the others are regular soldiers and members of the peasant militia, whose AKs lean against the wall of the next room, just beside the door.

There are two teachers, Ilena and Humberto. Like Angelita, who also helps them teach, but from her seat, Ilena is wearing pants. The other women in the classroom, except for two in the uniforms of the regular army, wear dresses. There is a blackboard across the wall in the front of the room. Both side walls are covered with drawings—pencil, crayon, charcoal, child and adult.

A large painting, done by the art teacher, who this week is teaching at another U.P., covers most of the back wall. In it Ronald Reagan, wearing a suit and tie, a shotgun lying across his lap, squats atop the shoulders of a campesina. He has a slight smile on his face; his hands hang over the stock and barrel in a way that indicates he is comfortable there. The woman holds her hands forward; there is blood running from her slit wrists. Behind them are fields of corn and beans and wheat surrounded on all sides by mountains. Reagan's eyes tilt slightly downward, hers straight ahead, so they are both looking directly at the viewer of the painting.

Primo understands why this is facing the teachers and not the students. It's much too distracting. It is realer, painted in the soft black and white of a news photograph, and more detailed and exact than the mural over the blackboard in his classroom in New York, or the one on the outside wall of this building, yet in its first impression there is the same simple and demanding immediacy. However, after that first burst of idea and feeling, it presents a deeper, more mysterious sadness. The sadness is not generated by the image, or the subdued color, but in the texture that each well-painted part of the composition has, when you separate it from the whole, and that becomes even more amplified when you put the parts back together. The two figures are a single figure. Unexpectedly fixed and permanent. The sadness then becomes terror.

The students seem self-conscious at first, having these ten strangers sitting among them. Since she is helping in the teaching, Angelita does not translate for the members who do not understand Spanish.

They each read what they have written in their softcover tablet notebooks. Periodically, Felix will turn to Manny, cup his hand and explain to him what has been said.

Anyone older than the ages we associate with the earliest grades of elementary school has already achieved the much more complex and far-reaching life of words. To learn to write, they must now decelerate their use of language, detach from the thinking and breathing that accompanies it, in order to learn its simplistic and unsubtle written form.

Por la cena los hombres y las mujeres comieron gallo pinto, y los niños comieron piñol y majadas.

It would be as if Manny, in explaining how to juggle, instead of surrounding the words *yes* and *no* with his moving hands, his stance and his energetic, comical face, were to say: *You must first remember how your left hand works and what it means in order to juggle oranges properly. Remember when you first discovered it was yours? And that you could touch yourself with it, bring food to your mouth with it, use it to protect yourself? Now manipulate the muscle and bone of the fingers, palm and wrist of just the left one, so that one orange may be caused to fly straight above it, before the other orange falls into it . . .*

21

The last sliver of sun hovers, waist high, between the trunks of the pine trees, on the opposite bank of the narrow stream in which a duck races to and fro, periodically submerging its head to snap up the M&M's Manny tosses into the shallow, murky water. He and Primo are sitting at the foot of a wooden frame—two beams that span the four feet to the other side—that once supported a walkway just wide enough to accommodate two people, strolling side by side. The wood is painted brown with fading stenciled images of green ivy and white flowers.

"Do you believe this?" Manny says. "A fucking chalet? If I were even slightly interested in figuring out what it's doing here, or what *we* are, I'd lose my marbles." He points at the duck, extending its gullet to swallow. "Look at that. M&M's: melt in your belly, *not* in your beak."

He looks farther downstream, to where Maryellen stands with Ken, Grace Berenson and Angelita, staring downward into the water, talking. "What a phenomenon," he says. "She is *something*."

Primo turns his head. The four of them look downward at the same angle, perhaps looking at the same thing. He moves his eyes to the spot their eyes have found on the water. What they see is in their conversation, not on the surface of the stream. A tired, late-day stillness has taken hold of everything.

"That this place," Manny says, "a fucking alpine chalet, could be here, like a mile from the *Upay* where they're picking coffee, cleaning their AKs, learning to read and write . . ."

"And juggle," Primo says.

"Fucking amazing." Manny turns, looks back at the wide, brown-painted side of the hotel, the Selva Negra, where they are to stay the night. "Forty-eight hours ago, I was watching the six o'clock news in the bedroom of my apartment in Massachusetts. I was eating a White Castle cheeseburger. No shit." He turns to Primo and smiles. "I buy them frozen, at the supermarket, then zap them in the microwave." He throws another M&M at the duck, who'd been paddling just enough to hold itself still, right in front of them. "I knew this country was far from there. But I had no idea *how* far. It boggles the fucking mind."

"I was just thinking about your M&M's," Primo says. "They started their life in Boston, and they'll come to their last rest here."

"Yeah, as part of the molecular composition of Nicaraguan duckshit."

Maryellen, now standing behind them, taps Manny on the top of his head. He turns, looks up at her, smiles.

"They're serving dinner." She takes a step backward, smiles at both of them. "Now that the duck has eaten, it's our turn." She walks up the small weedy incline to the door leading into the wide *comedor* of the hotel.

"I can't get over it," Manny says. "I don't think I see her sister Lisa anymore when I see her, but it's still weird. A different, new kind of weird. Did you notice those little deck sneakers? They're mint fucking green. She's like the prototype for flight attendants. You know, like the perfect apple? The one that makes the mold for plastic fruit?"

"Do I sense more in your feelings than idle curiosity?" Primo asks.

"Come *on* . . . And besides, she's married."

Primo looks at him, forcing him to look back.

"All right, all right . . ."

Primo stands up. Having been so still, even for a few minutes, after so much movement, makes him dizzy. The sun, were it as near as his eye chooses to perceive it to be, would be the size of a cue ball and at the height of his knees.

"She's got *something*," Manny says. "I don't know what it is, though. She's smart, she's hip, she's sexy, but *look* at her. . . . I'm talking *just* the externals. She makes the Brady Bunch look street-wise. It's a fucking enigma." He shakes his head. "I don't know. It's life in the eighties. I mean, the decade's nearly over, but shit . . . I haven't even *begun* to figure it out."

"You getting hungry?"

"This trip *and* this fucking decade . . ."

"See you later," Primo says. He walks toward the *comedor*. Either Manny hasn't heard him or he just isn't done talking. He can see through the window that the delegation members have gathered at two round tables. He notices, also, that Angelita is not at either of them.

"I don't know," he hears Manny say, as he passes inside. "I guess I should just buckle my seat belt. That's it. And enjoy . . ."

During dinner, rice and beans, *gallo pinto*, and *banana frita*, they talk about the chalet. Maryellen tells everyone what Angelita, who must be eating alone somewhere else, told her earlier. In the old days, the place had been a favorite of German tourists. Hence the name: Selva Negra, Black Forest. "She said that after the war and the embargo are only a memory, the tourists will come back."

They're drinking Victoria beer and Flor de Caña with Coca.

"This place belongs to a different kind of trip," Ken says. He shares a table with Primo, Manny, Felix, Grace Berenson and Maryellen. "It's like we're on a European tour, like tomorrow we'll see the Eiffel Tower."

Sarah and Theodore share the other table with Grace, Allen and John.

"A chalet wouldn't seem odd in the United States," Felix says.

"That's true," Grace says. "You know the London Bridge is somewhere in Arizona."

"And there *is* a little Eiffel Tower in Guatemala City," Felix adds. "I guess what I'm saying is that the Americas, whatever we mean by that, aren't really so different from each other. They are all the *New* World. At least in relationship to where I came from."

"You're right," Manny says. "But this place . . ." He looks around. "This place is Hitchcock. This place is fucking Mars."

Felix laughs. He and Manny touch glasses and drink.

Manny then toasts everyone else. "To our beautiful life on Mars."

They drink.

"*Nica libre*," Primo says. They drink again.

"*Nica libre*," Manny says.

"That's not just a toast," Primo tells him. "It's also the name of the drink."

"Ah," Manny says. "Like a Cuba libre."

"Yes," Primo says, "but it's *Jefe Comandante Fidel* who has the ice."

Primo, Felix, Ken and Manny are slowly finding their way to the small outcabin they are sharing for the night. The light of their combined flashlights is quickly absorbed by the thick darkness.

"How come we have to stay out here?" Ken asks. "Everyone else gets to stay inside."

"I think we've gone past it," Manny says. "It was much closer before."

"It was still light then," Primo says. "Everything seems closer when you can see things."

"He'd know," Manny says. "Last night he toured Managua by flashlight."

"Ah, there's a light," Felix says.

After a sharp turn in the path, they are suddenly approaching a faint square of light. It's the window of a cabin.

"That isn't ours," Manny says. "We didn't leave any lights on."

"We're close," Ken says. "I remember passing a smaller cabin earlier, just before we got to ours."

Their flashlights light up the painted wooden boards of the cabin's wall. Then Felix, swinging the beam of his light farther up the path, sweeping it across shrubs and shadowed tree trunks, finds their cabin, on the other side, less than a hundred yards ahead.

"There," he says.

"Ah," Manny says, relieved. "We're back on Mars."

As they pass the other cabin, Primo notices, through its lit window, Angelita, sitting cross-legged on a bed. The tight circle of light within which he sees her does not extend beyond herself, the clipboard she always carries, the sheets of white paper she is sorting through and arranging into stacks around her. She seems tired. When she moves her hand to write something, or to set a piece of paper on top of another, her movements are slow and deliberate.

"We should've left a light on," Manny says, aiming his beam at their cabin's door.

Primo wonders if her work is bureaucratic, something to do with the delegation, or if it's schoolwork: her attachment to the students she will return to as soon as these North Americans go home. She gives the impression that being tour guide and teacher to this group of foreigners disrupted a process of something more important. Something basic and mysterious and central to her life, to life here, that he and the other strangers he has come here with could never understand.

Lying in bed, his body relaxing for the first time since he awoke this morning, Primo realizes that the night is chilly. The first truly cold air he has felt since arriving.

Manny writes in his notebook by the light of his flashlight. Felix and Ken have fallen asleep.

It isn't the mystery of *what* Angelita was doing, when he watched her, briefly, through the window, that has held the image of her continuously in his mind, but her total absorption in it. In that moment, tired, occupied in her small task, she did not appear to lack for anything.

She knows what it is, her life. And she persists in the simple, consistent act of *being* it. It is what he has always sought: to fit the shape he imagines is his, but that has always eluded him. It makes him angry to think about this. And to compare himself, what he feels, to what someone else appears to feel. For everyone, life is a series of loosely wrapped orbits around a powerful and vaguely familiar gravity. It exerts its pull, and hides its face, especially if you look at it. No one gets any closer to it than that. This is true for him. And true for everybody.

"*What?* What *is* that?" Manny says this.

A sudden loud thump had woken them.

"I don't know," Primo says.

It wasn't nearby, and wasn't really loud. It was the kind of sound you feel to a greater degree than hear, and know would be very loud were you closer to its source. Then they hear a fast, loud, dense crackling.

"And *that.* What the hell is that?" Manny says.

The sound persists for a few seconds after Manny finishes speaking. Then nothing.

Primo heard the fear in Manny's voice. He tries to keep it from being audible in his own. "You've lived out of New York too long," he tells him. "You've forgotten how to sleep through noise."

They both shine their flashlights against the ceiling. The beams cross and recross. Then, at the same moment, they become still and form two circles of light on the rough wood. Neither Ken nor Felix seem to have awakened. One of them is snoring.

"At this moment, I'd like to unbuckle my seat belt," Manny says. "Just pull over here. I'm ready to get off."

"Go back to sleep. We'll find out in the morning that there's some factory near here. Or machinery, or something . . ."

"Primo, stop shitting me."

"Just go back to sleep."

Felix wakes. "What's going on?"

"This is a noisy country," Manny says.

"Who's snoring?" Felix asks. "Ken?"

"Since you've joined Primo and myself in the world of the rudely awakened, who else *could* it be?"

"Maybe that's what woke you," Felix then says.

"Wasn't that," Manny says. "It's this country. It's a very loud country."

"I know how it could get quieter," Felix says. He kicks Ken's bed. Ken makes a quiet growlish noise, smacks his lips and turns onto his side. "*Ahora, podemos dormir a piernas sueltas.*"

"What the hell does *that* mean?" Manny asks.

"It means now we can all sleep like lopped-off legs," Primo tells him.

"Delightful," Manny says.

"What's delightful?" Ken, now awake, asks.

"*Buenas noches,*" Felix says.

"*Buenas noches,*" Manny says.

They are driving back to the U.P. Fonseca. This morning they are to meet with Jilguero Santos, an organizer from the ATC, the *Asociación de Trabajadores de Campos.* He's currently living at the *Upay,* where he's helping with the coffee harvest. Yesterday, he was a student in the class they sat in on. Today, he will be *their* teacher. He will show them how the coffee is picked, and explain to them the role of labor in the revolution.

Angelita, standing in front, spends the short drive talking to them. "The campesinos were treated like farm animals before the Triumph. What the Somozistas did not realize was that their strong shoulders and backs would form the foundation of the *frente.* And still do. And in the years since, they have also become an integral part of its mind."

Manny, sitting with Maryellen in front of Primo, turns and tells him, "She's certainly in an ideological mood this morning. Wouldn't you say?"

They are passing an old campesino home Primo remembers from yesterday afternoon. The large patches of green mold on its dark gray walls look like islands on a dry, concrete sea. Its roof is made of unevenly laid sheets of red, corrugated tile. Yesterday, it appeared empty. This morning, four soldiers are standing out front. Through its glassless window, the size of two missing cinder blocks, Primo can see that inside there are more.

"Definitely *pre*-miniskirt," Manny says to Maryellen, pointing to it. "That mold is much older than the revolution."

That morning, at breakfast, Manny had asked her if she'd heard anything during the night. She hadn't. "But Grace talks in her sleep," she said.

"The older Grace?" Manny asked her.

"Yes. The poor thing seemed scared to death of something. She cried out twice. I woke her, both times, but she couldn't remember what it was." Then she asked, "What do you think it was? The noise you heard?" She looked at Manny and Primo, as if they knew the answer.

"I don't know. Maybe it was Ken," Manny said. "After two days of rice and beans . . ."

Another group of soldiers wave down the bus at the entrance of the dirt road that winds up the hillside to the *Upay*. They walk over to Horacio's window and talk to him.

Maryellen asks Primo and Manny if they think Grace's nightmares could have been caused by the stories told by the *madres.*

Primo is watching Angelita, who is now leaning over Horacio in order to speak to the soldiers standing outside the bus.

"Anything's possible," Manny says.

"My first thought was that they were. Then I thought, Those stories are the kind of nightmares we have only when we're awake. I think the dreams she was having came from somewhere deep inside of her." Then she points to a *cachorro,* wearing jungle camouflage, standing alone, farther in from the side of the road, leaning against his AK and staring blankly at the passengers aboard the bus. "My God," she says. "He's a child."

Horacio shifts into first gear and the bus begins to struggle up the hillside.

Angelita, still standing, faces the back of the bus and announces, with more than her usual formality, that their plans have been changed. There had been action on the *Upay* last night. "Nothing serious," she adds.

All eyes are on her. Maryellen lets out a loud sigh.

"Tell us what happened," Grace from California asks.

"We demand to know what happened," Allen says.

"We're just going up to the area we were in yesterday. I'll find out. We'll turn the bus around, and head back to Managua. I assure you, there is nothing to worry about."

Manny turns, leans over the back of his chair and says, into Primo's ear, "So much for your factory theory."

"What?" Maryellen asks.

A row of soldiers now fill the benches in front of the *Upay*'s main building. Everything appears the same, but the air is entirely different from the air they'd breathed yesterday afternoon.

"What?" Maryellen asks. She directs the question to Primo this time.

Before he can answer, Angelita is speaking again. She tells them they can get off the bus if they want to, but will have to remain in the small central area between this building and the building they were in yesterday.

"All I was saying," Manny tells Maryellen, "is that whatever happened here is probably what we heard." Then he stands and says, "Let's go."

"I think I'll wait on the bus," she says. "We'll be leaving in a minutes."

Primo stands and follows Manny to the front of the bus. When he steps down onto the dusty soil he notices Maryellen is behind him.

Primo walks over to the building where the class was held yesterday. Ilena, one of the teachers of yesterday's class, is sitting in the chair against the empty part of the wall. He asks her what happened during the night.

She lifts her arms, and looks at him angrily. "They fired a single round at us. From a *mortero*. This they do often. Then, as always, the soldiers fire back at them. We get out of our beds after it's already over. We get back into them. And we lie there, with our eyes open, waiting for the sun."

She says no more than this. After she falls silent the anger remains on her face.

Manny and Maryellen are standing right behind him, and had been when Ilena had spoken.

"That explains it," Manny said.

"All that explains is the noise," Primo says.

He walks back toward the bus, but stops when he sees that most of the other delegation members have gotten off and are standing in a crowd in front of the main building.

He's now standing in front of the section of wall where yesterday the children had sat, eating their oranges, getting their pictures taken. The campesinos with their rifles and their coffee beans stare dumbly back at him from the mural. They're too simply painted. They might as well be cows, he thinks. They're too incomplete, these people on the wall, not real enough and too stupid for anyone to give a shit if they get blown to pieces by a mortar round.

Beside the spot where he is standing, there's a hole in the ground, about the width of two graves combined, but not as deep and narrower at the bottom. He doesn't remember it being there yesterday.

Manny and Maryellen are now standing at the other side of the hole. There's a curved bit of shiny metal and some small pieces of black rubber lying near the bottom.

"The whole place feels creepy," Maryellen says.

A heavyset man walks out of the main building, and approaches them. Primo remembers him as one of the students in class yesterday. He's wearing a cap with a red, white and blue patch on its peak that says, in English: *I'M PROUD TO BE A FARMER.*

"I'm sorry you will not get your tour today," he says to Primo. He extends his hand.

"Me too."

He's Jilguero Santos, the organizer who was to teach them about harvesting coffee. "I think you would have found it interesting."

"We sure would have," Manny says.

"*This*"—he points to the hole beside which they are standing—"is a shame."

Primo suddenly realizes this is where the mortar round hit.

"This year, we didn't think they'd have the nerve to come this far south. . . . *Los carajos* . . ." He spits into the hole.

"There was a motorbike here," Manny says.

"That is what they hit."

"Holy shit," Manny says. "I was *sitting* on it."

Jilguero smiles at him. "Not when they hit it you weren't."

"And there were children," Primo says. He points to the wall.

"My God," Maryellen says. "There were children here."

"No one was hurt," Jilguero says.

Angelita now comes over to join them. "Maybe we can come back next week," she says.

"It is a shame this happened," Jilguero says.

"Thank God no one was hurt," Maryellen says.

"I was sitting on that fucking motorbike," Manny says.

"We've heard the yanqui have given them new laser aiming devices," Jilguero says. He points down into the hole. "But I still don't believe they actually aimed at it. They can't hit the roof of a house when they're near enough to throw stones at it."

"You're telling us they hit it by accident?" Primo asks.

"That's usually how it happens. They will fire a single round. Maybe two. Enough to cause fear and to disrupt whatever is happening. Then everyone on duty will empty their clip into the hillside it came from. When anyone hits anything, it's usually by accident. Last week, near Jinotega, they hit one of their own trucks."

"But the problem with these accidents," Angelita says—she seems angry at Jilguero, angry at everyone—"is that they can be deadly. And they often are."

"What will happen," Jilguero says, smiling again, "is that they will learn that a motorbike was blown up. Then they will announce over the *contra* radio that they aimed at it. They will tell all the farm workers to beware, because Ronald Reagan has given them a new aiming device, with which they can hit a motorbike." He spits again.

Manny gets down on one knee and looks at the pieces of shiny metal and black rubber. He then reaches into the small crater, pulls out a piece of bolt with a nut attached and hands it to Jilguero.

"Many of the parts were still usable," Jilguero tells him. "We have another, in the building where we keep the coffee beans. It has been broken more than a year. We will take the parts remaining from this one and combine it with that one."

Manny stands up. Jilguero puts his hand on his shoulder.

"Yesterday we had one working motorbike, and tomorrow we will have one working motorbike. The only difference is today." He laughs. "Today we don't have one. Today, what we have is this hole in the ground."

AL FIN CAYÓ EL PEZ

22

None of the four walls of Angelita's small bedroom are the same size. And because they curve outward as they rise from the floor, Primo felt, when he first entered earlier, that he was walking into a white bucket from a hole in its side. She told him that instead of rejoining the walls, after the earthquake, they just filled in the spaces with mortar and made them thicker. She told him she liked the room because it was designed by nature as much as by people.

"It's shaped like Iowa," Primo told her.

"I don't know that shape," she said.

"Actually it's not," he said, surveying the room. "It's much less proportionate. . . . Funny," he said. He spun himself around. "I feel like a saxophone in a violin case."

"It's just a room," she said. "Besides, a saxophone would not fit in a violin case."

"You're absolutely right. What it has is such a nonconstructed feel. It's like a chamber inside a living body. *That's* what it's like."

"*Biomórfico*," Angelita said.

"That's it. Like the cavity meant to contain a huge heart, or maybe a liver. Not two whole bodies such as ours."

Angelita looked at him. Seriously, at first. She then smiled and said, "Heart is better."

"I don't like liver either," he said. "Even with onions."

"Neither hearts nor livers have *those*," she said, pointing to the two windows, set widely apart, on the longest wall. "I relax by looking out of them." She held her hands to her face in the shape of eyeglasses, the two lenses unusually far apart. She laughed.

The bottom half of one window was filled with the top of a willowlike bush, growing against the house's side, and above that, at a distance, the upper branches of a cypress, spreading and long, like the lines in the palm of a hand. Through the web of thinning branches he could see the milky, dark blue dome of late-evening sky. The other window looked over the rounded top of an old, moss-covered stone wall that encloses the small courtyard they passed through earlier, on their way into the house, where there is a stone lavabo and a clothesline on which two pairs of white socks are hanging along with the same blue T-shirt, with its faded gray lettering, that Angelita had worn fifteen days ago, on the afternoon she met them at the airport.

There are two posters on the long stretch of wall between the windows, both the same size, hung at the same height and spaced evenly between. The impression is of there being four windows.

One of the posters is for a Spanish-language production of Chekhov's *The Cherry Orchard. El Cerezal.* The other is of one of the muraled walls of the church of Santa María de los Ángeles, where they attended a Mass earlier that evening. On it, a peasant Christ, nailed to the cross, is borne on the shoulders of campesinos and guerrillas, all of whose faces express the same steady weariness. They've been carrying him for a long time, and aren't yet near the place where they'll set him down.

Two hours ago, when the delegation members were boarding the bus to return to the Hotelito, Angelita placed her hand lightly against Primo's back and asked him if he'd prefer to walk. The small house she shares with two other women, both teachers and both, at the moment, in different parts of the country, is in the Riguero Barrio, a short walk from the church.

They are now lying on Angelita's bed. When they first came into the room the view, out the windows, was still clearly visible. She told him she never looks at the posters when there is daylight, or even when there is moonlight. They're only to be looked at by synthetic light.

Beside the lamp on the night table, there's a photograph of a young teenage girl, sitting on a park bench. "I can look at that"—she points to the photo—"any time of day."

Two weeks have passed since their trip to the north. A time so densely packed with new experience it took a lifetime to elapse, yet passed too quickly to measure its passing. Time has bent the way the walls of this room have. The moment he arrived here has already fixed itself in memory as the starting point of something that will complete itself long into a future he cannot, yet, fathom.

Earlier, when Angelita unbuttoned his shirt, she rubbed the palm of her hand across his chest and said, "*Pezones indios.*"

"What?"

She crossed her arms and lifted her own shirt above her head, then lifted the white cups of her brassiere and showed him her beautiful dark nipples. "See?"

Angelita is holding up in front of them, at eye level, the condom she has just slipped off Primo's penis. She studies the soft, wrinkled, lopsided, bottom-heavy cone. "It now has the shape of an old goat's beard. Or a tor-*nah*-do"—she looks at him to make sure she's said it correctly—"that has tried to lift off the ground something much too heavy, but is stupid and greedy and won't let go of it, so it just remains there, stuck, hanging still in the sky." She sets it on the floor beside the bed. "I have more," she says.

"We pronounce it tor-*nay*-do," Primo tells her.

She smiles at the space she'd held the condom in, lifts an eyebrow in a way that reminds him of Mr. Spock, lies back, her head against his arm and shoulder, and looks up at the ceiling. "Do you always have safe sex with your two women friends in New York?"

They had discussed their personal lives earlier, on the walk from the church and after they got here. Angelita, like Primo, had gotten married at twenty-one. She and her husband had a child, a daughter, soon after. In 1979 her husband fell in battle, in Estelí.

"I can't bear having a picture of him. It's been nearly ten years, but he's still with me, inside, when I need him to be. Too many walls in this country have pictures of the dead hanging on them. More than do not . . ." That was when she'd told him about her windows and posters. "Part of being free is choosing what I look at. And when."

She has another man in her life now. A compañero, not a husband. He had studied in the United States and speaks English fluently. He helped her to speak as well as she does. He's also a teacher and, at the moment, is living and working in Kukra Hill, a town near the Atlantic coast, north of Bluefields, where almost everyone is Creole or Indian and very poor. They mostly speak English there. "But not English like North Americans, they are *caribe.*"

"Do you really want an answer?" Primo asks her.

"Yes. I am concerned. I hope you always have safe sex." She thinks a second, then says, "*¿Impetuosidad . . . ?*"

Primo nods yes, leaning his head against hers so she can feel it.

"*Impetuosidad* can be dangerous."

"I don't want you worrying about me."

She laughs and then grows calm. "Do you like the works of Anton Chekhov?"

"I haven't read him since college. But yes."

"I love his drama." She points to the poster. "And I love his stories more." She's quiet for a moment; then she says, "Maybe I will worry about you . . ."

"Don't," he says. "I have safe sex."

"Are you being humorous?" She lifts her eyes and looks at him. "You know that's not what I'm talking about."

"You don't have to worry about me." He turns partially onto his side, sets his chin on top of her head and with his right arm, his free arm, strokes her hair. He smooths it, slowly, against her cheek and shoulder.

"Have you ever read the Chekhov story, 'La Dama con el Perrito'?"

"I may have. In college."

"You remember how the man and the woman met? They were on vacation and he saw her walking her dog?"

Primo starts to nod, then to speak, when she says, "Your memory isn't sure, but your chin has told the top of my head yes. And you remember how the man thought, after they had their *amorío breve*, that he would go back into his life and he wouldn't think of her again."

" 'The Lady with the Dog.' I do remember. Yes, he thought he'd never give it another thought. Like his other affairs. But after he went home, he couldn't stop thinking about her."

"*Affair*. I don't like that word. It sounds like business."

"If I remember correctly, she didn't expect she'd think about *him* either."

"Where in the story does it say that?"

"I don't think it does."

"So how could you know? The story is written by a man and, *principalmente*, about a man. Am I right?"

"You are."

"It never says what *she* expected to happen. So I'll tell you. She knew from the moment they made love. Do you remember, after? She was weeping, *he* was eating his watermelon . . . ? *Cabeza de cascarón* . . . *Tonto* . . . His skin was thick like that melon. . . . But she knew, from that moment, he would never be out of her thoughts."

"And did she know it would be the same for him?"

"I feel from your chin, which is more honest than *you* are, that you're smiling."

He's still stroking her hair, combing it into small tresses between his fingers. It occurs to him that her body, against his, is very still. And his, in response, is also very still. "You didn't answer my question," he tells her.

"Maybe. Or maybe not. I would have to give it some thought. But she knew *this*. That the man she had just made love to was stupider . . . You could say it this way, stupid-*er?*"

"Why not," Primo says.

"He was stupider than he ever could have imagined. He barely had an idea of what his life was really about."

"The thing is, however, you don't have a dog, and I don't have a wife and children and a job at a bank."

"Did anyone say I was talking about you? I was just making a comparison. Besides, neither of us has enough money to gain entry to that story. I was just trying, in some way, to answer your question about worrying."

"You don't have to worry about me."

"I don't have to do anything I don't want to do. And that applies to not *not* doing things I might want to do . . . I don't think I said that last thing clearly."

"What you're saying is that I don't have to worry about you worrying about me."

"What I'm saying is that you are frivolous and stupid and don't take things seriously enough. And yes, that too." She lifts her head, then leans it onto his chest. She slides her hand onto his belly. "I have more important things to do than worry about you."

He'd never noticed the door. Wood, big, dark. Thick and wavy-grained like smoke, but thicker, like water, and a glass doorknob. Just inside the front door, on the wall, on the wall of the narrow hallway that leads into the waiting room. How come he never noticed it? Because it was never there, that's *why. He doesn't want to go through it. It wasn't there and maybe what's inside wasn't there either. Maybe the inside is different now. He doesn't even want to be there standing in front of it. So he's not.*

He's walking down the block. There's the wooden front porch that sags on the side and the grouchy lady—that's what his mother calls her—sitting on a chair on it. But did his mother know the grouchy lady's round wrinkles, her hard circle-wrinkles, were around her own father's mouth, too? There's her big dog with no tail that she lets bark at him but she keeps the loop handle of the leash under the leg of her chair. She's Our Lady of Lords. *She's* Nostra Signora . . . *When she speaks it's in a harsh accent, it's like bricks. It's like she's still talking to someone in the place she came from. There must be a lot of smoke—just look at her—and it's really thick, and there's gray walls close together, where people aren't scared, but they're very unhappy, and don't even want to* be *happy. Everyone from there has legs like hers that are closer together at the bottom than at the middle and it's very hard for them to walk.*

Now she's not watching him. She's facing farther up the block, where the bus stop is, but he knows she has radar or something. She's aware of just where he is. Each step he takes, passing her on the porch.

She'd better paint the side of her house soon or those boards will fall off. If she ever let the dog go he wouldn't be afraid of it. That's what she doesn't know. He'd yell at it and he'd even kick it. He knows what she always thinks, sitting there, looking the other way, or at him sometimes. That he'd be afraid. The white boards have dark lines on them and they're going to fall soon. There are people on the floor inside. Next to each other. A father and a son. They're tied up, they're lying next to each other on the floor.

He isn't on the street again, he's on his way farther inside again, and he doesn't want to open that door. Why? Just because now *it's there? What if he just walks past it, but then would he have to be outside again?*

If you wrap all the string from a box that anything came in and if you do it slowly and carefully so each loop is the same size, you know you can use it again. You own things you like. You can keep the string where you keep them. *Why not? It's yours.*

No, he's not going in that way. Grandma has a glass doorknob but that's there. *There's the old way, too. It passes all the patients. Waiting against the two walls, in the chairs, with their feet on the floor. That's how it is in that part of the house. Not the part he lives in. He can walk through that way, Hello everybody, that's the way, and he doesn't have to go in any other way if he doesn't want to. But is somebody tied up in there? No, not there. Somewhere else.*

You get off the bus, and you walk up the block, and you climb all those steps to the door, and you go in, but then you still *have to go in?*

Of course they're all different. That's the outsides. There's wood, like the grouchy lady's, and bricks.

When you get inside there's also the pictures. One had all *the grouchy ladies in it. The fancy one. Now* he's *in it with his sideburns, Mariah too. You can laugh at his sideburns. She took* them *out and she put him in it. Then she was making the bed. She was unhappy and she really didn't like it, making the bed. He didn't either.*

Whoever put this door here can take it away. Don't say you can't make it not *be here . . .*

"Your eyes were open, these last few moments, but you weren't awake. Did you know it?"

Angelita's brown hair, closer to him than her face . . .

"And your feet moved. Like you were walking."

"What?"

"Are you awake?"

"Yes."

"Your feet moved."

He squints, looks toward her.

She touches his cheek, softly, with her curved knuckle. "And your eyes were opened a little, but you were still asleep."

He reaches for her hand, forms the thumb and forefinger into a circle, holds it over his eye, looks at her through it and smiles stupidly. He then turns his head, moving her hand with it, and looks out the window through the lens of her fingers, like she did earlier.

"Does my hand help you see better?"

The sky above the black cypress branches is a light, solid blue. "What time is it?" he asks.

"Time to get up."

Primo touches her hair. She leans her head against his hand. Then, sleepily, into the curve of his arm.

"Like when a dog has a dream," she tells him. "You know? They move their legs. They walk in their dreams."

He kisses her head. Her hair is warm and damp. He doesn't want to move. He doesn't want to sit up, turn, set his feet on the floor. He doesn't want to reoccupy his arms and legs.

"Sometimes they cry and move their noses like they're smelling things. And they walk. That's how I woke up. You were walking against my leg. Do you remember your dream?"

"Nope. Dogs can't remember their dreams. In fact, they can't remember half the shit that happens to them when they're awake."

"Well then. If you walk in your dreams, and if you can't remember them . . . I would guess that means you *are* a dog." She laughs and rubs her hand along his cheek. "*Vos tenés bigotes.*"

"*¿Cómo?*"

She rubs his cheek again. "You *do* have whiskers." She's still laughing. "And you know what I am then? I am the Lady with the Dog."

Primo is staring at the poster of the peasant Christ. He is looking at each face.

"You should be looking out the window," Angelita tells him. "It's daytime."

Many of the people bearing the cross, and Christ himself, look alike, as if they were members of the same family. "I'll look at whatever I want to. I'll look at the poster, I'll look at the wall. I'll look at you."

"Not for too long. We have to get up."

"And what is on today's agenda?"

"We're visiting a children's hospital. The director, a doctor, is also a poet. He's a great man. You will like him."

"How come?"

"He is funny, like you."

"I'm funny?"

"The way you say things. The way you look at me through my fingers, or tell me you feel like a saxophone."

"Let's just hang out in bed today. We'll listen to the radio, or look out the window, or snooze . . . When we aren't otherwise occupied."

"*Snooze?*"

"*Dormir* . . . *Sueño ligero* . . . Blow some Z's . . . Catch forty winks . . . Nod out . . . Hibernate . . . Get stupid."

"*¿Vos querés hacer siesta?*"

"Among other things."

"See? You are funny."

"*Yo soy un barril de risas.*"

"You are a barrel of laughter?"

"Close enough."

"We cannot *hibernate*, as you say, because we have responsibilities. What about the rest of your group?"

"Group? I came here alone. *You* said that."

"I have read that the North American male is a rugged individualist."

"I'm not the only barrel of laughter in this bed."

Primo, standing, leans onto the cool stone windowsill, and looks over the courtyard wall into an open doorway across the street. A scrawny, tiger-striped cat, half its body inside the bar of shade where the door edge cuts the morning sun, licks itself slowly.

"I'd rather be teaching than being a tour guide and translator for your delegation. . . ." Angelita's voice comes from the other room. "But it is a responsibility. *My* responsibility."

Primo doesn't answer. The cat rolls onto its back and pushes itself farther into the light. Primo makes a harsh meow sound, which it ignores.

"What?" Angelita asks.

"Nothing." The cat arches over its chest and begins licking its stomach. Primo makes another meow sound and then a *psssssssst . . . psssssssst.*

"You speak *cat* worse than you speak Spanish," Angelita, now standing behind him, says.

He turns from the window. She is now fully dressed. He's wearing only his undershorts. "How many dogs you know that can speak *cat* at all?"

"But what I said to you before, from the other room, I said in English. Did you hear me?"

"I did. And I know it's your responsibility."

"Responsibility is a boring thing in your country. A thing not desired."

"That's probably true." He walks to the chair beside the bed where he left his clothes the night before. He begins pulling on his pants.

"It is not responsibility that is the issue, but what you are responsible to. That's one of the main reasons North Americans come here. To observe people who are responsible because they want to be. There are only three reasons North Americans come here and that is one of them.

"What are the other two?"

"Their romance with revolution and violence. And to see peasants so primitive they have never had electricity in their home, or glass windows, and who cannot distinguish the letters of the alphabet from the footprints of chickens. I think they enjoy their own lives more after that."

"You said *their* lives, but you mean me, too."

"I mean you, too."

Primo, now dressed, walks up to her, sets his hands on her shoulders. "Let's enjoy *our* lives a moment longer."

"I am thinking in words. Out loud. And I am not finished yet. You must learn to listen better."

"I thought this was a bedroom, not a classroom."

"Everywhere is a classroom. Even dreams are classrooms . . ."

"I've already forgotten my walking dream. I guess that means I forgot what it taught me."

"*Escúchame. Y cállate.*"

"*A tus órdenes.* My lips are sealed."

"Last year, during coffee harvest, I brought a delegation of writers to the north. We visited the same classroom your delegation visited. They could not keep their mouths closed. They suddenly wanted to be the teachers, too. The next week, one of the students there—an old woman, she was learning for the first time to read and write—wrote in her *cuaderno* that the night after their visit, in her sleep, she visited the dream of one of the North Americans. In the dream there were not beans on the coffee plants, there were light bulbs."

Primo sits down again on the bed. Then he says, "You're not exactly a teacher. . . . You're something else."

"I'm sorry if I am going on. We have been intimate and I want you to know who you have been intimate with."

"Being here, being with you, I feel like I'm putting handfuls of things into my pockets without looking at them. Some of them are things you hand to me. Later, I'll take them out, one by one, and see what the hell I've been carrying around."

Angelita laughs. She walks up to Primo, shoves one hand in each of his pants pockets. "I like what you say sometimes. When I know you have been listening." With the tips of her fingers, she presses the cloth of his pockets against his penis, which responds. "These pockets are pretty full."

"That's what I was saying."

"You are very responsive."

"I'm a good listener. . . . How much time we got?"

"We are late already."

He presses his lips against her forehead. "You can't expect a dog to be too responsible."

Three times, on their walk back, they pass a house Primo thinks is the house in front of which he met Julio during the blackout. Each has three cinder-block steps leading to its closed front door; each, set in midblock, is surrounded by more ruined, less restored homes. Each time he projects the image of the darkened housefront he holds in memory against the new similar one they pass, it fits the shape better. He realizes, after the third, that he will never know that home, even if they do pass it. He had first encountered it in darkness, with people passing in and out of it. Each of these silent houses is held breathlessly still by the weight of the hot morning sun.

He remembers watching Julio's sister lean into the car's window, and knowing, with certainty, that even if they knew he was there, walking toward them, toward the red taillights, he was not seen. Or if he was, he was not noted. At the time it frightened him. A deeper fear inside the immediate fear of being lost in the dark. But the other side of that feeling, of being simultaneously absent and present, is a good one. It's being *meant* to be there, like a tree is meant to be there.

They pass a long, winding crack in the paved street he *does* remember. No two street cracks, like the whorls of fingerprints, are exactly alike. Watching it slide under the beam of his flashlight gave him the feeling of flying over a river in an airplane. Then it suddenly broke into a dozen short, straight cracks, stopped being a river and became a rake with a snake for a handle. They also walk past the car the three young soldiers were sitting on, drinking Naranja. He remembers a spot on the fender he did not make note of then, but now remembers, where the blue paint had faded to a rusty circle that, briefly, showed a bright orange—almost like the soda they shared—in the circle of light. Without tires, it couldn't have been moved. It's the same car.

"I've walked down this street," Primo says. "On my first night in Managua."

"Wasn't it dark then? How could you remember?"

"I have a powerful memory," he says. "So powerful I can remember things I never even knew I saw."

"And do you know why?" She stops their walking by standing in front of him. Then slips her hands into his pants pockets. "*Porque tus bolsillos grandes son llenos.*"

"I feel the weight, I just don't know what I'm carrying."

"If your customs officials knew, they would not let you back into your country."

"Then I'd have to stay here."

"That's *all* I would need . . ." She takes one of her hands out of his pocket and rubs the side of it across his sweaty forehead. She smiles. "*Ya tenés mucho sudor.*"

"I'm used to seasons changing slowly. At home I'd be wearing a heavy coat and a wool scarf."

"Where did you get your scarf? Did one of your New York women make it for you?"

"They are not *my* women. But it *is* my scarf. I bought it."

"I think you would not want anyone to know it if you needed somebody."

"We were talking about how much I'm sweating."

"We still are."

"I'm suddenly thinking of my friend Manny. You remember, the one swinging the camera last week . . ."

"The one who makes the jokes."

"Him."

"Do you know what he told me? That he will model a character after me in a novel he is writing. Do you know he took the title from something Chekhov wrote? I think that's exciting."

"Every beautiful woman he meets becomes a character in that novel."

"He thinks that of me? Do you think I'm beautiful?"

"I know you are beautiful."

"Your women in New York. They are beautiful?"

"They're not *my* women."

They start walking again.

"Why did you suddenly think of your friend? We were talking about sweating."

"Sweating . . . *That's* why. I remember the first sentence of his novel. There is more coincidence in all of this than the two of you being Chekhov fans. It refers to many of the things we've been talking about. It begins during a party at the White House on the day Alaska became the forty-ninth state. It was midsummer. About as hot in Washington as it is in Managua this morning. The President and First Lady were wearing sealskin parkas in honor of their guests. They had served a cake, so big you could walk inside it, shaped like an igloo. And at that moment, the air-conditioning goes off, and the heat is turned up full blast. Spontaneous combustion seems to occur in the fireplaces. Of course, all of this is arranged by the main character. But before you know any of this, we read this first sentence: *If he lived to be a hundred, Henry O would never forget the afternoon the air quality in the White House became harder to endure than the atmosphere inside a condom.*"

"I think someone can be funny and, at the same time, be a bad writer . . ." Angelita laughs. "I am now unsure if I want to be in this novel."

"I have the honor of being his only male friend to be included. We're in it together."

They are now walking beside the park. They are a block from the Hotelito.

"I bet they were talking about us," Primo says.

"I'd rather they were talking about what they've seen here."

Walking down this last block, Primo suddenly feels he's walking down the street he lived on as a child. He actually expects, just for a moment, to see the curbs, trees, the fading wood and shingled housefronts . . . It's the strangest feeling. If you don't hang tightly on to where you are it could suddenly become somewhere else. *Is that possible?*

A month ago, on his birthday, Olivia had told him her story of falling asleep, then waking and finding everything changed, but not realizing it until later. If it happened to him, he would know. He would know the minute it happened.

"You have suddenly become serious," Angelita says. They are entering the courtyard, walking toward the door.

He feels her hand once more slip quickly into his pocket, as if to leave something there, and then slip out again.

23

Dr. Fernando Silva, the director of the Hospital Infantil in Managua, is telling the members of the delegation, via Angelita's translation, the story of a young man he knew in the early years of the *contra* war. He had once worked in the hospital. His picture hangs on the wall just inside the entrance.

"He'd run from the office, to the laboratory, to the clinic, to the pharmacy, and back to the office again. I told him he should try and learn more. He could learn to do more than these little errands for the doctors and nurses. Instead he joined the Army. He told me he wanted to defend his revolution. I told him, you're too young. What he then told me was that a man is neither young *nor* old. An adult is someone who has dignity. I could hardly believe he said that. He was sixteen. . . .

"A month later he fell in battle. I had his body sent back here, to us. And the people who knew him placed him on a gurney and they wheeled it back and forth, from the pharmacy, to the laboratory, to the clinic, to the office . . . Someone who lives a life with dignity does not die."

"This too is hard-core, real shit," Manny says, leaning toward Primo. He's been using the phrase to express his feelings about each new startling thing, each discovery or event too complex, and too sudden in its burst on his perceptions, to comprehend at the moment. He said it the first time standing beside the crater at the U.P. Fonseca where the motorbike had been blown up.

Primo lifts a finger to Manny's eye. Brings it close to touching a patch of reddened skin just above his cheekbone, but doesn't. "That'll soon be black-and-blue," he says.

"That's all I need," Manny says. "To show up at next week's faculty meeting with a shiner. Maybe I'll tell them I did battle with the *contras.*"

Maryellen, standing beside them, looks at the bruised skin and grimaces. She touches the back of her fingers to his cheek, just below it.

"I assume by your gesture that your opinion concurs with that of the doctor's son," Manny tells her.

"Your father's a doctor?" Maryellen asks Primo.

"*Was,*" Manny says, saving Primo the trouble.

Maryellen looks at Primo, smiles warmly. "Mine was a dentist."

"Primo even has a stethoscope," Manny says. "So when he prophesies a shiner, I await its certain arrival. . . . But as I was saying before, I wouldn't be completely lying if I did say I earned my wounds in battle. Albeit against my wishes, I did engage in hand-to-hand combat with a *contra* sympathizer."

This morning, when Primo and Angelita walked in, they found John and Grace from California holding Manny, each by an arm. Allen, who was screaming at him, had blood running from both nostrils over his lips and chin. He periodically slapped Manny like an interrogator in an old war movie. Maryellen, in tears, was trying to hold Allen, but she couldn't. Breakfast was over; no one else was in the *comedor*.

"If I were you I'd kill myself," Manny shouted at Allen. "Do the world a service. Rid it of the *gaping*-est asshole that ever passed wind."

Allen responded with a slap.

Primo ran up to Allen and pulled him away before he could swing at Manny again.

"Don't touch him," Manny shouted to Primo. "You'll catch asshole-itis."

Allen twisted and pulled but Primo held him.

"*Ay, Dios mío,*" Angelita said. "Did I not tell you two to save your fighting until you were back in your own country?"

Grace and John let go of Manny. "Let me tell you what he did," Grace said, walking up to Angelita.

"Tell her," Allen said.

"*Tell* her," Manny mimicked. He shoved John against the wall.

Last night, after the Mass, Manny had been standing beside Horacio when Primo and Angelita walked off on their own. The rest of the delegation, except for Allen, had already gotten on the bus. Allen, still inside the church, struck up a conversation with one of the television news crew who had arrived, two weeks earlier, on the same plane, and who had also attended Mass. Manny asked Horacio if they were waiting for Allen, and Horacio said they were. Manny then told him that Allen had already left, he'd gotten a ride with the man from the news.

Allen, unable to speak Spanish, wandered the streets for hours, unable to find transportation. He eventually found his way back to the church where, luckily, the priest, who spoke some English, still was. Allen was pale and nearly speechless with hysterical fear. The priest made a phone call and a teenager—an altar boy, the priest told him—showed up a half hour later. The boy moved quickly, just ahead of Allen, guiding him more than walking with him, in complete silence. It was after midnight when they finally arrived at the Hotelito. Allen gave the boy every cordoba he had in his pocket, which the boy accepted. He then asked Allen if he had any batteries. He knew the word in English. Allen ran inside, then quickly back out again, and handed the boy his flashlight. When he walked inside again, John and Grace, now alerted to his presence, were waiting for him. He collapsed, in tears, in their arms.

They follow the doctor up a flight of stairs and through a hall, on the walls of which are cut-out cardboard images of Mickey Mouse, Bambi, Donald Duck, Goofy, Pinocchio, Snow White, Dumbo.

"I'm glad Allen's not with us this afternoon," Manny says to Primo. "That story about the teenager who fell in battle would be his cue to remind us we're getting the hard sell."

As their days there passed, the delegation members did more and more things separately. Felix borrowed a bicycle from the brother of Mercedes, the woman who works at the Hotelito, and spent the last three days at the Biblioteca Nacional. Allen, with the help of the network news crew member he was talking to at the church, had managed to get an appointment this afternoon with Doña Violeta Chamorro, at the offices of *La Prensa*, and brought John and Grace along with him. Sarah and Theodore are attending a literacy class, taught in a shut-down factory, in the nearby city of León. They had met the teachers there last week when they visited the home of Rubén Darío. Everyone else is here today.

"The truth is," Manny says, "though I hate to admit it, Allen would be right. It *is* the hard sell. It's Allen's aesthetics that suck. No, it's more. He'd never leave the inside of his own empty fucking head and ask *why* . . . I'm surprised that man can walk upright."

They walk slowly through the halls. They pass rooms in which there are children suffering from measles, appendicitis, colds. There are wards for children with pulmonary disease and nervous disorders. Through Angelita, the doctor tells them this is the only hospital in Nicaragua exclusively for children. It had been an empty shell—built with earthquake relief money from the United States—that never, until after the Triumph, contained a single bed. Tacho II used to drive visiting diplomats past it, to show them how he was using their financial assistance, but no one ever asked to go inside. The money meant for beds and equipment went instead into the pockets of the Somoza family. On *el Día de Alegría*, the day Tacho fled, he brought with him, in a caravan of cars, two coffins containing the bodies of his father and brother—he'd had them exhumed so as to always be near them—the living bodies of his wife and mistress, and every cordoba in the national treasury. "If he could have taken this empty building, and all the water in *el lago*, he'd have taken that, too."

The doctor points to a picture of Pinocchio above the door to a ward called *Unidad de Rehidratación Oral.* He smiles. Angelita, translating, smiles too.

"I wonder how anyone could think we're Communists," he says. "Could anyone with so many pictures from Disney be a red?"

"But Pinocchio isn't really American," Ken says.

Dr. Silva understands this without waiting for Angelita to translate. "This one is," he says, pointing up at the picture. "*That* Pinocchio is Disney's Pinocchio. Like most of you and like all the children here, I only know that one. Unless another one comes along, that one is the historical Pinocchio."

A woman, not in any kind of uniform, approaches the doctor, leans toward him and speaks to him quietly. They both read something on the clipboard she holds up for him. He nods, slips a pen from the breast pocket of his white doctor's smock and signs it. She then walks off in the direction she came from.

"I pass these Disney pictures every day," he says to Ken. "I dream of them at night, and I imagine they are in the dreams of the children as well. . . ." He starts to laugh. "In all, there are eleven Pinocchios on our walls. And of this I am certain: On each day that has passed, since the day Tacho left us, the noses have grown a little smaller."

Farther down the hall they pass a child, in an adult-sized wheelchair, with her legs and arms wrapped in gauze bandage. Three weeks ago, on an U.P. in the north, she'd been walking beside a cow that stepped on a land mine. The *contras* had planted it on a dirt path that ran from a cluster of miniskirt houses to the stream where they drew water. She incurred shrapnel wounds as well as third-degree burns. It took two days before the child was stable enough to be brought here.

Angelita stops translating a moment to explain what those two days meant. "Because of the embargo, the clinic on the *Upay* where she lives had nothing stronger than aspirin to dull the pain."

"There is no excuse," Grace Berenson says, suddenly furious, and now in tears. "There is no excuse," she says again, nearly shouting this time. "No explanation that could justify such suffering in a child. . . . The death of that teenager whose picture is on the wall, or the pain *this* child has been in . . ." She aims her remarks at Angelita, since it is she, translating, who mostly addresses the group. Angelita too has begun to weep.

"There is no agenda," Grace goes on, "no gain, political or

otherwise, I would accept in exchange. No one has the right. Not even God."

Dr. Silva asks Angelita what Grace has just said. He then tells Grace, in slow, broken English, that he agrees.

They proceed up another flight of stairs and stop in front of the milk bank. The doctor begins to explain how it operates, when the same woman who'd come up to him earlier, with the clipboard, returns and speaks to him. She has with her his stethoscope, which she hands him. He asks them to wait there, he'll be a few minutes, and walks off after the woman.

Maryellen reads aloud the sign on the wall.

SRA. MAMÁ:
SI UD. DESEA EXTRAERSE LA LECHE
Y NO HAY NADIE ATENDIENDO EL BANCO,
POR FAVOR LLAME A LA EXTENSIÓN 4
Y PIDA QUE LA ATIENDAN.
GRACIAS

Manny, standing beside her, his forefinger hooked in the cloth belt of her sundress, attempts to translate.

"*Extra-er-say?*" he asks her.

"Extract."

"Ah. Mrs. *Mamá:* If you want to extract milk and there's no . . . *hay?* Like, hey you? . . . Like cows eat?"

"Pronounce it *ay,*" Maryellen tells him. "And it means, like, there is, or are, or, in this case, there *isn't.*"

That morning, after they broke up the fight between Manny and Allen, Primo and Angelita sat at the table in the *comedor* and had coffee.

"They fight as if their opinions were actions," she said. "As if simply *feeling* them, thinking them, even expressing them, affected the outcome of events."

"Is that something like what democracy is supposed to be about?" Primo asked her.

"No, that is what watching baseball is about."

Primo had not realized, until she said this, that she was crying.

"They think they're on the floor of your Congress, or like gods up in Olympus, whose arguments become rain that falls onto us and becomes wars. The truth is, they are as much outside the control of our destiny as we are. Even more. . . . And when one side emerges victorious, or appears to, their team has won. And just by having an opinion, one way or the other, they are certain they have contributed to victory. Isn't that baseball . . . ?"

She slammed the side of her fist against the table. Primo put his arms around her, tried to pull her nearer, but she held herself stiffly apart, in her chair, and in her separateness.

"I'd like to kill them both," she said. "Better, I'd like to take away their ability to read. The money with which they travel. The freely spent time in which they *form* their opinions. You know what they then would be? Peasants. No, worse. They would be dogs. . . . I can't believe they are teachers."

She pushed Primo's arms away. She looked at him. "I don't care about opinions. I see *less* death, I see people learning to read, I see their lives improving to the point where dreams start—they actually believe life can be something other than a relentless struggle: *That* is good. And *that* is it. The beginning and end of my opinion. It doesn't involve ideology. It only involves what I can see.

"And you know what?" She looked at Primo to make sure he didn't think this a question to be answered. Not even with the shake of his head. "Maybe, sooner or later, all governments go bad. That's not an opinion, that's history. And maybe when a government has to defend its existence from outside enemies, that speeds up the process. Do *you* have an opinion on this?"

Primo was silent. He didn't know how to address her. He needed her to let him hold her. His heart was breaking.

He moved his chair up against hers. She leaned against him but did not relax her torso. He laid his head onto her shoulder.

"So much pain," she said. "More than can be spoken of. It began in the darkness before living memory. Nothing human can feel more permanent than that. Yet it has begun to stop. It *is* stopping. And perhaps for a while longer, will continue stopping. It isn't a government that is doing this, it is us. And when *your* government, one that has even less effect in the lives of the people it governs, at least less *good* effect . . . When that government destroys us—maybe tomorrow, maybe five years from now—one of your two friends will think he has won something.

"This is the last time I will do this," she said. She looked down at his hand which he had laid on top of hers. "I'm a teacher, Primo. I'm not a tour guide."

Angelita, now standing next to Primo, corrects Manny's translation of the sign. "Please call extension four and ask for assistance."

"Thank you," Manny says.

"You're welcome," Angelita says.

"No," Manny says. "Thank you—*gracias.* It's the last word on the sign."

"You are right," Angelita tells him. "You have had the last word."

"When my kids were young, I used a breast pump at home," Maryellen says.

"The issue," Angelita says, "isn't so much the pump, it's the refrigerator."

"I never liked warm milk," Manny says. Then, to Primo, he says, "Even this is hard-core. It's not just the big, obvious stuff. Know what I'm saying?"

The doctor returns. He smiles at Grace Berenson, then tells them he had heard there was a translator of poetry in the delegation.

Felix introduces himself. He tells the doctor he is currently attempting to translate Rubén Darío.

"I'm told that in the history of poetry, he's the hardest to translate," Dr. Silva tells him. "He is also the hardest poet to come after. He is so great that we poets who came after have to carry him around on our backs. And he's very heavy."

Everyone laughs at this.

Felix tells the doctor that he's originally from Spain and that Darío's influence had been great there, too.

"Ah, *Don Félix*," the doctor says, smiling. He then asks if he would help the delegation understand him if he were to read a poem.

"*A sus órdenes*," Felix says.

"*Gracias*," Dr. Silva answers. "Since you are all teachers, I thought I'd read a poem in which I, too, am a teacher." He takes a book out of the side pocket of his smock and shows them the front. *La Salud del Niño*. He nods to Felix, who takes over translating at this point.

Angelita stands beside Primo as they listen.

"*The Health of the Child*," Felix says.

"The title in this poem, like many medical terms, is the same in English: '*La Diarrea*.'" He holds the book open with one hand and, smiling, gestures emphatically with the other. "I think I can say, with certainty, that you have never heard a poem with such a title."

He slips on a pair of glasses, then proceeds to read a long, unusual, frightening, instructive and even funny poem, addressed to parents, about how to prevent diarrhea or find treatment for a young child suffering from it. The poem advises mothers to keep the child on the breast as long as possible. This way they will know for certain what goes into the child's body. Every so often he stops and allows Felix to render the last portion he read into English.

> ". . . *Only you can open your blouse and give*
> *the little prick just what he wants.*
> *Nothing delights him more*
> *than to be stuck there like glue* . . ."

Angelita laughs and pokes Primo.

"You are a wonderful translator," she then tells Felix.

He reads on. Felix, standing beside the doctor, looking at the book over his shoulder, continues translating. The poem instructs parents on what to do if the mother has no more milk and they cannot get to a milk bank. It tells them how important it is to act as soon as the symptoms of diarrhea appear. The effects of dehydration are devastating.

"And if he's so thirsty his little
open mouth is dry and anxious,
and he can hardly drink
the water you give him,
and he cannot pee, and his diaper
is dry,
and when he cries, screams like a kitten,
he cannot shed tears, and his eyes, tenacious
and rigid, have withdrawn into their sockets,
and the crown of his head
has fallen inward and softened . . ."

In poetry, he tells the parents of children there is always something they can do. And he tells them what it is. In the last part of the poem he tells them that he has only discussed the immediate cause of diarrhea. Not the injustice that creates the living conditions upon which these causes depend.

None of them had ever heard a poem on such a subject, nor one that instructs and, at the same time, is still lyrical, is still, finally, a poem.

Felix is in tears. "Imagine," he says. "Finding beauty even there."

Primo is beginning to get angry. It is the first response to his sudden realization that tomorrow, at this time, he will be aboard a plane flying toward New York. It isn't the restless anger he'd felt the day he arrived, it's a sad, unmoving anger made up largely of the weight of feeling he has carried with him since he and Angelita sat together in the *comedor* this morning. It is the first step on his trip home.

Manny is telling Maryellen and Angelita that if Allen had come with them today their fight would have certainly worsened.

Their fighting implies that they are each part of something larger than their own life, and that they can speak with conviction about this thing they are a part of. *But that's bullshit.* They cannot, they are not. They are no more connected to anything than *he* is. Any life lived from such a distance is absolute bullshit. It's only something *like* life.

"It's all bullshit," Primo says very loudly. "All of it."

Manny stops talking. "Pardon me?" he asks him.

"You and Allen. . . . The both of you are full of shit."

Angelita takes Primo's hand, leads him through the hall, down the steps and out into the afternoon air. She pushes him against the wall, looks at him, enters his arms.

"Did you see that guy's stethoscope?" Primo tells her.

"I didn't notice."

"I think it had a piece of Scotch tape holding one of the tubes together. You didn't see that?"

"I didn't."

"Can you believe it?" There are tears in his eyes. "When I get home I'm going to send him mine. It's much better. A million times better."

"*No puedo leer tu mente,*" Angelita says.

"What the fuck are you saying?"

"I cannot read your mind."

Primo starts to laugh. He sets his chin on Angelita's shoulder.

"*Pero yo puedo entender tus pensamientos,*" she says. "And I think you have begun to understand what is baseball."

24

Mercedes walks into the *comedor* and sets in front of Primo a small package, an overstuffed manila envelope, torn and taped in several places and bound with crisscrossing twine. Luisa, following her into the room, sets a tray crammed with bottles of Naranja, Coca and Victoria beer on the table beside it. She then leans toward Felix, sitting across from Primo, and whispers something into his ear. Mercedes also leans toward Felix and kisses him on the cheek. There are tears in her eyes. Before walking back into the kitchen, she points at the package and tells Primo that it had arrived this afternoon while they were out.

"Don't I get anything?" Manny says. He presses the palms of his hands onto the packet. "It's a pillow. You know, the small ones they give you on airplanes. Primo orders his own, custom-made." He tells this to Maryellen, Angelita, Felix, Grace Berenson, Ken and Primo, who are clustered at the same end of the long table. "Wherever he is in the world, he has it sent to him the day before he flies anywhere."

There's a note written in pencil on the outside of the envelope. *Profesor Primo Thomas: Esperamos que Usted podría llevar estas cartas a nuestra hermana Carolina. Mil gracias y* farewell, *Marta Benavidez.*

"It's correspondence," Primo says. "I'm back in the *cartero* business."

"It's five years' worth of letters," Manny says. "Or an autobiography."

"Look," Maryellen says. "She used *farewell* in English."

"That's like me saying *adiós*," Ken says, "which I often do, though I don't speak Spanish."

"This brings up something remarkable Dr. Silva said to me before," Felix says, "when I was telling him about the trouble I was having translating Darío. He said the English and the Spanish spoken in the Americas have much more in common with each other than with their European mother tongues. He said understanding this would make it easier."

"Fascinating," Manny says. "Illuminating. But what the hell does it mean?"

"He said they're both mestizo-mulatto languages, and that they're the same age, which, as languages go, is very young."

"This is very interesting," Angelita says.

"Darío liked geography. He would say something like, *Our young rivers, fed by fresher tributaries, flow more swiftly.*"

"*That* is so cool," Ken says.

"Beautiful," Grace Berenson says.

"Maybe I'm better at imitating Darío than translating him."

"It's a great name for a rock group," Manny says. "Young Languages."

"I like Fresher Tributaries," Ken says.

"This *is* very interesting," Angelita says again. "And true."

"I suddenly like the language I've been speaking all my life," Manny says. "That doctor's the *coolest* dude in the hemisphere."

"He's a teacher," Angelita says.

Primo feels something on top of his foot. He looks under the table and sees a bare toe rubbing the toe of his sneaker. It belongs to Maryellen, sitting next to Felix and across from Manny. When she sees him look down she brings her hand to her mouth, embarrassed and smiling. "A little to the right," Primo says to her, indicating where she'll find Manny's foot.

In their room, before dinner, Manny had told him that he could now say with certainty what Lisa, Maryellen's twin, looks and feels like, "ten years since I last laid eyes on her sans the obfuscating factor of clothing."

"Should I congratulate you?"

"This is serious business, Primo. Though you may not think so. They have the same face, and identical curves . . . I mean *identical*, like a key made from another key. They even have the same smooth skin. But they're *more* different than any two strangers I've ever met."

"I'm sorry if you thought I wasn't taking you seriously," Primo said. "I'm just not sure how to fulfill the requirements of my half of this conversation. Are you telling me you've learned something?"

"I'm not talking some shit about objectifying women. Or learning a lesson. I'm neither as fucked up nor as good as that. I'm talking magic here. I'm talking about the profound difference between two separate—*any* two—human beings. I'm saying you cannot comprehend it fully until you've been close, I mean *close*, with identical twins."

Mercedes walks in again with a large serving bowl of black beans and another of rice. Before leaving the room she leans toward Felix, as she did earlier, and again speaks to him quietly.

"What's with you guys?" Manny asks.

"We're just saying our goodbyes. You know I've been using her brother's bicycle. We got to know each other."

"He also gave them nearly everything he traveled here with," Angelita tells them. "Umbrella, flashlight, shampoo, clothing, and that knife with many blades . . . Mercedes and Luisa showed me."

"It's called a Swiss Army knife," Felix says.

"And I think you gave them some money, too."

"Just *rent*," Felix says. "For Verónico's bike." He seems angry that Angelita is giving this inventory.

"I am sorry," she says to him.

"Maybe we all should leave behind the stuff we really don't need," Felix says. "It's like poking a little hole in the embargo."

"I don't want to poke a hole in it," Grace Berenson says. "I'd like to blow the damned thing up." She then says, to Angelita, "I can't stop thinking of that poor child."

"I think that's a great idea," Manny says. "Leaving stuff behind." He lifts his bottle of beer in the air. "Fuck the embargo," he says. He looks down to the other end of the table, where Allen and John and Grace from California are sitting, to see if their glasses are lifted too. Sarah and Theodore, sitting across from each other, form a human buffer between the two groups. This seating arrangement had evolved in their first days here. Manny calls the two a living, breathing DMZ. He drinks. "*Ah,*" he says, and sets the bottle down loudly on the table.

Angelita then lifts her glass. "I'd also like to propose a toast. I'd like to thank you all for leaving your busy lives and coming here to the new Nicaragua, to learn how we live and how we teach."

"You're thanking us?" Ken says.

"Why?" Maryellen asks.

"You've given us so much," Grace Berenson says. "I can't begin to tell you . . . I've been transformed."

Manny lifts his glass. "Thank *you,*" he says to Angelita.

"I can't believe fifteen days have passed," Grace says. "It's been like a year and it's been like a second."

"What I can't believe," Maryellen says, "is that we actually did all the things on that itinerary. I remember, that first night, sitting here thinking, how could we *possibly* do all that? Everything we did and saw was memorable, but I think for me, what I will never forget are the *mothers* . . ."

"For me, the director of the *Centro de Derechos Humanos,*" Grace Berenson says. "Sister Hartman. She was something. To spend her days with hurt people . . . To spend her days investigating the people who hurt them . . . She is an angel."

"A very tough and earthbound angel," Manny says. "Not the fallen variety either, one that jumped from the heavenly penthouse with the intention of landing right here."

"That's the best kind," Grace says. "You'd think we would have heard of her outside of this country."

"The truth is," Manny says, "most great people never get famous. There's too much competition in the world of the *visible.* Most of the pedestals have the rich, the powerful and the beautiful on them."

"In that order," Grace says.

"The doctor is another one," Felix says.

"Most good and important things people do, big and small, get done in a kind of local privacy," Angelita says. "I think it's better that way. The people doing them, and those who benefit from them, are the ones who will give to history their meaning."

"You got to see Rubén Darío's clock," Manny says to Felix. "I bet that was your top moment."

"I liked the soccer game I saw in Diriamba," Ken says. "Professional-level players, and all of them wearing combat boots."

"By the time I got to see the clock," Felix says, "it had already taken a back seat to all the real, living stuff we saw. I mean, it's a *clock*, that's all, an idea. A poetic idea. I like poems and I like ideas, and the truth is, they're as enjoyable, as *experienceable*, from my living room in Colorado. The *real* clock was actually less exciting than the clock I've been envisioning for years."

For Primo, the first night they sat at this table and Felix spoke of Darío's clock, and the setting sun set the rough grain of the tabletop on fire, time had stopped, and it trapped him in its unbearable and endless stopping. The sudden halt roiled the sediment of memory: he wanted out of this moment, it was a chamber shaped like the inner wall of something living. Angelita had used the word *biomórfico*, a word he'd never used in English. He wanted out—the place was too densely flooded with himself—but couldn't find the exit. Like Jonah, you know only when the whale starts or stops moving, not its intentions, not its speed, not its destination. It has no knowledge of your existence, and shares nothing with you, other than to carry you inside it.

Primo looks down at the packet of letters he will carry home tomorrow. But time is not a whale, he thinks, it's a snake. His first night in this room, it had coiled back its head, held it poised for the smallest of moments, *its* moments, and then hurled itself, fangs first and at lightning speed, through the last fifteen days, to *here*.

25

"I know what happened earlier with Maryellen's foot," Manny says to Primo. Night has fallen. They're in their room, packing. "I heard you tell her, *to the right.* Next thing I know, her foot's on top of mine." He smiles. "Sorry about that."

"Sorry about what? Her foot was just asking mine for directions."

Ken walks over to their side of the room and drops a blue and pink T-shirt onto the pile of things they'll leave behind—flashlights, aspirin, batteries, half-rolls of toilet paper, pens, a portable umbrella, a plastic canteen, razors—forming on Primo's bed. Manny picks it up and holds it up to be seen. There is a picture of three blue women in pink bathing suits, holding hands, forming a line, each with one leg bent, in faunlike dance position. You can tell they're underwater because their long hair wafts above them. Primo reads aloud the words written underneath. *Weeki-Wachee Springs: Home of the World's Only Living Mermaids.*

"I envy the lucky recipient," Manny says.

"My mother sent it to me," Ken says. He smiles, embarrassed, then throws two wrapped bars of Ivory soap onto the pile and walks out into the sala, where someone has just turned on the TV.

"The reason I brought it up wasn't really to talk about playing footsie. There's more to what I was saying before that I couldn't say while we were all sitting at the table." Primo moves his bag off the bed so they both can sit. "I'm also not sure how much of my shit you want to hear right now. Before, when you walked out of the hospital, I knew you were getting tired of *life according to Manny Glass.* I talk a lot. Sometimes faster than I think. I know that, too."

"Sit, colleague. You've listened to a fair amount of my shit, too."

"I know you got a full head at the moment. I'm permanently blown by this trip and I know you've been too. And tomorrow we're flying back to the cave. We'll be quarantined from the real world. And I know you got something happening with Angelita and I know *you* never like to talk much about that kind of thing . . ."

"Manny, you do talk a lot. But your prologues are usually shorter. Just say it, man, whatever it is. I'll hear you."

"It has to do with this identical twin business. And that I'm feeling so genuinely *un*-cool at the moment. . . . I was saying how alike and how entirely *un*-alike these two women are. I was thinking, it's like what the doctor was saying about language. We can understand Brit and Aussie because they use nearly all the same words, and on a page they're as alike as twins. But they're worlds apart. Fed by different tributaries, as *Don Félix* was saying before when he was waxing poetic. But there's something more about this twinness stuff. There's one thing that *is* identical. It's how my heart now feels. With Lisa, I was just at the point I knew I *could* really fall in love, or worse, realized I already had, when our minute together was over. And Lisa never stayed anywhere for more than a minute. She always lived between arriving and departing. According to Maryellen, she still does."

"I think you're genuinely cool," Primo says.

"And her . . ." He points through the open door into the sala, where the TV has been turned louder, and where more people are gathering. "She shouldn't be lying in the arms of the likes of me. Not more than once, that's shit sure. She's got kids and a hubby. In a million years I never thought I'd fall for someone like her. Someone from a place where every year, on the first warm day of spring, everybody goes to the next house on the block, knocks on the door and borrows their neighbor's fabric softener. Not only somebody from such a place. Somebody who likes it—"

Ken rushes into the room. "They shot down a *contra* supply

plane," he says. "Someplace called Zelaya, in the south. At least a dozen people on board and most of them dead. They think one of them was American—"

Primo and Manny run out of the room and join the rest of the delegation, including Angelita, and the staff of the Hotelito, gathered in front of the TV. They're watching black-and-white footage of two soldiers carrying an unconscious man in a stretcher away from the wreckage of a large propeller plane. The midsection of the plane is broken nearly in two. The cabin is gouged open, spilling out wooden crates, twisted pieces of metal, a blown-up life raft. Two other uniformed men are squatting on top, their AKs lying across their knees.

An electronic caption tells them they are hearing the voice of *Teniente Coronel Roberto Calderón, Comandante de la Quinta Zona Militaria.* He says the plane, brought down by two missiles, had been air-dropping arms to the *contras.* He says evidence suggested that at least one of the eleven dead was from the United States.

Grace Berenson begins to cry. Maryellen takes her in her arms. Angelita, expressionless, stares straight into the screen.

"Real shit," Manny says. "Even when you see it on television, even when you see it after it happened."

The images on the screen are changing though the voice remains the same. An officer holds up a photograph of several uniformed men . . . the crates lying before the wrecked plane . . . the remains of a small blown-up building . . . a dozen grenades, the kind with tails, that are launched, not thrown, lined up next to each other on dusty ground. Then, suddenly, the screen and every light in the building flicker once, and then, except for the eye of light at the center of the screen, shrinking like a planet they are hurtling away from, there is absolute darkness.

26

In the foreground of the mural that covers the entire wall facing the booths in the restaurant in Miami International Airport where Primo sits are the pillars and low white marble pedestals of a portico you can imagine you are sitting on. Beyond it, and all the way to a tree-lined blue and pink horizon, a dawn or a dusk, are miles of shallow water in which flamingos wade, feed or stand on one leg, among hundreds of green lily pads. Periodically, the view is blocked by a large, amphoralike urn, balanced on the flat marble rail that runs atop the row of pedestals, adding to the composition the sensation of looking out onto an African savannah from a porch in ancient Greece.

He sits, by himself, at the outer end of the booth, his feet on either side of his bag. His muscles, though electric with caffeine, feel oddly solid and reliable, as if his nearly asleep and exhausted self were contained and transported within one of those stone urns. He is too weary not to let himself extend all the way to its inner walls, let them define his shape, rely on them to keep him apart from this environment and the vaguely dissonant activity that fills it. On the table are paper plates, Styrofoam cups filled with matches and cigarette butts, napkins, crumbs, a *Miami Herald* and a copy of *Barricada*, both carrying the same front-page photograph of the broken airplane he'd seen last night on the TV screen in the Hotelito, just before the lights went out. *Barricada* asserts there was at least one American on board; the *Miami Herald*, naming it for the first time, a DC 6 cargo plane, states that there were none.

The AeroNica flight that brought them to Miami had arrived an hour late, and by the time they passed through customs, he'd missed his connecting flight to New York. The next flight with an available seat on it isn't until six p.m. The other members of the delegation, singly and in small groups, dispersed as they boarded their planes. A dense and growing cloud of smoke is settling around him from the five German-speaking people sitting in the next booth, all of whom are smoking. It's 3:55 Eastern Standard Time.

Primo unzips his bag, removes his leather jacket, reaches into the pocket and takes out his keys. He hefts them, tosses them a few inches into the air. He hasn't seen or held them for close to four hundred hours. He shoves them into his pants pocket and lays his jacket between the handles of his bag, even though it will be a wholly different part of the day, a different season, before he'll need either of these things. He gets another cup of coffee and returns to the booth.

Last night, after the lights failed, he and Angelita went for a walk in el Parque del Carmen. They went without a flashlight, as the Managuans do if they are out of doors when the lights go out. You navigate by feel, memory, voices, whatever light the heavens make available, the occasional candle, headlight, lantern, lit cigarette. They sat at the base of the same tree he'd sat under with Julio his first night there. It felt the same, as if he'd arrived at the far end of the same moment. Even the lizard was scratching around in the branches overhead. However, some of the noise he'd carried there with him had escaped. It was just as loud—he could hear it when he concentrated—only it took up less space.

"We're used to this kind of thing," Angelita said, referring to the news of the plane being shot down. "I think it is more frightening to all of you."

"It's the kind of thing we read about after the fact, and at a great distance *from* the fact," Primo said. "Being far from it makes it less real. Like it's already history, and somebody else's history."

"We have one moment of terrible fear when something like this happens," she said. "Like feeling the first tremor of an earthquake, and hoping there will not be a second. Most of us are afraid there will be a big invasion from the United States, but don't know when or where it will happen. So our first response to such news is: *It has come.* When we learn that it is only one plane, we know it is the same slow, familiar invasion we have grown used to. Then we go back to our rice and beans."

She took his hand, laid her head on his shoulder. "*Al fin cayó el pez,*" she said.

"*¿El Pez?*" Primo said. "It was a plane that fell, not a fish."

"That is an expression," she told him. "It has nothing to do with that plane you are still thinking about. *Or* fish. You say it when something you have waited for, something good, finally occurs."

"And what *good* thing has finally occurred?"

"I don't think I will tell you."

"Why not?"

"Because you are being, as your friend Manny would say, an asshole."

"I am sorry," Primo said. "But what has happened? What has *fallen?*"

"I think that during your time here, you have learned, just a little, to listen. And to hear what you are listening to."

"*What?*" Primo said. "*What* did you say?"

"I am sorry I ever said that you are funny. I know you are new at this, Primo . . ." She touched his ear with her fingertip. "But try. When I first talked with you, that night after your friends came for their package, I felt, watching you, very curious."

"I was *curious* too."

"I knew that, as well. But I also knew, in that moment, that you were . . . *a puño cerrado* . . . with closed . . ." She pressed the knuckles of one hand against his cheek.

"Fist?" Primo said.

"Yes. Now this can mean brave, but it can also mean frightened." She tried to explain more, then held her clenched fist in front of him. "If you could see my hand in this darkness, I would say, look closely, that is what you looked like to me. And I thought, someone who lived inside a closed hand would hear very little from the outside. I thought this, selfishly, because the voice I wanted you to hear was mine."

"Thank you," Primo said.

"You are welcome," Angelita said back.

He took the hand she held in front of him, opened it, kissed it. "*Al fin cayó el pez,*" he said to her.

The screen of his sleepy mind can barely hold the image of what is immediately around him. It has begun tracing lines, through totally vacant space, between recurrences. The way lines on a road map imply that the space between cities is empty. The first and last blacked-out nights, sitting beneath that tree, his seeing the plane's image on the about-to-fade TV screen, and again, today, on the front pages of *Barricada* and the *Miami Herald.* His having the same kind of piecemeal experience last year, the first night he spent with Pamela, when he saw the image of the one survivor of that locked boxcar on the silent screen, saw it again the next morning in the newspaper, *heard* it the next night on Manny's radio: two clusters of recurring events *themselves* recurring. Restating that they happened, not louder, just again, and in doing so, becoming possessed of a greater realness. Getting nearer. The lines are forming a web, like the diagrams of flight routes in the airline magazines. These silly Greek columns in front of the flamingos—the Parthenon, under a blue sky, not *there,* on television. *Shit . . .* The smoke from the next table is making it harder to breathe, keeping him in that last level of awakeness before being fully asleep. Floating in the warmer water near the surface. There are men lying on the floor, they're bleeding, and their bound wrists and ankles stink. *Les apestaban.* Of course they do. *Las muñecas, los tobillos.* They've been like that so long they're rotting. Could they have thought it was the smell of their own deaths? They were still alive.

This smoke is impossible. They light up one after the other.

A man is now standing in front of him. He has rolled a cart up to the table with a plastic bus tray on top and a green trash bag, its top clipped open, underneath. He removes the empty plates and napkins and cups from the table and tosses them into the bag. There is also a small plastic bowl and a metal spoon from the soup Maryellen had eaten over two hours ago, and these he sets into the tray.

"*Gracias*," Primo tells him. The man nods. Primo takes the last sip of coffee from his own cup and drops it into the plastic bag.

He gets up. There's enough caffeine in his tank to go for a walk. He drapes his coat over his shoulder, and picks up his bag. He moves out of the smoke cloud and approaches a shoreline where the water-and-sea-grass pattern of the restaurant's indoor/outdoor carpet ends and a landmass of smooth gray concrete begins.

Manny and Maryellen went off on their own to spend the last minutes alone together, before she boarded her plane to Little Rock. Manny then came back just minutes before his own flight, for Boston, was boarding. While saying his goodbyes, he offered Allen his hand. Although Grace and John urged him to, he refused to accept it. "Asshole-itis is indeed a permanent and incurable condition," Manny said, in a single exhalation, loud enough to be heard but not specifically addressed to anyone. He shook John's and Grace's hands, then embraced Felix and Grace Berenson. When he embraced Primo he sighed and said the words, "I don't know . . ." Then he kissed him on the cheek.

Last night, this morning actually—the sun had half risen and Primo was about to head to his room for the half hour of sleep he would have before they left for the airport—he'd said, to Angelita, the same thing: *I don't know*. They had been arguing about whether they should write to each other. Primo wanted to but she didn't. She said it didn't feel like a natural extension of the time they had spent together.

"But worrying about you," she said. "To worry about you feels completely natural. And I will do that if I want to."

He told her it was different from his side. "I can't stop you from worrying, you can't stop me from writing. If I do, you don't have to write back."

"Don't expect me to," she said. And as she said it she pressed herself into his arms.

It was then, holding her against him, her damp hair against his face and neck, that he said it. "I don't know . . ."

He still has to make more than an hour pass before his flight.

The air smells like a lot of things but mostly like new upholstery. Moving at a slow and steady pace through the maze of walkways and interconnected concourses, past the gift shops, and magazine stands and restaurants and duty-free shops, is easier than sitting in one place, but the weight of his body, and his bag, tires him.

The tiredness he feels is not simply the tiredness of losing a night's sleep, nor the aftereffect of more than two weeks of exhausting travel. He is weary from the labor of holding at a distance, out of range, the life he will return to.

A girl, six or seven years old, appears, riding toward him on a small bicycle with training wheels. She swerves as she approaches, and stops in Primo's path, then sets her feet on the indoor/outdoor carpet, and looks up at him.

"What's your name?" she asks him.

"Primo," he says. He barely has the energy and focus to remind himself he isn't dreaming. Her light brown hair is gathered into a ponytail, right at the top of her head. "What's yours?"

"Manda." She smiles. She has been eating or drinking something that left an orangy-red stripe around her mouth. "We're seeing my grandma off," she says, in an adultlike manner. "She's flying in a plane."

"Me too," Primo says. He sets his bag down.

"You going home?"

"I am. To New York."

"That's where *she* lives. And I been there." She points to Primo's jacket, lying on top of his bag. "And it's cold there, right?"

"It sure is."

She looks at him, curious, like there's something mysterious about him, something not quite right. "You a teacher?" she asks.

"I am."

Her look relaxes, her curiosity satisfied. "I thought so."

"How come you thought so?" Primo asks her.

"You look like Mr. Sanford."

"Who?"

"*My* teacher."

Primo imagines her knowledge of black people limited to two kinds. The ones she sees at a distance, from the window of a passing car, in a department store, on television, being angrily, silently, exotically or unremarkably different, absorbed in the occupations of their separate world, which has always seemed to share the same planet with hers; and then this other kind: teachers. She would most often see teachers in school, not at the airport.

"What color is *your* house?" she then asks him.

Primo looks at her, at her smile, at the small fountain of hair that is her ponytail. The bricks on the front of his building are a dark, sooty tan. He has never looked at them closely. "Kind of a light brown," he tells her.

"I know that house."

"You do?"

"A little down the block and across the street there's one just like it and it's a green one. You know that one, right?" She's giggling now. She sets her feet on the pedals and rolls the bike back and forth, a few inches each way.

"I think I may have seen it."

"Of course you have. It's *so* close. And you know who lives in it?"

"I don't."

"My grandma. That's where I go when I visit." She swings the bike around. "Wait here, okay?" She pedals quickly down the walkway. He watches her swerve into the tide of people walking toward him, which parts and then closes again when she enters it.

Primo has awakened slightly. He slings his jacket over his shoulder and lifts his bag. He then notices he's standing near the open entryway of a small coffee shop. He takes a few steps nearer and looks inside. A number of people are wearing uniforms. It must be where the terminal employees gather. Only Spanish is spoken and this draws him in. He doesn't want to speak English until he has to. The language is the last thing he has to hold on to.

He sits at the counter and orders *tostadas y café.*

"*¿Mantequilla?*" the woman serving him asks.

"*Sí,*" he tells her.

No one has noticed him enter and no one seems aware he is sitting there. There is a tacit acceptance in their indifference and Primo likes the feeling. In fact, as feelings go, he likes it best.

PART III

LEAP YEAR

27

Primo, walking downtown on Avenue A, crosses Sixth Street—the second block south of Tompkins Square Park, and the point at which the Saturday-night crowd, spilling out of the bars and restaurants, begins to thin out—then Fifth Street, where the avenue becomes even emptier, darker and quieter. This walk home, on a weekend night, is like moving in time, not just space, through the last moments of a party, toward its completed ending, when the place it happens in has fully returned to the state it was in before it began. Just below Fourth Street, he encounters a woman, who steps out of a doorway and asks him for money.

"I need a dollar," she says. "At least."

She had begun speaking before he'd realized she was talking to him.

"Of all the people on the street tonight," she says, "you're the only one who'll stop and talk to me." She speaks louder than is necessary. Her jaw clenches as if she has to force it open and closed to get out each word. Her eyes are glazed, and do not hold steadily to his eyes as she speaks.

"I haven't spoken to you," he says.

"My car was towed, then somebody snatched the purse right out of my bag." She holds open the top of her wide shoulder bag so

Primo can see. At the bottom there's a bunched-up paper bag, and something white that could be a handkerchief. "It had all my money, keys, my credit cards, everything . . . I need a token, and I need five dollars to get back to New Jersey."

Primo puts the bottle of wine he's carrying under his left arm, which also holds tomorrow's Sunday *Times*, pressed against his side. He then hands her seventy-five cents, all the change in his pocket. "I'm sorry," he says.

She's wearing designer jeans, a worn but fairly new down jacket, and zippered musketeer boots that come above the knee. She probably *is* from New Jersey, or once was, and perhaps has owned a car, though not recently.

"You're the only one who'll talk to me," she says again. She looks at the three quarters he handed her, then at the paper and the bottle he's holding. "You live around here," she says, slightly energized, not a question, a statement, and like it's the beginning of something else she's going to say, but then chooses not to, or becomes distracted. "That's *Linda?*" she says. She's now looking beyond Primo, at a woman walking toward them, half a block away. "What is *she* doing here?" She smiles, squints to focus, shakes her head, then frowns. "No." She seems disappointed. "Somebody else. It isn't fair," she says. "I never saw anybody look so much like someone I knew, and then turn out to be somebody else." She then looks curiously at Primo, as if she's forgotten why they are both standing there, facing each other.

"Good luck," he says.

"Good luck to *you*," she says.

Primo walks into his apartment, and sets the paper and the bottle of wine on the table. As he takes off his coat, he notices, in the middle of the front page, a wide photograph of a balding man in a windbreaker, changing the number on a sign that displays the number of days—534—that his brother has been in captivity, along with nine other American hostages, in Beirut. Primo hangs his coat and scarf over one of the chairs, walks back to the front door, closes it, locks both locks and then drops onto the couch in front of the TV, which he'd left on when he went out a half hour ago. He remembers, some months ago, seeing a news photograph, or the image on a news broadcast, of the same sign, and the number of days being 300 and something. Since then, as Primo slid through this past season of his own life, the man in the photograph imagined each passage of light and dark, each period of sleep, each meal his brother ate, then changed, by one day, the number displayed on the front of this sign. It would be the only way to believe he was still alive and might return home, the only way to believe he'd ever been there, in *his* life, in the first place.

Primo had been reading *Lying to the Holy Ghost*, which Manny has nearly finished in a fit of creative energy in the month since they returned from Nicaragua. He'd switched the TV on when he sat down to read, but barely watched it. It became another live presence, independently occupied, with which he shared room. *Wheel of Fortune* had elapsed during his first half hour of reading, and nearly all of the movie *Somebody Up There Likes Me*, with Paul Newman playing the boxer Rocky Graziano. Primo had seen it before, which made it easy to mostly ignore yet listen in on, and occasionally lift his eyes to, when he wanted a break from Manny's relentless, funny, angry narrative. There was an old and familiar companionship in the sound of the forties, New York-street-smart, white English that every character in the movie spoke. He looked up at the screen at the exact moment Rocky gave himself the name he would henceforth carry. A fight trainer asked him what he called himself. The war was on and Rocky, at that time, was AWOL. He needed the money he'd get from prizefighting, but also needed to keep his identity secret. He was lost for something to tell the man when, like a sudden gift from heaven, he noticed the label on the wine bottle he was holding and read the name aloud: "Graziano." "*Tanks, God,*" Primo said, also aloud, in a voice that sounded like Rocky's, but took its tone from Manny's novel. "*Tank God it wasn't Inglenook, or Pino-fuckin-Car-duh-nay.*"

In that moment, it also occurred to him that tomorrow was Sunday, and if tonight he didn't get the wine he was to bring to the dinner Carolina was making for him tomorrow, he would arrive at her apartment in Williamsburg empty-handed.

He is in the middle of chapter 28, the last in the manuscript Manny had sent him. Now, on the screen, there's a crowd of teenagers dancing to house music on an inner-city rooftop. Black, Latino, white, all of them young and pretty. Something about the scene is familiar. It's summer, and they all dance with an easy, athletic, sexy grace. A teenage boy dangling a cigarette from his mouth, like wise guys did in forties movies, holds an enormous boom box across his lap. Behind him are the lights of New York City.

The phone rings twice. Primo then hears Manny's voice squeezed through the speaker in his answering machine. "If you're back, and if you're still reading, don't pick up the phone. I don't want to hear from you until you've read everything I gave you, and then listened to my last message over again. I'm sorry it was so long. I couldn't bear finishing this damn book and just keeping it to myself. But call me as soon as you've finished, okay? The very moment. I want to know what it feels like to have just finished reading an Emanuel Glass novel. . . . Oh, and here's another scoop. What a night *this* has been. Maryellen called me just this minute. She thinks she's pregnant. Do you believe it? Next thing she says is that she's nearly certain it's her husband's. I'm just standing there holding the phone, my lower lip bouncing on the carpet. I don't know what to say. I don't know what she *expects* me to say. After a yearlong moment of silence, I finally utter something brilliant. 'Are you sure?' I ask her. *Not* meaning is she sure she's pregnant, but is she sure it's her husband's. I mean a *month*—that's cutting it *awfully* close. Instead of saying yes or no she says, in that voice of hers, 'Manny, we *were* careful, weren't we?' A *question*, not a statement. I told her we were, and that being careful, the *way* we were careful, has always worked for me. Then she was kind of relieved and asked what I was doing home on a Saturday night, and I told her. 'Completing the first novel of an American master.' 'You mean you're reading?' she says to me. I could *not* believe it. I thought she had at least *some* tender feelings. I don't know what the statistics are, but I think the chances are like ten in a hundred the baby *could* be mine. . . . A slap on *each* cheek. That's how I see it. How I *feel* it. Anyhow, I told her, I'm not reading, I'm writing. I've finished my novel. And she said, 'Congratulations. I'm so happy for you.' And she says it in the tone of voice you use when someone you're *not* in love with, but who you *know* is in love with you, gets a raise. *I'm* so *happy for you* . . . Both cheeks *and* my libido are stinging. . . . Anyhow, sorry again for the long message I left before. Come to think of it, this one's pretty long too. Anyhow, don't call till you've finished, okay? But that means call the minute you do. The staggering ego of this brilliant, creative artist needs your help regaining its feet. May God bless and preserve you . . ."

Primo watches as the answering machine resets itself. Once it has, the small light blinks twice, followed by a two-second beat of solid red light, then twice again. Manny's two messages are the only ones. His last one couldn't have taken more than a half hour, because that's how long he was out. If it's not too late when he finishes, he'll call back tonight. If not, in the morning.

Since they returned from Nicaragua, Primo has received cards and notes from Felix, Grace Berenson and Maryellen, and spoken to Ken Steiner on the phone. Ken had written a letter to be sent to members of Congress, and to the press, describing their trip and asking that our government discontinue all military aid to the *contras.* He had solicited the signatures of everyone on the delegation, except Grace, Allen and John from California. He asked Primo if he thought he should ask them and Primo said he should. You never know. As it turned out, Grace and John did sign.

The week he returned, Primo sent a postcard to Angelita with a picture of the Manhattan skyline at dusk. *If you visit New York City,* he wrote, *we can watch the sun set over New Jersey.* He signed it with the name of the male character in Chekhov's "The Lady with the Dog." *I think of you. Gurov.* He has not heard from her, but then she had said he wouldn't, and besides, the mail to Nicaragua is slow and unreliable. It might have just reached her. It might never reach her. This week he will send another.

In the story, Gurov, at first, had no idea what Anna, the woman he'd had his brief affair with and then left behind, was thinking. He only knew what the afterlife of their time together was for himself. As months passed, his mind was increasingly filled with her. He found himself less and less able to occupy the world he had always lived in. His feelings for her led him to believe that everything of value to himself, everything that had meaning, was what he kept hidden, gagged, held captive. And everything people knew him to be, the version of himself that was free to walk around in public, in the brightest daylight, was bullshit. If he lived today, and in the real world, he might say, *My life is fucking TV*. "And so, at the moment," Primo says to himself, "is mine. . . ."

He picks up a page of Manny's manuscript, but doesn't read. A commercial comes on, and as if an invisible hand has adjusted the volume, the sound, a single male voice speaking over happy, tropical music, becomes louder. *Have you heard the rumors going round lately? The earth is flat, the moon is made of green cheese, and get this one. Someone's saying there's no escape from winter* . . . On the screen a beautiful, tanned young woman, wearing a white two-piece bathing suit and dark, round-lensed sunglasses, lies on a raft in the sun. Two hands appear, reaching from below up onto the deck of the raft. Then a man pulls himself out of the water, his skin and hair dripping. The look on his face, at first serious with physical effort, gives way to a smile. Cut to nighttime—the two of them are dancing at an outdoor club among tables at which people sip tall, brightly colored drinks through straws. The voice falls away and the same music, played by four black musicians in brightly colored island shirts that tie in front, grows louder.

There's a knock at the door. Primo's body hears it too: his head swivels in a fast, tight turn. His shoulders follow. He first imagines that the person knocking is on the inside.

A knock on this door, up here on the fifth floor, especially at night, is a rare occurrence. Someone coming would ring downstairs, or, more likely, call first. The Lower East Side is not a neighborhood where people just drop in.

Primo looks through the eyehole and sees the face of the young son of his downstairs neighbor, close against the door on the other side, swollen by the small fish-eye lens. He unlocks and opens the door. The son is sitting on his father's shoulders. They're wearing matching green bathrobes with pajamas underneath. The child's hair is gathered into short dreadlocks.

"Evening, neighbor," the father says.

His son smiles.

"Come in," Primo says.

They come in, the son still riding atop his father's shoulders, and stop, just before the couch. He looks at the screen, then says, "Ah, you know already."

"What?"

The father points to the screen. His son points too and smiles.

"Keith," he says, looking up at his son. "You think he's watching it but *doesn't* know?"

Keith points again and laughs.

"Ah-*hah*," Primo says. "I *thought* it looked familiar."

"We figured we'd just pop up during the commercial"—he bounces Keith once as he says this—"and tell you, just in case you didn't know it was on. Didn't want you to miss the moment the whole world gets a look at the street our humble asses reside on. Me and Keith: a walking, talking, two-headed *TV Guide.* That's us." He looks up at his son. "You ready?" He turns them both around and heads back toward the door.

"What's it called?" Primo asks.

"*Above the City,*" he says.

"The mystery is finally solved," Primo says. "Wait," he then says, just before he shuts the door. "Didn't you say you *weren't* going to watch?"

"You have a good memory, brother. But me and Keith, we're not the type that holds a grudge." Keith begins moving his legs up and down. "You want to walk?" he asks him.

Keith giggles and nods yes.

He reaches up, lifts him over his head and sets him down. Keith, holding his hand, pulls at him to get started.

"He loves walking downstairs," the father tells Primo. "But he hates walking up. He likes a little help when traveling against the pull of gravity."

Primo goes back to the couch and the movie.

One of the girls he remembers from the shoot last June runs up a flight of stairs, shoves open the bulkhead door onto the nightscape of the city, then rushes out onto a tenement roof and joins the two young men and the other girl. He remembers them all now. She is crying. She tells them that her mother's boyfriend, who lives with them, and who beats her mother when he's drunk, has just tried to beat her, too, because she refused his sexual advances. He was holding her against the wall in the kitchen, about to strike her, when they heard her mother's keys in the door lock. When her mother walked in, she rushed past her, without explaining, and came right here. She was mad at her mother for allowing that brute to live in their home. But now she was worried for her. Her mother's alone with him, and he was in a crazy state when she left. *If he hurts her* . . . she says.

The next scene, the four of them rush out the front door of the building on the corner and then head up the block.

Primo hears the voice of his downstairs neighbor shouting loudly. "Yeah. . . . Whew. . . . All *right*. . . ."

When they get to the girl's building, they find police cars and an ambulance on the street out front. They run upstairs and push past the uniformed policeman guarding the door of the apartment. Two paramedics carry her mother on a stretcher from another room into the kitchen and past them, out into the hall. She is unconscious and her face, all that can be seen above the blanket, is badly bruised and bleeding. A detective in street clothes, one who apparently knows the girl and her friends, tells her that her mother was hurt pretty badly, but she'll be all right. He then asks her if she knows the whereabouts of Rico Jones, her mother's boyfriend, and she tells him she doesn't. She goes into the room they had just carried her mother out of, a bedroom, and shuts and locks the door. You can't touch anything in there, the detective shouts. She doesn't answer. He pounds on the door. She slides her hand under the mattress on the double bed, brings out a revolver and slips it into her bag. She then opens the door again, just as the detective is preparing to break it down. She smiles at him. He gives her an angry look, shakes his head, then lets his mouth loosen into a slight smile.

Another commercial comes on, this one for a singles telephone hot line. It's only ten-thirty, and it occurs to Primo that on weeknights they don't start running these ads until after the eleven o'clock news. The word from market research must be that on Saturday nights the lonely and dateless, sitting in front of their TVs, start getting restless during prime time. This isn't the commercial aimed at the domestic singles, sitting alone on a couch at home, just like he is, who suddenly smile as the thought occurs to them, energize, pick up the phone, dial and quickly enter a conversation. In this one, active men and women, black and white and Asian, attractive and well dressed, all talk to each other from portable cellular phones as they step off airplanes, walk along midtown streets and ride in limousines.

The four of them are back on the roof. The girl, whose mother is now in the hospital, is crying. They all embrace her. She's been angry at her mother since her father left five years ago. Angry at her father, too. What she didn't tell the police was that she does know where to find Rico. But she wants to get to him first. She shows her friends the gun she has in her bag. It belongs to Rico, she tells them. So it's fitting I use it on him. She smiles. You won't need that, one of the young men tells her. Because when you find him, we'll all be with you. It's what we *got* to do. We're the only family any of us really have. If we don't take care of each other, no one else will.

In the next scene they're walking out the door again and back up the block. This take looks more like the one Primo watched them shoot.

He had just brought himself back to the neighborhood. He was restless and energized and exhausted all at once. He was standing aside, at a distance, watching them, as he is doing now; only now, transformed by their own unreality, he feels nearer to them than when they were actually here and he was standing less than ten feet from where they walked. Again, he hears the shouts and cheers from his downstairs neighbor. This time there are other voices, too. A man and a woman from an apartment across the street, and a New Year's Eve crank noisemaker from somewhere else in the building.

Primo turns off the set, gathers the last pages of Manny's manuscript and brings them into the bedroom. He's sleepy, and he's seen enough of *Above the City.* He falls onto his bed, and lays the pages on his chest.

It doesn't feel as if he'd just spent a quiet Saturday night at home, alone, reading. The night has been crowded with people, and busy. It's as if he spent the last several hours out on the streets, where the woman he gave the seventy-five cents to still is.

He begins to wonder if it could ever really happen, say sometime in the next century, that families made up solely of teenagers actually came to exist. Not gangs or clubs but real families, with dinner plates and TVs and coffee tables. Perhaps, even, families made just of young children. Children who are real, like the children he sees on the streets, or encounters at airports, not Peter Pan or *Little Rascals* children.

He tries to imagine himself, as a child, coming home from school to a household made up of other children. What would they do in the kitchen, the living room? His father's office? The image will not hold. It doesn't scan. Could never happen.

His mind now replaces the thought with the image of the building the four actors walked out of. The doorway and walls looked normally lit, as they appear in ordinary daylight, not the scorching, electric glare the lights and mirrors projected on the day they filmed. It's like a flash camera. It leaves you blinded for a second and even leaves you seeing a bright white aura around everything. But when you see yourself in the photograph, you are no more brightly lit, no clearer, than if you were looking into a mirror. Even less so.

28

Primo, standing beside the phone, is drinking coffee and rewinding Manny's two messages from the night before. He hears two kinds of sounds. And they make a kind of sense together. The reverse, accelerated string of chatter rising from the answering machine, and the church bells from St. Brigid's on East Tenth Street, each spherical body of gong-sound clear, whole and separate, even after traveling through seven blocks of inner-city air. They are the polar extremes, the freezing and boiling points, on a scale that registers every kind of noise humans make and have filled the world with.

Less than a half hour ago, he'd woken from a dream in which he was a teenager. He and his father and someone else, another teenager who was somehow related, maybe a brother, were tied up by their wrists and ankles, and were lying on the wooden floor of a one-room house. The door and windows were open to the outside. In fact, there was no glass in the windows, no door in the doorway. There was no one in the room but the three of them.

They'd been there, bound as they were, for some time, and had resigned themselves to the fact that they would remain that way. No one spoke. The third person couldn't have been a brother, because Primo was really himself in the dream, and his father was really his father, and in their house there was no brother. He was the first, the *Primo*, and the only child. Who was this guy?

He didn't like dreaming that dream, nor waking from it. Reading the last pages of Manny's manuscript this morning was a relief, and a diversion. The voice that tells the story, not unlike Manny in real life, immediately understands everything it sees, and everything that happens to Henry O. It's a powerfully observant, but limited understanding—angry, humorous and usually exaggerated—an understanding arrived at for the purpose of making a point. Yet there is nothing more comforting than a reliable comprehension of everything. While in its arms you can look inside things, and not be frightened. You know there exist words to mark the path, however long, between what you actually see there and what it looked like from the outside.

He is about to play the messages when the phone rings.

"Hello?"

"Haven't heard your voice in a while." It's Pamela.

"Actually, I was going to call *you* today. Did you by any chance see *Above the City* last night?"

"Who?"

"The movie with that handsome young actor Felicia's going to marry."

"Oh, him. Nope. She's forgotten him. Her taste in men ages at the rate she does. Only the chronological gap, fifteen years or so, remains the same size. *Prince* is her current heartthrob."

"Her taste is improving. And how is *your* current heartthrob?"

"I gather you're referring to the film they shot on your block last year. And that you, rather than visit your dear suburban friends, stayed home to watch."

"I did."

"And it moved you beyond words."

"It did."

"I am fine, thank you. Though that's not exactly what you asked."

"Good. Me too, thank you."

"I was wondering if you were angry because of the change in our arrangements. You're not, are you . . . ? It's just that you haven't called since we spoke about it, and we miss you."

Last month, Pamela had told him she had begun to see someone whom she might, in the future, want to live with. He has a child too. She liked him, and so did Felicia, who was getting to know his daughter. The sleeping-over part of their relationship, hers and Primo's, could get difficult at this point. But she so loved his visits, and their dinners. She told him there was a spontaneous familyness to their evenings together that both she and Felicia hoped would continue.

First he'd said, "Shouldn't we sleep together *once* in the new year?" Then he said, as if she had answered him, "Good. Now I won't have to get up so goddamn early." He told her that he, too, wanted to keep up their newly established, half-year-old tradition of monthly dinners.

"Good," she said to that. "And get your ass up here soon. We missed January since you were away for so much of it."

But in the course of the month, he found himself detaching from his thoughts about it, about going to dinner, and *not* staying over. Not angry, not anything else, simply that each time he thought of calling, he didn't follow through.

"Me and Felicia miss the full moon of your face rising above our kitchen table once each month."

"This is not, I hope, something poetic in the making. It seems the best poems get written about me *after* the fact. You and your West Coast friend can do an anthology. A poetic duet. *The Man We Knew.*"

"That was not a poem, just meant to be a nice thing to say. Maybe I *have* written a few poems about you, and maybe they're *not* retrospective, but you ain't likely to see them. I got a daughter. I got a different kind of chance. Something I never expected I'd have. Or even to want. That I do—want it, that is—has mostly to do with you, sitting there chewing your food and enjoying the fact you were doing it at a table with two other people, and that from a few feet away we actually looked just like a family. That gave *me* something too. Then there was *after* dinner. *Our* part of the evening. My memory of that is in more places than the brain. Places it don't leave so easy."

When she told him, he felt something he'd enjoyed and possessed was no longer his. But he understood. He knew how to feel this, how to digest it and go on. He lived light. If you don't possess much, you don't lose much. And besides, she's not the only woman he's been seeing. But his insides have been roiled and unsettled since he returned from Nicaragua, and he can't keep this more immediate loss, one he *can* fully embrace with his understanding, from touching an older sense of the things he's had in his life but no longer does.

But he can't tell Pamela about this. His hope is that if he doesn't give it any more attention than he has to, this other thing, this feeling, will pass like a cold.

It's like dreaming without going to sleep. It's like knowing what you're seeing when you lose yourself in a stare, without losing a clear sense of the patch of wall you actually *are* staring at. It's like listening to a stereo that has a different song coming out of each speaker.

Images float upward, break through the surface of the moment he's in, and demand *they* be what he feels and sees. Some of the footage is not familiar. Not even his.

"I'll be up to visit you two lovely ladies soon. The new semester has been busy. Things keep coming up . . ." He begins to laugh.

"What's so funny?"

"Lot of *up*'s in what I just said. Did you notice? I used it in two different contexts. One meaning to travel northward, one meaning to arise. *Arriba* in Spanish means up, and in Managua it means east. And *that's* on the up-and-up."

"What's up, Primo?"

"Hah! *You* got it. I think *up* is the direction things travel in from the past and into the present. From the present to the future. It is otherwise a very relative term. To go to Westchester, where you reside, I travel up. *Up*-state, we say. I go to Central America, I travel down."

"Very interesting."

"This is the stuff poems are made out of."

"That's true. But at the moment, I'm more interested in the prosaic world in which you and I live. You have things on your mind, Primo. I can feel it."

"I do. One of them's that I miss you both. A few more weeks to chill, I'll be up to see you. And tell Felicia I approve of her taste. Her friend in the movie, the one with the high-top fade and the cute butt, doesn't strike me as having much depth. Prince, however, got a lot more of what it takes."

"I'll tell her. By the way, she thinks you're pretty cute too."

"The two women who comprise your household both love my company, and both got their eyes on other men."

"Look who's talking. You've been spreading your love around the entire hemisphere. I'm just working the Greater New York region."

"I'll visit soon."

"Please do. We miss you. What *has* been keeping you so busy, anyway? Aside from the search for love, that is."

"Well, I just finished reading the first twenty-eight chapters of *Lying to the Holy Ghost.*"

"That the novel your friend's been writing?"

"The same. It's almost done. There's one more chapter and I think last night he read the whole thing onto my answering machine, though I haven't played it back yet."

"Is it any good?"

"I think it's too weird to be bad or good."

"If it's too weird, it's usually bad."

"Don't jump to conclusions. Listen to what happens in the twenty-eighth chapter. It seems that a famous senator, a longtime friend of big business, is himself in business. He produces child pornography films."

"Nice. But not weird. Maybe not even fiction."

"No one would have known about it if Henry O, the book's main character, hadn't arranged to have one of his films broadcast in place of a weekly televangelism program."

"Also nice. So what happens?"

"A special committee is formed to investigate this senator's activities, which, finally, exonerates him of all charges."

"It still sounds more like news than fiction."

"The senator offered three points as his defense. The first was that the business he owned was, in fact, an advertising agency, and that the films alleged to be pornography were actually commercials for toilet paper, automobile brakes and fabric softener. They simply had children actors in them. People liked them so much they began to order them directly."

Pamela laughs. "I've seen those commercials. This is definitely *not* fiction."

"The second was that his business in no way represented a conflict of interest that could impede his carrying out his role as senator. And the third point was the fact that his business was a success. He submitted his tax returns, which indicated that business doubled during each of the last five years. He told the committee that he personally would deem it a great insult to Americans, believers all in the family, to think they would spend that kind of money on filth."

"You're right. Too weird to be bad *or* good. He has a good imagination, though. Good and scary. You might tell him the rest of us stopped taking acid these twenty years and more."

"I'll do that when I talk to him later."

"You also tell him to remind his friend, in case his friend forgets, that there's people *up* north, though not too far, two of them to be exact, who miss him."

"I will."

"Now when I say bye, we both hang up. *Bye.*"

What felt familiar, last night, while watching *Above the City*, was not, simply, that he'd seen the actors on the day they were filming, but something more. He remembers the next morning sitting in front of the TV, like he was last night, and suddenly finding himself in tears. He hated that moment. It overturned him. What he feels now, and has been feeling, is that the thing that rose inside him that morning, like an air-filled sphere that suddenly broke free of the chain that anchored it to the ocean's bottom, has risen again, slowly this time, and has climbed to a depth just below the reach of his senses. It has stopped its ascent at that point, where it hovers, menacingly, underneath every single thing he does. Though he can't actually see it, he can, increasingly, perceive the deliberate exertion that holds it there: the mysterious pressure of water, and the gravitational pull of his own anger.

Manny's first message begins with the voice of Ray Charles singing "America." After the song plays in its entirety, Manny's voice comes on. "Wait a minute," he says, He starts it again, lowers the volume, raises it, lowers it again until it's soft enough to serve as background music.

He then begins to narrate what he calls the ending of the end of *Lying to the Holy Ghost:*

" 'We've had automobiles for a century,' Henry O mused to himself. 'But they still look more like something drawn by horses than something that came into existence because of the discovery of the internal combustion engine. We have overthrown the idea and, ostensibly, the reality of aristocracy, yet establish our relationship to the wealthy and powerful in its image. Though we have abolished the evil of slavery, we continue the dehumanization of racism, and the working conditions of the laboring classes, born during its terrible reign. It takes us a very long time,' Henry O thought to himself, 'to get an idea *entirely* out of our heads, and to replace it with a new one.'

"Each of Henry O's planned and executed interventions was a weapon aimed at our collective denial of the class system that has survived the social/political upheavals of history, as the Roman chariot can still be seen in the body of a Chevrolet. And, alas, they have had no more effect than a single pair of oars would have in changing the direction of an ocean liner.

"It is humanity that changes the course of history, not conceptual artists. Revolutions are made by people, not by individuals, and certainly not by ideas. That lambs are gentle, that lions are ferocious, that there is one God, that Harvard offers a good education, that the color tie you wear can affect the outcome of a business negotiation, that the sun never sets on the British Empire, that yellow jaundice results from standing too long in the sun: these are all ideas. And Henry O has arrived at an understanding of what ideas truly are: gaseous emanations that escape from that part of humankind that seems to benefit most by explaining things. And continues benefiting, by proving, again and again, to each successive generation, that their explanations are correct.

"We can make a world in our image, which seems, to Henry O, the hardest job of all, yet are then unable to change it. Why?

"In his search for an answer, Henry O reviews the basis of his own life's work: that the struggle to amass and maintain wealth has been, and will always be, the largest root cause of human suffering. To our hero, this one fact remains irrefutably true. But he must now add to that his discovery of how human we all, in fact, are.

" 'Yes,' Henry O thinks, sadly, 'we *are* only human.'

"There is a simple universal truth that cannot be denied. When presented with the sensuous appearance of the garden of earthly life, the first response on the part of all of us who are not rich is to *want* to be. This fact, because Henry O himself is the possessor of nearly limitless wealth, had, until this moment, eluded him.

"But humans *can* make change. Only they do so collectively, in a way larger than individual will, and at the speed of nature. Change occurs at the rate human life is actually lived: the speed at which one word, spoken to be understood, follows another, a pace our beautiful, anxious, hungry hearts keep trying to accelerate, and that the regimes governing us strive to slow down.

"Thus, his life, as conceptual artist and trickster, is over. However hard the task will be, he will give all his money away. Not through institutions, and not through trickery, as he did in so many of his interventions . . .

"*Primo*," Manny says here, "open parentheses.

"(He sadly remembers his third intervention. . . . Having gained access to the IRS computer files, he randomly sent tax returns of one hundred thousand dollars to earners of less than fifteen thousand a year. Of the eight thousand people to whom he sent checks, over seven thousand returned them. Of those that kept their surprising refunds, two hundred were audited and asked to explain the sudden swelling of their savings accounts. No, no more trickery. He would stop his meddling.) . . . *Close* parentheses.

"Henry O would spend the next phase of his life, however long it took, traveling the world, its poorest parts, giving gifts of hard currency and precious metals to each person in need that he encountered personally. He would simply say he was a sinner, which he was, struggling to repent, and beg them to accept his offering . . ."

Manny had, during his narration, changed the music several times. "Blowin' in the Wind," "The Star-Spangled Banner" and "Amazing Grace" have all played. He now puts on Ray Charles's "America" again.

"And when every last cent was gone, Henry O's plan was not to live the life of the homeless beggar, the penitent hermit or the cloistered monk. He will not denounce the world which had given him so much. He will organize people on the community level, one at a time. The oldest, hardest, slowest route to change: to be a subversive brick in the wall, rather than a stone thrown uselessly against it. And he will do this in the workplace: after he's divested himself of each and every cent of his vast holdings, Henry O, against the very grain of anything he has known prior to this moment in life, will get a job."

Manny raises the volume once more, then slowly reduces it until it fades to silence. He then speaks the words *the end* and hangs up the phone.

After the beep, a silent pause and another beep, Manny's second message begins to play itself. "If you're back, and if you're still reading, don't pick up the phone. . . ." Hearing it for the second time, and right after the slower, more oratorical tone with which he read the end of his novel, Primo realizes how quickly Manny normally speaks. Much faster than his metaphorical rate of human change.

His rapid understanding of the world is dependent upon its immediate expression. But in this message, his voice has an even faster and more urgent tempo. ". . . Oh, and here's another scoop. What a night *this* has been. . . . I don't know what to say. . . . 'Are you sure?' I ask her. . . . That's cutting it *awfully* close. . . . I could *not* believe it. . . . *I'm* so *happy for you*. . . ." His voice moved the words like a 33-RPM record played at 45. "Call me as soon as you've finished, okay? The very moment. I want to know what it feels like to have just finished reading an Emanuel Glass novel."

29

Carolina and Primo are sitting at the small Formica table in the kitchen of her two-room apartment. They both have small plates of salad in front of them, glasses of wine and empty bowls for the pasta now boiling on the stove. Against one wall, beside the sink, is an old claw-footed bathtub. Across its top is a white enameled steel cover, on top of which are a drainboard, a bowl of green salad, a covered pot of hot tomato sauce with the stem of a ladle sticking out the top, a cutting board with a loaf of bread on it, an open bottle of red wine, a white plastic bowl containing an apple and two oranges, and a spiral-bound notebook, with a pen marking a place in the middle.

The walls and slanted wood floors have recently been painted. The skin of new white paint covering the walls is not stretched flat but tumescent and wavy, from a century of small, urban, geological heavings, plastered repairs and coats of paint. The floors are painted a dark red. There is, in these new clean surfaces, a sense that if they are maintained they can hold back the advance of decomposition forever.

Marta had written in one of the letters Primo brought back from Nicaragua that Carolina was to make a dinner for Primo, in thanks for his carrying their messages and gifts back and forth.

"She wrote," Carolina says to Primo, "that I am to make for

Profesor Thomas his favorite meal. However, I don't know what your favorite meal is. So I have made you what is mine."

"Pasta's one of mine, too," Primo says.

"I've made zitis," Carolina says. "Twice, when we have eaten out, you ordered them."

Primo corrects her. "Zi-*ti*. . . . English is what I'm supposedly qualified to teach, but I know one or two things about Italian. If a noun ends in *i*, it's already plural. I guess just one of them would be a *zito*."

"A *zito*. What *is* a *zito?*"

"I don't know."

"Then how do you know what is plural and what is just one of them?"

"Do you know what a *flink* is?"

"No . . ."

"You don't know what *flinks* are?"

"I said no."

"But you didn't question that one was singular, and one plural. Just because I added the *s*. In Italian, with a masculine noun, if it ends in *i* it's plural. That was my only point."

"I see. But what is a flink?"

"If you don't know, I don't know."

"You have made up a word."

"I guess so. You might say *these* are flinks." He points to the little boomerang shapes in the Formica tabletop.

Carolina shakes her head. "I think *you* are a flink."

"You might be right. Come to think of it, I do remember one use of the word *zito*. It's not a noun, though."

"Please don't make up another word. I'm still learning the old ones."

"Seriously. It's the way my mother told me to be quiet. She'd say, *Zit-to!*"

"That means 'Be quiet'? *Cállate?*"

"Actually it means 'Shut up.' "

"I like that. *Zi-to*."

"My mother didn't say it like the pasta. She'd accent the *zi* and harden it with her tongue. Like *pizza.* Then slam the *t,* like hammering a nail. *Zzit-to.*"

"*Zzit-to,* Primo. You are no longer my teacher."

"That's right. I'm off duty. Permanently. *And* hungry."

"In a minute, we will eat our *Shut up*'s."

"In a minute, we'll shut up and eat."

"I am also making for you something I know you like, apple pie. I always see the boxes in your refrigerator. The kind from the market with the ugly smeared windows on them through which I can see the part of the pie you haven't yet eaten. If it were my pie, it would remain that way."

"What way?"

"Uneaten."

"Thank you."

"You are welcome."

Carolina gets up, takes the pot of boiling ziti off the stove and pours them into the colander sitting in the sink. She then takes the salad plates and empty bowls off the table.

The pattern on the Formica tabletop, a gray field of smoky, blossoming cloud shapes covered with pencil-thin white and black boomerangs, is brighter and clearer on the extension wings, which Carolina has raised in order to fit the two of them and their dinners.

"Whoever owned this table before you did, must have often dined alone," Primo says to her.

"Why do you say that?"

"That person used the wings much less than the middle."

"Is that a hint? *Un acertijo?*"

"A what? What is an *acertijo?*"

"A riddle. What you just said: . . . *used the wings much less than the middle.* I thought it was a riddle. But I think I know what it is." She fills the bowls with pasta. "A clue from the game show *Jeopardy,* where they tell you the answer and you then say the question. Right? *Uses the wings less than the middle.* That is the clue."

"You've lost me," Primo says.

"*What is a bird that prefers to walk?* That is correct, no?"

"A bird? I meant the sides of the table that fold up and down."

She ladles sauce on top of the steaming pasta, sets the two bowls on the table and sits. "I believe what you meant to say is *leaf.* Birds have wings, as do airplanes, buildings and political parties. Tables, and *trees*, have leafs."

"*Leaves.*"

She sits down, mixes her ziti with the sauce and begins to eat. She looks back at Primo, who is watching her, smiling.

"As your teacher of English, I have created a monster."

"We are done with English. I can now continue learning it on my own."

"That's clear."

"Can you now teach me Italian?"

"There's only one word I want you to understand," he says. "*Zitto.* And no others for a while."

"This is delicious," she says. "How come you are not eating?"

"I thought I'd first digest the linguistic antipasto. It was very filling. I was also wondering if there was any grated cheese."

"In the refrigerator."

Primo gets up, brings back the small plastic container and shakes some over his pasta. He then sets it in front of Carolina.

"I don't like it. Too salty. I got it just for you. My sister said to prepare for you a meal that will please you. Are you pleased?"

"I am."

"Then shut up and eat."

"The reason I have waited until tonight to make this dinner is because it's Leap Year's Day Eve. *Es la víspera del día del año bisiesto.*"

Primo is washing and drying the salad plates so they can use them for the pie cooling on the bathtub top. "I never heard it called that."

"No one calls it that. Not in Spanish, either."

"Except you." He sits down again, takes a sip of wine.

"And you too, if you want to. I have been researching leap year and learned a lot about it. In this country it is the time when women ask men to marry them. Did you know that?"

"I did."

"I want to first say that I am not interested in marriage."

"I think you have the whole year to decide, in case you change your mind."

"About this I would never change my mind. Since I was a child I knew it was my sisters who would be the wives in our family. Perhaps I will become a mother someday, but never a wife." She smiles. "I see that a calm look is now on your face."

"I wasn't worried."

"You are a good teacher, and you are a bad liar."

Primo lifts his glass. "This is, by far, the best Leap Year's Day Eve dinner I have ever eaten."

Carolina lifts her glass and touches it to his. "That, I know is true. Even if you do not receive a proposal of marriage. Maybe *for* that reason."

"Is this *Jeopardy* again? Let's see. The clue, which is actually the answer, is: *Not receiving a proposal of marriage.* And the answer, folks, which is actually the question: *What, for Primo Thomas, makes it the best Leap Year's Day Eve dinner he's ever eaten?* Am I right?"

"You are correct. And you are other things also, that I will not say at the table."

"Actually I was not correct. The clue that's meant to get that answer has nothing to do with marriage proposals. It is simply: *Homemade apple pie.* The smell is driving me crazy."

"What I started to say before was that I wanted to follow the North American *año bisiesto* tradition as far as asking you to dinner. You have never been in my home, and have never eaten food I have cooked."

"Another toast," Primo says, still holding his glass. "To the delicious pie we are soon to partake of, to your gracious hospitality . . ." He stands, raises his glass toward the ceiling. "And to us: *Zitto* and *Flink*, connoisseurs of *non*-marital bliss."

"Sit down," Carolina says, laughing. "And listen to the interesting things I have learned about leap year." She takes the notebook off the bathtub top, opens it to the page held by the pen and sets it in front of her.

"Do you know that an actual solar year consists of three hundred and sixty-five days, five hours, forty-eight minutes and forty-six seconds?"

"How long before the pie cools off?"

"This is very important. To have a calendar, the years must be balanced. And to do that, we have had to measure time in units of four years: three years at three hundred sixty-five days, and every fourth year at three hundred sixty-six."

"What does that have to do with women asking men to marry them?"

"I don't know. They don't think that in El Salvador."

"It's like Sadie Hawkins."

"Who is she?"

"I don't know. I just know if you have a Sadie Hawkins dance, the women ask the men to dance, not the other way around."

She writes down the name. "I will research that."

"You are the most natural researcher I've ever met. You love to learn. . . . My grandparents were the serious teachers in the Thomas family. So is my aunt. They'd have loved to get you in their classrooms."

"You too are a good teacher."

"You learned English well and quickly, and actually, quite privately. It wasn't until we began talking outside the classroom that I realized how much you *had* learned. You're a natural. It's like whatever else you're up to—eating, sleeping, walking, cooking—learning's also what you're doing. I'm not sure how good a teacher I am. But I know this: Even if I were awful, you'd have learned just as much."

"In ancient Rome," she says, "someone they called the Pontifex Maximus was in charge of regulating the calendar. He would make the year longer when there were senators he liked in office, and make it shorter when he didn't like them."

"That would be a great job for my friend Manny."

"He's the one who's writing the novel?"

"He finished it last night. It's a fascinating book. And I told him so, but being a novelist might not be his first calling. But Pontifex Maximus–ing . . . That's something he's cut out for. The whole gang in Washington would wake up tomorrow and find their terms had ended during the night."

"I like that idea."

"If you control time, it gives you the same power as controlling space, or even people."

"I have also learned that the word *leap-year*, in English, can be a verb. It can mean to skip over something. One can leap-year a bad day. Or if your father was a cook and your grandfather was a duke, you can leap-year your father, and take your title, or inheritance, or even your name, from him."

"It's like playing leapfrog."

"Frog?"

"*Sí. Una rana de saltos.*"

"A leaping frog?"

"A game."

"Ah. *Pídola.* But in that game you leap over one person at a time, no?"

"Correct."

"When you leap-year, you can jump over many. And backwards. You can take your name from your great-great-great grandfather."

"That would be a slave's name. I wish it could work the other way. That he could leap-year to the future, not just his name, whatever that was, but his whole self. To a time beyond the abolition. Beyond all these years we're going through now, and a ways into the future. To a time when *this* world is the *old* world. The *last* world. But only a name can travel through time, like a word through telephone cable. The rest of you has to stay put. The only name I know from my mother's side of the family, beside hers, is *Zit-to.*"

"You are a good teacher because you are wise."

"I've been told my ass is wise."

"I know this expression, and about you it is also true. Although you sometimes say strange things, or sometimes don't say anything —which is *your* way of saying a strange thing—you have a wisdom. You're *kind* of wise."

"I thank you, my dear, for that left-handed compliment."

"*Left-handed compliment?* I will write that down."

"The New York Public Library has something called the information number. You call it and you get someone who is probably sitting among piles of books, and staring into the screen of a computer. All they do, all day long, is answer questions. You call them and say, 'Could you tell me about leap year? What does *zit-to* mean? Who was Sadie Hawkins?' And they'll give you an answer."

"I will find that number and write it down."

"Even better, you should get a job there."

"You are wrong. You think I just want to know *things.* What I really want to know is what it feels like to know something very well, and to use what it is that I know. What it feels like to be an astronaut, or a surgeon, or the person that controls the days of the calendar. *That's* what I want to know."

"I hear you," Primo says.

"Are you hearing me, or just waiting for the pie to cool off?"

"*Zit-to.*"

"You can wait another five minutes."

"I can."

"Since tomorrow is February twenty-ninth, and since this semester you do not teach on Mondays, I would like to take you to lunch."

"Aren't we skipping breakfast?"

"You don't want to eat breakfast when I do. I get up too early. It's still dark."

"Lunch, then. It's a deal. But let's finish this meal before we concern ourselves with the next one. Can we possibly *leap-year* those five minutes till the pie is ready?"

"*Zit-to,*" Carolina says. "Leap-year the *flinks.*" Tonight we have words that are just our own. If we were with other people and said these things, they would not know what we were saying."

"They'd think we were crazy."

"No, they would be curious. And they would be envious. Do you know why?"

"I do not. I only know why they would think we were crazy."

"Then I will tell you. They would envy us because all the secrets in the world are in those things we hear other people say, but cannot, ourselves, understand."

30

The string of linked chirps emitted by the small alarm clock reaches into Primo's sleep and forms a rope up which he climbs, without effort and without waking, through the atmosphere of a dream he's already begun to forget. There was a dog in the dream, and the side of a house: the last things to fall away before he climbs into the late morning. *Dee—dee . . . dee—dee . . . dee—dee . . . dee—dee.*

A shaft of bright thin light falls across the red floorboards and across the foot of the bed. The room is otherwise dark.

Snow has fallen in the night and clings in hard white bars to the rungs of the fire escape just outside the curtainless window. Above the buildings across the street, and at a distance, a string of cars, one close behind the other, ascend the entry ramp of the Williamsburg Bridge and pass beyond the window's edge before they reach the horizontal span. *Dee—dee . . . dee—dee . . . dee—dee . . . dee—dee.* He awoke briefly, in the dark, when Carolina reset the alarm.

She begins her workday at seven-thirty and has lunch at eleven. She wanted him to sleep as late as he could and still wake up in time to meet her. To his awakened ears the alarm sounds like a cricket whose body is made of hard plastic.

His hand, beside his head on the pillow, smells of Carolina's body. Her hair, her skin, even her breath. She had slipped out of bed more than three hours ago, without disturbing the small environment they'd created around themselves, generated by their lovemaking, their sleep, their combined smells. He notices her denim jacket with the sports car insignia on front lying across the foot of the bed. He vaguely remembers her taking it off, setting it there, walking to the window, talking quietly to herself as she got ready, and putting on, instead, a long green overcoat.

He lifts the blankets and feels the nearest part of the outer world enter, diminishing Carolina's presence. The place he is in, wherever it is, is always a place wrapped in layers. Skin, blanket, room, atmosphere. And those are just the ones you can touch, and feel the weight of. Each day you somehow move upward, and during the day's course occupy each successive layer. At night you pass out of the system entirely, like completing a short life. The next morning, when you wake, you're back at the bottom, beneath a pile of blankets.

This morning he'd like to *leap-year* the entire day and remain in phase one, the first layer, skip the rest of the process until tomorrow, then start over again. If it were last year, or next year, this day wouldn't even exist.

He thinks of an Ethiopian painting his Aunt Olivia has on her wall. The sky, high above the ground, is filled with another, different civilization, walking around in what, for us, is substanceless air, seemingly unaware of and unconcerned about the lives being lived below. *If I pass their level, on my way through, I'm getting off.*

Who, in their right fucking mind, needs another day? *Dee—dee . . . dee—dee . . . dee—dee . . . dee—dee.*

He reaches across the bed to the small white clock on the seat of a chair set against the empty side of the double bed. On its face is the image of Mickey Mouse, dressed as a sorcerer, against a blue-black sky filled with small stars. When he turns off the alarm, the steady purr of late-morning traffic and the hiss of the steam radiator assert themselves in the small room, until his first whole waking thought—*It's cold*—readjusts the volume so that he will not even hear them again, in the half hour he has yet to remain here.

Following Carolina's instructions, Primo walks south, between the spans of the Williamsburg and Manhattan bridges, until he comes to York Street, where he turns left, and then walks toward Navy Street and the East River just beyond it.

The streets are nearly deserted. Less than half the floors of the old brick factory buildings seem occupied.

He notices two women walk into a building in which all the floors, except two, are gutted. All the windows on the third floor are covered with plywood and sheet metal. Only on the floor above that do the windows have glass panes, and the light and shadows of activity sliding across them. The window casements on all the other floors, below and above, are open and glassless. Nothing inside but the same cold air he's breathing.

Nearer the river, where he is to turn left, are the tall hurricane fences that surround the old Brooklyn Navy Yard, now filled with Con Ed's generators and transformers, the newest structures in his field of vision.

He remembers his mother telling him that the husbands of her two aunts, her mother's older sisters, had both served here, in the Navy, during the First World War. They were new citizens, the first members of her family to come here, and could barely speak English. Day and night, they were sentries. Their wives would bring them food in those old-fashioned lunchboxes shaped like barns.

"They were very choosy about what they ate," his mother had told him. "Like you." He was eight or nine at the time. He was home from school with the flu, which is what occasioned her telling the story. She had brought him chicken broth he didn't want to eat. "At that time," his mother said, "there was a terrible flu epidemic in New York."

"In-flu-enza," his father, who had just walked into the room, said. He was wearing his stethoscope. "And in those days, it wasn't just a bad cold . . ."

"We're lucky to live when we do," his mother said.

His father then sat down on the edge of the bed and placed the palm of his hand across Primo's forehead. "I'd say your fever is down from this morning." He smiled, set the earpieces of his stethoscope into his ears and placed it against Primo's chest. "Clear and strong," he said. He then moved the round disk below Primo's ribs. "Your stomach's trying to tell me something," he said. "But stomachs are very hard to understand. Here." He put the earpieces in Primo's ears. "Maybe you can tell me."

Primo heard a slight gurgling, and a squeezed, liquid, washing sound that might have been his own breath. He laughed.

His father put them back into his own ears. "Ah," he said. "I think I got it now." He sat up. The sides of the stethoscope fell back around his neck. "It's saying it wants some more of that chicken soup."

After his father left the room, his mother continued with her story. She used the voice he imagined was the voice *she* had heard the story in. "So one night, when they're on duty, another sailor tells them, *We can rest easy wit choo guys around. Between dose smelly* Eye-talian *cigars, and all da garlic in da food ya wives bring yas . . . Whew! Da flu wouldn't come near da place. Neither would da Germans!*"

It was his mother's mother, and those two aunts, whose photograph had been in the frame that later contained the wedding picture of Mariah and Primo. He remembers visiting his mother in Queens, on the day she replaced the picture. He and Mariah had come for dinner. They were both twenty-one, and newly married. When they walked into the house the frame, usually hanging on the wall, was on the kitchen table, and now their wedding picture was in it. His mother was nowhere in sight.

He and Mariah found her in the bedroom, angrily snapping the bedspread, unfurling it over the tucked-in blankets. Each time it floated down onto the bed, she pulled it up and snapped it again. There were tears on her cheeks, but when they came into the room she wasn't crying. She always made beds first thing in the morning, he told Mariah, later that day. And Mariah told him that she had. She'd just unmade it so she could make it again.

She sent them back inside, told them she'd be out in a minute, and they left her alone. After dinner, Primo helped her mount the photo on the wall. She never spoke of what was bothering her.

Years later, his aunt told him what happened that day. His mother had called her mother to tell her Primo had gotten married. "She'd spoken to her maybe once or twice since that day she dragged you to church. Remember? Anyway, when she told her her grandson had been made into an honest man, she wasn't interested. All she wanted to know was what color your wife's skin was. Your mother didn't answer. She hung up. She was used to her own eviction from the family. She'd already had over twenty years of practice. But by then, the world was changing, and for some reason she thought that if it kept changing, you might someday get to know her family. She'd held out some hope, even after all that time. She wanted to believe the rift could heal in the next generation. That maybe your children would get to know her mother's other great-grandchildren. This could soothe her, give some meaning to what she'd already endured."

Primo, walking along the cold street, thinks of the word *leap-year*. What his mother had wanted to do was leap out of the mess they lived in, jump so high that the planet would go through an entire rotation before she lit down again. When she did, she wanted to land right in the middle of the same family, but after the world had somehow healed itself.

"But she knew," Olivia had said, "after that call, it wasn't going to happen. Not if anybody was forecasting from that moment. Not in her mother's lifetime, not in hers . . ."

On the first blocks beyond the hurricane fences that edge the Con Ed facility, the buildings are even more desolate: their basic structures are still sturdy and standing, and they do not appear older, but their disuse is more complete, and has been their state longer. The cold wind coming off the river has penetrated his coat and sweater. He walks faster.

A pair of trolley tracks, set into the paving stones, runs up the street where the building in which Carolina works is located. She had told him to look for the rails. Although nothing has rolled on them since the Second World War, they still shine in the sunlight. Between the thin icy patches, the paving stones, tilting in different directions, form hills and valleys, as if the earth they are set in were as thin as a blanket and the river, just a few blocks east, extended just beneath it, forcing upward the shapes of its own heaving surface.

The building's only unlocked entrance, a wide steel door that scrapes the pavement when he pulls it open, leads directly into a freight elevator as wide as a two-car garage. Carolina had told him he would probably have to wait there for the operator to arrive.

Primo walks into the dark empty cabin of the elevator. The air is as cold as it is outdoors and smells strongly of cigarette smoke. There is another, smaller door at the back, as if the elevator itself were also the first in a chain of several rooms. He thinks of Carolina's joke: *¿A cuál piso?* It does not seem funny inside this strange, airless chamber. The company she works for is called CuddleCo and is on the third floor.

He steps out front again and waits in the sunlight. He notices that another set of rails branches off from the main track running along the far side of the street, moves toward this doorway and then passes under the cracked pavement of the sidewalk. Whatever vehicle those tracks once bore probably brought materials to this factory, fed them into the elevator and then brought finished products back toward the world.

From inside, he hears voices speaking Spanish. He walks back into the elevator. There are three people in the car with him, standing beside the back door, and from their voices Primo can tell they are a man and two women. The first thing about them to realize itself, the moment his eyes readjust to the darkness, are the unusual and unnaturally bright colors of the clothing or costumes they're wearing. Were there more light, the colors would be electric. Draped like a mantle over the head and shoulders of one woman is a sheet of strange, vivid cloth, several layers of it in fact, printed in the pattern of a yellow zebra with electric-green stripes. The man is wearing a cape, as long as Superman's, with two corners tied in the front. It's covered with the skin of a purple-spotted cheetah. The other woman is wearing several different-colored layers over her shoulders. At the front, where she holds the sides closed, and at the bottom, edges of blue, red, green and orange show. The outer layer might be the coat of a nappy-furred orange bear. She wears a blue watch cap on her head.

A short man enters through the inner door, a cigarette in his mouth. He pulls a wooden lever and the elevator suddenly jumps upward. They rise too quickly for the first few feet of the ascent, then very slowly. There are no gates or doors, just the walls sliding by.

Primo can now see that the bearskin is actually the pattern of several smaller bears. Distributed evenly across the material are small constellations of eyes, ears and whiskery snouts. He begins to laugh, audibly. The funniest part of it is that no one smiles or even finds this unusual. He breathes deeply and looks down at his feet to stop himself.

When they stop at the third floor, he steps off into an open, hangar-sized loft, in which hundreds of people sit in rows at sewing machines and other kinds of devices. More than half of them are wearing the same kinds of comic-book animal skins around their shoulders. The others wear jackets and overcoats, and gloves with the fingers cut out. He now understands. The icy clouds of breath that pass out of their mouths, and his, explain.

He takes a step into the room and hears the elevator begin to move. He turns, watches it descend. He knows, from outside, that the building has six or eight floors, but it doesn't continue going up. He wonders if this could be the only floor that's occupied.

The three other people from the elevator walk out into the room. He moves his eyes along the rows of workers but can't find Carolina. There are men and women operating machines that cut the cloth, and machines that sew it into shapes resembling large empty gloves. There's a row of tables on which people hold the cloth forms over the mouths of hoses that suck something from deep canvas carts and force it into the heads and bodies and embryonic legs of small bears and cats and giraffes and zebras.

There is suddenly someone standing beside Primo. A tall, heavy-set smiling man in a Mets baseball cap and earmuffs. He must have been standing somewhere close to the wall alongside the opening to the elevator. His odd and sudden presence is both awkward and threatening. He's some kind of guard or bouncer, yet it feels like he simply happened to be there, hanging out in the space beside the space Primo is now standing in.

He says good morning to Primo, loudly and in Spanish. Primo now notices a second thin band, encircling the back of his cap, which holds the headset of a Walkman, tucked beneath the pads of his earmuffs. He is shy, friendly and menacing. He asks Primo if he can be of any help. Again he speaks in Spanish, and loudly.

The man takes a small step and leans unusually close. Primo can hear the thin stream of electric music that escapes the earphones and earmuffs. There are guitars and a heavy bass line. It's as if the sound were coming out of his ears and not going into them.

Primo still can't locate Carolina, and the man's too-near-ness makes him angry. He turns to him and points to the Mets symbol on the front of his cap. He then says, in English, "Center field, am I right? I always wondered what you guys did off season."

"Is there some way I can help you?" the man says again, this time in English.

"Yeah. I'm going to guess the tune I *think* you're listening to, and you can tell me if I'm right. Ready? 'My Girl' . . . The bass line gives it away."

"Are you looking for someone?" he asks Primo.

"Not looking, waiting. I'm meeting someone for lunch."

He tells Primo the person he is meeting should have told him to wait downstairs.

As he is saying this, Primo sees Carolina walking toward them up an aisle between machines. The guy, who also sees her approaching, reaches to the wall behind Primo, and presses the button that will bring the elevator.

They walk through the door at the back of the elevator, through a hall that leads to an exit on the other side of the building, across the street and into a small, crowded coffee shop. Loud music is playing. It's the first heated room he's been in since he left Carolina's apartment.

She directs him to a stack of plastic trays and then to the back of a short line that leads to a counter in front of two cooks standing at a grill.

The woman ahead of them sings the refrain of the sweet ballad that fills the room. "*Me duele la cabecita* . . ." Ahead of her a man and a woman speak loudly to the cooks.

"I love this group," Carolina tells him. She hums along too. "They are the Hermanos Rosario."

"They're not the only ones with a headache," Primo says.

"When the music is loud it takes you into it quickly." She smiles. "It makes a little vacation out of a lunch hour."

"If you work where they do, where *you* do, a little vacation isn't enough. You need one that lasts the rest of your life."

"It *is* unpleasant."

"Un-*pleasant* . . . ? Do you know it's illegal to work under conditions like those? When the heat goes off, you're supposed to send people home. And that fucking elevator . . . Is that the only way in and out?"

"You know my English isn't yet so strong and there are better words for this than *unpleasant.* I know what they are, in any language, and so do the other people I work with."

"And who is that goon in the baseball cap? I didn't like him one bit. Judging by his articulate response to me, I'd say it was mutual."

He notices that in the time they have waited only one person, the woman ahead of them, has moved to the counter in front of the grill. Both she and the woman who'd already been there seem to be bargaining with the cooks.

"Okay," the woman says. "If I get the french fries and the hot dog and the little cakes . . ." She points to a package of Drake's cupcakes. "How much is *that?*"

"Two-thirty."

"Then I don't want that. And for *two* hot dogs and the little cakes?"

"*Lo mismo.*"

"Then a hot dog and two little cakes?"

"Bingo," the man says.

Primo smiles at Carolina. "*Bingo?*" he says, in a whisper.

The woman sets the hot dog on her tray and puts the two packages of cupcakes into her bag.

They all move a step forward. The woman ahead of Primo is conducting the same kind of negotiations. Both she and the cooks use the word *peso* for dollar.

"What the hell is this?" he asks Carolina.

"Order," she tells him. "We have only one hour, and other people are waiting."

When they are sitting at a table eating, she explains that their boss has paid, for each of them, in this restaurant, two dollars a day toward lunch. "So everyone tries to get as much food as they can for that amount. No one wants to spend more. And no one wants to get less."

"You mean a free lunch?"

"If it does not cost more than two dollars."

"Since I left your apartment, less than an hour ago, I've felt like I've been traveling farther and farther from Earth," Primo says.

"Eat your cheeseburger," Carolina says.

"Yet, as far as I know, lunch isn't served elsewhere in the solar system. And there's the fact that *you're* here." He touches her cheek. Maybe it's just what the world is always like on Leap Year's Day. In four years it's easy to forget. Tomorrow things'll return to normal."

"I like my neighborhood much better," Carolina then says. "More people live there."

"That's the least of it. To start with, there's the interesting fringe benefits you get in this neighborhood: a two-dollar lunch and all the stuffed-animal skins you can wear when the temperature drops below freezing." He turns his head toward the counter. "Are they playing that same record over again?"

"It is very popular here."

He notices that a man, now facing the cooks, is waving his arms and arguing loudly.

One of the cooks waves a spatula back and forth to emphasize *no*.

"Yesterday you gave me the hamburger *with* the cheese," the man says, "*and* the french fries for two dollars!"

"My first response to this free lunch," Primo says to Carolina, "was that your boss, whoever he is—maybe that goon in the baseball cap—has one valve of his heart still working. But I quickly realized I must be wrong. How much does he pay people?"

"Different. People get different amounts. There are different machines. The sewing machine operators, and the stuffers. The cutters get the most, and the people who have worked there a long time."

"How much do you get?"

"How much do *you* get?"

"Not much, but on a different scale of *much*."

"Three dollars and thirty-five cents."

"An hour?"

"Yes. And the lunch."

"Yes, the lunch. And you have a green card. Everybody who studies at *Solidaridad Humana* has to have at least a green card. How much would you get if you didn't have one?"

"Less."

"How much less?"

"You ask me questions like I have done something wrong."

"I'm sorry. That isn't my intention."

"I think you are mad at Franco, the man you have called a goon."

"I am. Because he *is* a goon. But that's just part of it. How *much* less?"

"Two."

"Jesus. What's the minimum wage, four-something . . . ?"

"Three dollars and thirty-five cents."

"You can't live on *that.* It's a struggle to get by on *my* salary. How could anyone live on two dollars an hour? With or without a fucking two-peso lunch."

"You are speaking too loudly."

"No one can hear me. Not with all the bargaining going on over there, and the Rosario Brothers getting another headache at a million decibels."

"Most of the people who I work with cannot get other jobs. And they are afraid. The free lunch makes them feel like American workers."

"I got news for you. They *are* American workers."

"You are speaking too loudly again."

"But these conditions are monstrous. Are you aware they're also illegal?"

"I am. We all know this."

"Then why do you show up every day? Shouldn't we call somebody? The police, the unions, a priest? Somebody?"

"Last night I said you were wise. But today I don't think so. Today you are making me angry."

"Why?"

"Have you heard the term *at-will employment?* It is not a term you will hear on *Jeopardy.*"

"I haven't."

"It means, simply, that unless someone is a member of a union, or is otherwise protected by law, they can become . . . *desempleado* . . ."

"You mean get fired."

"Yes. A strange use of that word. They can become *fired* for any reason their boss wants them to. Maybe because they are too fat or have pimples, or because they don't want to be touched by their supervisors, or don't speak English well enough, or maybe because they speak it too well."

"How do you become a *not-at-will* employee?"

"Most people are *at-will* employees. They just don't know it, or think about it. Something other than laws or unions protects them. What protects them is that *they* are the people who come home from secure jobs every night in the movies and on television. The screen they see themselves on is like a mirror. You do not see in a mirror what isn't there."

"I hear that."

"The people I work with are not on this screen. According to your government, there is no such thing as the people I work with. And most of them prefer it that way. They are, in the official words, *undocumented* workers, the most *at-will* employees of all."

"I'm sorry if I'm making you angry. But there must be something they can do."

"You are a fool if you think people must think the way you do. Even if you are right. What they can do is wait and hope something better will happen." She looks around, then quietly adds, "A chance to get a green card, or a better job."

"I'm going to find out about this. I'll see what the law has to say."

"Keep your voice down."

"I'll keep my voice down."

"We are supposed to be enjoying a Leap Year's Day lunch."

"The food sucks. The ambience is worse." Primo stops, is quiet for a second, then lifts his hand, palm upward. "But I like the company."

"I am glad," Carolina says.

Primo lifts his can of Pepsi. "*Zit-to* and *Flink*, *at-will* lunch partners."

"We can at least have this small moment of calmness."

"We could, if that goddamn record wasn't playing again. The fucking thing's worse than your alarm clock."

"Now you don't like my alarm clock?"

"I like your alarm clock. I like Mickey Mouse, and even more, I like the person who sets it every night. However, I am not fond of the noise it makes."

"I like the noises you make, especially the strange things you say. Though today you are making too many." As she speaks, she looks at her watch.

"You have to go back soon," he says.

"Five minutes."

Primo stands up.

"You are still angry," Carolina says.

"If I leap-year those five minutes in my mind, I see you back in that fucking sweatshop where it's too cold to sweat. And that goon standing there like a fucking watchdog."

"He *is* ugly, isn't he?"

"Unpleasant."

"Yes, unpleasant."

"And speaking of noises, he has noises coming *out* of his ears."

Carolina laughs.

"And if I *leap-year* to tomorrow," Primo says, "to this same time of day, I'll be in Manhattan, but even from there I'll probably hear them playing *'Me Duele la Cabecita'* again and again and again, and why the fuck not, if it makes a little vacation out of the time it takes to eat a two-peso lunch. . . ."

SELF-TALK

31

The conversation Primo had spent the last hour having with the students in his evening class continues itself in his head, as if they were still with him, walking up Avenue A toward East Third Street. They'd begun by looking through the newspaper, not reading, just passing it around, holding it up, looking at the photographs and naming things. Not the subjects of the pictures but things in the background: stop sign, hubcap, awning, nightstick, umbrella, steeple, cirrus cloud? No, look, *cumulonimbo* . . . Sparrow, dusk, clear, *nublado*, cloudy . . .

The clouded sky over the Vatican—the President was visiting the Pope—began a series of transitions that carried their conversation from the newspaper, out the window, and then back into the classroom, like a drummer moving a roll from the high hat, across the snare, and onto the skin of the tom-tom. They searched the room, looking for words they hadn't yet spoken in English. Transparent, casement, steam valve, lapel, yogurt, polka dot, corduroy, varnish, light fixture, paint chip, dust ball.

Primo, now alone, walking up the avenue, is talking to himself. He doesn't move his lips, or speak aloud, but his tone is more formal, the words internally louder and more clearly enunciated, than usual self-talk: *Fender, piss, hydrant, bottle cap, skid mark.*

Although spring has recently begun, and the air is getting warmer, everything still appears cold.

Class, amidst this profusion of persons, places and things, I espy something uniquely interesting on the corner just ahead. There, *see it? Sitting right on top of that city garbage can is an uneaten piece of toast. White bread, I believe.*

And there's a young couple, see them? They're arm-in-arming toward the setting sun, the westerly side of the neighborhood, where orange juice costs five cents more per quart.

And now look here. That *is a closed window gate. What is behind it is harder to explain. A storefront. It once had shoes in it. Then people eating. Then works of art and people looking at them. Then something I can't remember. Now, if you look through those diamond shapes in the window gate, and through the glass, you will see that the inside of the window is coated with newspaper. The business inside is changing again. That space has entered the* bardo *between incarnations.*

Bardo. A word Mariah had used a lot. The period between things. The transition, the passage. She wrote a series of poems entitled "Bardos." He remembers her saying, "It's what milk must go through to become cheese." *How do I explain, class? No, nothing to do with Brigitte Bardot. Let's see . . . Tibetan lamas use this word a lot.* No, *not* llamas. *It's* between *things. That's* all, *folks. It's the moment between the rinse and spin dry. In fact, it's the very sound a washing machine makes when changing cycles. Chug*-bar-do-*chug. That's where the word came from. It's not English, Spanish or Tibetan. It's the language of washing machines.*

Primo walks up to the storefront. There's not a space he can see through in the covered window. The door is locked and inside it's quiet. He tries to remember what was there after the gallery. He's been too preoccupied lately, while walking to and from things, to notice.

Primo raises the door of his mailbox, reaches in and pulls out a small stack of letters wrapped like a tortilla in a coupon circular from the Key Food supermarket.

It's always cooler in the entryway, since the sun can't reach into it and the heat that escapes from the apartments reaches only as far as the building's inner hall. *Architecturally speaking, this is just an entryway, class. Metaphorically, however, it's a bardo.* A chilly one. His breath couldn't create steam on the street, but it does in here.

He unfolds the circular and looks through the small stack of mail. On top is a letter from Local 613, Distributive Workers' Union. He opens it to take a quick look. There's a note and a small pamphlet.

> The enclosed tells you a little bit about how we work. When reading this, bear in mind the things I told you over the phone.
>
> Sincerely,
>
> N. Jacobs

The day after he met Carolina at work, he wrote to the Department of Labor for information on the rights of aliens, legal and not, in the workplace. He told them he was a prospective employer. He learned, from the information they sent, that even illegal immigrants, since they are working on American soil, have rights. "If their specific job description and work area fall under the protection of the National Labor Relations Act of 1935"—that is, if they are not supervisors, and if they are not farm or domestic workers, public or federal employees, transportation, small interstate or intrastate commerce employees—"they are guaranteed, in their entirety, the rights provided by the Fair Labor Standards Act of 1939." The people who work in CuddleCo, as far as Primo can determine, are not among the above exceptions. Thus, according to federal law, the rights that are their due include minimum wage, a forty-hour work week, two weeks' vacation, reasonable working conditions and environment ". . . and the right to self-organize, and to form, join, or assist labor organizations." Primo then called Local 613, and spoke to a business agent. The man asked Primo if he worked at the place he just described, and Primo asked why he wanted to know. He said no union can even talk about organizing a workplace unless they are asked to by its employees. Primo told him he did work there, he just started last month. The man said there were more shops like this one in the New York area than anybody could imagine. "It'd make your hair curl," he said. Primo liked that expression. He told the man his hair was curly enough already. He said to Primo, "Yeah, they have rights. *As* workers. But not as citizens. How can you defend those rights when to announce that they are being violated is to announce your presence to Immigration? They don't want us in there. Not just the employers, who are rarely happy to see us, the workers too. If you *do* work there, talk to your co-workers. I'm afraid they'll tell you what I just did."

"You don't have to save that," a voice, from behind Primo, says. Mrs. Karbash and Lady had come in while he was reading.

"What?" Primo asks her.

"That." She points to the circular. "You know, when you walk through the automatic door and then, to your right . . . ?" She motions with her hand.

Primo doesn't know what door she's talking about.

"Where they line up the shopping carts. Right there, in the first ones nobody ever uses, they keep big stacks of them."

"I don't use coupons much anyway." Primo hands her the rolled-up circular.

"You *should.* Let's face it. If we were rich we wouldn't be here. If we were rich we'd be in Miami Beach."

"You're right," Primo says. He smiles, reaches down and pets Lady.

"Oh yeah," she says. "You can save a lot of money with coupons." She shows the circular to Lady, who has her forepaws on Primo's knee. "Can't you, girl. We'll use this later, to clean up after your business."

Primo looks through the rest of his mail. A bill from Con Edison, a letter from Felix, a postcard advertising the grand opening of a new store in the neighborhood, a catalog from a small publishing house addressed to Mariah and a ticket-sized card from a local locksmith with a number to call if you lock yourself out.

"Weren't you married once?" Mrs. Karbash asks him.

"I was," Primo answers.

"What happened?"

Primo retains his smile but returns his gaze to the pieces of mail in his hands.

"Isn't that her?" Mrs. Karbash asks, pointing at Mariah's name on the catalog.

"It is."

"How long since . . . you know?"

"Divorce?"

She nods.

"Five years now."

"That long? Goodness. And still she gets mail here."

"Just fourth-class."

"I was asking because for a long time I haven't seen her, but *that* long . . . I hadn't realized."

Primo opens the inner door. He holds it so she and Lady can pass through.

"I was married once, you know."

"You were?"

"Close the door. You're coming in too? It's chilly."

Primo lets the door shut, then walks to the bottom of the steps.

"Yeah," Mrs. Karbash says. "I lost him in Korea." As she speaks, she looks at her hand, gripping the wide painted knob atop the first upright of the iron banister. "We got married in 1950. That's when we moved into the building."

"I was born that year."

"And I was *married* that year."

"I know."

"You want to hear another coincidence? His name was Tom. That's why I like seeing your name on the mailbox. *Thomas.* When I see it there, it's like Tom's still here. It's like he just moved upstairs."

"My first name's Primo," he tells her. He reaches out his hand. They shake.

"Ah. Like a ballerina." She laughs. "A prima donna." She's still holding Primo's hand. She shakes it again. "I was just kidding," she says. "You don't strike me as a prima donna."

Primo smiles. He's now standing just ahead of her on the first step.

"Goodness. Born the same year as my marriage, and your being named Thomas." She smiles at him, then asks, "Do you keep in touch?"

"In touch?"

"You and your wife?"

"Rarely."

"You should, you know. I watched you two. You were together a long time. You were so young when you moved here, the two of you were like brother and sister. And you know what's most important? That she's *alive.* That's a blessing. Family's still family. I never cared much for this divorce business."

Primo looks down at his mail.

"You know I'm right," she says.

The postcard advertisement is for a clothing store called House. It opens next week. *Not just garments: jewelry, stationery, lampshades, knickknacks, lapel buttons, toys, et al. Grand Opening April 1st. No fooling!* Primo reads the address and realizes that House is the next tenant in the now closed storefront he just passed.

"The shoe store," he says.

"On Avenue A?" Mrs. Karbash says. "They got a new business going in there."

"This is it," he says. He shows her the card.

"I got one too."

"At least they're selling clothing," Primo says. "Maybe they're heading back in the general direction of a shoe store."

"Oh yeah. I remember that place. For a million years, he was there."

"Tell me," Primo asks her. "In all the time you've lived here had it always been a shoe store?"

"Yeah. He repaired shoes too. I used to get half-soles. Morty, his name was."

"And did he always have the same brown shoes right in the middle of the window? The high ones with the seam across the front?"

"*Shoes.* The window was always shoes."

"But do you remember the high brown ones? On the top, in the middle."

"Let's see. I remember all the shoes being there. In two rows. Good shoes. Well made, but not fancy. A lot of them, maybe half of them, were brown. The rest were black. That's all I remember."

"That's okay."

"Are you looking to buy that kind of shoes? The kind Morty sold they probably don't make anymore."

"No. I just want to remember them."

"Huh," she says. "I tell you what. If I think of anything else, I'll tell you the next time I see you. Okay?"

"Thanks, Mrs. Karbash."

"I will, I promise." They both begin climbing the stairs.

"I'm old, you know," she says.

Primo stops and turns.

"I climb stairs slow. I remember things slow. But if I remember anything about those shoes you're interested in, I'll let you know."

"Thanks," Primo says again.

"See you, Primo Thomas." She smiles, having used her long-term neighbor's name for the first time.

Primo walks in, looks across the room at his answering machine, sees the tiny, nonblinking red eye—no messages—drops his briefcase and jacket onto the couch, sits at the table and looks through the pamphlet sent by the union.

It contains little information that is new, or that he finds useful. At the request of the employees, a union representative will come to their workplace and speak to them, and their employer, about the possibility of organizing a union. A majority of the workers must want one for this to happen. The next step, the most difficult, also involves the employer: negotiating a labor contract. If people found acceptable the conditions and compensations their employer wanted them to find acceptable, or if they already had a relationship that allowed for the negotiation of these things, no one would have called the union in the first place.

He opens his Con Ed bill: $35.19. Two dollars less than last month. The next bill, with each day's additional daylight, will be cheaper.

He opens the envelope from Felix and unfolds the letter. Felix had said he would send copies of the poem Dr. Silva read to them in the hospital, after he'd translated it into English. Primo imagines this is it. There's something attached but it's not the poem, it's a news clipping in Spanish. The headline reads: *Tres Personas Murieron en Ataque de Morteros.* He looks back at the letter.

3/22/88
Dear Primo,

I hate what has happened, and what has become my responsibility to tell you. I have just received word from Luisa. You remember her, she works in the Hotelito. There was a mortar attack last week at an Upay *in the north, near Jinotega. After we left, Angelita had gone there, to work. The house that she and a family of three were staying in was hit. They said everything inside burst into flames. They said it all happened very quickly. Primo, Angelita has died. An eight-year-old boy and his father also died. Only the mother survived. Their family name is Núñez. Angelita had told Luisa that she had become close to you, that you were very important to her. Luisa asked that I write you and give you this terrible news. She sent this article, from* El Nuevo Diario. *She said that Angelita's daughter has come to Managua and will stay with her and Mercedes until she goes back to school. If she learns anything more, she will write. Dear Primo, I am so sorry. Please, when you get this, call me. If you want to, that is. Call me anytime.*

Primo looks carefully at the article. It restates what Felix had said in the letter. Between the two columns of print is a grainy black-and-white photograph of a peasant home. Half the ribbed metal roof is missing. Had it been blown off? It's impossible to tell from the photograph if it had simply been lifted off by human hands, had at some point fallen off or had never been there in the first place. There's a crack, as wide as two adult humans, in the concrete wall. There are some chunks of broken concrete, but they could be rocks. The dark areas at its edges, where it had once been joined, could be the burnt-black results of fire, or could simply be grainy photographic shadow. The place could've been like that for years. It could be any fucking ramshackle miniskirt house.

I see nothing indicating she was inside this house. Where was she, in the front or the back? Was she asleep? Was she anywhere near the fucking place?

These things are so fucking rough-built and jerry-rigged you can't tell from a photograph if one has been blown up or not. You can barely tell in real life. These fucking things are built in a demolished state. They always look blown up. *I'd rather live in the subway.*

He stands up. He pushes the chair he was sitting on under the table. He walks toward the door, stops.

If he goes through the inventory of everything that filled the last hour or so, from his class onward, all the way up to right now, he can make *this* less real than the rest of it. *Stop sign, awning, clouds, steam valve, polka dot, paint chip, storefront, mailbox, minimum wage, shoes, brother and sister. See you, Primo Thomas.*

He asks their realness, their presence, to grow. To overpower everything else. *Get louder, get brighter.* He calls on them to become *realer.* Each thing, each sound. Realer than a fucking letter, a scrap of newspaper, a mortar attack two thousand miles away.

But they can't, because now they're words. The class had changed all these things from news photographs, from the world outside the window, from the room they were in, from the street he walked on, from right *there,* into words.

Then make *this* a word.

You change something into words and you do the job right, it never comes back.

Even the space the dove *had* been in, or the bouquet of flowers, before the magician said *Abracadabra* and waved back his black cape, *even that empty fucking space is more substantial than a word.* It's filled with the *absence* of dove, of flowers and also, for a long moment, the possibility they might come back. A word doesn't lack for anything. A word never changes what it is.

This happened far away. Change *this* into words. Nothing is farther away than words.

32

Between this evening, when he passed the storefront that once displayed the brown shoes in its window, on his way home from school, and now, someone has dragged the garbage cans from the front of the building out to the curb, arranged them in a line and set bricks on their lids so they'd remain in place atop the overfull cans.

There are six of them, ready to be emptied in the morning, when the garbage truck passes. They're ugly and they stink, and tomorrow morning, when the sun rises, they'll stink even more. A six-pack of trash. A family of fat, squat, nasty people, who snarl at children when they pass by. Each lid has black phone wire tied to the handle on top and tied again to one of the handles at the side, just in case anyone might want to steal them. It looks like the members of the garbage can family are all wearing Walkmans, the wires running from their fat waists and up into the rice paddy hats held atop their fat heads with bricks. They listen to the same song over and over: *Stick out your can, here comes the garbage man* . . . Thank God for these wires and bricks. Those metal lids are worth their weight in gold. Who knows—thieves might want to use them as cymbals, shields, pizza trays. People'll do anything these days. Maybe put them on top of their own garbage cans. *If suddenly there was no law and order and no police around to keep me from doing whatever the fuck*

I wanted to, I know what I'd *do. I'd go right out and steal these dented, piece-of-shit garbage can covers. Maybe I'd take the cans, too. They're even more beat-up-looking. Kicked in, split open. They might even go all the way back to the days of Morty.*

Primo went out earlier and brought home a bottle of wine, most of which he drank, quickly, sitting at the table. He downed the last few ounces sitting on the stone steps of the Most Holy Redeemer Church farther down the block. He knew he'd want more, he figured he'd finish on the way. The plastic letter-set sign beside the church doors, with the times of Masses and services, had been missing two letters since before he'd moved out of the city and come back again. *Mo— Holy Redeemer.* They'd better fix that. The brothers'll be reading *More* holy. And in the language of superlatives, *Mo Holy* is less holy than *Most Holy*. Could be a lot less.

He then had a shot of rum in a small, dark bar near Avenue B. Though it was the nearest one to his building, he'd never gone in there before. Through the window, day or night, he'd see the same handful of older, quiet, white men, leaning over their drinks. In his passings by, they never appeared to move or speak: it was as if the small, dark room emanated from their few motionless, angry selves, and would disappear if they all left it at the same time. No one else, white or otherwise, ever went into this last outpost of a generation that began moving to the boroughs, or farther out into America, in the years after the war. The bartender was eating a take-out hero sandwich and watching the TV with the sound off. The only other person at the bar, a silent man drinking shots with short beers, had an indecipherable blue tattoo on his forearm. He'd laid the arm across the bar as a border, kept it there and stared into the ashtray in which he would set down his cigarette each time he lifted a glass to his mouth.

Afterward Primo walked to another bar, on First Avenue and Seventh Street, which was always crowded with people wrapped up in their drinking and talking, sitting at the bar or at the row of tables next to the wall, or just standing around. If there was a seat at the bar, and tonight there was, he could just sit there, in the middle of the smoky clusters of people, get drunker and jam all his frequencies with thick noise and conversation, and not talk to anybody if he didn't want to.

Now he has wandered back onto the street. He wanted to buy another bottle of wine, to bring home with him, but the two liquor stores on Avenue A have closed.

When he was sitting at the crowded bar, he noticed the bartender had skin about as dark, and as light, as his. Primo looked at him, then at his own reflection in the mirror facing him behind the rows of top-shelf bottles, then back at the bartender, who was younger than he was. Maybe in his late twenties. He had light brown eyes, like marbles, and loose, hip, nappy curls. There had to be a white person somewhere in his genetic haystack, and probably nearby. Primo was drinking doubles of straight rum.

"Yo," he said to the bartender, who was gliding down the bar, evaluating the condition of people's drinks. "My name's Primo."

"Hiya, Primo," he said. "Need anything?"

"I do." He tossed back the last sip in the rocks glass in front of him. "You can fill this again."

The bartender refilled Primo's glass, without moving it. His hand, holding the bottle, moved up and down like a yo-yo, and the stream of dark rum, sliding out of the chrome pourer, was the string. He then cut off the flow with a sudden uptilt. "You want some more water behind that?" he asked.

"I'm fine, thanks."

He slipped a five-dollar bill out of the stack in front of Primo, the remainder of the twenty with which he paid for his first two drinks.

When he brought back the change Primo smiled at him. "What's your name?"

"David," he said.

"David," Primo leaned forward and said to him, "I don't mean to pry or anything . . . so don't answer me if you think this is too personal. But what else you got in you besides the blood of Mother Africa?"

David smiled. "What else *you* got?" He emptied the ashtray being used by the couple sitting to the right of Primo.

"I'm only asking," Primo said, "because *I'm* mulatto." Primo paused, started to laugh, then said, "You know? I just realized something. This is like the third or fourth time in my whole life, *as* a mulatto, I ever used that word out loud." He slowly shook his head. "No shit. I don't like it. It's too anthropological. You know what I'm saying? Too *National Geographic*."

"I agree." David set his elbow on the bar and leaned toward Primo. "That's the cold, scientific meaning. There's also the interracial-cinematic-erotic-Mandingo version. That's when the word *mulatto* comes up, in reference to oneself, and you get to watch whoever else is in the conversation imagining just how you got made. Black sweaty flesh humping pale skin."

"Or vice versa," Primo added. "The island version of that one's better than the plantation version. With the island version you get palm trees and drums and pounding surf and shit."

David reached across the bar and shook Primo's hand.

"My mother was Italian," Primo told him. "You might call me a *moolin-yatto*. And from the look of you, you handsome devil, I was wondering if you ain't got a bit of the Mediterranean floating around in there yourself."

David laughed. "My father's a Turkish Jew," he said to Primo. He took a step back, and quickly surveyed the bar.

"Wow," Primo said. "Really? There ain't too many of them around."

"Not around here," David said.

"This is cool," Primo said. "I don't get to talk about this stuff very often. I think that's because I don't like to use the word *mulatto* unless I'm talking to another one. In mixed company it sounds too much like a white word."

"Or unmixed company," David said.

"On not mixed enough company."

"You can say that again."

"You're getting me all mixed up," Primo said.

"That's cause we're like these drinks, though not the one you're drinking, *mixed*."

"One Primo on the rocks. One David with a twist of lemon."

"I like it," David said.

"David, I don't know how old you are, but you're so cool right now, you'll be cool forever. I can tell that."

"I thank you, Primo."

"You're welcome, my friend." Primo shoved his empty glass toward David's side of the bar.

"On the subject of drinks, and blood, I get the impression you were already hitting it pretty hard before you got here. And you just put three away *fast.* Listen to your mixed-race bartender. I got some hot coffee back here . . ."

Someone called David's name from farther down the bar. Primo watched him open two beers, then mix and pour a martini. He drank back the new shot. He'd just mentioned his mother to David and now, as much in a dream as in this crowded public room, he saw her, snapping the bedspread over her bed. It floats slowly down to the bed, she snaps it again. He looked for David but he was nowhere in sight.

Primo wanted another drink. He wasn't halfway there. He wanted to be drunk enough to have complete control over the conversation, and who he'd be in it with, the next time he was alone and talking to himself. He could see the whole space behind the bar but couldn't see David. Conversations *that* exclusive require being much drunker than he thus far was.

David then rushed past with a tall, thin, green drink in one hand, and in the other a mug of coffee, which he set in front of Primo on his way by. After he dropped off the green drink he returned, briefly. "On me," he said.

Primo didn't want coffee. He wanted another rum, and he wanted, for now, to keep talking to David. He was cool, this guy with his Turkish-Jewish father. Maybe that was why he could pour rum like an Arab pours tea. He wanted to see him do another one of them magic, smooth-ass, up-and-down piss-pours. This other *mu-la-to-re-mi-fa-so-la-ti-do* . . . Cool. *Now, where the fuck's he gone off to* this *time?*

If David was too busy, he'd get another bottle from the liquor store and head home. You don't stop in midconversation, not when there's more night to travel through. He didn't need David to continue, to make it the rest of the way to the other side. When you're drinking at home, and by yourself, you have the most pleasing discussions. Everyone's so interested in what you have to say. And no one ever says a thing you don't want to hear.

Primo steers his body through a long swerve, then another. He doesn't stagger. He aims himself through the pattern of a slalom ski course, holding out his arms for balance, away from the row of trash cans toward the corner of East Third Street. He wonders if Angelita had gotten any of the postcards he'd sent her. The one with the view of the Manhattan skyline, or the front of the Abyssinian Baptist Church, or the Brooklyn Bridge.

He sees her and he stops walking. He sees her completely absorbed in looking at the pictures on each one, the way she had looked at the papers she was sorting the night he saw her, through the window of her cabin at the Selva Negra.

He starts walking. He thinks of stopping in again at the old bar he'd been in earlier. Not much ambience, but a drink's a drink, and nobody'll bother him there. Maybe the rest of the gang has showed, all of them sitting there, growling privately over their shots and short beers. Maybe the two guys from before have turned to stone from sitting still so long and the next owners already have the place undergoing renovation. Maybe he'll find another bar. Like magic he'll find one he's never seen before, one that was a drugstore last week, a laundromat the week before.

Earlier, he had read the date on the article. It happened *la noche pasada, a las once*, according to the March 17 issue of *El Nuevo Diario*. Eleven o'clock, March 16. Ten days ago. He'd sent the last card around the fifth. She might have gotten it. Hopefully, she got at least one of them. Or two. He'd touched each one of them, written his name on them, before a hundred other hands touched them, but after that, she touched them. *Oh, please, one, at least.* Maybe that's why she had told Luisa they'd become close. Because she got one.

Of course she got *one. More.* In the letter, the phrase, as it passed from her to Luisa to Felix and, finally, to him, was: *She had told Luisa that you were very important to her . . .*

But . . . He stops again. He's just reached the corner. He turns himself around, heads back along the stretch of sidewalk he just walked on. *But,* Carolina had said, the night she asked him to carry the package with him to Nicaragua, *No tengo confianza en los correos.* He stops again. She'd never received even the first one. That's also possible. But then, how do Felix and Luisa keep getting each other's letters? What can anybody have *confianza* in? *Please, just one.*

Primo is standing in front of the garbage cans again, facing the storefront. *Just one.*

He turns, lifts a brick off one of the lids, spins around and hurls it at the window. It slams against the gate, jangles it loudly against the glass, which does not break. *Too big to fit through. Fucking brick's too big.*

"Congratulations!" he shouts, at the top of his voice. He grabs the lid, rips the wire, and in pulling it spins 360 degrees until he's facing the street again. "Keep a lid on it, buddy," he says aloud, and laughs. "Hurray!" He hurls the lid into the air. *Like a Frisbee, like a graduation hat . . . what do you call them, mortar-fucking-boards . . . mortar fucking rounds,* kaboom, *like a bonnet . . . fucking hurray . . . like Mary Tyler Moore used to do every week at the beginning of that ridiculous TV show that Mariah actually* liked *to watch. . . . I sure got a lot of shit in my head. Too much of it is words. Primo, you're just too much.*

The lid lands on top of a van parked farther up the block, with Chinese characters painted on its side. He notices a man in a white T-shirt, standing inside a second-floor window across the street, watching him.

He kicks over the can and garbage spills out onto the sidewalk. "Let's see, anything good in here? What's that, Cool Whip?" He holds the empty plastic container up to the man watching from his fire escape. "Shit," he shouts to him, "everybody knows these containers are *not* biodegradable." He kicks the garbage around. "Let's see. What else we got here? This is a milk container, class. This is a Popsicle stick. This here's some kind of disgusting meat somebody chewed up but didn't swallow. Anything good here? A piece of toast? A squash racket?"

He looks up. The man is still watching him. *Shit, just do one thing. All right, two. Just do two things. Fling a garbage can cover into the air and throw a brick, just like fucking Ignatz, at a window that don't even break . . .*

He walks up to the window. The brick had broken into two pieces when it hit the sidewalk.

He picks up one of the halves, walks back to the garbage cans, does a pitcher's windup and flings it right through one of the diamond-shaped gaps in the window gate. It crashes through, immediately tripping the alarm. It leaves a hole in the glass three feet in diameter.

He walks up to the window, reaches through the gate and pulls away a sheet of newspaper that still covers half the hole. When he does this, another section of glass, from the top of the pane, falls and shatters. He tries to look inside, but it's too dark to see anything.

"Hey," he shouts into the space. "Hey in there, fuck you." He listens for an answer. He smells wet paint coming from inside. "What color's it going to be now?" Again he listens. No answer. "Hey," he then says, more softly this time.

The alarm is a steady, fast-clanging bell. Old-fashioned, like a classroom bell, or a firehouse alarm from the old movies. *Morty might've installed this sucker himself.*

There's a doorway beside the storefront that leads to the apartments upstairs. Primo leans against the door, sinks down, lets his feet slide out from under him and sits.

He begins to hear the sound of his own voice. He'd been talking for a while, but this is different. He's not *making* this sound. It's not words, it's like water, and it's pouring from the inside of him to the outside. It hurt when it started because it had to push so hard. But now he hardly feels it. The sound is growing, even pushing the alarm farther away.

Primo is looking into the face of a black police officer. "You don't, by any chance, know who did this?" he says to Primo, who vaguely remembers being lifted to his feet by the front of his jacket. "Did you hear what I asked you?" He's holding Primo erect, against the wall beside the doorway.

There are the sounds of footsteps crunching glass from inside the storefront. The alarm is turned off. Footsteps again.

"That's better," the cop says. Another cop, a white one, appears beside him. He shines a flashlight into Primo's eyes.

Primo squints into the white glare. "Why?" he says.

The cop turns it off.

"Can you hear me?" the one holding him asks again.

"It's a good thing you're here," Primo tells him. "But you're too late." Then he says to the one with the flashlight, "That was like a third degree, right?"

"It's a good thing we're here?" the one with the flashlight says.

Primo notices that neither of them is over twenty-five.

"Does that mean you know who did this?" the one holding him asks. The name on the plate above his badge is Evans.

"Sure I do."

"You think you might tell us?" Evans asks.

Primo points to the swinging red and white light on top of the patrol car. "What's with all this light?" he says. "Officer Evans, do you have to leave that thing on? I mean, you guys need it for *getting* here, not for *being* here. It's attracting a *lot* of attention."

The second cop smiles. Evans, holding Primo by his lapels, does not. "Tell us what happened here," he says.

"I will, I will." He squints into the swinging beam from the car. "That shit's bright, though."

"I'll turn it off," the white cop says.

He walks over to the car, reaches into the driver's window, and the light stops. He then reaches further in, pulls out the handset from the radio and says, to Officer Evans, "Since I'm already standing here, maybe we should find out what the computer can tell us about this piece of shit."

"I sense a distinct change in tone of voice," Primo says. "In the movies you got to at least kill somebody to get yourself called a *piece of shit.* You guys'd know that. I can't believe you think I'm *that* bad."

The cop at the car is leaning into the window, holding the handset, looking at Primo.

"You haven't even asked me my name," Primo says. "You can't just tell the computer, Negro, middle–late thirties, articulate, handsome. There's too many of us out here."

"Primo Thomas," the black cop says. "You weren't very responsive when we first got here. We took the liberty of examining your wallet."

"Did you put it back? I know how much money I had in there. And how do I know you guys didn't make any untoward advances, me being in such an unresponsive state."

"You'll never know," Evans says.

"Now, we actually turned the fucking light off," the other cop, walking back from the car, says. "We didn't have to. *We* cooperate, you cooperate. That's the way it works." When he's standing in front of Primo he says, "You're the first person I met born on New Year's Eve."

Primo's whole body clenches. He tries to raise his arms.

Evans shakes his head. "Don't," he says.

"Too bad you can't celebrate with the rest of us adults," Primo tells the white cop. "Tell me . . ." He looks at his name plate. "Officer Rico. How long before you reach drinking age?"

"Ricci."

"Sorry, Officer Ricci. I couldn't see it in the dark."

"The sun was out, you wouldn't see any better."

"There was a Rico *Something* in this movie I saw on TV a few weeks ago. *Above the City.*"

"I saw that," Ricci says.

"Only this Rico was a bad guy. He beat on women and did other bad stuff. Now *he* was a piece of shit. But you, you're a good guy."

"That's right," Ricci says.

"What were you doing alone on a Saturday night?" Primo asks him.

"Maybe home," Ricci says, "but not alone."

Primo smiles at Evans. "Your partner's a devil," he tells him.

"Why'd you break the window, Primo?" Evans asks. He doesn't smile back.

"I didn't. I was about to tell you . . ."

"We're ready," Ricci says.

"There was these two young brothers. Just walkin up the avenue and they be *blisted.* Maybe you seen em somewheres. One of em wearin a do-rag, the other got the highest bald fade ever cultivated. Looked like a cigarette standin on end, that nobody ever flicked the ashes off of. So I'm standin right here, in this doorway, an I'm thinkin, it's a *shame.* Just teenagers. I *know* you guys know what crack'll do. I mean, how these kids gonna get anywhere? Disadvantaged to start with, comin outta the hood. And now handicapped from suckin all that butter. How they gonna do on the SATs, bein so whacked out?"

"Do I have any reason to keep listening?" Evans asks.

"This is what went down," Primo says. He smiles at Ricci. "Word to life."

"Why do I get the feeling he's full of shit," Ricci says.

"Maybe because his storytelling voice got a slightly different music to it than his *teacher* voice," Evans says.

"You learned a lot, walking around inside my wallet," Primo says. "But since you know I'm a teacher, I'll take a moment to teach you something. I just be talkin American, which, for your information, happens to be a mestizo-mulatto language. And to that I would like to add just this: I'll talk however the fuck I want to."

"Handicapped *and* disadvantaged," Ricci then says. "He left out broken home, didn't he?"

"He must be fun to work with," Primo says to Evans. "Now you want me to finish or not?"

"Why not," Evans says.

"Where was I? Oh yeah, they were having an argument, and they were getting angry and loud. Something about foul shots. Then one of them runs up to those garbage cans, pulls the lid off one of them, runs back again and begins dribbling an invisible basketball. Do you believe it? That's what crack does to you. A shame, man."

Ricci shines the beam of his flashlight over the scattered garbage, across the sidewalk up to the window, and over the broken pieces of glass.

"Anyway, when he gets like ten feet away from the garbage can he stops and turns around. Then he gets real still, bends his knees a little, dribbles that make-believe ball just one time, holds it right in front of his face, rocks it a little and lets it fly."

Primo follows the ball's arc of flight with his eyes. Both cops watch him closely.

"The weirdest shit is that the other one sees it too. He runs right up to the can, steals the ball off the rim, dribbles back to half-court, turns, shoots and sinks the invisible motherfucker."

"I don't see nothing over here," Ricci says. Then he says to Primo. "Your story fascinates me. But mostly, what I'm hearing is that it's you broke this fucking window. And since we ain't got time to stroll down the mile of shit between here and the end of your story, why don't you skip right to that part. Where you tell us how you did it." He then says to Evans, but keeping his eyes on Primo, "I'm gonna look around inside."

"I wouldn't leave if I were you," Primo tells him. "This's the whole truth and nothing but. And it gets better."

"I didn't mean *really* leaving. I was just going to have another look around. Probably find something of yours near that broken window. We'll probably be taking you along when we *really* leave."

"I just thought I'd save you guys a whole lot of trouble," Primo says. "I know about all that paperwork and shit."

"You've revived my interest," Ricci says.

"I'll make it quick," Primo says. "I know you don't have all night. Now listen carefully. . . . So the one who took the foul shot yells, '*I been vicked, man.*' And you know why he says this?"

"You tell us," Evans says.

"Cause you can't steal a man's second foul shot. Not if he has *two.* Everybody knows that. That's what they were fighting about the *whole* time. Whether he had one coming to him, or two. So then the one that took the first shot gets so pissed at the whole business he picks up one of them bricks they got holdin down the lids of those garbage cans . . . You see them over there? And he throws the fucking thing right at his friend's head. That's when *I* enter the picture. I yell, '*Heads up!*' That brick would've killed him. This is *real* life, not *Ignatz* and fuckin *Krazy Kat.* So thank God, he hears me and ducks just in time. But the brick sailed right through the window."

Ricci shines his light on the garbage cans again, then on the broken window.

"Next thing I know, they start laughing, being so fucked up and all. Then they run down the block . . . and *with* the quickness." Primo points his finger. "That way."

Both cops look in the direction he points.

"It's almost better, their being out of here before you guys arrive. They were crazy motherfuckers. Even so, you ever arrest them, I'll testify in court."

"You're not funny," Evans says.

"Oh, he's a little funny," Ricci says.

"Listen," Evans tells Primo. "Now I'll tell *you* a story. This is what we got. We got an alarm going off, and we got a phone call from a neighbor who thus far hasn't shown his ass on the street, that says someone looking an awful lot like you was disturbing the peace and, as a crowning achievement, broke this goddamn window. Next, we show up and what do we find. A broken window, a fucking mess and you sitting in the doorway wailing like some kind of banshee. You were louder than the fucking alarm, my brother."

Primo is furious. And sickened.

Ricci is smiling at him.

"What does that look like to you?" Evans asks him.

"What does *what* look like?"

"*My* story," Evans says.

"It don't look like shit."

"You're the one looks like shit," Ricci says. "I'd say you're the one got a little *blisted* tonight."

"You talk too much," Primo says. "I'm surprised my brother here lets you hang out with him."

Primo pulls himself back, shoving his own weight against the wall. He cannot bear the idea of their finding him this way, of this cop helping him stay on his feet.

"My partner thinks you broke this window," Evans says. "And I think he's right. I'm not sure what to do with you." He looks straight at Primo.

Primo starts to sag, his legs weakening. Evans pulls him erect again, holds him that way.

"You know," Primo says. "I look at these black-white police partners, on TV, or even on the street, and I think, *this* is cool. This is just how the past was supposed to become the present. Know what I'm saying? Like Bill Cosby and that other guy in *I Spy*."

"Robert Culp," Ricci says.

"That's right, that's right. And there's this other situation you always see in the movies and on TV, where the black cop's the lieutenant or the captain, and he's always yelling at the white cop cause he gets a little too enthusiastic about enforcing the law. That ring any bells?"

Ricci smiles. "It ain't too far from the truth."

"Is there a point to this?" Evans asks.

"It's what I said. I see it all over. Cops being cops before being a color, before being *anything* else. I like that. It's the future." Primo stops, exhales, looks at them both. "And then, on my part, there's something real personal happening. Something strange. And that part of it's, like, embarrassing."

"You can tell us," Ricci says. "We been around."

"Well, I *did* get smashed tonight. That's no lie, but I know I'll be sober real soon. Know why that is?"

"Uh-uh," Evans says.

"Because I look at the two of you, who have just encountered me in this unfortunate condition. Big guys, in uniform, able to stand up a little straighter than I can at the moment, holding me on my feet, and suddenly I realize that the two of you, standing right there in front of me, roughly approximate the genetic makeup of this noisy, drunken . . . for lack of a better phrase, piece of shit who stands here addressing you. And that, Mr. Cosby and Mr. Culp, my new and dear friends, is a *very* sobering thought."

"Is that an insult?" Ricci asks.

"I don't know," Evans says.

"No insult, my young friends. It's myself I'm talking about.

Maybe too much. I should talk about those two kids, instead. *Do-rag* and *Fade.*"

"Even if they don't exist," Ricci says.

"They *were* disadvantaged, *and* handicapped. From the hood, poor, strung out."

"Enough," Evans says.

"You got me, Sheriff," Primo says. "Officer Ricci knows I've been talking about myself all along. I'll tell you what. I'll talk about my mother, God rest her soul, instead. She was Italian. Probably like your mother, Officer Ricci. You just have to look at me to know my father's bloodline. And my mother, she loved my dark ass. She loved me so much I got tired of hearing about it."

Ricci smiles, looks down, looks back at Primo.

"My father, God rest *his* soul, he was busy a lot and when he was around, he was always wrapped up in some kind of shit. I never could figure it out. That's how fathers are. So what happens, according to psychologists, is that the child looks toward the mother. . . . I know you're both hearing me."

They nod, seriously caught up in what Primo is now saying.

"Okay. So I look at myself. And I look at you two guys, standing there, being cops and all, and I think about advantages and disadvantages. Then I look at you, Officer Evans. Being dark, as we are, I look at you and me together, and I think of some very specific disadvantages."

"I hear you," Evans says.

"And now, Officer Evans, I'll tell you about handicaps. The person with whom I felt the safest, in my life, my whole fucking life, the person who still shows up in my dreams to make me feel better, God rest her soul, was the same color as this handsome motherfucker you're standing next to. Now *that's* being handicapped."

"Now that *is* an insult," Ricci says. He steps toward Primo, his shoulder against Evans.

"Insult? This is just truth, my friend. Look, I'll come clean about the window, if you at least admit I'm telling the truth. Being in the predicament *I'm* in is being the king of the handicapped-and-disadvantaged. Your dreams *and* your waking life are at war with each other. I'm a fucking quadriplegic. I'm Helen Keller squared. Let me tell you boys, this shit ain't at all fair."

"Be cool," Evans says. He looks from Primo to Ricci and back to Primo again. "Both of you."

"But you know," Primo says, "you can't just see it that way. You'd lose your fucking mind if you could only see life *that* way. It's like if one day you guys forgot your first names, or who they referred to, and all that was left were these two uniforms called Evans and Ricci. Your lives would be the same size as what you did. You'd be nothing, you'd be Starsky and Hutch *during* the commercials, that's the same as being dead. You'd lose your minds. First you'd forget to brush your teeth, lose the ability to hold a fork, stop enjoying sex. Then your eyes would get all funny."

"I don't understand all of what you're saying," Ricci says.

"He doesn't either," Evans tells him.

"But there's *something* in it," Ricci then says.

"There's method to my madness, as Mr. Shakespeare once said."

"The madness part is right," Evans says.

"You know," Primo says, "I've lived in this neighborhood over fifteen years. There used to be a shoe store right here. And they had these shoes on display, right in the middle of the window. Beautiful, high-top, brown ones. And you know how they got there?"

"The guy selling them put them there?" Ricci says.

"Of course. The same way mannequins get in Macy's window," Evans says.

"Yeah," Ricci says.

"No," Primo says. "Not these shoes. These shoes *I* put there. They were mine. Brand-new too. I bought them but I never wore them. They were just too damn beautiful. Not made to be worn, I decided, just to be looked at. They were so beautiful I wanted everybody to see them. That's the kind of guy I am. So one night I slipped in, just before Morty closed—that was his name, Morty—and set them right on top of the display. All shiny, their toes facing frontward, side by side, as if the person who might have been wearing them was standing at attention. Fifteen years they sat there, fifteen years, and nobody even noticed. Not even Morty. He didn't do much business and he was getting pretty old. Well, that was back then. There's no more shoes there now. Haven't been for years."

"You think you can walk?" Evans asks.

"I wish you guys could've seen those shoes. But you were children at the time. Shit, who was president then, Nixon?"

"I remember him," Ricci says.

"Can you walk?" Evans asks again.

"Sure," Primo tells him. He pushes himself off the wall, takes a step, then another.

"I think it's time you got yourself home," Evans says.

"You're not arresting me?"

"Bringing you in would be a royal pain in the ass," Ricci says. "We'd have to cuff you *and* gag you."

"I'm tired," Evans says.

Primo takes a few steps, staggers, regains himself. "I'm all right," he says. He starts walking again, slowly toward the corner.

"Good night," he hears Ricci say. He then hears footsteps crunching broken glass.

Primo turns. Evans is still standing outside the storefront, watching him walk up the avenue. Primo waves at him.

He reenters the conversation as he walks. "Can you imagine, fifteen goddamn years and nobody even noticed those shoes.

"They were just too beautiful. They just couldn't handle it.

"Problem is, if you don't notice them while they're *there*, how's anybody going to remember them? Tell me *that*."

In the course of the night, for a few moments, he had achieved a consciousness so transformed, so angry, so fractured that he could travel inside of himself, slip between the broken sensations of his recent life and cross the endless space to a distant corner of memory, so distant the part of himself residing there never knew Angelita had ever existed. There were just a few such moments. And they were brief ones.

He continues talking as he walks down East Third Street, enters his building, slowly climbs the stairs, unlocks the door and lays himself down, fully dressed, on his bed.

33

Primo, standing in the shower, holds his forehead up to the stream of water so that the column of spray splits around his head, a river's course divided by a rock. He holds himself perfectly still, allowing the skin of water to swathe the top and sides of his skull, and so that the sensation does not know itself as water, or as moving water, but as the larger, formed and unchanging thing, as a river is itself a thing, and the water that moves within it another, lesser thing. As hands that part, and become the beginning of arms that extend from another body toward your body, are a thing, and as the memory of hands that have parted, extended, touched you, is a wholer, and unchanging thing.

It's early afternoon. This is his third shower. He's taken six aspirin and drunk a gallon of water, but standing under the shower is the only thing that eases his throbbing, metallic headache.

He managed to call in sick this morning but otherwise has done nothing other than lie on the couch and stare out the window. Sometimes he'd see the roof and chimneys of the building across the street, and beyond them, the distant, higher buildings of midtown. Sometimes the reach of his vision didn't extend to the window itself. It would stop and diffuse, the way a car's headlight loses itself in close, thick fog.

On his way back to the couch, the phone rings. Manny's voice comes over the machine. Felix had called him and told him of Angelita's death. Manny had called last night, while Primo was out, and again early this morning.

"Where are you? Primo . . . ? Call when you get in. And if you're screening calls, just call briefly and tell me that's what you're doing."

He sits this time. Looking out the window, tunneling his focus and aiming his vision through the point where the sashes and mullions intersect. Like looking through crosshairs.

If he holds his head perfectly still, the hairs cross on the scrawny trunk and branches of a tiny ailanthus tree growing out of the brick chimney of the building across the street. It's a tree, yet in aspect and nature, it's a child. Cover it with raggy clothes, maybe just a white T-shirt that's filthy and torn and too large, and bull's-eye, there you have it: the dark, arboreal, Managua–*Loisaida*–Oliver Twist street urchin it actually is.

Then what he sees is nothing. What he sees is not what his eyes rest on but what is inside, and what he does not delineate, as the outer eye does, and what he does not mark or retrieve when the phone rings again, restoring his focus to the room, the window, the light gray afternoon light.

It's Olivia. "Your friend Manny just called. He told me about the death of your friend. He also told me he hasn't been able to reach you. The way I see it, if he's got reason to worry, so do I. I hope you're okay, nephew. I'd appreciate a call from you reaffirming that fact. Shit, I hate these machines. I've had one ten years and I still hate them. I feel like signing off, as if this were a letter I'm writing to you. Call me. And soon. Shit, that's just what I *will* do, sign off. Your loving aunt, Olivia."

He gets up, walks to the machine, watches it reset itself. Then to the kitchen, where he takes two more aspirin with a tumbler of cold water.

A thought occurs to him. A thought he first wants to think, because it would please him, but then wants to stop thinking, because it hurts to think it. Angelita had said she would worry about him. He could write, on his part, but she wouldn't. On her part, *if she chose to*, she would worry. That was *her* part.

It's as if *her* worry has mixed in with Manny's and Olivia's.

As if she's behind it.

That would be nice. No it wouldn't.

Time has passed. The rectangular bar of light that had been as wide as the window, but longer, has withdrawn from the tabletop, which, this morning, it had crossed entirely, and now falls onto the floor at the foot of the window, shrunk nearly to a perfect square.

The phone rings again. It's Rosario, an administrator at *Solidaridad Humana*. "If you're in bed, stay there. If you're out, you're out. If you're near the phone, pick it up and let me know if you expect to be in tomorrow."

Rosario Núñez. He remembers her name from the little name plate that introduces her to everyone who approaches her desk. Like Evans and Ricci. *Núñez.* Same family name as the one whose house was hit by the mortar. *House. Not just garments—knickknacks, lapel buttons, jewelry . . .*

Against the darker sky, the window's sashes and mullions are the incurved lines of mortar between the cinder blocks of the muraled wall at the U.P. north of Matagalpa, next to the wall where the children sat, eating their oranges, and next to the wall in front of which stood the single, universal chair.

It's still late afternoon. Angelita doesn't look at anything on the inside until it's so dark you can't see a thing on the outside.

Primo walks to the bathroom, pisses, walks to the kitchen, drinks another glass of water. His headache has begun to abate, but the ache and roiling in his torso has not.

As he walks, he feels as if the slight tilt of each step causes a wash of liquid to roll from one side of him to the other. This is not, simply, hangover sickness but something the hangover has caused to be more violent in its heaving and, thus, more detectable. Hangovers do this. They amplify the clock's ticking, distill it out of the wash of noise it's usually an undetected part of.

He's more than half filled with something: *shit and piss and blood.* And something else, a different substance. *He* washes back and forth inside himself. In the immeasurable brief stillness between completing one step and beginning the next, he comes close to being filled with something. Himself? As close as he ever gets. Then he leans into the next step and he rolls back toward the other side. He can stay in the emptying half, in his own brief death, or allow himself to be carried, as he always has, to near fullness again, and then into the next washing back.

Is there a hole in my dehydrated brain?

Left, right, left, right.

It's like he's about to become something entire, to know himself as something entire, he comes *this* close, then begins to decrease again.

Of course: Primo.

Not Primo *the first.* Primo *the before.*

Primo at the end of the last thing, just before the next one. Replaying its ending over and over. Retreating from the next thing just before arriving at it, slipping back down into the *before.*

His father had said it. It's luckier to be born at the beginning of something than at the end of something else.

Primo sets a chair beside the phone, picks up the receiver and asks the information operator for the Kendallville, Indiana, area code. He then calls their local information number and asks for the number of the Kendallville Chamber of Commerce. He dials it. He leans back in the chair. He does this all in under sixty seconds.

"Good afternoon." A woman's voice. Gentle and clear.

"Good afternoon."

"May I help you?"

"Good afternoon." He pauses. He hadn't actually decided to pick up the phone and make this call. It was like throwing the brick through the window last night.

"Yes. And how may we help you?" the voice asks.

"I'm on the staff of the *Wall Street Journal*," Primo says.

"Yes," she says. Nothing more this time.

"I'm writing an article on inter-American trade relations. Would you know if the company that exported towel dispensers to Central America is still doing so?"

"Dispensers?"

"Bathroom fixtures, metal cabinets, sheet metal products, stuff like that." It starts to get easier, becoming this person, a voice with the life span of a single conversation.

"Oh, *sure*," she says. "Now I know who you're talking about. They went out of business so long ago I've even forgotten their name. I could look it up for you if you want."

"No thank you."

"Bedsprings are now our largest export. And cereal boxes, but they're just for Kellogg's up in Battle Creek."

Primo falls silent. By the sound of her shallow breaths, and by the way she occasionally swallows, he can tell she's holding the phone pressed between her cheek and shoulder.

"So, I guess no one's making towel dispensers in good old Kendallville anymore," he tells her.

"You're right," she tells him, in her clear, soft voice, "on that score. But we still do a *lot* of manufacturing here. A *lot*, and more each year. You don't hear the word *recession* in Kendallville. We have very little unemployment, which, as you know, is in contrast to the rest of the country. Commercial real estate is affordable, that's one of the reasons. You just have to look at a population map for the other. Geographically, we're nearer the east coast than the west, but in terms of America's population distribution, we fall right in the middle. The perfect place to ship materials to and, of course, products from."

"Do you think that company—the one that made the towel dispensers—went out of business because of the trade embargo?" he asks her.

"The what?"

"Trade embargo. For over six years we've maintained one against Nicaragua. And they were *big* importers of that stuff. I'm asking because an executive I interviewed down there—you may have heard of him, Señor Julio Septentrión—told me that in Kendallville, they manufactured the best sheet metal products in all of the Americas. And as you know, this is a big hemisphere."

"Pardon me," she says. "I don't think I'm familiar with what that is. An embargo?"

Primo explains.

"*Now* I see," she says. "We were having one against *them*. . . . Now I see."

"That's right. And it hurt a lot on their side, businesswise I mean."

She is silent again. This time Primo doesn't hear her breathing. He imagines she has put her hand over the mouthpiece, and is talking to someone else.

Her voice returns. "They're a pretty small country," she asks, "no?"

Primo tells her they are. "By our standards of big and small," he adds.

"Well then," she says. "Small country, small market."

"But every hotel and restaurant there used this company's products," he says.

"Ah, but if they were *already* using them, wouldn't that make the market even smaller?"

"I guess."

"Nope," she then says, her voice more energized, and assured. "I'm certain they went out of business for entirely different reasons. The loss of a market *that* small couldn't hurt anybody."

The moment Primo hangs up, the phone rings. His body shivers. The ring is louder, so close to its source, more startling. He allows the machine to answer. There is a silence that's not a silence but a sound like the palm of a hand sliding across a smooth, hard surface, and then the clicks of the machine resetting itself. Whoever was calling left no message.

He walks to the table, gets the pamphlet he got yesterday from Local 613 and calls their number. He asks for Mr. Jacobs, the business agent whom he spoke to the last time, and who wrote him the letter.

Primo thanks him for the information he sent, then tells him he should come with him to visit CuddleCo and see the working conditions there for himself.

"Tell me," he asks Primo, "do you *really* work there?"

"Yeah," Primo tells him. "If it matters so much."

"If it matters? For the purpose of this conversation, and any subsequent ones about my possibly visiting this workplace, it's *all* that matters."

During their last conversation, Primo sensed something familiar in this man's voice. He's sensing this again.

"Did you hear what I said?"

"I heard you."

"Have you talked with your co-workers, as I suggested?"

"My name's Primo Thomas."

"Primo? That sounds familiar. Do I know you?"

"Tell me yours?"

"Nazz Jacobs."

"Nazarino, am I right?"

"How'd you know that?"

"City College and Bartleby's Bookshop, nineteen seventy . . . three."

"Primo? You? And your girlfriend, what was her name?"

"Mariah."

"Mariah. Yeah. I think I read one of her poems in a magazine not too long ago."

"You probably did. In fact, she wrote a poem about that bookshop. The story of how we got fired."

"I remember that day. How is she?"

"Fine, as of our last communication. We've been married, then not married."

"Me too. On both counts."

"*Fifteen years.* You were an overworked graduate student and, if I remember correctly, a father. Now you work for the union. That's a long way upriver."

"Yup. I got fired shortly after you did. So I found work in another bookstore, a Local 613 shop. I worked my way up, or out, from there. My daughter's a senior in high school. My ex-wife's already somebody else's ex-wife. I spend too much of my daylight in the places other people work . . ."

Primo feels a wave of nausea. He stands up, sits again.

"By the way," Nazz says. "I got even with that bastard who owned Bartleby's. In 1978, his establishment became a union shop. Of course, with a little help from yours truly. When you next speak to Mariah, let her know that. She'd be pleased to hear it. . . . Wow. But tell me, Primo. For real. You work in this place?"

"I don't. Got a good friend who does."

"Does your friend want a union there? Do the people he works with want a union?"

"*She.*"

"She."

"I don't know."

"There's not much we can do to help, Primo."

"Can't you just come and look?"

"What's the point?"

"You'll see. You'll be able to understand it better."

"Primo, I hate to sound cynical, but I've been there already. I've seen dozens of places like it."

"If you come, I'll buy you lunch. I'll buy you the best two-dollar lunch you've ever eaten."

"Let's have a five-dollar lunch somewhere else. We'll split the bill."

"For old time's sake."

"If I come, it's not as a representative of a union. If I come, I'm with you, visiting your friend."

"After all these years, you haven't changed. You had a good heart then, and you got a good heart now. The dark ages haven't hurt you."

"Everything I eat is bad for it. My heart, that is. I love milk shakes and I'm addicted to hamburgers."

"You always were."

"They got french fries in this place you're taking me to lunch?"

"Plenty. You can have seconds."

"It's good to hear your voice after so many years. Since you're not working in this factory, what *are* you doing with yourself?"

"I'm a teacher. English-as-a-second-language."

"And is your connection to this workplace somehow connected to that? I mean, is this friend one of your students?"

"You sort of, but don't quite, have the picture."

"I have the feeling you'll fill me in. But I got to say something. Don't get your hopes up. Don't *even* have expectations."

"I won't. But it makes me feel a lot better, knowing you'll have a look."

"It's hard to make *anything* happen these days. The last time we knew each other, it was a *very* different time. You know that, Primo. A different world."

"A few months ago I visited Nicaragua. I saw teachers there, and union representatives. There were people there *making* things happen. I'm not sure what it all meant, not yet anyway, or what actually *is* possible, but I never saw that before."

"I'm not sure what it means either, but I *do* have an idea what's possible. If I remember, their labor situation sucked the big one when Washington was running things down there. As far as I know, they're still running things up here."

"I hear you. And I'm still glad you'll have a look. You'll also get to enjoy a strawberry shake, two hamburgers, a bushel of french fries and my delightful conversation."

"I can't eat them all at once anymore. Just two out of three, and that's too many. How about one hamburger, french fries and a glass of seltzer."

"Perrier with a squeeze of lemon."

"Seltzer will do fine. Listen, I got a lot happening this week. How about later in April? I don't imagine that company . . . what's its name?"

"CuddleCo."

"How nice. I imagine CuddleCo will still be there in a few weeks."

"Thank you. It sounds like you've seen a lot of shit, but I have the feeling you'll find this place *original.*"

"I hope not," Nazz says.

When Primo sets the receiver back into the cradle, he finds himself exhausted from the work of maintaining the conversation.

He returns to the couch, sits, looks through the cross-hair view at the small ailanthus tree and jerks the finger of his right hand. "*Pow*," he says.

He hasn't eaten all day, and there's nothing much in the refrigerator. He decides he's ready to walk outdoors, go to the small bodega on the corner, if he can't walk farther, at least get some bread and cheese.

The first downstairs flight isn't bad. He fears coming back up might be harder. The sway inside, the back and forth of himself, continues, but the flow has less volume. It continues as it did, but his awareness of it is lessening. As time passes, as his hangover abates, he will gradually release his entire awareness of the process, but not of its effects.

Just ahead of him, on the third-floor landing, he sees Mrs. Karbash locking the door of her apartment. He stops and waits. He doesn't want to encounter her. He'll wait for her to go downstairs ahead of him, and leave the building. She is telling Lady not to bark while she is out. She tells her she's going to the bakery and will be back in ten minutes. "Good girl," she says, then closes and locks the door.

She begins walking down the steps. "I'm old," she says.

Primo leans himself against the wall. "I *could* make cabbage," he hears her say. It doesn't sound like she's making a decision, but speaking from the middle of a conversation that had been going on inside her, that had been interrupted by the act of her leaving. In this conversation, she speaks clearly and softly.

"I *could* make it. I know you like it. But that means making *two* stops. And you know it takes longer to cook."

She is now more than two full flights below him. Primo leans over the banister to hear her.

"*Okay*. I guess if I made enough, we could have it again Saturday. But so soon after? We could wait till Monday. Any longer than that, I'd have to freeze it."

THE GATES

34

As the elevator bringing Primo and Nazz Jacobs up to CuddleCo slows jerkily to a stop at the third floor, they find Franco already standing there, facing them. It's as if they are standing on a fixed plane, and it's Franco who is moving. His legs, waist, his arms folded across his chest, finally his face, arrive in a slow, staggering descent, down to their level. He looks over Nazz, then Primo, then takes a single step back, marking the extent of the floor space he will allow them to occupy.

He's wearing his Mets hat, but no earmuffs this time, and the Walkman with the headset resting around his shirt collar. The last time Primo came he was waiting off to the side, and didn't appear until he'd already stepped off the elevator. This time they were expected. Someone, perhaps from the street, perhaps from downstairs, had signaled that they were coming. Primo wants to tell this to Nazz, but Franco is already standing too close for Primo to say anything without his hearing it.

Franco tells Primo, in Spanish, that his *novia* isn't here. He suddenly smiles with an overstated, dramatic curiosity.

"She's *not?*" Primo says.

Franco doesn't answer.

Primo looks out into the room as if to find her and prove him mistaken. He decided to bring Nazz on a day when Carolina was off. He'd hoped their unexpectedly showing up on the wrong day would provide a reason to prolong their visit, and enable them to talk more to Franco. He also didn't want to involve her in this. She was opposed to their coming in the first place, and he didn't want to jeopardize her job.

Nazz had told him that if they came on a Saturday, as opposed to a weekday, they were likely to find a larger number of undocumented workers.

"I was certain she'd be here," Primo says.

Franco offers an oddly confused, yet significant smile. He's telling Primo the rules of today's engagement. The confused aspect communicates that he will not speak English today, not even let on in front of this stranger—probably here in some official capacity—that he understands. The other aspect of the smile, the knowing one, has in it the spirit of the private game the two of them, since Primo has chosen to come this second time, are now playing. Against the faint possibility Primo didn't know Carolina was off on Saturdays, he aims at him a small additional communication, mostly with his eyes and the corner of his tightened mouth, that says anyone who thinks his woman is in one place when she is, in fact, in another has a major problem.

"I'm surprised to find *you* here on Saturday," Primo says to him. "Don't you take any time off?"

"*¿No puedes volver el lunes?*" He isn't sure if this stranger speaks Spanish, he's playing it straight.

"*Yo trabajo el lunes, como tú,*" Primo says. He will draw it out. And, since Franco has begun to do so, in the familiar.

"*Pero la última vez . . .*"

"*La última vez fue un día feriado. Muy importante.* Leap Year's Day. I was off that day. *¿No lo conoces?* In the whole world, the only people working were in this place. I was very surprised, my man."

Primo senses Nazz surveying the room and looks out into it himself. It's warmer than the last time he was here. There's no need to wear the animal skins or overcoats. There's not a single empty machine or worktable.

"Business must be good," Nazz says.

"They had a full house last time, too."

"There's as many people needing these jobs as the better-paying, legit ones."

Primo turns to Franco and says to him, in Spanish, "Since we're here, why don't you join us for lunch. In the café, downstairs."

Franco smiles broadly now, at both of them, then says he's eaten already, thank you.

"What did you tell him?" Nazz asks. "I heard him say thank you."

"I asked him to join us for lunch."

"Damn it. I thought I'd be your only guest. What did he say?"

"He's eaten already."

"Good."

"Remember." Primo leans close to Nazz's ear. "He's savvy to English."

Franco tells Primo the cafeteria is closed on weekends.

Primo tells this to Nazz.

"Saturday's crowd don't even get *that* fringe benefit," Nazz says in an undertone, still surveying the room.

Primo then turns to Franco and tells him that perhaps it's a fortunate accident that they showed up on the wrong day. His friend, who just happens to be with him, Mr. Henry O. Bartleby, owns a company that distributes gifts and notions—*¿nociones, regalitos?*—to church bazaars and Woolworth's and such. All over the country. These stuffed animals are just the kind of thing he handles. There might be some good business done, if he could meet the boss.

This seems to make Franco happy. He tells them their boss is in Hollywood and that she rarely comes here. That's where the home office is. "*La casa matriz,*" he says. "Hollywood." He then laughs.

Nazz smiles.

Franco smiles back at him. "Hollywood," he says again.

"What's so funny?" Nazz asks.

"Hollywood," Primo says.

"*Sí. Pero Hollywood en Florida. Cerca de Fort Lauderdale.*" Even smiling, he does not loosen his clenched, erect posture, nor has he uncrossed his arms, which remind Primo of the blades of a manual lawn mower.

Nazz laughs politely. "Do you, perhaps, have a business card?" he asks Franco directly.

He waits for Primo to translate before answering.

"No, but if you have paper, I can write down her telephone number."

He writes down a number on the inside cover of a matchbook Nazz hands him. When he finishes he hands it back to Primo. Then he tells him that they both should now go back to Manhattan, *where he lives*, and have lunch there. No more false goodwill in his voice, just menace. He wielded this small bit of information—*where you live*—like a weapon. Nazz, without understanding the words, hears this too.

Primo moves his face in front of Franco's. "I don't like the way you said that," he says, in English. "Tell me, man, how do *you* know where I live?"

Franco doesn't answer.

"I'm tired of this I-don't-speak-English shit. Answer my question."

"Have you lost your appetite for lunch because you cannot find your *novia?*" Franco asks, still using Spanish.

"What did he say?" Nazz asks Primo.

"He was just telling me who his heroes are. His namesake, the Spanish dictator, and Mr. Clean, who taught him everything he knows about posture."

"I don't think he said that. He doesn't know who Mr. Clean is."

"This snake-eyed motherfucker knows who I'm talking about. He knows a lot." Primo is still facing Franco. "Don't you?"

Nazz then says, "I think it's time we had lunch. I've seen all I need to here."

Hearing what Nazz just said enrages Franco. It implies there is an official and yet undisclosed purpose for his visit. It implies danger.

Primo, seeing this, smiles. "I wish you could understand my friend," he says to Franco, in English. "You know I teach English, and I'm good. *Very* good. Yesterday I taught a fire hydrant all the words to 'Ain't Nothing Like the Real Thing.' "

"I *love* that song," Nazz says.

"If I could do *that*, Franco . . . shit, I might even be able to teach *you*."

"Let's go," Nazz says.

"I wish you could've seen this place two months ago. Everybody wearing animal skins, looking like chimneys from all the steam their breath was making. Franco here was making music come out of his ears."

"He was what?" Nazz asks.

"Making music come *out* of his ears. I tell you the truth. Franco, could you show my friend how you do that?"

Franco looks past Primo at someone walking toward them, along one of the rows between worktables. Franco seems to grow calmer. He uncrosses his arms as the man joins them.

"I speak English," the man says, to both of them.

"That makes four of us," Primo says.

"No," he says. "I mean that I can help."

"Thanks," Primo says. "But me and Franco understand each other perfectly."

He shakes their hands, then proceeds to tell them the history of his getting this job. "Like so many of us here, I got my green card through the amnesty program. I'm going to be a citizen someday and soon! And best of all, that was what enabled me to get this job."

"What did?"

"Getting my green card. I got it last year, and started here right after that, and this year, on my two-week vacation I'm going to visit the Catskill Mountains. My wife and children have always wanted to go there. My name is Rafi," he says.

"I hope you enjoy your vacation," Primo says.

"I recommend a place with both indoor and outdoor tennis," Nazz says. "In case it rains."

"Franco," Primo says, "why didn't you tell us you had a public relations man? We didn't even have to talk to you."

Franco smiles. He has recovered his uncomprehending, awkwardly calm appearance. He points to the matchbook Nazz is holding in his hand. "*El número,*" he says.

Primo and Nazz look down at it. Beside the number is a name. Rosa Guzmán.

"You call her," he says, for Primo to translate, "because she won't be here until the Fourth of July. That's her favorite holiday. She comes here for the Macy's fireworks. But if you want to talk with her sooner, you can call her at this number."

He extends his arm toward the elevator, which hadn't left the floor the whole time they were there. They step onto it.

"You should probably find out where your *novia* is," Franco says to Primo.

"I think I know," Primo says, in English.

"*¿Sí?*"

"She's probably gone to buy me a present, a surprise. She's always doing things like that. She knows I want a Walkman just like yours."

"Women can give many surprises," Franco says. "And then again, they can easily be surprised."

The threat in his tone causes Primo to step back out of the elevator.

Nazz puts his hand on Primo's shoulder. "You've learned to speak Spanish very well," he says.

"Not as well as this asshole speaks English."

"You would know," Nazz says. "You're the teacher."

Primo steps back inside.

The operator crushes his cigarette out on the floor of the car, pulls the lever, and the elevator lurches into movement.

"*Adiós,*" Nazz says to Franco, just before they descend below the floor.

35

Primo, sitting on a bench in Tompkins Square Park, smells woodsmoke. He turns and sees, twenty feet behind him, in the enclosed grassy area at the center of the park, two men sitting on plastic milk crates, cooking hot dogs on sticks held over a small campfire. They have made a tent out of a yellow tarp slung over a rope tied on one end to the fence that edges the paved walkway, and on the other to the handle of a shopping cart. They'd built their fire inside a small circle of bricks and stones.

The smoke had awakened Primo from his absorption in a series of thoughts that began ten minutes ago when Nazz stood up, told him he had to run, shook his hand, said, "Okay," and walked off.

Nazz had to rush. He was going to pick up his daughter. Tomorrow is Mother's Day, and the two of them are flying down to Florida to visit his mother.

They drove back to Manhattan in Nazz's car. While they had lunch—sandwiches from D's—they spoke about CuddleCo. Nazz was certain there was little anyone could do to improve conditions there. They spoke about Franco. They spoke about marriage and divorce, and about the fifteen years since they'd last seen each other.

Nazz told him that on his way to get his daughter, he had to stop and pick up flowers for his ex-wife. "Our marriage ended ten years ago, but this will be the seventeenth time I've given her flowers for Mother's Day. Some things continue even after other things stop. My daughter, who likes geography, once told me she feels like a river that runs between two states."

Primo reminded Nazz that CuddleCo's home office is also in Florida. "Going anywhere near Hollywood?"

"Nope. Doesn't matter, though. Franco's boss won't be there." He handed Primo the matchbook with the phone number written in it. "The only useful thing in this is the matches. You call that number, whoever answers will have no idea what you're talking about, even if they do. Most likely, he thought up the numbers as he wrote them down. You wouldn't think he had that much imagination. Then again, his fingers were in sight the whole time." He opened the cover Primo now held in his hand. "Yup. Not one of the numbers is higher than five."

Both of them looked at the matchbook and at the name. Primo said it aloud. "Rosa Guzmán."

"I don't think she exists either. Nice touch though, making her a woman. It has a certain realism. Tells us Franco is a man of our times. My suggestion is you use those numbers the next time you play the lottery."

That was when he stood up, shook Primo's hand and said, "Okay."

On the last night Primo spent in Nicaragua, after the lights went out, Angelita, sitting close against him in the park, raised her hand, closed into a fist, and told him that if he could see it, in the darkness, he would know what he looked like, to her, the first time she saw him.

"Since I can't see a thing," he told her, "I'll never know what you saw."

"You know what I saw because you understand what I'm saying."

Primo then said, "Okay," in Spanish, imitating the way she said it. "*Bopway.*"

Angelita laughed. "*Va pues,*" she said. "Say it the correct way first.

Va pues. You must learn to pronounce *nicaragüense* before you can learn to *mis*-pronounce it."

He told her that she was the best teacher he'd ever known. And in his life he's known some awfully good ones. He told her he admired her, not just for being so good at it, but because it was *who* she was, every moment of her waking life.

"I am other things," she said.

"Yes. You are a mother, you are a widow. You are beautiful, if that's a thing. That's all I can say with certainty, beyond your being a teacher."

"You know countless other things. I have felt you learning them, taking them from me. I feel you *having* them."

"Maybe these things I know about you are mixed in with all the stuff you put in my pocket. I haven't even looked at what's in there." He kissed her after saying that.

She said the best teachers are rarely those who try to teach you something, they are those whose actions or whose generosity, or just their presence, makes you feel some understanding of your life. "As it is made up of people, not a span of days filled with things that happen."

"Like the lights going out."

"Are you listening?"

"I am."

"That people suffer so much has no meaning," she said, "other than what we give it. And we give it very little."

They were quiet for a while. Then she said, "*Bopway.*"

The first time she'd said it, he had to ask her what it meant. It didn't sound Spanish, it sounded like a funny word in English.

"It means okay." she said. "Not like, I'm *okay*, it's all right. It means *okay*, it's understood, we are in accord."

She used it as teachers do: to help collect what she had just said, and what has been said back to her, into a package of understanding, before going on to the next thing. A word for the silent point in a medley just before a new song starts, a segue, a bardo. It can also, simply, be the act of taking pleasure in agreement.

She then said that the best teachers, those who teach us the most important lesson, are feral children. She didn't know the word in English. She called them *niños salvajes.*

"That could be the weirdest thing anyone's ever said to me," Primo told her.

"You don't know what they are?"

"Sure. Children raised by animals. Wolves, mostly. Tarzan too."

"That's correct, but I'm not talking about Tarzan. He's another kind of teacher."

"I know. I had him for geometry when I was in high school."

"Then I feel sorry for him. Having had a student who never listens."

"*Lo siento,*" Primo said. "*Bopway.*"

"What these children teach us has nothing to do with wolves." She said this as if he understood her already. "What they teach us is just about ourselves."

She was leaning against his chest and the inside of his arm and he leaned their combined weight against the same tree he'd sat under with Julio. He remembers, in that moment, feeling he could see her voice in the pitch dark.

"*Niños salvajes,*" he said. "In English we call them feral children."

"Ah," she said. "And if they never had a name, not in any language, they would still teach us the same thing: that we can become anything. If the *becoming* starts early enough, and if the circumstances are right. That is our beauty, and that is our curse."

The word *okay* began his series of thoughts and ended it. But it was not a round trip through a maze that brought him back to the entrance. It was more like a journey that traced a single line through the splayed stretches of cracked pavement on the streets of Managua, that led you to an identical intersection in an entirely different part of the city. You don't decide where the switch tracks are, the journey *is* the navigator. *Okay.* The destination just happened to have the same name as the starting point. You can travel from Leone in the province of Naples, where his mother's family came from, to León in Nicaragua, where Rubén Darío's clock is still counting the years.

Franco, during both of Primo's visits, said *okay* the same way as Angelita: *Bopway*. Primo wondered if he could also be Nicaraguan. He doesn't want him having anything in common with her.

She used the term to gently align her understanding with his, to assemble their agreement. Franco used it to wash back over a string of simple, calmly voiced words, and transform it into a threat: *I know you live on the other side of the East River. Why not go back there.* Okay. Tough, cool, gangster-movie talk. A voice that doesn't inflect a question, or flatten out a statement, but clenches around words you hear, but that have not been said, like fists you cannot see in the dark.

Nazz told Primo there have been a few cases, very few, in which organizers, working on their own, have had some small effect in situations such as CuddleCo.

"The unions don't want you fucking around in places like that. And if you do, it's *Mission Impossible* undercover shit. You get caught, we disavow any knowledge of your existence. A dime, a quarter more an hour. A coffee break, better lighting, an extra hour of steam heat. It's been done. You get the management worried you'll talk to your very good friend at Immigration, the Department of Labor, whatever. That's all you got to deal with. One of the problems is finding the bosses. They're always in touch, but never nearby. If you do find someone, you find they usually have friends too. They've heard it all and aren't easy to threaten."

"But it's been done," Primo said to him.

"It has. About as often as an oyster turns up a pearl."

Last week Mariah called from California. It was their first verbal communication in nearly a year. She had learned, from Manny, that someone close to him had died. Beyond offering her condolences, her concern, they did not talk more, not specifically, about Angelita.

In the course of their conversation, they recalled his mother's funeral. There had been friends at the wake, though no relatives from her side of the family. Primo, Mariah and Olivia were the only mourners in attendance at the burial.

"I wish I could be there," Mariah said, after they spoke of Angelita's death. "I'd like to help even out the sides again."

The director of the funeral home stood at his mother's graveside and read the service. Primo didn't hear a word the man said other than her name, Giovanna Thomas, which infuriated him, hearing it spoken by this stranger. Afterward, two men, who had been standing off to the side, stepped up to the coffin, slung a harness underneath it, removed the frame that held it above the open grave, and lowered it with a winch. Primo led the way, at a fast walk, back to the entrance. He wanted to reach the sidewalk before it touched bottom. They had been silent before the grave, and before these strangers. Just outside the cemetery gate, Olivia began to cry, angrily, sadly. Primo stood aside, leaning against a parked car. Olivia took Mariah in her arms and told her that she had evened up the sides. "It would have been awful," she said, "if there were more strangers than family members."

On the phone, they spoke about friends in common. About Pamela's new friend who was moving in. He told her he'd encountered Nazz Jacobs again after all these years.

She told him she had just gotten tenure at the college where she teaches. That was as close as they got to discussing the time they have been apart, and the distance. It was a way of acknowledging that the path between them has continued to become overgrown, and enough to free them to fall into the kind of easy, familiar, indirect dialogue in which they can exchange something yet remain safe.

He told her about Julio's theory that they each live in an armpit of the continent.

"I wonder what Pablo Neruda would think of that," she said.

"I bet he'd like it. That people keep chewing on his metaphors."

"When you think of it, the whole thing, I mean, it's an awfully strange body. Got these enormous hips thrown all the way out toward Africa. And what about the Caribbean, all those islands?"

"This is how we used to talk when we were students, remember?"

"I do," she said. "We'd take an idea and roll it in the weirdest direction, like a bowling ball across a tennis court, then follow it, wherever it went."

"I'd say the islands were bracelets and a pocketbook."

"Ah, so you're telling me it's a woman?"

"Men don't have hips that big."

"Some do."

"Not with waists that small."

"You would know. I've watched you *watch* women with hips that big, and waists that small."

"I didn't notice you noticing."

"Tell me, what's up with Nazz?"

"He's a union organizer now."

"He was always deadly serious."

"He still is."

"Unlike your other friend Manny the comedian. He wants me to help him find a publisher for his novel. He sent copies to ten different places. As of the last time we spoke, he hadn't yet heard anything."

"What he's heard since hasn't been encouraging. But the magazine you told him about has agreed to publish an excerpt."

"Good for him."

"He's worried he won't fit in, though. Their last issue was devoted solely to poems and stories about whales."

"What's wrong with whales?"

"Nothing I can think of."

"You have to start somewhere. I don't think it will hurt his career, such as it is."

He heard a call-waiting click on her side.

"I think that's work," she said. "I'm in my office."

"Thanks for calling."

"Wait . . ." she said. She put him on hold, then reopened their line.

"Now *they're* holding. Primo, give Olivia my love, and listen, Primo, I hope you're doing okay over there in the left armpit."

Two policemen, nightsticks in hand, are loudly telling the two men, still sitting beside their fire, to put it out.

"And you too," one of them yells to another man, farther back from Primo, who has started a charcoal fire in a hibachi set in front of a huge cardboard box. The cardboard is sagging and dark. It has been rained on and then dried again. Across its side is the word *Frigidaire.*

The number of homeless here has doubled in the year since he came back from More, and doubled again just recently, since the weather has grown warm.

One of the cops walks over to a drinking fountain on the paved walkway just outside the fence. A man who had been washing a shirt in its concrete basin stands aside and holds down the button while the policeman fills a two-liter soda bottle with water.

The cop then walks back to the small campfire and pours the water over it. It hisses and smokes.

The two men whose fire it was are now standing beside the policemen. The four of them watch the wet ashes smolder and the dark smoke rise and thin out.

Talking to Mariah was like seeing a needle suddenly poke through the surface of a piece of cloth after covering a lot of distance on the other side. It startled him at first, then, as suddenly, became familiar. There was a tone in her voice, warmth, interest and the expectation of his accepting her communication, that made him feel they had just spoken yesterday. She's had this tone ever since they first lived apart.

They don't share a child, like Nazz and his ex-wife. No river connects their two states. But there's something.

Mrs. Karbash said they seemed like brother and sister.

Their communications don't seem real to him, until after they've already happened.

Mrs. Karbash had said, "But she's still alive."

Mrs. Karbash just looks at his name on the mailbox, Thomas, and sees *her* Thomas. Like a train of thoughts starting with *okay* and ending with *okay*. His name travels through the life and imagination and pain of this woman, and when it came out again it looks and sounds the same. But it's not.

This tent and this campfire, this cardboard shack: his neighbors. Close enough to shout over to, introduce himself. It's like watching the war in Nicaragua on Nicaraguan TV, or hearing gunfire from a mile away. There's all this life near him. And all this life that's not. Nearby, but not his.

He knows someone who works in that shithole sweatshop in Brooklyn. *What else do I have to do with it? Nothing.* It's as far off, and as nearby, as people who were once in your life and aren't anymore.

Like the two *Thomas*es, the two *okay*'s: each a set of perfect strangers, so near to each other they live inside the same word.

One of the men whose fire had just been put out tells the two cops that their nightsticks don't match.

"What the hell does that mean?" one of the cops asks him, loudly.

Primo turns around.

"Just look," the man says. He points to their sticks. "Yours is new and shiny. And his is old. All scratched and dented up."

The cop with the newer stick says to his partner, "Hey, we don't match." They both laugh, but not along with the man who caused them to.

The man with the cardboard shack then walks over to where the two policemen and the two other guys are still standing beside the wet ashes of the campfire. He asks the cop with the older, battered nightstick if he hits a lot more people than his partner does.

"Looks that way to me," one of the two other men says.

"You're lucky we're just making you put out the fire," the cop says. "You know that later you'll *all* be hauling your asses out of here."

The two policemen climb over the railing, beside the bench Primo's sitting on, and walk down the paved path toward Avenue A.

Primo stands, stretches, throws the paper his sandwich had been wrapped in into the garbage can, then walks toward the exit, on the same path the two cops are on, about twenty yards behind them.

He couldn't see Angelita's hand when she held it in front of him in the dark, and he can't see it now, in the bright afternoon.

Maybe that's good. *Not* seeing it, it wasn't fully there. Something only partially there can only come partially to an end, when everything *completely* there is history.

As he walks, Primo lifts his hand, pushes it out in front of him, at eye level, closes it tightly around something, lets it drop again to his side.

36

"That movie was like a dream," Carolina says to Primo. "And I'm still having it."

"Wake up," Primo says. "We're on Fifth Avenue."

"There are angels all around us. I have always felt them being there, I just didn't know what they were." She waves to the empty space ahead of them. "Hello, everybody."

They have just seen the movie *Wings of Desire.* They're walking downtown, slowly, toward the subway station on Fifty-first Street.

"Look," she says. She points upward. "There is an angel on top of that building."

"Inside the penthouse?"

"Look on the roof."

There are thin strands of orange and gray cloud, interrupted by the tops of buildings, crossing the entire dusk-blue sky. "I lack your special vision for them," Primo says.

"It feels *right* that they are here. I like it when a movie or a book or a song touches what my life feels like, and says it for me. I then feel like *I* said it."

"I'd like to think they are there."

"I know they are. I feel it that they are. They touch us slightly. *That's* what I feel. I feel something always touching me slightly."

"I like the way you explain things."

"Do you feel that? That there are angels, or something, always *slightly* there?"

"I wish they were there. But that's not the same as feeling they are."

"It's not that different, either." She waves again to the space ahead of them. Then she says, "If *you* were an angel, would you be happy?"

"That's a funny question."

"Would you be happy to stay an angel, or would you rather become mortal, like that angel in the movie, so you could experience life?"

"I don't know. I *do* know that once he gets to know life as we live it, he'll want his wings back, fast."

"I loved what he said about life on Earth. He made it seem enjoyable."

"He said, *I want to feel my skeleton when I walk*," Primo says. "That's enjoyable?"

"He also said, *I want to suspect, instead of knowing all . . . I'd like to feel the wind and say*, Now."

"And he said that he wanted to get excited by a meal, which is why he hung up his wings in the first place. That bring anything to mind?"

"Dinner?"

"Your mortal friend is hungry."

"Wow," Carolina says, looking at a display in a shop window they are passing.

"Does *wow* refer to my being hungry, or what has caught your attention in the window?"

"Both," Carolina says.

"There is no *both* in the world," Primo says.

Carolina smiles. "You are right," she says.

"Is that your whole answer?"

"We will eat soon. Right now this window is more interesting than your appetite. Look."

The window is decorated with a Victorian dining room scene. A mother sits at one end of the table, the father opposite, and their children, a boy and girl, face each other on opposite sides. The mother is holding up the red, velvety cover of a box of candy and looking inside. The ribbon that had wrapped it, and a greeting card with three names written in it, lie on the table beside her plate. With her other hand, she shyly covers her open, smiling mouth.

The window is divided by a screen and on the other side is a contemporary mother, wearing a business suit, sitting at a desk, with a painted Manhattan view out her office window. The door to her office is slightly open, and looking into the room, where she cannot see them, are the smiling faces of her husband and two children, who are about to surprise her. The husband is holding a box of candy. On the desk, in front of her, is a stack of white papers, and on the top one, in bold, is the word *Memo.* Beside it is a framed photograph of the same family scene on the other side of the divider. The identical mannequins, posed and dressed differently, play the same roles in both scenes.

"Do you think mannequins have mothers?" Primo asks.

"*¿Maniquís?*"

"*Lo mismo.*"

"These ones do. And grandmothers."

"Grandmothers?"

"The modern woman is the granddaughter of the old-fashioned woman." She smiles. "And that would mean that one of the children in the first scene is the parent of the woman in the second scene."

"What about the other child?"

"You can't tell from what you see here."

"I can tell."

"No one can tell."

"You can see angels, and I can see things like that," Primo says. "Things like what happened to the other child in the first scene."

"Tell me, then."

"The other one married a black person. And they never have mixed-race families in store windows. People would say, *Oh look dear, Macy's has a mulatto window.* They wouldn't even notice if it's a Christmas window or a Mother's Day window."

"Was it the boy or the girl?"

"I can't tell that much. I only *slightly* see them."

"I loved it when the angel sat beside that man on the subway, and then that woman in the laundromat," Carolina says. "I'd like to think the homeless man who just spoke to us on the street has an angel watching over him, too."

A moment earlier, the man had asked if he could walk along with them on the last block before the station. He didn't want money or anything else, just to walk this short distance with them.

"He was so sad, and so funny," Carolina says. "And after that movie, he reminds me how hard life on Earth really is."

They're on the subway, heading to Carolina's apartment in Brooklyn. They both look at the other people in the car, as if, among them, there are angels, listening in to the thoughts of the people who are not.

Carolina then says, "I'm mad at you."

"Still?" Primo asks.

"It was a stupid thing to go there, and to bring your union friend with you. I asked you not to do it. I keep forgetting about it, then it comes back to my mind and I'm mad at you again." She shakes her head, leans back against the seat, folds her arms.

"I'm sorry. I guess I had to learn for myself how little anyone can actually do."

"I told you and you did not believe me."

"I don't always listen so good."

"So *well.*"

"So well."

"And it was wrong for you to feel you could not tell me . . . *me*, about the death of your friend."

"Tell me," Primo asks. "Will it affect your job there? When I asked you before, you were too angry to answer."

"I don't think so."

"I wish I could say I'm glad about that. To tell you the truth, I wish they would fire you. I wish they'd close the damn place down."

They had argued about this before the movie, walking in Central Park. Primo kept telling her he had to do it, show someone else the horrible conditions at CuddleCo. It was the only answer he could give her.

She became furious, he got angrier and they both fell into silence. It was then that Primo told her, for the first time, about Angelita. For some stupid reason he hadn't earlier. A kind of guilt. A fear of jealousy or anger on her part. He also felt that since he was close to Carolina, he'd have to share with her what he carried of Angelita inside himself. He didn't want to, and that, for Primo, became an unspoken part of their argument. But Angelita—what he'd learned from being with her, *taken* from her, as she had said—was part of the explanation for his going back to CuddleCo.

In that moment, what angered Carolina the most was that she wanted to know *why* he did it, and he couldn't tell her. He had to tell her about Angelita.

They were walking when he told her. She stopped, faced him, lifted her hand to her mouth. She began to weep.

Primo could not tell why. At first, she wept as if she'd also known Angelita. Then, it seemed, because *he* had known her, had been in such pain these last weeks since learning of her death, and had not told her about it. He felt these things in her weeping. But that still wasn't all of it.

"I am now angry about two things," she said.

Primo started to speak but she stopped him.

They walked for a while. She led them off the path, across a small stretch of grass that led to the benches at the edge of the lake.

"There is now something I want to tell you about," she said. "Something I have not told you before. I want you to know why you made my father so angry, in Managua, when he thought you had said you were his cousin Tomás."

"I wondered about that," Primo said.

"Tomás is dead. It was just after he died that we left El Salvador."

"I'm sorry," Primo said.

"We lived in a town called Aguilares, which is in the province of Chalatenango. Though Tomás was older than my father, they had been close since childhood. They both loved mathematics. My father took over the small grocery store my grandfather had owned, but Tomás, he became a professor at the *UCA*, the Catholic university. My father had a blackboard in our house, covered with numbers and formulas, and when Tomás would visit us, he would also visit my father's blackboard. They would write numbers and *X*'s and *Y*'s. They would erase them, and write them again. In the world they were in, they couldn't hear when you called them to dinner.

"Four years ago, the Army began arresting students in Aguilares who they suspected of being FMLN sympathizers. The guerrillas controlled most of the countryside in Chalatenango, but not the cities. In the cities the Army had no restraints. Tomás allowed three of his students, who they were hunting, to hide in his house. He was an old man by then. He was a widower, he had no children, and he knew what they would do to these three young people if they caught them. Somehow the soldiers found out and one night they arrested them all. Two days later we received word that Tomás was dead. The Army said a sudden heart attack. They sent a . . . *partida de defunción* . . ."

"A death certificate, I imagine."

"They used the medical term, to make it sound official, and to make it sound true. . . . *Miocardíaco* and something."

"Myocardial infarction. A sudden heart attack. It's how my father died."

"But it was not how Tomás died."

"What happened?"

"They never released his body. My father wrote letters to the Army, to the government. No one could help him. Then he wrote to a newspaper and they printed what he wrote. The following week, on the same day, he received a letter in the mail and a phone call. Both with the same message. They said that sudden heart attacks might run in his family.

"On that day, he told us we were leaving Aguilares. He and my sisters went to Managua, where Marta's husband could find work. I went first to my aunt in Miami, and then to here."

"I'm surprised your father didn't hang up on me."

"At first he thought it was the people who had called him in El

Salvador. He then thought that anyone with such a strong gringo accent would probably not be the one to make such calls."

"Is my accent *that* bad?"

"Don't ask me to make you feel better when I am still mad at you."

Now, on the subway, Primo puts his arm around Carolina's shoulder. They are moving slowly through the tunnel that runs under the East River, the longest stretch of track between stations.

"I was just thinking about before, when you were telling me about Tomás. I felt a little like I was one of the angels, in the movie, listening to your thoughts."

"You are not an angel," she says.

"I enjoy my meals too much."

"That's not the only reason." She points to a Spanish-language advertisement for paper towels. "When I first came to New York, I learned a lot of English from these. They have them in Chinese and in Haitian French, too. I would say that most people who come to this country, and read these signs in their own languages, didn't come here simply because they wanted to. One way or another, they probably had to."

"The extreme case being how I, this many generations after the fact, am here, in this train, in this tunnel, under this fucking river, seated beside you, the person who is angry at me."

Carolina leans her head against his shoulder. "History is mostly bad. But I am glad you are here, at the same time I am. Do you understand that?"

"I do." Then he says, "Tell me, honestly, how bad *is* my accent?"

"Actually, your accent isn't bad. Your weakness, in Spanish, is your overuse of it."

"You've lost me."

"You often try to say things in Spanish you aren't ready to say. Or you speak English in Spanish. Like before, when you were trying to end our argument. I didn't know you were going to tell me the terrible news of your friend. You said, *Yo quiero echarte la toalla.* That means, I want to throw a towel at you. Luckily, I knew you did not intend to say that. If I had thought you did, we would still be arguing. However, I did not know what you *did* say. And I still do not."

"I wanted to throw *in* the towel."

"Why?"

"It means to give up. Give in. It meant I was wrong and that *you* were right.

"Of course I was right."

"How would you say that?"

"Yo quiero tirar la esponja."

"Throw the sponge?"

"I wouldn't try to say it that way in English. And that is how we're different. I am aware that other people think differently than I do, and wouldn't assume there is just one way to say it."

"I throw in the sponge."

"I have already accepted your towel."

37

As Primo and Carolina climb the last of the stairs leading from the subway to the street, Primo sees Franco standing at the exit. Then two other men step into view, one on each side of him.

He is not here by accident. That Primo immediately knows.

He grabs Carolina's hand, turns her around and heads back down the stairs. Three other men, one of them Rafi, the guy who had told him and Nazz about his green card and his forthcoming vacation, are standing at the bottom.

They turn again.

He must keep thinking. This sudden, weird change in everything. He must keep thinking.

It would be better outside. More people, more room.

When they reach the top of the stairs, Franco says, in English, "How was the movie?"

He was there? He was, *somewhere*. He knows.

I must think.

"Get out of our way," Carolina yells. Franco and the other two close the space between them. Primo knows the others are climbing the stairs right behind them. He shoulders a space. The guy to the right of Franco takes a small step to the side. Primo presses through and pulls Carolina with him.

It's completely dark now. They're walking down the street toward

Carolina's building, four blocks from here. The six of them are walking with them. Franco and another man in front, two in back and two in the street, just outside of the row of parked cars. There is no one else in sight.

"What do you want?" Primo asks Franco.

"Just to know if you liked the movie."

"I give it four stars. You guys leave now, you can still catch the late show."

"He is funny," Franco says. He turns as he walks, lifts both hands.

Franco is wearing rings on every finger. Gold bands. Three and four on some fingers, even the thumbs.

To Primo he says, "I enjoy it when you visit me and act funny. It amuses me."

There's not a car moving on the street. Primo sees, at the other end of the block, a woman walking a dog. Holding Carolina's hand, he quickens their pace.

The six stay with them, contain them, like a three-sided vehicle. If they knew they were at the movies, and knew they were getting off the subway here, and *now*, they must have been following them for most of the day.

"I think you are a Communist," Franco says to Primo. "Am I right about that?"

"When did you start following us?" Primo asks.

They must have been there when he and Carolina left his apartment earlier. On the subway uptown, in Central Park, outside the theater . . . How did he *not* see them? How did they communicate with each other?

"I must be right about that," Franco says. "Because you didn't even visit your mother today. Communists have no respect."

"You guys have walkie-talkies?" Primo asks.

"You are being funny again." Franco pokes the guy walking next to him, and the guy reaches into the inside pocket of his sports jacket, pulls out a small cellular telephone and hands it to Franco.

Franco unfolds the top and bottom, speaks into it.

"Yes. Could you please send six orders of fried rice. What would you two like?" he says to Primo. "The same? And could you send an ambulance?"

"*Déjenos en paz*," Carolina says to him. "*No tiene derecho*."

"He didn't know where you were yesterday," Franco says to her. "If you two had these"—he holds out the telephone—"you could keep each other informed as to your whereabouts."

"*No hay porque hacerlo*," Carolina says.

"Of course there is," Franco says. "There are reasons for everything we do. And they are simple." The other men laugh. He hands the phone back to the first guy, who pockets it.

The woman walking the dog is still on the street. She is walking ahead of them, away from them, but they are closing the gap. If they get near enough he can shout to her to call the police.

Franco turns again, walks backward, facing them. He places his forefingers next to his eyes, pulls them into slits. "I love Chinese food." He laughs. Then says to Primo, "You did not answer my question."

"What question?"

Franco turns forward again, keeps the pace. "Are you a Communist?"

"I thought your guys were following me today."

"That does not answer my question."

"Yes it does. They would have told you I did celebrate Mother's Day. Only with *your* mother."

He translates what Primo said into Spanish. "I want everyone to hear that one." He laughs loudly.

A teenage boy riding a bicycle crosses the intersection on the corner. The woman with the dog is now stopped in front of the first building. If they get to the corner, or near enough, and if they shout, someone might hear them.

"He must make you laugh all the time," Franco says to Carolina.

She does not answer.

Primo and she are still holding hands. It feels, in this moment, like the two of them are children, frightened by these angry adults menacingly in control. This fear makes him furious.

"You will not answer me?" Franco asks. He turns, reaches behind him toward Carolina and touches the tip of her nose with his finger. "You will not answer me?" he asks again.

"*I'll* answer," Primo says. "Fuck you."

"Everyone knows that one," Franco says. "I don't have to translate."

A tall hurricane fence, closing in a lot the size of two buildings, runs between the point they are now at and the last building on the corner. From here, they could only escape in one direction, out into the street, where the two guys are still walking. If they suddenly rush through the space between two parked cars, and he pushes Carolina ahead of him and starts punching and shouting, perhaps she can run free, and perhaps the woman walking the dog, or someone else at the corner or inside one of the buildings, will hear.

As he finishes the thought he moves. He tightens his grip, pulls Carolina along with him. Already they are both off the curb. The men in the street converge ahead of them, Primo shouts, breaks into them, one falls, the other grabs his arm. He shouts again. He shouts *Help.* He shouts *Call the police.* He lifts his elbow and slams it against the chin of the man holding his arm. The man falls back.

Primo starts to pull Carolina around him. When she gets to the front he pushes her. "Run. Run toward the corner—"

He feels something crash against the side of his face. He hears it and he feels it. "Run," he shouts.

He then feels Carolina pull away from him, not ahead of him, farther out into the street, but backward, toward the sidewalk. She screams. He stops moving. He feels a fist hit him from the other side.

The woman walking the dog is not in sight. He can't see anyone. They hit him again.

One of them, standing against the fence, is holding Carolina from behind. She is stomping on his foot, trying to wrench herself free.

Two of them hold one of Primo's arms, a third, Rafi, holds the other. Primo's back is against the fence. He can't see anyone on the street. He tastes blood.

Franco is standing in front of him. Next to him is the guy who holds the phone.

"Let go of her," Primo shouts.

"You did not even tell me if you liked the movie."

"Let go of her."

Franco walks over to Carolina. Stands in front of her.

"*Hijue puta*," she spits at him.

"Now you have both spoken badly of my mother." He shakes his head. "And on Mother's Day."

He reaches out both hands, takes hold of her collar. "Tell me, *cipota*, are you a mother?" He rips open the front of her blouse. The act pulls her torso forward.

Carolina pulls herself back, looks at him but doesn't speak.

Primo tries to tear his arms free.

Franco holds his face close to Carolina's. "You can't be," he says. He then takes a step back, shakes his head and says to the other men, "This one is no mother."

The man with the phone now helps Rafi hold Primo's arm.

"I can do anything I want," Franco says. He holds up his hands, showing off his rings. "*¿Te gustan mis anillos?*" He smiles at Carolina, then at Primo. "*Todos son de boda.* And all of my wives are mothers. I become angry when Communists disrespect this holiday."

He again walks up close to Carolina. Primo pulls an arm free, grabs the hair of the man who'd been helping Rafi hold it, and pushes his head against the fence. He then feels someone hit him, hard, from the other side.

They're holding him pressed against the fence again.

Franco is standing in front of him. "Don't worry about her," he says. He waves his fingers in front of him. "I got too many already."

"Rafi," he then says. "I want you to show him your new possession."

The guy with the phone walks over to Primo, takes his arm, leaving Rafi free to walk over to Franco, and stand beside him. He looks at Primo and smiles.

"Go on," Franco says. "Let him see it."

Rafi reaches into his pants pocket and takes out something small. He walks up to Primo and holds it in front of his face. It's a bottle cap. He shows him the top. Pepsi-Cola. Then the inside.

"Can't you read it?" Franco asks. "You're a teacher, no?"

Primo doesn't look at it. He only looks at Franco.

"Read it for him," Franco says.

Rafi holds it right in front of his eyes, then says, "*Congratulations. You and your family have won a two-week vacation to Disney World.*"

"Show it to her, too." Franco throws his head up, slightly, and smiles at the other men.

Rafi moves in front of Carolina, holds the cap in front of her face.

"I'll tell you something that will surprise you," Franco then says. "Rafi hates Pepsi. The caffeine prevents him from falling asleep. I don't think he's ever bought it. Rafi, have you ever bought Pepsi?"

"No," he says. "I prefer wine." He steps back and stands beside Franco again.

"You both must be wondering how he got this," Franco says. "I will tell you. Last night the man who owned it showed it to Rafi, and Rafi knew, right away, that he wanted it. So he waited. He waited until later in the evening when the man was alone. In fact, he was walking on a quiet street just like this one. Rafi knew how happy the man was to have it, and he knew he wouldn't just *give* it to him. So he didn't waste this man's time, or his own, by asking him for it. He just killed him. And now Rafi and his family will have a wonderful vacation this summer."

"I have changed my plans," Rafi says. "I think my family will enjoy this much more than the Catskill Mountains."

Rafi and the man with the phone change places.

"Whatever it is you want, you want it just from me," Primo says. "Let her go."

"*Un caballero*," Franco says, "*¿no?*"

"What do you want?"

"I have been instructed to teach you something. Actually not you. I don't think you can learn anything." He points to Carolina. "Her."

"Who instructs *you*, you sick motherfucker?" Primo spits blood as he says this. He sees it fly out of his mouth.

"I have to confess something. Rosa Guzmán is not my boss. She is, I think . . ." He holds up his hand. He points to the second ring on his index finger. "She is this one."

He steps close to Primo. "I am to teach *her*"—he points at Carolina—"that what *you* did yesterday was wrong. And you. My instructions are to stop you from ever making that mistake again." He punches Primo in the ribs.

Primo feels the rings grind into his skin. His legs are weakening. He pushes his back against the fence.

"Just answer one of my questions, Primo." This is the first time he has ever used his name. "Are you a Communist?"

"Franco, this Communist shit's old-fashioned." Primo lifts his head, looks at him. "Besides, you don't have opinions, you don't have reasons. You're doing this because somebody ordered you to. And because you know how much I hate you, you sick fuck."

"See," Franco says. "He cannot be taught anything." He walks up to Primo, leans toward him and holds his face close, like he did the first time Primo showed up at CuddleCo. "Even so, I will try," he then says. "I will try to teach you just one thing. And then you will know why I'm doing this. And you will understand why I'm happy, and why I'm rich. And also, you will learn why you are not."

He laughs at this. Some of the other men do too. "It's because I know a simple truth," he says, "and I will teach it to you."

He steps in front of Carolina, touches her neck with his finger. "You listen too. You are also in my class.

"When somebody is hurt," Franco says, "somebody *else*—for example, the man whose vacation became Rafi's last night—when someone else gets hurt, *you* don't feel it. You don't feel a thing. I think that is pretty easy to understand, don't you? Whether you read about it in the paper, or you make it happen with your own hands. If you did it a thousand times, or if you did it once, it can't touch you. Never, for your whole, long, happy life. That is my lesson."

"How to be successful and influence people," Rafi says.

"If you have truly learned that lesson," Franco says, "even a *moreno* like yourself, there is nothing you cannot do."

He punches Carolina in the stomach. She screams, she doubles over.

"You animal, you sick fucking animal," Primo shouts.

"I am right," Franco says. "You cannot learn anything."

The man with the phone walks close to Primo. Primo kicks out. Connects to his groin. Then presses his back into the fence, kicks out with both legs, hits him in the stomach.

Franco hits him. Hits him again. He feels the rings breaking skin, but not the pain. He hears each blow, against his face, his arms, his body, but no longer feels them.

He hears Carolina screaming. He hears Franco tell her, "Don't worry. You will be the audience."

Primo can hold his head up, but it keeps moving back and forth. He looks at Franco. His eyes are wet with his own blood.

Franco will not let him live. Primo knows this now.

With each blow he watches time push him into the next moment. With each blow he sees that they are all together. More so each time. He can see as they see, and he can see as the buildings and the parked cars see. This is all it is. He will not live longer.

Primo is trying to speak. His mouth is filled. "Please don't hurt her," he is saying, but he cannot hear it. He will say it again.

He still hears the blows, but now they're getting farther and farther away. He will try to keep hearing them. *Don't hurt her anymore.* This time he does hear his voice. Good. . . . His voice, too: *Please don't. Don't hurt her. Not anymore. Listen.* He can still hear the blows. He can still hear himself.

38

There are two chairs facing him. Beyond them is an open doorway leading into larger, shadowed space. There must be light farther away outside the door: the white basin of the sink, between the chairs and the doorway, has a star-shaped glint around the outside, near the bottom where it curves, and the glint flickers sometimes or partially disappears.

He is inside. He tries to look around the room he's inside of.

But he can't see more without moving his head and it moves less than it usually does. Above him, a smooth white shadow, and if he turns as far as he can, there is the pleated top of a long curtain. He can't see where it ends on either side or on the bottom. His head doesn't move enough, and he must look over the clouded ridge of his nose.

A sound comes from that side. A hum. But it's easier to let his head fall back to where it was. Not because his head moves easier that way. But now, in the room he's in, it's the eye on this side that he uses.

He'd seen Olivia. She was sitting next to someone else. More than one person. A man, and then a woman.

Olivia's face was different. It was her. Her short gray hair and her eyes. But the way she looked at him. There were a lot of things in how she looked at him that made her not *just* her.

There's a bicycle ahead of him, it's moving, it passes by, and now it's not there. And there's a woman, but he can't see who. She's all the way up the block, standing in front of a building.

Olivia, and the people sitting next to her, kept saying his name. They said it like a question. They kept saying *Primo, Primo,* like he would know all they wanted him to know just by hearing them say it. Of course he knows his name.

The light in the basin of the sink goes out and then there is someone in the doorway. He doesn't know her. She comes near him, closer than the chairs. When she touches his forehead he can't see her hand anymore. She places her face near his, he still doesn't know her. She says something and she smiles. She's gone.

There might be people on the other side, where the hum comes from. He can't see them, but that's probably where they are, on that side. Oh, he wants to see them.

Whenever Olivia said his name, when she was sitting in the chair, she wanted him to say something back. If he could have said it, she would have stopped being sad. She looked at him the way she looks at television, *not* the way she looks at him.

39

Primo is sitting up in bed. Light falls into the room, across the thin white blanket, and across his left arm, lying beside his breakfast tray on the stand in front of him.

A minute ago, when the aide brought his meal, he just set the tray on the flat top of the movable stand, and started to leave the room. Olivia, sitting beside the bed, said to him, "Is this mine?"

He smiled. "It's *his*," he said.

"Then swing this goddamn tray over his bed so he can eat it."

Primo hasn't touched his food yet.

"Who eats dessert with breakfast?" Olivia asks. She unwraps the small brownie that came with his meal. "Especially with orange juice." She takes a bite out of it, sets it back on the small plate beside his scrambled eggs and toast.

With his left arm, Primo slowly lifts a forkful of eggs to his mouth. He sucks in a small portion of it, then lets his arm fall back onto the stand. His right arm is too sore to hold lifted. He slowly lifts another forkful. This time Olivia helps him steer it to his mouth.

"Your hand-eye coordination isn't what it usually is. But I'm glad to see you're finally hungry."

He nods. He cannot taste the eggs in his mouth.

"Does it hurt to chew?" Olivia asks him.

He swallows. "It hurts," he says softly, "to chew." His swollen lip causes him to slur each word. "It hurts not to."

"My ancient friends say things like that." Olivia lightly touches the side of his mouth with a napkin. "You might see this whole experience as a brief warm-up exercise for old age."

When she came in earlier, the first thing he said to her was, "Wednesday?" and she said, "Yes."

He lifted his head just above the pillow. "Carolina?"

"She's okay," Olivia said.

He didn't say anything for a moment. She then said, "I can't imagine why such a wonderful, bright young woman is hanging out with the likes of you."

He shook his head. "Tell me," he said.

"She *is* fine, Primo. They sent her home Monday morning."

He dropped his head back onto the pillow. The movement sent a fast wave of pain up the right side of his body, that started above his waist and reached up through his neck and face into his forehead. "What happened?" he asked.

"You got beaten up, Primo." Tears filled her eyes, then. But she didn't look like she did the last time she sat there. "Badly."

"I know that."

"To her?"

Primo nodded.

"Did you hear the sirens?"

He shook his head.

"Carolina said there were suddenly sirens. More than one, and coming closer. Before she knew it, the bastards who did this to you were gone."

He knew why she had looked at him so differently. It wasn't because he was seeing her with just one eye. She didn't believe he was really there.

"She's not sure which way they went, she said they just ran off in different directions. The poor kid was too frightened to notice more than that."

"Where is she?"

"At my place. The cops said these guys spent some real energy figuring out where you two would be. That being the case, I didn't think she should stay in her apartment right now. Or alone. She said she'll be here later."

A nurse walks in with a tall plastic cup. "Will this do?" she asks Olivia.

"Perfect."

The nurse runs water into it, from the sink just inside the door, hands it to Olivia, and then leaves the room. Olivia places into it, one by one, the daisies she has brought with her.

Primo watches her concentrate on each step of this act. He keeps being startled, in memory, by how different she looked the last time she was here. When she's finished, she sets the arranged flowers on the small chrome and Formica table beside the bed. She then arranges the two paperback books she also brought with her, so they are nearest his side of the tabletop, and props against them a photograph of her two turtles. Written across the top are the words *Pat & Mike say get well soon!*

"Last night was really the first time you said anything back to anybody," she says. "At least something remotely connected to what they'd said to you."

"Wednesday," Primo says. He hasn't been able to understand how three days have passed. Early this morning a nurse opened the curtains behind him, flooding the room with light, and said, *Mr. Thomas, welcome to Wednesday.*

"How was I?" he asks Olivia.

"How were you? You were just here. You just looked at people when they spoke to you. Or said something entirely unrelated. You seemed curious. Annoyed too. You had this look on your face that said, 'What do these people want from me?' You knew your name, at least."

She helps him steer another forkful toward his mouth. He shakes his head, and she guides his hand back to the tray.

"I have to tell you, nephew, I was worried."

A wave of pain shoots up his right side. "Did they catch anybody?"

"Nobody *to* catch. The police said they'll be by later too."

Primo turns toward the window, which fills an entire wall. Turning this way, toward the right, is harder. His right eye is covered with a patch of gauze. The sky is clear, and the day looks warm. A thin trail of steam rises from a pipe on the next rooftop.

"St. Vincent's?" he asks Olivia. He doesn't turn his head. He has just realized he doesn't know what hospital he is in.

"You got it on the first guess."

There is no wind, and the steam climbs straight upward, holds the circumference of the pipe it escapes from, and gathers slowly into the shape of a drill bit. When it reaches the height of a human, it begins to swirl outward, grow thinner, and lose itself in the clear morning sky.

"Your friend Nazz came by yesterday," Olivia says. "He's kind of cute, in a strange way, but that name. . . . Sounds like the noise I hear inside my head when I blow my nose."

Primo starts to laugh but it hurts too much. "It's short for Nazarino," he says.

"He looked kind of familiar. I asked him if he remembered any of his teachers from way back, like during the Kennedy administration, and if perchance I had been one of them, but he said no. So I told him there was a strong possibility we'd had a romance in a past life."

"What did he say to that?"

"Not a thing. He just blushed. Now, when I think about it, what looked familiar was the worried look on his face. The same one I'd been seeing on my own when I looked into the mirror."

An aide comes in and takes the tray with Primo's unfinished breakfast. As he lifts it Olivia takes the brownie, uneaten except for the bite she'd taken earlier.

She then gets up, pulls back the tray arm and shifts her chair nearer to the side of Primo's bed.

"Your friend Nazz and the police went over to this company where Carolina used to work and looked for the men who did this to you. The one called Franco wasn't there. No one knew where he'd gone."

"It was my fault. I really fucked things."

"She's doing okay. We've been talking the last couple of days. I think I might be able to massage her a job as a teacher's aide in the school where I used to teach. The pay has got to be better. They might even help her out in terms of tuition. She wants to go back to college. You know, she almost finished before she came here. Like I said. Can't understand why such a delightful young lady's hanging out with you. I could never figure out what women see in the Thomas men."

Primo lifts his arm, reaches upward and across his face and touches the gauze patch over his eye.

"Your vision's fine," Olivia says, looking sadly at him. "I think they told you that much already. But you got a few stitches at the top of the eyelid and they don't want you opening and closing it for another day or so."

"What else?"

"You're ready for the inventory? The doctor'll be by later, you can wait for him if you'd rather."

"No, you."

"You've got two broken ribs, both on the right side. You've got bruises and a lot of cut skin from your hip up to your head on that side. Some on the other side, too."

"The rings."

"Carolina told us about them. That's what broke a lot of the skin."

Primo feels more stiffness than pain. His body feels absent: inert and barely his, just lying there connected to this sore face and this sore arm, which are also mostly numb, until he tries to move them.

"You had a concussion, too. Probably a severe one. That's what scared us the most." She started to weep again, saying this. "You didn't know who I was, Primo. That scared the hell out of me."

"I remember you yesterday, sitting here, talking to me."

"That was Monday."

"What about yesterday?"

"When you saw me, did you know it was me?"

"Yes."

"Why didn't you answer?"

"I don't know." It was as if she were somewhere else, and her face was responding only to what was happening where *she* was. Not where he was.

"Primo, if you didn't know who I was, it would be harder for me to know who I am."

"There's nobody. . . ." Primo pauses, he had spoken quickly and it hurt him. ". . . who knows who *they* are . . ." He pauses again. ". . . more than you do."

"That a compliment?"

Primo nods.

"Remember what your mother used to say about somebody who thought they were hot shit, you among them. In fact, you especially. She'd say, *He thinks who he is.* Remember?"

Primo nods.

"I never understood how the words all worked together, but I got the gist of it."

"Your face was different."

"My face?"

"I could see you were worried, but I didn't know why."

"Worried . . . ? I wasn't sure if I was about to become the last of the Mohicans."

He pauses, exhales. "You were you, and you were someone else at the same time."

"Who else was I?"

Primo can't answer.

"Faces are a whole different ball game at my age. Especially since you don't go showing too many other people the rest of you. Among us older folks, the face does a lot more of the talking. No, that's not true. It might even talk less. But what it says is usually true. You understand that?"

Primo shakes his head.

Olivia holds up the last bite of the brownie, to make sure he doesn't want it. Then she pops it into her mouth.

"When you start getting old—not aging, getting old—aside from all the other crap that happens, your face starts to take on a life of its own. The face you'd been thinking of as yours starts to recede into the background. It's like the face you were born with, the strange one you often see in photographs, and don't like very much, has been running a race with the face you've been thinking of as *yours.* The one you made for yourself. When you get older, the face you were born with starts to take over. There's no stopping it. That's probably the one you saw."

They hear a siren, faintly, from the street below.

"You sure you didn't hear those sirens Sunday night?"

Primo shakes his head. Then he nods.

"That's right. You answer yes to affirm a negative question. You should know that by now."

He nods again.

"You were unconscious until early Monday morning. But even after that, after your eyes were open and you were talking, you weren't fully conscious. Not until last night."

"Go on," Primo tells her.

"On this face business?" She does a military salute. "*About* face."

Primo smiles, shakes his head, grimaces at a pain in the side of his neck and cheek.

"I assume it was my humor caused that reaction."

Primo nods.

"Actually, what happens is that you stop looking just like you, and you start looking like your whole family. Somebody looks at you, they can see what your brothers and sisters and parents look like too. Even your ancestors. The face you've been holding out in front of you begins to spend more time deeper inside the house, where it's calmer, simpler, farther from the windows and street noise. It's not like you don't have the strength to keep squeezing yourself into those eyes and cheekbones, you just stop caring so much. You let the face God and the genetic lottery gave you do the work of greeting the world. Truth is, neither face, the one we make, the one we're born with, has much to do with who we are."

She smiles, stands up, turns herself around like a model.

"I've finally learned the truth," she says. "Look."

Primo just looks at her.

"This is what life is: clothing and accessories." She points to the belt pouch she's wearing on her waist. She opens the zipper in the front, takes out a roll of Lifesavers, unwraps it, sets one in Primo's mouth, one in hers, puts it back into the pouch and sits.

Primo lifts his arm, touches the skin beneath his left eye.

Olivia touches her own eye in the same place. "What?" she says.

Primo shakes his head. He has been crying, quietly, with his breath, not his voice, and his face is still too numb to know if a tear had fallen.

"These are the hippest things." Olivia lifts her arms. "Look, no handbag. Everybody's wearing them. The whole city, everybody walking around looking like marsupials."

She begins to weep again. "Sorry," she says. She leans over the bed, takes Primo lightly in her arms, leans her head against his.

40

It's night in the room. He has slept and now he's awake. The star-shaped glint is back in the sink.

It is clear, in how he sees the things in this room: chairs, ceiling, sink basin, doorway—how he sees them now, as opposed to when he first registered their existence, hours, days ago, and since—that he has, in a larger way, and from a state farther removed from consciousness than sleep, been slowly, and increasingly, waking up.

Carolina came in before Olivia left. She had called a friend from CuddleCo, who told her the police have been making visits there all week. Other people too. Not all of them in uniforms.

"Shit," he said.

"What?" Olivia asked.

"Immigration?" Primo asked Carolina.

"I don't know."

"People will lose their jobs," he said.

"That hasn't happened yet," Carolina said. "It probably won't. Strangers have visited before."

Carolina told him she was fine. She was lucky. But she still feels frightened.

Olivia set her hand on Carolina's shoulder.

"I became even more frightened afterward," she said.

"That's no mystery," Olivia said.

Carolina told Primo that he'd collapsed onto the sidewalk the moment they let go of him, and she went to him, instead of watching to see where they ran to. Franco and Rafi were the only ones who had worked at CuddleCo. And they're both gone.

"And you?" Primo asked her.

"They only hurt me that one time. I think mostly they wanted me to watch them hurt you. That was my lesson. They are animals."

"*Niños salvajes,*" Primo said.

"Worse than that."

Olivia left then.

Her friend from work had also told her that they were going to get a raise. Twenty-five cents an hour. Everybody.

Carolina smiled when she told him this. "There is a new *jefe* and this was the first thing he told everyone. This has made them happy, but they also know it's so they don't talk to the police or the other strangers when they come around."

"There was a pearl in the oyster."

"What are you talking about?"

"*La perla de la septentrión.*"

"Your aunt told me your head was better. Was she wrong?"

"Nazz said it was nearly impossible that anything good would come from our visit." He tried to shake his head. It barely moved before the pain started. "There must be easier ways for people to get a raise."

"Sometimes there are not."

"What? It was you who thought I was crazy . . ." He spoke too quickly and had to pause. "Now you've changed your opinion?"

"I have not. It can be harder, even than that, for people to get a raise. That's all. And you *are* crazy. And I'm still angry at you. Cannot all those things be true?"

"I'm sorry," Primo told her. "I'm so terribly sorry. They could have hurt you much worse than they did." He lifted his hand to his forehead.

She sat down next to him on the bed and lightly touched his head where he had.

"And they did hurt you," he said to her.

"There is no crying over milk that has already spilled," she said.

"*Spilt* milk."

"That is incorrect, no?"

"That is incorrect, yes."

Carolina slipped off her shoes and curled her legs onto the bed. She leaned back against the wall above Primo's head on the pillow.

"Remember the man on the street?" she asked him. "The one who walked with us on Fifth Avenue, before we went into the subway?"

"The homeless guy?"

"Yes, him. I remember him now in a way I never thought I would have."

"How so?"

"It was a beautiful night. The sun was setting, there were angels, remember?"

"And devils, too, somewhere nearby. Rafi and his cadre. I realized that's why Franco introduced him to Nazz and me. So he could get a close look."

"For a minute let's not think about the devils. He was a good man, the one who spoke to us. An angel from the world of that beautiful night."

"An angel from midtown?"

The man had appeared beside them on Fifth Avenue, and walked with them along the last block before they entered the subway. He was small, had a froggy, harsh, breathy voice, and deep creases of skin around his eyes. There were no laces in his shoes, which were too large, and his heels scraped the pavement with each step. On one wrist was a plastic hospital name-tag bracelet.

"I don't want no money," he'd said. "Don't you worry, I don't want no money." He smiled. "In fact, you need any, my brother and sister, I'll give *you* some. I just want to walk along with you, if that's okay."

"Okay with us," Primo said.

He then walked around them to the inside of the sidewalk, arranging their formation so that Carolina was in the middle.

"You see," he said, "I want to make believe, just for a minute, that she's my girl, and *you*"—he pointed to Primo, his face cracking open with his smile—"*you* walkin with *us*."

They all had laughed. The man walked along with them, in silence after that, for half a block.

Carolina fell silent. Primo could feel a wave of fear pass through her, then through him. In recovering the moment, she had to now place into it, whole and real, the knowledge that Rafi and his friends were near, watching them, as they walked with this man.

He remembers something she had said just moments before this. She said she had always sensed the angels, but didn't know that was what they were. Perhaps we can sense the presence of other people, whose attention is on us, but not their intentions. Just feeling their presence can make us happy, because we are too stupid, needy, childlike, to know when they mean us wrong. These thoughts frightened him, were the language of his fear, and he would not speak them to Carolina.

"You were talking about our friend," Primo said to her. He slid his left hand across his torso and tapped the white plastic hospital bracelet on his right wrist. A pain shot up to his shoulder. "The one whose jewelry matched mine."

"Oh yes." She smiled, touched the wide part of the plastic band with Primo's name typed on it. "I would have remembered him just as another poor man I saw on the street," she then said. "There are so many of them. A sad and funny one. But now I remember him as . . . as *un retrato* . . ."

"A portrait?"

"Yes. But not just of him. Of the last moment before everything changed. We went down into the subway and when we came back up again the whole world became different. It will never be the same."

"Your world has changed once already. When you came here, to the United States."

"This has also been such a change."

Two policemen then appeared in the doorway. Although they had all seen each other, one of them tapped his knuckle against the doorframe before they entered.

Primo had little to add that they hadn't already learned from Carolina and from Nazz, but they asked him everything two or three times in case anything new came to mind. He told them he probably still had the matchbook with the phone number Franco had given them.

"You all handled it after that, right?" one of them asked.

Primo nodded.

"Then the matchbook itself is of no use. If it's all right, we'll call you at home, in a couple of days, and you can give us the number."

"*Oh*," Carolina said. "I just remembered something."

Both policemen looked at her.

"Olivia asked me to call your machine today and see if you had messages. You did," she said, and smiled. "You had one. From your friend Manny. He said, Maryellen had admitted it was probably *his.* He said this like it was something good. Then he said, 'Can you believe it?' and that was all. Do you know what that means?"

"I'd sure like to know," one of the policemen said.

"It would be indiscreet to tell," Primo said.

"I had a feeling," the policeman said. "But if you remember anything else, relating to what happened to you, call us. Sometimes, in situations like this, people remember things later."

"We're glad to see you're doing okay," his partner said.

As they were leaving, a doctor came in.

Carolina stepped off the bed, slipped on her shoes and leaned back over Primo. "When I come back tomorrow," she said, "will you tell me what your friend meant by his message?"

"I will," he said.

She kissed his forehead, then left the room.

It wasn't until the doctor, with the help of an aide, removed Primo's hospital gown that he realized his torso was wrapped. The doctor then cut away the tape and layers of gauze, and examined the bruises along the side of his rib cage.

"I was told the guy who hit you wore a lot of rings," the doctor said, lightly touching Primo's side.

"He said they were wedding rings."

"Last I heard, polygamy was illegal." He lightly tapped one of Primo's ribs with two fingers, then another. "This hurt?" he says.

Primo shook his head.

"It will soon. Maybe tomorrow, maybe sooner."

Primo tried to look down at himself. It felt as if he were holding someone else's body forward for this stranger to examine. There were lacerations, mostly small ones, up and down his side and rib cage. They were like small ships moving among continents of bruised skin.

"He hit me a lot," Primo says.

"He did," the doctor said. "I think the bastard was left-handed. He did most of the damage on your right side."

"He might have planned to get around to the other side, and just didn't have the time." The sight of his own body frightened him. He held his focus on the brown plastic rims of the doctor's glasses. "I barely feel it," he said. "I barely feel anything."

"Drugs can do remarkable things. So can shock."

"Am I in shock?"

"No longer. But sometimes the body decides the rate at which it will let you feel things."

Before he rewrapped Primo's rib cage, he listened to his chest with a stethoscope. "You're doing fine," he said.

He began to remove the patch over Primo's eye. "Please don't open it until I say." He lifted off the gauze, then removed a ball of cotton with tweezers.

Before he could stop it, his eyelid sprang open and blinding light closed it again, caused him to close both eyes and sent a sharp pain up into his forehead.

"Take your time," the doctor said. He was examining the area just above the eye.

Primo opened his eyes again. This time the glare subsided, as it does in the moments after a flash photograph has been taken. He now felt the wider range of vision. The edges of things were sharper, but the objects themselves were slightly less clear.

"I think we can leave this off now," the doctor said. "Let you see more of the world." He placed a smaller dressing just above the eye.

He tested Primo's reflexes as best he could, and stuck something sharp into his toe and the bottom of his foot.

The last thing he did was slap a tuning fork against the heel of his palm, hold it to Primo's ear, ask him if he heard it and then to tell him when the sound stopped.

Now, in the dark room, the small star in the sink flickers off, then on again, each time someone passes through the shaft of light that has its source somewhere down the hall. He has no idea how near the light is, who it is that passes between it and the open doorway, what else there is outside of this room.

His body is still, and calmer than he ever remembers it being. He barely feels the electric sensation, the abrasive music contained in his arms and legs and trunk, that has been the most consistent part of his awakened life.

A wave of fear suddenly rushes through him. "Shit," he says aloud.

He has relaxed too much, allowed a hand to break through his skin, squeeze his heart, forcing blood into his numb body, and waking it terribly to all its pain. "Don't kill her," he says aloud, in the dark room.

He begins to grow calm again.

When he had realized that they would kill him, his acceptance of this was, at first, the beginning and end of the entire thought. It wasn't that he didn't care, had given up, or wanted them to. It was simply what was happening.

He understood the point of view of these men who were going to kill him. He had detached from himself, and could see everyone's relation to what was being caused to occur. He could feel their expectation, and their terrible and certain knowledge that before they were done, he would be dead.

But then he felt Carolina's fear, saw them, and saw himself, from inside her.

He thought, deeply inside of what was happening, that from the point of view of these men, there was no reason to kill her. They had said she would just be the audience. "*So don't.*"

But they were going to kill *him.* What would they do to her after they did that? He knew, then, what they would do. It didn't hurt him anymore. He hardly heard it. *That* was what reawakened his fear. *Oh please, don't.*

He heard the blows then, louder. He heard his voice.

Another spasm seizes his body. "Don't." He shouts out loud.

He is calm again, but then another spasm comes. After each one he feels more and more of the pain in his sore body.

The nurse comes in. The one who had been in last night. Or the night before. "What?" she says. Again, and more softly, "*What?*"

The first time he looked up at her, it was as if he were seeing her from underwater, and she were looking down into it.

"It's time," she says. She holds out to him a small paper cup in which there are two red-and-white capsules.

He tries to smile at her, at the little cup. "For ketchup," he says. "McDonald's."

She brings the cup to his lips, and holds the back of his head. "I keep my earrings in them when I'm on duty," she says.

She then hands him a larger cup, half filled with water, which he tries to take from her—he wants to bring this to his mouth himself—but it hurts to lift his arm and it trembles and starts to spill, so she guides his hand.

"This will help, now," she says.

After she leaves he has another spasm. He knows he'll have another, and another after that, but he knows, also, that they will stop.

They are the aftershocks of the bruises and trauma he has just undergone, and they are something else. They are the last difficult steps toward something he almost is. The back and forth, the almost becoming, then receding, the almost becoming again: it is slowing to a stop. Between spasms is a different and new calmness.

Primo the *almost* is almost over. The sensation of near-ending is over.

He's beginning to float, now. The mattress sags and falls away beneath him but his body doesn't sink along with it.

He's been walking *into* something. It might have been a room, it might have had people in it, from outside it might have appeared warmly lit. Just before his foot touched the floor inside, it disappeared. And to a degree of absolute, traceless self-erasure that could only be achieved by something that was never there in the first place. He has crossed *the rest* of the distance.

When his body heals, his life will seem pretty much the same. He will go back to work, he will eat the same foods, he will be as curious, as angry, as stupid, as horny, maybe even as isolate as he has always been. But a word he has carried around inside himself his whole life has finally spoken itself.

He now hasn't the slightest sense of his body. Not even the light cloth of the gown against his skin.

He remembers the hum of the tuning fork the doctor had held to his ear.

He remembers the late afternoons when his father was at the hospital and he would sneak into his examining room. He'd do it because he was bored, or just because the door was open, and he was passing on his way into the house.

Before he left, he'd always bang the chrome tuning fork against his knee and hold it to his ear. It continued its high-pitched hum long after he'd expected it to stop. He could no longer see the tines move, or sense their vibration in his hand, or even feel the thin, sharp tickle of wind, but the steady sound continued.

He'd wonder if everything that shook or trembled kept doing so after you thought it had stopped.

The hum would then settle into a faint, steady purr. It would stop its decrease and hold at that timbre. At that point, if he moved the fork away from his ear, set it down, even left the room, the hum would continue: the small engine of sound had become his.

He'd take it with him into the rest of his day, gradually lose the sense of its presence, and later would have no awareness of the moment it actually came to a stop. He'd be watching the world that pressed against him from the outside, too occupied in this to notice that just before the sound stopped, it shook, it thundered, it shouted, it gathered its last self into a storm of noise louder than any sound it had owned since the moment it first leapt out of silence.

ACKNOWLEDGMENTS

EPIGRAPHS:

The quote from James Baldwin is from: "Down at the Cross, Letter from Region in My Mind," in *The Fire Next Time*, Dell / Doubleday, copyright © 1962, 1963 by James Baldwin.

The quote from Arthur Stanley Eddington is from *The Nature of the Physical World*, Cambridge University Press, 1933.

The quote from Muriel Rukeyser is from *The Gates*, McGraw-Hill, copyright © 1976 by Muriel Rukeyser.

The film summarized in chapter 5 is *Made in Heaven*, directed by Alan Rudolph, Lorimar Motion Pictures, 1987.

The quote in chapter nine, included in the letter written by the character Manny Glass, is from *The Sandinista Revolution: National Liberation and Social Transformation in Central America*, Monthly Review Press/Center for the Studies of the Americas, New York, copyright © 1986 by Carlos M. Vilas.

The quote from Chekhov referred to (and partially given) by the character Manny Glass in Chapter 19, is from "Anton Chekhov's Diary, 1896," *Notebook of Anton Chekhov*, trans. by S.S. Koteliansky and Leonard Woolf, The Ecco Press, New York, 1987. Copyright 1921 by B. W. Huebsch, Inc., and is as follows:

"February 19. Dinner at the 'Continental' to commemorate the great reform [the abolition of serfdom in 1861]. Tedious and incongruous. To dine, drink champagne, make a racket, and deliver speeches about national consciousness, the conscience of the people, freedom, and such things, while slaves in tail-coats are running round your tables, veritable serfs, and your coachmen wait outside in the street, in the bitter cold—that is lying to the Holy Ghost."

The poem partially quoted in Chapter 23 is "*La Diarrea*" by Fernando Silva. It appeared originally in his book, *La Salud del Niño*, Ministerio de Cultura (Colección Popular), Managua, 1986. It first appeared in English in "Hanging Loose," 1992, trans. by Chuck Wachtel.